PANDORA'S BOX

After gaining a BSc at King's College London and MSc at City University, Giselle Green worked for British Telecom and Unilever. Giselle is now a full-time mum to six boys, including twins, and a part-time astrologer. In 1999 she qualified as an astrologer with the Faculty of Astrological Studies and now specialises in medieval astrology. *Pandora's Box* is her debut novel. She lives in Kent with her family.

Find out more about Giselle at www.gisellegreen.com

Visit www.AuthorTracker.co.uk for exclusive updates on Giselle Green.

GISELLE GREEN

Pandora's Box

AVON

AVON

A division of HarperCollins*Publishers*
77–85 Fulham Palace Road,
London W6 8JB

www.harpercollins.co.uk

This production 2011

First published in Great Britain by
HarperCollins*Publishers* 2008

Copyright © Giselle Green 2008

Giselle Green asserts the moral right to
be identified as the author of this work

A catalogue record for this book is
available from the British Library

ISBN: 978-0-00789-978-4

Set in Minion by Palimpsest Book Production Limited,
Grangemouth, Stirlingshire

Printed and bound in Great Britain by
Clays Ltd, St Ives plc

Mixed Sources
Product group from well-managed
forests and other controlled sources
www.fsc.org Cert no. SW-COC-001806
© 1996 Forest Stewardship Council
FSC

FSC is a non-profit international organisation established to promote the
responsible management of the world's forests. Products carrying the FSC
label are independently certified to assure consumers that they come
from forests that are managed to meet the social, economic and
ecological needs of present and future generations.

Find out more about HarperCollins and the environment at
www.harpercollins.co.uk/green

A big thank you to Penny Halsall, for her enthusiasm, help and encouragement. To my editor at Avon, Maxine Hitchcock, for enriching suggestions.

To Dot, my agent for her input and advice. To the RNA, an organisation which enthusiastically supports published and unpublished authors alike. To my mum, Yolanda, who was the first person to look over the manuscript. To my friend Val Chiltern-Smith for advice and support. To the Arvon Foundation, for providing me with a space to go to, to 'get away and write' and to make more writer friends.

And last – and perhaps most of all – my thanks to my husband Eliott who has long supported my writing endeavours, and to all my boys for not just putting up with, but being so proud of their 'writer mum'.

To dearest Jonathan, who is a hope and inspiration to us all.

When at last I saw her fall, it was exactly as I had imagined it would be. Her face was a white flash of shock, eyes wide open and full of surprise. I watched her hair riding up in tumultuous curls behind her, the light filtering through every strand, all in slow motion like some scene from a film where they slow everything down to savour every last agonising detail.

All the while that she fell I had the worst feeling in the pit of my stomach. It was the knowing that, oh god, I did that. It's my fault. I should never have let her go. I could have saved her but I didn't. I can't believe that I didn't. And the shocked, horrified part of me that had let her go turned on the bit of me that had wanted her to fall all along.

You needed to be free of all this. How many times have you thought that? You needed her to fall so that you could be free, didn't you, Rachel? So you just let it happen. By the sins of our commission and omission . . .

You were responsible for her safety and her wellbeing and you knew this was going to happen and you just let it.

And I could not deny it.

How many nights had I lain awake fantasising about just such a scenario, my escape route from the prison that *my life had so long ago become? Would it have made any difference if I had not succumbed to temptation and looked inside Pandora's box? I really cannot say. I'm feeling too numb now. My world has crumbled, everything has gone. I don't know anything at all any more.*

And so she fell and I did nothing. And why? Because although I loved her, as long as we were yoked together I could never be free.

1

Rachel

Pandora's box arrives on a grey Saturday in March, wet on its cardboard bottom where the postwoman has laid it down in a puddle outside our front door. My first thought is: I *told* my mother not to send it. I know what's in it and I don't want it.

I'm not even going to open it.

The box has '*This will cheer you up*' scrawled in my mother's handwriting along the top. But I know that it won't. My mother, Pandora – who is emigrating to Sydney with her new 'boyfriend' – has already told me exactly what she is sending:

'Just some of your childhood things I've been holding on to. All your stuff, you know. Your school certificates and your medals and some old letters I kept. Photos of you and Liliana doing your dancing. God, what *promise* you two girls once showed!' she had sniffed, remembering. She didn't have to spell it out to me that we'd never lived up to that promise. 'But there's nothing I can really take with me all that way.'

Of course she can't and, fair enough, I thought, I am

3

forty-two after all. I can't expect Mum to hang on to all my childhood paraphernalia forever.

I just wish she'd chucked it out herself instead of sending it on to me. There is something disquieting about having this stuff turn up at my door this morning; something I can't put my finger on. I look at the box. It's 7.45 a.m. and the children aren't even up yet. The hallway is still dark when I pad through to the kitchen with the box, hoping for a tiny bit more light. The fact that she's sent this to me . . . it's as if *I've* been left holding the past in some way. My stomach catches tight at the thought. I feel as if I've just filled it with a bowlful of cold porridge.

What I *want* to do is just chuck the whole lot out without even looking at it – after all, why waste the time? Time is precious. Time is something I never have enough of, these days. The lino on the kitchen floor is freezing my feet and the scissors aren't in the drawer where they're supposed to be. My little kitchen faces north but when the sun shines I can see the blue sky in the distance over the tops of the houses and trees. When the sun shines all the pansies and daffodils struggling through in the garden don't look so battered and lifeless. It isn't shining today.

It's all very well for *Pandora*, I think suddenly. She gets to jet off to sunnier climes with a new life and a new man. 'I couldn't believe it when Bernie asked me to join him out there.' The memory of her voice fills my head again. 'You know I've always wanted to emigrate but the time never seemed right till now. Bernie said he couldn't *possibly* set up his new PR

4

venture without me. Just think, at my age!' The cold feeling in my stomach resolves itself into an uncomfortable patch of envy.

I've got the wintertime blues, that is all.

The cardboard box – underneath all the masking tape – looks vaguely familiar. Surely it's got to be the same one that my mother has kept, tucked away in the back of her wardrobe for the last, oh, century or so?

It must be at least that long because that's how old I feel. I set about one corner of the box with my little vegetable knife. It must have been at least a hundred years ago that I was young enough to have won certificates at school and drawn pictures that anybody judged worth keeping and . . . had Mum said *medals*?

I hadn't won any medals. I pull a face as the brown tape sticks onto my hands, winding itself around my fingers as if it wants to tie me up. Liliana had won all the medals. All those championship rosettes for the under-fourteens' ballroom dancing events. Yuck. I had *hated* those events. I was the taller one so I always had to be the 'boy'. I didn't remember anything much about them except that I hated them.

'You *will* come out and visit us, won't you? Just as soon as we're settled.' Pandora's voice over the phone had been breathless, just the slightest edge of anxiety to it had warned me: just say yes, say you'll come. Don't bring up Shelley and the fact that she can't fly so you won't ever come, even assuming you could get the money together in order to do so . . .

We are trapped, basically: Shelley and me and her brother Daniel. I pull vengefully at one long piece of sticky tape that has been wound interminably around the top of the box.

My mother can't – or won't – see that.

Hell, she doesn't even really accept the fact that Shelley is dying.

'Hope springs eternal', as she likes to tell me gaily every time she calls. Well, she is Pandora, so maybe in *her* world it does. I just wish I could tap into that eternal spring when I get faced with things like Shelley refusing to go to school because it is 'a waste of the precious little time she has left'. And maybe Shelley is right. What does school matter, for her? She won't need the exams. She won't ever be going to university. She won't live long enough to ever get herself a job.

It is an unfathomable thought, but it is the stark reality, a truth that winds itself like a steel cord around my heart every time I think about it, threatening to cut me in two.

I cut the masking tape away from my fingers with the knife and flick open the door under the sink to throw it in the bin. *Damn it*. Why did things have to work out this way? Nothing matters any more. Things only ever matter when you've got hope, and today I don't have any.

My daughter might *seem* fine, but I know she isn't. Recently her consultant has been keeping an even tighter check on Shelley. Our one-monthly check-ups have become fortnightly. Lately he even offered to make them weekly, even though there has been no real change in her condition for a long while. But there has to be a reason why he is tightening up on her care, doesn't there? They warned me last year, after her friend Miriam died with the same condition, 'Shelley doesn't have long.' But how long is 'not long'? How long is a piece of string?

And how long do I really want to waste this morning, going through all this old junk? I stare at the space behind the little pedal bin. There is just about enough room in there for me to store this old box away without ever having to give it another thought. What do I care about old certificates and photos, anyway?

'Mum? What was that, Mum? What did the postie bring?'

Shelley can be deadly silent on that wheelchair of hers. She must have oiled the wheels because I didn't hear her come in at all. She looks wan in the pale morning light, I think, even younger than her fourteen years without all her usual Goth war-paint on.

'Um, just some paperwork your gran sent through. I'll have to plough through it sometime. Nothing for you to concern yourself with.'

'And you're putting it in the *bin*?' She leans forward in her wheelchair to see what I've been up to.

'No. *Behind* the bin.'

'You don't usually put stuff there,' she notes. She knows I'm angry. She can tell, just like I can always tell what she is feeling. We spend too much time in each other's company for it to be otherwise.

'Are you upset because Granny Panny's left the country?' Shelley enquires sagely. 'She was never really much use to you anyway, even when she was here.'

'Well, what use would you expect her to be? She's got her own life to live, hasn't she?'

Shelley sits back, slender shoulders slumped. She is

7

wearing the same pink pyjamas she wore last summer. She hasn't grown much in the year when most of the girls in her class have shot up to about six foot, it seems. The rest of them have all begun to blossom out.

But something in Shelley's face has definitely changed. There is a different look in her eye that I don't remember being there before, a certain angle to her jaw that has made her face more defined, another year older, more worn by life.

And she shouldn't be worn by life, why should she? She's never had any fun, never been anywhere, never done anything. She doesn't know yet what it is like to love or to be loved. How can she be so worn by life when she has never really *lived*?

'*This will cheer you up*' indeed! I shove the pedal bin in front of Pandora's box with my foot and close the cupboard door. I'll give the whole lot to Liliana when I see her. She's into nostalgic memories and memorabilia. It isn't of any use to me, that's for sure.

As far as I'm concerned, the past is dead and buried, and all my hopes were buried years ago, right along with it.

2

Rachel

'*Why* can't I pull it down? I don't want any "New Year resolutions" hanging up there for me. Daniel can keep his own if he wants to but I don't see why I have to have any. It's just plain silly.' Shelley grimaces at me as I squeeze past her to get milk from the fridge. 'It is *March*, after all.'

'No.' I push the door firmly shut with my elbow and take another look at the list her brother had Blu-Tacked onto the fridge door in January.

**Family New Year's Resolutions List
(by Daniel Wetherby)**

Daniel
1. Find mate for Hattie.
2. Ride bike without stabilisers (before I am eleven).
3. Help mum more.

Mum
1. Become famous artist and get rich.
2. Find cure for Shelley.

3. Buy the house on Strawberry Crescent.
4. Have a proper holiday.

Shelley
1. Get cured and be healthy and walk.
2. Get a boyfriend.
3. Do well at school.

'If it's March, that still gives us the next nine months of the year, doesn't it? All we've got to do is find you a cure, make me a famous artist, buy that gorgeous property up on Strawberry Crescent and get you a boyfriend.'

'Huh. Granny Panny is the only one of us who's ever going to get herself a boyfriend, Mum. And the fame, the house and the cure are all non-starters, wouldn't you say?' She gives a little laugh. 'I mean, *you*, famous? What could you ever be famous for? You don't actually do anything, do you? Daniel's mad. And you haven't done any art since you left art college.'

'He's just a kid, Shell. You've got to let him have his dreams. Don't you dare take his list down.' I stay her arm as she reaches out to pull it off.

I don't *care* if there's no point in you going to school any more, I think suddenly. At least it gave us some respite from each other when you did.

I should never have given in to her on that point. I should have made her keep on going.

'It doesn't matter if it's silly, or if none of it can come true. It matters that he's still got things he's hoping for in his life. That's all. He wants us to have things to look forward to as well. That's why he wrote us lists, don't you see?' Her comment that I don't actually do anything is one that I choose to ignore. Oh, I do things all right. She just doesn't see it because everything I do is invisible. I'm like the invisible thread that holds the whole fabric of our household together – but she's right, it's not something I'm ever going to become famous for.

'Oh don't worry, Mum.' Shelley's voice is suddenly dripping with sarcasm. 'He can leave it up there if he likes.' She turns to gaze through the window where a sudden squall has sent a splatter of rain across the glass. Outside, a disused flowerpot is rolling up and down on the patio. We are supposed to be planting seeds this weekend. I don't suppose we'll get round to it now.

The kettle boils and I fill up two mugs with some coffee. There is a moment's silence. A truce.

'So. Are you going to tell me what's in the box from Granny then, or what?' Shelley's voice is amicable, conciliatory. She seems to have forgotten about the resolutions list already. She feels more like the old Shelley when she's like this, more like the daughter I remember. When she's all done up with that black lipstick she favours these days I hardly recognise her.

'I think I'll go for "or what".' I pull a face at her. She should just take the hint that I don't want to talk about it or accept what I tell her at face value. But teenagers never do.

'It's something to do with Aunt Lily, isn't it?' Shelley sucks on her lower lip, pensive. 'Why don't you two ever meet up? Are you making arrangements to meet up sometime soon?'

'You've been eavesdropping,' I accuse her.

'I can't help it if I occasionally overhear things,' she counters. 'This house isn't exactly massive, is it?'

'Well no, it isn't.' Not as big as the one we lived in before Bill and I split up, which is the subtext to her comment, I know. But there is nothing that can be done about that. 'However, it would be polite to . . . move somewhere else in the house if that happens.'

'If I moved far away enough in *this* house I'd end up next door,' she observes. 'Come on, Mum,' she adds before I can reply. 'What's the big secret? Just tell me what's in the box? Why are you trying to hide it?'

'Oh, fine!' I kick the pedal bin out of the way and heave the box out again. The cardboard sides are soft and a bit mushy and the whole thing smells musty, like the dark secret place at the back of unused cupboards where nobody ever goes and the spiders breed, un-molested, for years. You'd think Pandora would have rummaged around for a new box before she posted all this stuff off.

'Here we go, if it will keep you quiet, madam.' It isn't a big secret after all. There is nothing in there that matters; just a load of old dust and memories I'd rather not be dredging up at this moment. But it's guilt that makes me cave in to her, guilt about the fact that she might not be around to ever see any of it, if I wait too long. 'It's just some old keepsakes, photos and things that Granny sent over. Most of it will go to Lily. *When* we meet up.'

Once the masking tape is all off the side flaps of the box fall open limply, revealing a pile of yellow-stained envelopes. Most of them seem to contain photos. A few hold old birthday cards, flowery and beribboned with 'to our darling daughter' on the outside. On the inside of one of them, all embellished in curlicues, are the words 'from Pandora and Henry'.

'Who's this, all dressed up like a dog's dinner?' Shelley pulls my attention back to one of the photos. 'She looks vaguely familiar.'

She's found a picture of me and Liliana in our dancing outfits. I, as usual, being the taller, slimmer one – albeit two years younger – got to be the 'male' partner, dressed up in a tuxedo with my dark red hair cut appropriately short. Thankfully, though, Shelley hasn't even noticed me. It is Lily she is frowning at; Lily with her long blonde bubbly curls and that frilly dusty-pink dress with all the sparkly sequins sewn into the hem. I take the photo from her for a minute, feeling my fingers trembling, even after so many years, as a gush of unhappy memories comes flooding back.

'I can't believe she kept that!' I make as if to tear it in two and then change my mind because, after all, Lily might still want it.

'It's Aunt Lily, isn't it?'

'It is. She always got to wear the most beautiful dresses.'

'Oh, Mum!' Shelley's face crumples in mirth. 'You didn't really think that dress was *beautiful*, did you? The only thing she's got on that's halfway decent is that string of blue beads around her neck.'

'Well, actually . . .' I do a double-take of Lily's glammed-up version of a ra-ra skirt before dropping the photo back into the box. Shelley is right. How things change! That dress really does look rather hideous. 'Okay. Point taken. It was the kind of thing we thought was beautiful at the time. One of these days you're going to look back at yourself wearing all that Goth war-paint . . .' I stop and catch Shelley's eye. 'Oh, Shelley, I'm so sorry. You *won't*, will you? I can't think that way. I just can't get used to thinking that way, it's so *unnatural*.'

'It's all right, Mum.' Shelley's wide blue eyes are calm and focused. 'It's funny how Pandora kept all those things for so long, though, isn't it? Look, she's even – she's even kept that necklace in here. The one that Lily's wearing.' Her nimble fingers dive in and pull it out. She holds it up to the light so we can both see. Oh, but I had forgotten that necklace! Its pale blue nuggets of rounded sea-glass are all held individually in place by a tiny filament of gold wire. The central portion of the necklace is a darker blue stone – also sea-glass though you'd never know it – it's so dark it could be lapis lazuli – and that is framed by the iridescent halo of a cut-out piece of mother of pearl.

'It looks just like something a mermaid might wear,' Shelley breathes. Exactly, I think, and her comment makes me smile. I designed it with a mermaid in mind, all those years ago. I collected all those bits of blue glass myself, on solitary walks, trawling along the coast of Cornwall.

'Can I keep it?' my daughter begs, and I shrug. Why not? If Lily were here she would claim that it was hers, that she always wore it. But the truth is, I found the glass, I designed it, and I fashioned it up with the limited tools that I had at my disposal. My friend – a lady in the second-hand jewellery shop – had cut the mother of pearl into shape, but she'd shown me how to do everything else. The only thing I *wasn't* allowed to do, I realise

14

now, was actually wear it. It so happened that the colours and the theme were a perfect match for the dance outfit that Lily was wearing that season. I had to give it over to her. Oh, I wasn't exactly *forced*. It was just the kind of thing we were expected to do, back then.

'All these things – I mean, they must have been so precious to Pandora once. Maybe to you too?' Shelley glances at me curiously but I look away. She will never really know the truth about that.

'The things that matter to us change,' I say simply. 'What mattered so much yesterday doesn't matter so much today. What matters today, we might not give a fig about tomorrow.'

'When you look at it that way,' Shelley is scanning Daniel's list on the fridge again, this time looking quiet and thoughtful, 'maybe those resolutions aren't so stupid after all. Maybe it means we should just make the most of things while they're important to us. For instance, we could still get Daniel the second tortoise, couldn't we? Hattie could have her mate. And I was thinking . . . we could still take that holiday. Just you and me. Daniel's away on scout camp the week of my birthday. I'd really love it if we could go down to Cornwall, back to Summer Bay for one last time. It could be this year's birthday present for me. That shouldn't break the bank too much, should it?'

'Do you really mean that?' I watch her fasten my necklace around her throat and I feel my heart thudding in my chest. It's been so *long* since Shelley expressed any real interest in anything at all. If my daughter could only be interested in something, if she could only have

15

something to live for, then she might live a little longer, a little better. She might have a little more joy in whatever days she has left to her. 'I would love to take a trip down there with you. Are you sure you don't want to go when Danny can come too?'

'No!' Shelley comes back vehemently. Then she recovers herself and smiles. 'I just want some special time with you. While we still can, you understand?'

'Of course I do.'

'And Dad won't mind?'

Bill, of course, will have to be consulted. He always likes to be included in whatever plans are made for Shelley, and that's fair enough. But my ex-husband has his new wife and their young child to think about these days, doesn't he?

'I'll square it with your dad,' I tell her decisively. And Daniel will have to be managed somehow because he'll no doubt want to be in on it too. But then Daniel has his scout camp to look forward to, so why shouldn't Shelley have her special time?

'Don't you wonder when it happens?' Shelley is still thoughtful, looking at the box. 'When do all those precious things become . . . just a pile of old junk?'

It happens when we're not looking, I think. At the same time that those crows' feet appear, which we tell ourselves will disappear when we get a good night's sleep. When our dress size creeps up from a ten to a twelve and then a fourteen. When we're not looking.

'It happens when we cease to care,' I tell her.

'But if you don't care,' she whispers, 'why were you so upset that Granny Panny sent it all on to you?'

'I'm not . . .' I begin, but there is little point in lying to Shelley. I edge over to the kitchen sink and throw the dregs of my coffee away. 'Maybe you have never heard the story of Pandora's Box?' I say to her at last. 'In Greek myth, Pandora was a beautiful and foolish woman who, out of insatiable curiosity, opened a box that she had been warned she should never open. The minute she opened it, out flew all the spites: Old Age, Sickness, Envy, Disloyalty, Deceit . . . in short, everything that makes mankind miserable.' I trail off.

'Come *on*, Mum. This isn't a magical box. It isn't going to release a load of nasty stuff into the air just because we've opened it up to look inside. You don't really believe that, do you?'

'Of course not literally,' I say. A shiver goes through me then. I'm not superstitious. I'm not really going to be opening up the past just because we've opened up that box, now, am I? I was never allowed to look inside Pandora's private box when we were kids, that's all. Old habits die hard, and all that.

'I think we should put it away now,' I say. Shelley opens her mouth to protest but I add, 'Maybe I'm just scared that there'll be something in there I don't want to see.'

My daughter nods wisely. She doesn't ask me what this thing might be. Instead, she comments, 'I *have* heard the story of what was Pandora's Box, Mum, and you've left one of them out.'

'And what might that be?' I arch my brows. A ray of sloping sunshine appears for a moment across the kitchen worktop, making long shadows of our coffee

17

cups. Outside, the squally wind is chasing the clouds across the canvas of the sky, opening up small patches of blue.

'Hope,' she says simply. 'You've left out Hope.'

3

Shelley

I have decided that when dawn breaks on my fifteenth birthday, that is the last day I will ever spend on this planet.

I am not depressed and I am not angry with my parents.

I am not insane, neither am I frightened of Death.

I *am* frightened of dying, however, in the way that I inevitably will if I don't take matters into my own hands. I meant what I said to my mum about hope, though. I do have hope. But it's for the others who are going to be left behind after me, that's all.

I have a poster-sized photograph of me and Daniel in my bedroom. It's one of my favourites of the two of us and it was taken nearly ten years ago because in it I'm five and Daniel is just one. It's an 'action' shot. We're both in our swimsuits on this huge empty beach in Cornwall. I'm jumping off a rock with my eyes closed and my arms in the air. I love the smile on my face. Whenever I look at that photo I remember what it must have felt like to be free. We called that our 'jumping rock'. It seemed so huge to me then, but we went back to

Summer Bay three years ago and the rock was still there in the same place, same green algae and footholds all over it, jutting out of the sand at the head of the beach and, guess what . . . it had shrunk!

Well of course it hadn't really shrunk. The rest of the world – including us – had just got bigger. Daniel kept jumping off it, showing off, because in my photo he's just a baby sitting on the bottom waiting patiently for me to jump and here was his chance to take on a more active role. I wasn't completely confined to Bessie – that's my wheelchair – three years ago, but neither were my legs strong enough to jump. This time I was the one sitting on the sand waiting, so Mum took a photo of that and Daniel's got it on his wall, and it kind of evens up the balance of power as far as he's concerned.

He's like Mum there, see. They both have this immaculate sense of fairness and justice about things. I may only be fourteen but I know damn well that life isn't fair. Maybe it's genetic or something, I don't know, but some people never seem to work that one out. That's Mum's fatal flaw; that's how I'll get her to come round to my way of thinking in the end. You'll see.

Anyhow, this photo of the last time I felt really free, it's given me the idea of how I want it to be on my last day.

I have decided that I will go down to Summer Bay in Cornwall and I will jump off a cliff, and that way, for those last few moments of my life, I'll be flying. I won't die in my bed all shrivelled up and cold as my limbs finally atrophy to the completely withered stage. I'll be flying through the sunshine. It'll be a hot, peaceful,

20

blue-skied day. We'll do it in the early morning – I was born at 6 a.m. – so there'll be no footprints in the sand. The sea will have wiped everything clean from the night before. There will be no marks there before I make my mark.

I'm not bothered about the impact. It will be so quick I just won't feel it. I'm focusing on just that one moment when I go over the edge. I'll be like a white bird – a seagull – twinkling in the sunshine. I'll feel the warm air rushing up through my hair and I'll be . . . well, I'll be released.

I've struggled with this whole plan for a while because I was worried that I might be being a bit, well . . . selfish. Everybody else is going to suffer and I hate the thought of that. Then I think – hell, they are going to suffer anyway. This way we'll just get it over and done with. A long, protracted death with every vein stuffed with needles, tubes down my throat to aid breathing when the lungs cave in and a tiny bump under the bedsheets where my shrivelled legs should go is even worse.

I haven't forgotten Miriam. One day she was just like me – she was okay enough, with the same disease, but still okay. Then suddenly . . . poof! It all went downhill for her. I heard them say she was lucky; that it could have taken much longer, but no, she was *lucky*. What if I'm not so 'lucky'?

'Did they give you an initial diagnosis of MS?'

The first time I ever saw Miriam we were both sitting on the green benches outside Neurology. She had brought crossword puzzles and drinks and things and she seemed to know everyone in the department by name. I, on the other hand, was just sitting on my hands, feeling sick to my stomach with nerves. I remember I couldn't take my eyes off her wheelchair. I wanted desperately to ask her if she'd always been like that or whether it was this illness that had done it to her but at the same time I really didn't want to know.

'Hi,' she'd started again when I didn't answer her. 'I'm Miriam.'

'Uh, yeah. I'm Shelley. Yeah, they did. They thought it was MS. At first.'

She had taken a thoughtful sip of her juice carton through a straw.

'And now?'

'Now they think it might be something called AMS.'

'Atypical Myoendocal disease.' Her eyes had beamed at me. 'Same as me, then. Welcome to the club! We're very unique, you know. We're less than one in five million.'

'I feel honoured,' I'd muttered under my breath.

'You should feel honoured,' she'd laughed, and I remember her blue eyes had been warm and bright with humour. 'It means you now get the best consultant on the block; the gorgeous Doctor Ganz.'

'Uh-huh.' I'd already met him. He seemed kind. I didn't think there was any danger I would be falling in love with him, though.

'Just remember that I saw him first,' she added, but there was a more important possibility rearing itself in my mind just at that moment.

'Does it mean, if it's *atypical* MS, that there's any chance we could get better?'

22

That was the one and only time I ever saw a shadow cross Miriam's face.

'You don't get better from this, Shelley,' she told me. 'It's atypical, because it actually . . .' she hesitated, 'look, I guess I'd better let them explain it all to you when you go in. They'll put it so much better than I ever could. Have you had an MRI done yet?'

'That thing where you go in the tunnel and they look to see if there's any nerve damage?' I'd nodded but she didn't say any more and I'd guessed, correctly, that she'd just been trying to distract me. Miriam was the one good thing to have come out of all of this. She was the best friend I ever had. She really was one in five million.

But the thing is, it was like she was a friend travelling the same road as me, only she happened to be further up ahead than I was. Every time she got a new symptom, I knew it would be only a matter of maybe six months to a year and then I would get it too. She never had any pain until the end, and neither have I had any yet. Nor do I want to. Dr Ganz kept saying to me that these things were all very individual. Nobody could predict how it would go. Not enough people had been studied to make any hard and fast conclusions. The only hard and fast conclusion that I know of is that the condition is, in the end, fatal. Miriam came to the end of her road. It's a year later for me. I don't need anybody to spell out what that means. I guess the thing I detest most about my situation is the *inevitability* of it. I'm like a fish caught in a net. There is no way out. Apart from the way I have thought up.

Which brings me back to my plan. At least this way

I will be drawing my own last breath. And the air I draw will be warm and sweet and full of birdsong and the gentle crash of the waves on the shores of Summer Bay.

I can't do it by myself. It's not something I can do alone, and I don't really want to be alone at the end. Now all I have to do is persuade someone to help me do it.

4

Shelley

SugarShuli has come on MSN just now. She must be having a day off again. Like me, she doesn't see much point in going to school but her reasons are different to mine. Her parents are bringing a boy over from Pakistan for her and she's supposed to marry him just as soon as she's legally allowed.

SugarShuli says: *I'm off sick. How are you?*

ShelleyPixie says: *Okay. What's up?*

SugarShuli says: *Nothing really. Just didn't see much point in going in. What are you doing?*

ShelleyPixie says: *Right now, talking to you. I'm waiting for Krok to come online so if I go quiet . . .*

SugarShuli says: *Krok your bf?*

ShelleyPixie says: *Sort of. Online thing.*

I haven't actually met Krok of course, not in the flesh, but he's sent me a picture of him and his mates when they were doing a gig in a pub in Hammersmith. Krok plays the bass but what he really wants to do is produce music. When he grows up, he says. He's nineteen now, so I'm not sure when that will be.

Krok has got this dream: he's going to set up his own

recording studios one day and bring on a load of new young bands playing real music – real musicians, he says, not just pretty people prancing and miming. He says most real musicians are ugly. He isn't. He has longish hair and the deepest blue eyes. Irish eyes, he tells me. He's got a cheeky smile.

SugarShuli says: *You two going to meet?*

She means him, I suppose. Are we going to meet? I *wish*, I only wish I could. Don't know how it would happen, though. I also worry that he might be put right off me if we ever did. It's better this way. On the other hand, Daniel might be right with his list of resolutions. We don't get forever. And I'm getting a lot less of forever than most people count on. I keep thinking that if there are things I want to do then I'd better get on and do them.

ShelleyPixie says: *Yep. Sometime soon. I'm going to meet him.*

SugarShuli says: *I'll be meeting Jallal soon too.*

Surinda – that's her real name – takes all this marrying Jallal business in her stride. She doesn't seem to mind. It's all part of her expectations, she tells me. She says it's much harder for those people who have to go out and find someone and decide who to marry all for themselves. Hmm . . .

ShelleyPixie says: *Good looking?*

SugarShuli says: *I haven't seen a picture yet. He comes from a good family and I am assured they have money. That's what counts, isn't it?*

ShelleyPixie says: *Christ.*

SugarShuli says: *You know how it is.*

Hang on a minute, I think Krok has just logged on so she'll have to shut up for a bit. Krok is more important. I haven't spoken to him since last Thursday. He's got a busy schedule at the moment.

Krok says: *Hey Pixie.*

ShelleyPixie says: *Hey Krok. How's it going? Been missing you.*

Krok says: *Sorry, Pixie mine. Been following up on your advice so don't be cross.*

ShelleyPixie says: *How so?*

Krok says: *I've been trying to get some funds together. My mate Bruno and me, we're going in for that quiz show you were telling me about.*

ShelleyPixie says: *You never!*

Krok says: *We are. Don't know if we'll get selected but we've been short-listed down to the final fifty so keep everything crossed for us!*

ShelleyPixie says: *You're going to be on* Beat the Bank! *OMG!*

Krok says: *Well, maybe. We'll find out in a couple of days. Just wanted to let you know, sweetheart. It was U gave me the idea. What if I win the million pounds? What then?*

ShelleyPixie says: *You'll make your dream come true. Yay!*

Krok says: *Send me a pic.*

ShelleyPixie says: *I haven't got any recent ones.*

Krok says: *Send me one anyway.*

ShelleyPixie says: *I'll see.*

Krok says: *Are you afraid I won't like what I see?*

ShelleyPixie says: *No. I'm not that ugly.*

Krok says: *You have a heart of gold, Pixie. How could you ever be ugly? Marry me?*

ShelleyPixie says: *Only if you win the million. LOL.*

He's joking, by the way. He knows I'm on this time-limit thing. He knows I'm not going to last all that long. I told him about all that at the beginning. He's gone quiet now. He's probably talking to three girls at once. He's asking them all to marry him. Guys who look like him don't lack for girlfriends. Oh well. Where's SugarShuli?

ShelleyPixie says: *Still there?*

SugarShuli says: *Still here. Where'd you go?*

ShelleyPixie says: *Krok just came on. You won't believe it. He's been chosen as a finalist on* Beat the Bank.

Surinda watches this every Saturday evening. It's what brought us together in the first place. She's hooked on it, like me.

SugarShuli says: *He never is!*

ShelleyPixie says: *It's true.*

SugarShuli says: *When will he know? OMG. Could he get us tickets to be in the audience do you think?*

That's a thought that hadn't occurred to me.

ShelleyPixie says: *Might do. If he gets in. Would you even be allowed to come? Don't know if Mum would take us.* Actually I don't even *want* my mum to take us. Mum always has to be in on everything. I want to do this without her. Maybe Surinda could help me?

SugarShuli says: *I'll tell my parents it's a school project. I'll come if your mum can take us.*

ShelleyPixie says: *No, Mum can't do it. Can yours? What about we two go alone?*

Krok's back.

Krok says: *Sorry, Pixie. Phone call interrupted there. I'm supposed to be working at the moment too.*

ShelleyPixie says: *Who wants to hire DVDs at this time in the morning?*

Krok says: *You'd be surprised. Never mind the shop, though, Pix. I've got a stint at the recording studio this afternoon.*

ShelleyPixie says: *Cool. Hope they give you a job.*

Krok says: *It's all good experience. They like me helping out. Maybe they'll hire me eventually!*

ShelleyPixie says: *They should.*

SugarShuli says: *Hey, Krok, I'm Surinda.*

Hell, where did SHE come from?

ShelleyPixie says: *Private conversation, SugarShuli.*

I'm going to kill her.

SugarShuli says: *Sorry. Good luck with the* Beat the Bank *thing, man.*

Krok says: *Thanks.*

Krok says: *Who's that?*

ShelleyPixie says: *Just a friend who wants to come with me when you send me tickets to see the* Beat the Bank *being recorded.*

Krok says: *Will do. Got to go now, Pixie.*

ShelleyPixie says: *Speak soon?*

Krok says: *Very soon. Bye bye, sweetie.*

He's gone.

SugarShuli says: *He's cute, Shell.*

ShelleyPixie says: *You've been looking in my photos file?*

SugarShuli says: *Why not? You can look in mine.*

ShelleyPixie says: *You've got nothing in there. Not even Jallal.*

SugarShuli says: *Are you sure your mum can't take us? Ask her again.*

ShelleyPixie says: *Yep, okay, speak later.*

Silly cow. *She* could help me get there. We could take the train.

I shouldn't complain I suppose. At least Surinda from my form class still keeps in contact with me, which is more than Michelle and the others have done since I stopped going to school. They say they're really busy. I know some of them are seeing boys and the ones who aren't are just hanging out hoping to see some boys or else they're studying. I don't know why I don't want to hang out with them any more. I just don't see the *point*. Sometimes I just wish I didn't think so much. Life would be a lot easier.

If Krok sends us the tickets I think I'll have to make an excuse. I don't even want him to have a picture of me, much less actually see me in real life. I couldn't cope with that. It's not going to happen. I'm not even going to ask Mum so Surinda can forget all about that. I know what she's like, though, she won't let it go now.

I wish I'd never told her.

5

Rachel

'Coo-eee?' Annie-Jo's special-edition turquoise Mazda Berkeley MXS just pulled up in the drive. I can hear her Josh and my Daniel clambering out, chasing after one another, laughing. They'll be round the back in a minute, dark curls crashing against short blond spikes, racing up the new treehouse my old friend Sol has installed in the oak tree for Daniel.

My hands are deep in the earth. I've been digging a trench so I can insert a palisade of sticks like a little fort; somewhere we can put Daniel's tortoise Hattie so she won't be able to escape. It's seven thirty and the last rays of the sun are beginning to slope over the rooftops, bright yellow and a bit chilly now, the sky just getting shaded in with patches of grey.

'You're back early?' I scramble to my feet, wiping earthy hands behind my back before hugging my old friend. She is looking far too nice for me to get soil all over her. I take her in a little wistfully: 'You've been out celebrating something today?' She's dressed in an elegant skirt and a soft white blouse and she looks . . . radiant somehow. The thought that she might be pregnant again crosses my mind. She is five years younger than me; it is still possible, after all. Her new husband Bryan has adopted her two but they don't have any children between them. Not yet.

'Oh no!' she laughs dismissively. 'Just been running around town doing errands, you know the sort of thing. Nothing special. We're going to be "lunching" next week, though. Would you like to come? Say you will. My treat.' For a moment she smiles at me and I catch a glimpse of the old Annie-Jo; the one who would have come to visit me wearing torn jeans and a faded T-shirt with baby-food stains still on it. That Annie-Jo would have flopped down beside me on the grass and we'd have finished off Hattie's palisade of sticks together in no time. This Annie-Jo looks like she's just had her nails done. She isn't going to be up for any digging.

'See what day you're going. I might come. I'd like to.' I do want to have lunch with Annie-Jo, but probably not with all her new friends. We'd see. 'I suppose we'd better get you inside then. I can't have you out here drinking tea in your finery.'

'Where's that old garden bench we used to sit on?' She looks around, frowning.

'I threw that away two *years* ago, Annie-Jo!' I laugh at her, but it surely can't have been two years since she last came and sat out in the garden with me? When our children were little we practically used to *live* in this garden. Her daughter Michelle is just a month older than Shelley, and she had Josh pretty much around the same time I had Daniel. In those days Annie-Jo was a single mum, struggling on her own in a bedsit. Now she's married to Bryan and they live in what I can only describe as a mansion in the better half of town. How times change!

Now that she's noticed the missing bench, she's looking around at other things, reluctant to go in, taking in all the modifications that have crept up on this garden over the years.

'Where's that orange rose "Maria Tierra" I bought you for your thirtieth?' she asks suddenly.

Heavens, we are talking about over a decade here; where is it?

'Bill kicked a football into it repeatedly one summer and it never recovered,' I recall at last. He broke my rose bush, I think, with an unexpected flash of irritation, and now he isn't even here to help me with Hattie's palisade, not to mention the children.

'You've got a vegetable patch,' she comments, '*and* a herb patch!' For some reason the enthusiasm in her voice warms me right through. I don't let on that I only put those in because I thought they might save me a few pennies. 'I've been telling Bryan I want one of those put in, for ages, and you've got there before me,' she accuses.

'The vegetable patch is something Sol does with Daniel, on and off. The herb patch is mine, I planted it a year ago and I've managed to kill off even the mint. You remember I gave you a bunch of mint last summer?'

'Oh yes,' Annie-Jo is still looking around as if she's never been in this garden in her life, 'so you did. Sol helps Daniel with his vegetable patch, does he? Lucky you.'

'How so?'

33

'He's a good-looking guy, Rach,' she grins at me coyly. 'There are plenty of women I know who wouldn't mind having your boss around to help out with their gardens . . .'

I figure I'd better not mention that it was him who installed the treehouse or there might be 'plenty of women' putting two and two together and ending up with five.

'If you're thinking of him as a potential partner for me, darling, I thought you knew, he doesn't swing that way.'

Annie-Jo laughs dismissively as if this is just a tiny-weeny little blot on the horizon; some minor irritating male habit that any good woman could train him out of.

'Last I heard, he'd broken up with his partner – *Adam*, was it? Maybe he's not gay after all? It does happen, you know. Sometimes the right woman comes along . . .'

'No,' I laugh at her. 'No, no, no!'

'He's got his own successful antiques business,' she carries on regardless, 'he's delightful. He clearly likes your children. And he likes you. Maybe more than just a bit?'

'Such a pity I don't fancy him, though.'

'*Fancying* is a luxury afforded only to teenagers and rich women!' Annie-Jo scoffs. 'You're forty-two now, Rach. If you don't want to be stuck on your own forever you've got to start getting realistic. Take what's available, if you catch my drift.'

Whatever makes her think that Sol might be available? He might have broken off with Adam ('He's getting so *old*, Rach, he's really let himself go!') but now he is besotted with Justin. Hell, I'm not even going there.

'That smacks of desperation, my dear, and I'm not desperate.'

Whatever has brought that on, I wonder? I'm not even looking for a man. All I ever think about are the children, especially Shelley, she takes up all the space in my thoughts.

She is dying, how can it be otherwise?

'How're you and Bryan doing?' I glance surreptitiously at Annie-Jo's belly as she perches on the low garden wall. It is as flat as ever, but that's just Annie-Jo; she could be six months gone but she'd keep her figure to the last.

'Doing great. Just great.' Annie-Jo smiles. Her right foot is swinging languidly, crossed over her left leg. 'A little tired, that's all.'

'I thought you were looking a little tired,' I prompt. Is she going to 'fess up here?

'His mother's just downsized and we've inherited all her antique rosewood furniture. It's Japanese. Very rare. Absolutely gorgeous, but I've had to redecorate and rethink the entire *lounge* to make it fit.' She pulls a 'this is so tedious' face but I know underneath she is thrilled. Being hooked into someone like Bryan means she can inherit the kind of things she once would only have dreamed of.

'Wow!' I enthuse. I'm just hoping that the growing sensation of envy I'm feeling isn't showing in any way. Annie-Jo gets to inherit antique Japanese furniture. I get Pandora's bloody box. But I don't want to be envious. Envy is one of the Spites, isn't it? Pandora's box is working overtime here.

No, I'm happy for my friend, of *course* I'm happy . . . it's not that I even want any more babies or to get married again. I mean, okay, once upon a time I did. Bill and I were actually discussing the possibility of going for a third child when all Shelley's troubles appeared, and, like a tropical storm, blew our whole lives away.

Anyway, maybe it's just as well that never happened because I've got too much on my plate now as it is. I just want . . . *hell*, I'm not sure what I want. I want a miracle to happen and for Shelley to be well. If you live in hope of a miracle then it doesn't seem fair to hope for ordinary things like a normal life as well.

'And of course, Bryan's just got the Risling contract. I mentioned that, didn't I? He's taking us to Barbados in fact, in a couple of weeks. He says he'd like to celebrate it in style.'

'Wow.' What else can I say? I'm dying to ask if the Risling contract is *all* they are celebrating, but if she isn't telling then I'm not asking. I cast my mind back to the day, eleven years ago now, that I'd driven her down to the chemist for a pregnancy test when she was expecting Josh because she'd been too frightened to do it by herself. I don't know if she's thinking about the same thing herself, or whether she's thinking about anything very much at all. Her gaze spreads out over the garden, back to examine her nails and then to some non-existent specks of fluff on her skirt.

'Sounds great,' I enthuse, but she doesn't elaborate. We both fall silent for a bit after that. Is she *bored*? Maybe it is me? I don't have much to talk about these days that comes within her sphere of interest, that is the problem.

What is she interested in, though? She has Bryan, and they have an idyllic lifestyle. They always seem so besotted with each other. I wish she and I could just *talk* to each other, the way we used to. We used to be able to talk about anything. I remember the time she thought her fella of the moment was seeing someone else and I'd ventured to tell her that I thought maybe Bill was seeing someone too. Because he'd become all withdrawn and defensive. I'd only said it to make her feel better. I hadn't known then that Bill really *was* seeing someone else. I had never even imagined it could really be true, but afterwards Annie-Jo had been convinced that I'd 'sensed it all along'. For ages, she'd been the only person who'd known about it, till he moved out and the cat was out of the bag. 'So . . . things still as good between the two of you?'

'Of course!' She's been biting her nails and she stops abruptly. I remember A-J used to be an inveterate nail-biter but she obviously doesn't do that, these days, and gives me a dazzling smile. 'Bryan is all I ever wanted in a man. I just hope that one day you find the happiness that I have,' she tells me solicitously.

'You've been lucky,' I tell her, and I push down the bitterness that surfaces suddenly and forcefully from nowhere. A man in my life would be great; maybe, one of these days.

Just at this moment I would settle for far less, though, just the friendship of an old, long-time friend. The kind of friend that takes on board your troubles, wherever you're at in your life at the time. We used to be like that. I remember the time Annie-Jo had been so fraught and sleep-deprived that she'd taken her daughter out to the shopping mall in her pushchair and left her there, outside Mothercare. I hadn't believed her at first but when she didn't produce Michelle I'd got straight in the car and gone down there myself. Lo and behold, the child had still been there; fast asleep in her buggy. I'd suffered the few dirty looks I'd got from onlookers in silence as I'd wheeled her quickly away. I wondered if Annie-Jo remembered any of that now; the way we used to be.

I want the old Annie-Jo back, but she isn't the old Annie-Jo and I'm not the Rachel I used to be when I was 'Rachel-and-Bill', either. Whatever happened to us?

'The boys will be all right up there, will they?' She glances towards the treehouse, which is a super-duper all-singing all-dancing one with bells on, typical of Sol. Of course they'll be all right. Annie-Jo never used to fret about Josh either. It was me who was the fretting type. These days I've realised we actually have control over so very little in our lives, I just coast along as best I can.

'They're going on scout camp, aren't they?' I remind her. 'They'll have to put up their own tents and grill their own sausages.'

'Ah yes, that reminds me.' She turns at last and is following me into the house. 'You have to pay the remainder of camp monies owing before next week. Arkaela needs the money before Thursday.'

Shit, I'd forgotten. I didn't like to ask Bill to help out but I was going to have to; it was either that or the gas bill would get put off again.

'Fine.' I wave a nonchalant hand at her. I know that one hundred and fifty pounds is precisely nothing for

38

Annie-Jo these days; I don't want her to guess what hardship it is for me. It is stupid pride on my part, I know. When Annie-Jo was in her bedsit days I couldn't count the times Bill and I helped her out with food and nappies and things. We never had much either, but we had so much more than she did. She'd probably help me out too if I let her.

I turn away, so I don't have to catch that hint of detached pity in her eyes.

'I've got the money,' I tell her, 'I just forgot.'

'Well it's hardly any wonder.' She follows me through the lounge into the kitchen. 'You've just had that fabulous treehouse put up; Daniel was telling us all about it on the way here. It must have taken a while to do. And workmen about the place can be so distracting.' She nods towards the boys in their den. We can see the treehouse quite easily from the kitchen table and she doesn't take her eyes off it. 'That must have cost you an arm and a leg.' She glances at me sideways. 'Unless Bill did it for his elder son?'

'Not Bill.' I shake my head.

'No?' She sips at the tea I put in front of her. No sugar these days, I've remembered that. 'Mind you, he wouldn't have too much time on his hands as I hear. Things being what they are at home.'

This is Annie-Jo in her incarnation as gossip queen. It's what they do at the Maidstone 'Domestic Goddess' meetings when they've done with other matters. It's taken her off the scent of who put up the treehouse for me, though, so I'm grateful for that.

'How *are* things at Bill's home?' I smile at her.

'Fraught, I hear.' She gets the gen from her sister-in-law who goes to the same NCT group as Stella. Annie-Jo still thinks I want to hear all the gossip about Bill. I used to, five years ago when we'd first split and it was still rankling that I was the one left on my own while he'd moved on and found someone else. I don't any more.

'Poor things.' I sidle over to the sink and give my hands a good rinsing under the tap while she stares out over the garden as if the boys might disappear any minute. 'Nikolai isn't letting them get much sleep, I hear.'

Annie-Jo gives me a significant look, but her lips remain firmly pressed together. Is she remembering the 'pram in the mall' incident or is she thinking about something else altogether?

I am resisting the temptation to ask when Shelley suddenly wheels herself in the kitchen. She wants to back out straight away, I can tell by the look on her face, but she's been spotted so she can't.

'Aunt Annie-Jo! Hi. How's Mickey?'

'Michelle is . . . she's doing great, Shelley.' Annie-Jo averts her eyes. She sounds embarrassed. 'She said to say "Hi" and she'll come over and see you very soon.'

'It's been a while.' Shelley's eyes narrow. She hasn't missed that Annie-Jo is practically squirming and neither have I. 'Did she get my birthday card?'

'I'm sure she did.' Annie-Jo is looking vague again. 'Thank you so much for that, dear.'

'Did they have a good time?' Shelley wheels over to the fridge to pour herself some milk. 'At Mickey's birthday meal, I mean. I heard they went to some lovely restaurant?'

'Oh, yes, thank you, dear!' Annie-Jo clears her throat. 'She had a lovely time, thank you. She thought you . . . maybe wouldn't . . . with the wheelchair, I mean, as you can't dance . . .' She takes a great gulp of her tea and uncrosses her legs. 'I suppose I really should be making a move, though. I'll tell Michelle you asked after her.'

I've got the strangest feeling, like I've gone pink right up to my ears. The girls had been going to each other's parties since they were *one*. I have whole albums full of their party pictures. They spent years doing horse-riding and ballet together and then, later, when Shelley got ill and became too weak for all that they used to go round each other's homes and do things that Shelley could do, playing board games and sewing, listening to music. I know they haven't been as close for some time, like Annie-Jo and me they've drifted apart, but I didn't realise things had got this bad. Why hadn't Michelle asked Shelley to her party this year? Annie-Jo is clearly embarrassed about it. I want to ask but something stops me . . . they will have their reasons. There will be some excuse. It is too late now, whatever the reason is.

'Look, I'll give you a ring about lunch next week, okay?' Annie-Jo has picked up her keys and is rapping on the kitchen window to draw Josh's attention.

Sod lunch. She can stuff it.

'I've got a feeling we might have some work for you if you do come. Do you still do that calligraphy? It's a shame, really. What with your qualifications in the fine arts and so forth. You even got a diploma, didn't you?'

I shove both our teacups into the sink. A degree,

actually! I got a degree. But I am so steaming that I don't even want to answer her.

'You always said you'd like to use that professionally, didn't you? I remember that. And calligraphy was something you always wanted to do.'

No I bloody didn't! Whatever makes you say that? I think. I never wanted to do calligraphy *professionally*. It calls for a degree of perfectionism and skill that, yes, I can muster, but it nearly kills me. I'd far sooner be slapping paint randomly over a huge canvas. In fact, what I *really* wanted to do, the only thing I ever really wanted, was to design and make my own jewellery. I haven't told many people in my life about that particular ambition – even Shelley doesn't know – but I know for a fact that I shared it with A-J. Even now I can see us, sprawled in front of the kids on the swings in the park, and scheming, the way mums do, about what we were going to do with our lives once we'd regained some measure of freedom again. I was going to design this fashion jewellery line, and A-J was going to be my model and dazzle everybody showing off my pieces on the catwalk.

It was a pipe dream. We never did anything about it, of course. We never got the chance. But she knew damn well that I never wanted to be a *calligrapher*!

'Yes, Mum does the most beautiful calligraphy.' Shelley jumps in and answers for me and I am so surprised that I say nothing. 'What's the work?'

'Invitations. We've got a big "Domestic Goddess" do coming up in the summer and we want someone who can do the invites professionally. The woman who used to do it has just moved and we usually use one of our

42

own for any little jobs.' Annie-Jo looks at me encouragingly. 'So you see, it might be worth your while joining us. There is quite a bit of this kind of work over the course of a year.'

'She'll think about it,' Shelley puts in for me again. 'Thanks for the offer, Aunt Annie-Jo.'

'Thanks for the tea, Rachel. It's been so nice to talk to you again. We'll have to organise to get together just you and me sometime. We'll do it next week, when you come to lunch.'

'Sure.' I keep washing up the cups and I don't see her to the door. I feel stung to the core about Shelley not getting a birthday invite, even if it is stupid of me.

The door shuts behind her at last. The atmosphere in the kitchen is thick with my unspoken resentment. It isn't me that she's hurt, I could cope with that. I just can't bear that she did that to Shelley, my Shelley, who has such little time, so few parties left to go to. Why had they done that?

'It's all right, Mum.' My daughter has seen my guest out and chivvied Daniel up the stairs to get out of his scout uniform. 'I don't mind. I really don't. You don't have to be so hurt on my behalf. Michelle and I haven't been close for *months*.'

'That's not the point, though, is it?' My throat is tight. I'm not really sure what the point is, but this feeling of rejection has cut me to the quick so I go back to the sink to wash up all the bits and bobs of cups and teaspoons and plates that gather during the course of the day. Outside it has grown dark all of a sudden. There is a wind stirring up the leaves in the garden and I have a feeling that tomorrow it will be quite cold.

'If she can get you some calligraphy work then you should go to the lunch. She might prove a useful contact for you.'

If Shelley feels rejected at all then she really isn't showing it. And maybe she is right. Maybe I should think of Annie-Jo as a contact if I can't think of her as a friend any more.

'She's still your *friend*,' my daughter reads my thoughts in that uncanny way that she has, 'she's just a different kind of friend than you are.'

'A disloyal one, you mean?'

'Mum,' Shelley laughs, 'compared to *you* the whole world is traitorous and harsh!'

'What on earth do you mean?' I look at Shelley in astonishment. Daniel has just bounded into the kitchen and he's ravenous as usual. His look of disappointment that there is nothing cooking on the hob is a picture.

'I mean that there is no one on this planet who is as good and true a person as you. You are the best mum in the world.'

Disloyalty, I think. That's what this is all about, really. I feel let down. I feel trampled over. Disregarded.

'I always thought of her as a friend.' I give Shelley a lopsided attempt at a grin. 'There we go. No sooner do I open Pandora's box than all the Miseries start flying out at me.'

If there is one person I would have laid money on remaining loyal to us, it would have been Annie-Jo.

'Not, of course, that there is any connection whatsoever between Annie-Jo becoming a turncoat and

Pandora's box of old junk arriving at our door . . .' Shelley reminds me.

'No. None at all,' I concede.

'What's a turncoat?' Danny looks from one of us to the other and his face seems worried. 'And what do you mean, Pandora's box makes miseries shoot out at you, Mum? Is there something inside Granny's box? Like – like *germs*, you mean?'

'Mum was making a joke, dunderhead. No germs in there. No miseries. Nothing. It's just that Mum's a bit sad because A-J, well, she doesn't appreciate that our mum's the best.'

'Mum's the best,' Daniel echoes his sister, and I pull a face and go to rummage in the fridge. If I am quick enough maybe I can pretend that these tears welling in my eyes are just the onions?

'Did you get to speak to Dad yet?' Shelley speaks softly to me, peeling the garlic in the corner. 'About the trip?'

'I've left a couple of messages. I'll get on to him tomorrow, definitely.' I don't add that he's already got back to me this morning with a resounding 'No!'

'What if he says no?'

'I won't take no for an answer,' I tell her. 'How did you find out about Michelle's party?'

She shrugs. 'The girls were all talking about it on the Internet last night. Bryan hired out the whole of the top floor at Maxime's for her, apparently. It was formal attire. Not really my scene, though, you'll agree?' I look at her closely, searching for any hint of regret at having been left out, but I can find none. Shelley accepts it; it is me who can't accept it.

45

'You'll go to Summer Bay,' I tell her. 'No matter what happens, you'll have your wish, I promise you that.'

'Okay, Fairy Godmother,' Shelley grins, dropping the peeled garlic cloves onto the chopping board. 'I'll leave it in your capable hands.'

If I know Bill, though, it is going to take more than a wave of a magic wand before he will let her go.

It is going to take something more akin to a miracle.

6

Rachel

I feel so . . . so pathetic and stupid and helpless now that Annie-Jo has gone. I've got all those I-should-have-saids twirling round in my brain like a snowstorm in a bottle and to what end? For what?

I've just pulled the tray out of the bottom of the toaster to get to all the crumbs. This is a job I never do, not ever. It is one of the least necessary things in my life and yet I am doing it now because . . . if I don't do something constructive with all this energy I fear I may pick a chair up and hurl it through the window.

I am never going to mention to Annie-Jo how hurt I was that Shelley didn't get an invite; I won't, because there is simply no point. It's gone. You can't bring the past back. I can't change anything, can I?

It's the same reason why I don't see any point hanging on to all the trash that people accumulate about the past. Like all the things Pandora sent me that I've shoved behind the pedal bin. What could possibly be in there that anyone could have judged worth keeping for all these years?

In fact, now that I'm down here throwing the crumbs

away I can see I really need to clean out this cupboard under the sink, too. There are no less than three dried-up used teabags under here that never quite made the bin. And Pandora's blooming box is taking up too much space. It makes the pedal bin stick out at the front so the door won't close properly. It's a darn nuisance having to hang on to all this for Lily, it really is. Pandora should have sent it all to her in the first place. Still, there is nothing stopping me from sticking it all in a slightly smaller (and fresher-smelling!) box that will fit more neatly behind the door. I don't know where else I would put it; we're bursting at the seams as it is.

Oh my god, there's my old diary. I can't believe she kept that! I just hope Pandora never read any of it. How embarrassing. I must have written pages and pages, what on earth did I go on about? Better take *that* out before Lily gets her mitts on it!

8 February 1978

Today my feet hurt and my legs hurt so much. We have to strengthen all our muscles, Mrs Legrange says. We have to keep on practising daily, practising and smiling, all the way through the pain because that's what the pros do. Ha, if only she knew there is no way I am ever going to do this as my grown-up job, no way, ever! The competition season is coming up again and that means extra lessons which we've got no option but to go to because once it's paid for, Dad says, it's paid for and we go. But – here is my big secret – at the moment I don't mind.

There's this boy called Gordon. He's sixteen. His

partner is called Amelie and she's two years younger than him. They aren't boyfriend and girlfriend, though. You can tell it by the way they automatically separate once the dance is over. Their gaze goes to different things. She looks up to the balcony where someone else is watching her. He looks around at the edges of the dance floor, scanning the other couples, sussing out the opposition. He's very focused. You can just see, he so much wants to win. He's got what Dad calls 'the hunger'; he says he's one to watch. So I do; oh, I do.

I watch him when he's dancing with Amelie; I watch the way that he looks at her, his eyes melting right into the very heart of her, and I find myself wondering, what might it be like if only he looked at me like that? Just the thought of it is enough to make me shiver. Just thinking about what it might be like if – just for one day – I could be his partner instead of Amelie, it's been enough to get me into trouble with Legrange for not 'paying proper attention' already.

Oh, wow, I remember him now. I do. I remember how I used to hang about after class, looking out for him. He used to turn my insides to jelly! Just thinking about it is bringing a smile to my face because I can remember how it used to be, god, what it is, to be in *love*. I suppose it must be just a teenage thing, because I never remember feeling anything like it with Bill. Not that I didn't love Bill, I did, but it wasn't this kind of head-over-heels, all-consuming thing that I felt for this boy Gordon. And here's the strange thing. When I think about it, I can hardly remember Gordon at all. I cannot bring to mind his face, or hear the sound of his voice any longer, it's all faded. What I do remember, reading this, is how I *felt* about that boy!

4 March 1978

He asked me my name today. He's been looking out for me. Well, that's what I think anyway. My class finishes ten minutes earlier than his but three weeks in a row he's come through the door into the hall at exactly the same time as me – can that be a coincidence? I told him, 'Rachel'. He said that's real nice. He's got a soft voice but it's got a strength about it, you can tell. He might be a dancer but he's not the kind of boy any of the other lads would want to mess with. He told me his name was Gordon, and I already knew that but I pretended I didn't.

I got some other info from his partner, Amelie, too. He's got a younger sister who's only six, and he's got a dog called Blanche and he's into Guns N' Roses. She told me all that without me having to probe too much and I don't think she even suspects I'm interested in him yet cos I was pretty casual about it.

Gordon didn't say anything else to me apart from 'That's real nice' and then he kind of shrugged and said, 'Well, see ya.' And then Lily came out at that moment so I was pretty glad he was gone because I don't want her getting involved. Next week I'll get to talk to him for longer because she'll be at the dentist and I'll have the field clear, all to myself. I don't know how I'm going to get through the next seven days without seeing him. It's torture. But a kind of wonderful torture at the same time because him being there has made going to practice so much more exciting. I've been trying to find out what other times he and Amelie are there but I've got to be careful. If anyone finds out they will make so much fun of me that my life will be one Holy hell, as if it isn't bad enough already.

It's all because I have to be the one to dress up and be the 'boy', of course. When we were younger it didn't matter. Nobody cared. But now that the other kids are older it's the kind of thing they notice and they laugh at me for it and I hate, hate it! I don't want to be a bloody boy, I never did. But now Mum and Dad say me and Lily have got to stay together for at least one more season because we've been dancing together for so long nobody else is going to be able to partner her as well as I can.

I don't want to have my hair cut short any more. I don't want that nasty top hat or to have that moustache painted onto my face.

Gordon doesn't know because he only sees me on a Tuesday evening after we finish general dance fitness classes. Then I'm allowed to wear my pink leotard and look like any other girl so he doesn't know. If he did he'd probably hate me and call me nasty things like all the other boys do. God, it doesn't bear thinking about, it really doesn't.

Ugh! It brings it all back, it really does. I would never have thought that just a few simple words written in a diary could have such a strong emotional impact, but it's almost as good as a time-machine, this. I'm transported. I'm actually *there*.

'*Mu*-um, are you coming? *Mu*-um?'

'Just one second, Dan. Do the bits of your maths that you can and I'll be along in a moment.'

He's waiting upstairs. I said I would just finish in the kitchen but I'm taking an age over it because I was feeling so upset about Annie-Jo.

'I've already *done* the bits that I can do.' His voice is languid. He's probably hoping that I'll get sidetracked and forget all about it but I can't, I mustn't.

'Okay. I'll be up at exactly quarter to. Five minutes.'

Five minutes – just one more and then I'll have to leave reading the rest of these diary entries till later.

11 March 1978

I had to make the most of it tonight, I knew that and I went for it. I kept thinking there's never going to be another good time like this when Liliana is out of the picture. It couldn't have been better really. First, she and Dad got stuck behind a long appointment at the dentist. I got a message through the office that they were going to be delayed. Then that was nearly ruined when my class overran by fifteen minutes. My heart felt so tense in my chest it was just unreal. I kept thinking he's going to be gone by the time I get out of this bloody lesson, my whole week of waiting will have all been for nothing and I can't stand this, I really can't.

But when I finally got out, blasting through the

double-doors like a bat out of hell, he was still there, leaning all casually up against the doorway opposite, waiting for me. I could feel it. He smiled at me and then he . . . just sort of put his head a little to one side, indicating the courtyard, and I followed him out without speaking. And outside there was a chill spring wind blowing, I could feel it goose-pimpling up my arms but I was too excited to feel any cold at all. It was getting dark, quarter to five already, and there was only the lamplight from the street opposite for us to see each other by. It didn't matter.

I was worried I wouldn't know what to say. Gordon was so quiet at first I thought maybe he's shy too, but he wasn't. Not at all.

They say you always remember your first kiss, but what do you remember? Is it the surprise of first having someone else's ardent lips on your own, that feeling of having them so near, dangerous and exciting as it is, the heat of their body up close against yours? If we'd had more time to get to know each other, more opportunities during the week to meet, I would have hung back forever shy, I would have taken forever to let him get near to me.

But tonight . . . all I could think of was, I won't get to see him again for another seven whole days. And when I do, next time, stupid Lily will be there. And by then maybe someone will have told him about my nasty tuxedos and painted-on moustaches and he will have gone right off me. Hell, if I were him I would have!

So we kissed. And I didn't feel shy and awkward

53

about it, not at all. I felt powerful and feminine and
beautiful even though we didn't say a word, no, I
swear, we didn't speak. We didn't need to. Only when,
after an entire age had passed at last I heard my
father's voice calling through the corridors inside; I
heard his footsteps coming quickly and the janitor
following behind him saying grumpily 'I'm already
locking up here'. And only then did Gordon let me
go. He had this peaceful smile on his face. He said,
'See ya'. That was all he said but it echoed in my
heart all the way home and for a long time after-
wards. I think it will echo in my heart forever.

Reading that has just lightened up my day, it really has.
I didn't always feel like such a dried-up old husk of a
fruit bat like I do now. I did once know what it felt like
to fall in love with someone. Puppy love, maybe, but
who cares what it was? It's all come rushing back and
it's made me feel all funny inside.

'Mum, it's quarter to already!'

Hell, so it is, and I did promise Dan.

I don't want to read on, though. I'm not really sure
why. It reminds me of who I used to be, I suppose. It
reminds me of the person I might still be, inside, underneath the crusty layers of all the years and all the vicis-
situdes. I'm not sure if that's a good thing or not.

'Coming, Danny. I'm coming.' I jump up, pushing the
journal back in Pandora's box. I'm going to have to find
some other hiding place, well and truly hidden out of
sight. I don't want any of the kids cottoning on to this
before I have a chance to destroy it.

'Okay, Mum?' Shelley's caught a glimpse of the smile in my heart, I know she has, because she's just looked at me curiously, passing me on the way to the stairs.

'I'm fine,' I tell her automatically. Maybe I am, too, I think. I've just had a reminder of the fact that, after all, I am still human. I am still capable of remembering what it feels like to love and be loved.

Maybe at the end of the day that's the only thing that counts?

7

Shelley

Miriam's mum came round this morning. When she came through the door I thought she was someone else. She didn't look the same. Her hair has gotten much thinner than it used to be, much lighter, almost white. Her face has been leached of all its colour, of all its life. I think she was wearing a thin beige jacket; the kind that the old ladies wear who queue up at the post office on a Thursday morning. She's gotten old.

She's not that old, though. She's only the same age as my mum is. She shouldn't look like that.

'I'm getting there,' she said, when Mum asked her how she was coping. 'Slowly.' She wanted to see me, to say hello, and I wanted to see her too, but when I came into the hallway she looked at me so long and hard I felt she might be X-raying me with her eyes. It was as if she was trying to look right through to my bones, to see how they were holding up, assessing just how much longer I might have left.

She told me I was looking well, but she didn't say it with any happiness in her voice. She made me feel guilty. When they went to drink their tea I left them and went into my bedroom, which is downstairs nowadays. My heart was pounding. My arms felt all weak. I needed to stay there for a minute and just rest. I didn't want to be with them, but I still peered at them from where I was behind my door. I felt hypnotised.

Miriam's mum and her husband David have split up now, apparently. She said they didn't know how to be together any more; they couldn't remember who they each were.

I wondered if my mum would remember who she was, once I'd gone. It seemed a strange kind of thing for Miriam's mum to say, and it stayed with me for a long time afterwards.

'Well at least that's one bridge I won't have to cross.' Mum had smiled tightly at her. She had no one to split up with. I guess that's what she meant.

'Splitting with David was the least of my worries,' Miriam's mum had shrugged. 'I'm leaving for Spain in three months. I'm leaving this country for good. I'm taking her ashes with me. I plan to plant them beneath an olive tree under the glorious Mediterranean sun.'

'I'm sorry about David,' Mum said.

'Look, I just don't care any more. When you see someone you love – your child – go through that suffering, everything else in the world . . . it just turns a shade of black or white or grey. Nothing matters. In the end,' she looked at my mum sharply, 'I just wanted her gone.'

'Was it that bad?'

They had lowered their voices. They were talking in loud whispers but this house is full of echoes. I could still hear every word.

'It is far worse than they told us to expect, I'm afraid.' She shot Mum a pitying look. 'I won't go into the details but you will have to brace yourself for it. We were desperate, in the end. To say that her passing away was a blessed relief would be an understatement.' She stopped, then, as Mum put her hands over her face and began, noiselessly, to cry. I wanted to go and smack that woman in the face just then. I would have liked to storm in there and tell her to get the hell out. What business did she have, coming in here doing that to my mum, just because she'd been through a terrible time?

All that she'd been through – it must have changed her. She never used to be like that, and now she was regretting it because I could hear her saying, 'I'm so sorry, Rachel. I shouldn't have said that. I wanted to warn you, that's all, so that you would be prepared for what is to come. Maybe there is something you can take some strength from?' She hesitated. 'Do you ever go to church?'

Mum shook her head at that. She blew her nose into a tissue. 'It might not be the same for Shelley,' she said when she put her face up. 'Research is giving us new medicines all the time, things are getting better. And maybe the new doctor, Ari Lavelle, maybe he'll be able to come up with some things that Doctor Ganz never thought of?'

'I won't hear a *word* spoken against Doctor Ganz,' Miriam's mum flared up and you could see Mum had hit on a real nerve there. 'Doctor Ganz was the only one out of the lot of them who really cared. If you had your eyes open you'd know they've only taken away his consultancy and his research post to allow that *Lavelle* man to come in and . . .' Our visitor sniffed loudly. I could see her fingers clutching tightly on to the handles of her bag. 'I blame Doctor Lavelle, personally, for what happened to Miriam. She only started getting much worse when he came in and began messing around with her dosages and asking questions that Doctor Ganz never asked us. Messing things up, basically.'

'I really think that might be a little . . .' Mum didn't know what to say, I could tell.

'You got Doctor Ganz back for a little while, though, didn't you?' There was a hint of resentment in Miriam's mother's voice now. 'I heard Doctor Ganz came back because Lavelle had some more *important* work to do at his other base in the US. But I hear the old man's back at the department now, causing mischief again?'

'I . . . I really don't know about that. I believe that Ari Lavelle has very good credentials. And I still think . . . I think maybe there's hope for Shelley yet. She may react differently to the drugs they give her. Everybody's different you know.'

'They are. You watch out for him, that's all I'm saying. At least you can't say I didn't give you fair warning.' Miriam's mum stood up then and pushed a small white card into her hand. 'Anyway, I've taken up enough of your time. We're having a memorial service for Miriam. The details are on the card. Let us know if you can come. Shelley, too, of course, if she's able.'

'Why would I be coming if she *weren't* able?' Mum's voice had a new energy to it. I watched her as she shoved the front door closed with her foot. It slammed more loudly than seemed polite. I hoped Miriam's mum hadn't

59

got offended. I don't know why I cared, but I did. I thought maybe we should still try and be kind to her.

I remembered how many times she had brought Miriam to our house and what good friends we had all been then, Miriam's mum and my mum, Miriam and me. The last time they had been here Miriam had been laughing and joking because she'd just made her mum buy her a bright green coat which made the ginger of her hair stand out even louder. She might have been sick, but she was still so full of life.

Now Miriam was ashes. I tried to think about that but it was more than my head could take. Where did the person go if they were ashes? Where was I going to go? What if I didn't want to go there?

I'd talked about this sort of thing before, with Solly. Solly is very spiritual. He told me that Miriam would probably reincarnate sometime; that I shouldn't worry. I told him that if I'd had the shit life she'd had then I wouldn't bother reincarnating. Besides, it might sound selfish but I was more worried about myself just at that moment. It was going to be my turn next. I didn't want to disappear into a pot of ashes under an ornamental tree.

'I suppose you heard most of that?' Mum reappeared from the front door looking tired and worn; and *angry*. I nodded.

'Just who the hell does she think she is?' she stormed.

'She hasn't come to terms with it,' I muttered. 'She's angry that she had to go through seeing Miriam suffer so much. It's that which has made her bitter.' And the change of doctors, I thought. She hadn't got over that yet, clearly. What if she'd got a point, though? I pushed that thought out of my mind quickly.

'I know, I know. I feel sorry for her too. Even though I'm angry with her.'

'Don't be.' I looked Mum straight in the eye for a minute. 'She's just jealous, you know, because you've still got me.'

'You're right.' I could see Mum had tears in her eyes, though she was trying to hold them back. 'It's just . . . why do people have to change so much?' she muttered under her breath. 'First Annie-Jo, now her.' She picked up the cushion where Miriam's mum had been sitting and gave it a good punch then set it back down again. 'Why can't things ever just stay the same?'

They don't, though. The unspoken thought hung in the air between us. I wasn't going to stay the same, either, even though we were both in the habit of pretending otherwise.

Sickness.

That's what was coming.

I looked at Mum's face and I could tell exactly what she was thinking.

'It's not going to be the same for me, Mum, I *promise* you that.' I don't know if that made her feel any better, me telling her that I wasn't going to suffer. It made me feel better, though, knowing that I wouldn't be putting her through that final hell. It strengthened my resolve, as she would say.

Maybe Miriam's mum had done us a favour after all.

8

Shelley

SugarShuli says: *Hi Shelley. Am I the luckiest girl in the world or what? Sending you a jpg of Jallal so you can see why. (Isn't he fit?) Got it through last night. Please don't be jealous, just be pleased for me. Mum and Dad want to hold the wedding in the summer, so you should be okay to come, yes?*

ShelleyPixie says: *Jallal looks nice.*

SugarShuli says: *Nice? Is that all you can say?*

ShelleyPixie says: *He looks nice, Surinda. I hope he's good to you when you get married. What is he like?*

SugarShuli says: *Haven't met him yet. He comes over next month. My parents sorting him out with a job, that sort of thing.*

ShelleyPixie says: *Sounds real strange to me, to think of marrying someone you haven't even met.*

SugarShuli says: *To you it does. We spoke over the phone for the first time yesterday too. I couldn't sleep all night after hearing his voice. He sounds seriously sexy, my friend.*

ShelleyPixie says: *Sure.*

I'm thinking maybe what Surinda is doing isn't so very off after all. Krok jokes all the time that he'll come for me one day to marry me and sometimes I pretend that it's true. Only because I have nothing better to do. I know it's just his online chat. But sometimes I pretend; and if it ever really did come true – let's just say 'if' – I wonder if I really would elope with him. Maybe I would.

SugarShuli says: *I've never felt like this before. Have you ever been in love, Shelley? I mean, really, head-over-heels type in love?*

ShelleyPixie says: *No, what's it like?*

SugarShuli says: *You can't stop thinking about the person. It's like an addiction. Some people need a drink or a chocolate to make them happy. I know what I need is Jallal.*

Phew, she's derived all this from a photo and one long-distance telephone conversation. Love must indeed be a powerful thing.

ShelleyPixie says: *I'm just wondering – how do you know it's love and not just a crush or something?*

SugarShuli says: *Well – you've read about it, haven't you? It just takes over your whole world, just like Mystical Crystal said in 'Superstars Secrets' last month. All I can think about is the wedding. It's, like, taken over my brain.*

Surinda doesn't have an enormous brain, so that shouldn't be too hard, the uncharitable thought pops up.

SugarShuli says: *All I can think about is . . . you know, the actual night. I'm working on my mum to buy me some nice stuff, lingerie, you know the type of thing. She says I won't need it. It won't matter. But I'm working on her; it's all part of the fun, isn't it?*

ShelleyPixie says: *I guess.*

How would I know? She's talking about sex. I've never

even been kissed. I'm never going to be. I'm not much of a friend, I know, but her joy is making me miserable. The more wonderful Surinda assures me that her life is, the crappier I feel about my own. Not that any of that is her fault. Krok hasn't answered my emails for ages and he's never online these days. I don't know how he spends his time. Having fun making music and going out with girls who can go out with him, I suppose. I want to ask him about the *Beat the Bank* tickets. Not that I'm planning on going, it's just a thing we talk about online.

ShelleyPixie says: *I don't know how you can get so enthusiastic about someone you've never met.*

There I go. I don't want to rain on her parade, not really.

SugarShuli says: *You're enthusiastic over your Krok, aren't you?*

ShelleyPixie says: *I'm not marrying him, though.*

I wish I were. I can't believe I just thought that. I'm jealous. I admit it. Surinda sees this Jallal as the easy way out of her life as she's living it at the moment, stuck in that tiny house with her five brothers and sisters and her strict 'do-as-I-say' father and her timid-mouse mum. She was always a dunce at school so marriage is her only way out of it.

I wish I had an easy way out of my life too.

I guess I do.

I've already gone through all my options on that score and I've made my decision but it isn't a very thrilling one. I'm going to have to tell someone soon because keeping it all to myself is killing me. Ha ha.

It has to be someone who won't say anything, though,

or my plans will be ruined. I have to tell Mum, of course, but I want to tell someone else as well. I don't know if I can trust Surinda. I want Krok.

SugarShuli says: *I wish you could be happy for me.*

ShelleyPixie says: *Don't think I'm not. Once you're married you're stuck with him, though, aren't you, Surinda? I mean, with your family being the way it is, you won't have the option of a quickie divorce if things don't work out.*

SugarShuli says: *I'm content, girl. I couldn't be happier. I see your Kieran boy was in the papers this morning?*

She means Krok. Kieran is his real name.

ShelleyPixie says: *Was he? What for?*

SugarShuli says: *He must have got them places he was after. They were doing a piece about how today's youth have such high expectations and it's all because of the hype surrounding game shows. They all had to say what they hoped to gain if they won. Kieran's bit got the biggest coverage – they said because he'd tragically lost his parents and here was a lad who wanted to do something positive in their memory, but I think really they're targeting him because he's so photo . . . photoginetic.*

ShelleyPixie says: *Photogenic?*

SugarShuli says: *'God damn gorgeous, girl! Anyway, he's on tonight's show.*

Christ, is that what he's been up to? I didn't know. He hasn't even bothered to let me know . . . I feel like not even watching it now. Plus, now there's the added worry that everybody else is noticing him. I don't want everyone else making a fuss of him. He's *mine*.

ShelleyPixie says: *Not been talking to Krok lately.*

SugarShuli says: *He pissed with you?*

ShelleyPixie says: *Why would he be?*

SugarShuli says: *Dunno. Maybe because you won't send him a photo? And he hasn't sent you them tickets.*

ShelleyPixie says: *NOYB, is it? Anyway, even if we did get tickets – assuming he's not eliminated in the next few weeks – how would we get there? Mum won't take us so how would we . . .*

SugarShuli says: *Yes she would. Your mum is the best mum in the world. She gives you everything. You're so lucky. She'd give you the lingerie I'm after if it was you in my place.*

ShelleyPixie says: *If it* were *me.*

SugarShuli says: *That's what I said, if it was you.*

ShelleyPixie says: *If it* were *me,* not *was* me. *Anyway, why don't you ask Jallal if he's so loaded? It'll be mainly for his benefit, won't it?*

SugarShuli says: *lol. Big brother wants the computer off me – he's looking for jobs now. Speak to U tomorrow.*

ShelleyPixie says: *Okay, CU then.*

God, she's so excited. She's like a jumpy bunny. I'm a cow, I know, but I don't want to hear all about it really. I wish I had some proper friends I could speak to, like Miriam, not just Surinda. I wish Krok would come back online. Maybe I could phone him and speak to him at the DVD shop? Just the thought of doing that gives me butterflies in my stomach. What if he doesn't want to take my call? I'd be so embarrassed.

I was thinking about that last night. I looked up his shop but they aren't listed on the Internet and Mum keeps the telephone directories upstairs so I can't get to them without her wanting to know why, and I don't want to tell her so I'm stuck. Unless Surinda does it for me?

ShelleyPixie says: *B4U go – could you look up the telephone number for David's DVDs for me? It's in Kensington somewhere.*

SugarShuli says: *Did you think of trying directory enquiries?*

ShelleyPixie says: *I haven't got the full address – you might have to hunt for it.*

Surinda's brother works in telesales. He's got a huge pile of directories beside his bed at home. Surinda told me he keeps his collection of top-shelf magazines hidden underneath them too, but that's more than anybody wants to know.

SugarShuli says: *Give me a little while. If Yusef goes out later I can search for you, otherwise not.*

ShelleyPixie says: *Thanks for that, Surinda.*

She's not so bad after all. It's not her fault her life is on the up and mine isn't. I think I'll make out a 'May resolutions list'. I've got such little time left. I need to focus on what I want to get done before I go. It's a pity I won't make Surinda's wedding like she thinks. I would have liked to have seen her all decked out in her orange sari.

But I promised myself I wouldn't do the 'if-onlys'.

I said I'd never do that.

My 'May resolutions list' would look like this:

1. Meet Krok. Okay, I do want to meet him. I want to say hello and goodbye. I want to know if I

really would have fallen in love with him. I want to know what that must feel like. I can't leave earth without doing that.

2. Sort out my stuff. I'll make a list. Danny gets my computer. Surinda can have the emerald ring that belonged to my dad's mum. That can be my wedding present to her.

3. Be independent. Find out who I am. Do something brave.

I reckon I can do those things before my birthday at the end of May. I can if I put my mind to it.

9

Rachel

Stella is having a difficult time with little Nikolai. I can hear him kicking and struggling in the background.

'He's always like this whenever one of us gets on the phone!' Stella tells me. She sounds strained, distantly polite as always. I wish she would just accept that the last thing on my mind is any desire to steal my ex-husband back from his new wife. I don't want Bill back. If they are happy together then I am truly glad of it.

'Nikki and I were just about to go and play in the garden.' The tone of her voice suggests that I have phoned at a *most* inconvenient time. The sun has been beating down all day in Surrey, apparently. Lucky Surrey. We, on the other hand, have been blessed with unremitting rain since the beginning of April. My garden is a veritable sea of mud.

'I'll see if I can locate Bill for you.'

Stella could be a secretary screening calls for a high-profile executive. I bite my lip irritably. I've already phoned Bill *twice* this week about our daughter's birthday; the least he could do is get back to me.

I must be frowning more deeply than I realise because

Sol – out there in the treehouse fixing a leak for Daniel – catches sight of me through the window and pulls a face. I pull a face back at him but then force myself to smile. I *am* going to be pleasant to Bill, no matter what it takes.

'Hi, Rachel,' Bill's breathy voice comes down the phone suddenly. I get a momentary vision of him, a half-eaten piece of toast in one hand, his jacket half-on and scooping up the car keys from the sideboard as if he needs to be off, quickly, somewhere else.

'Bill, I'm phoning about Shelley's birthday. Have you got a minute?'

'A minute, yes.'

Hi Bill, yes, I'm doing just fine. The kids are well too. So kind of you to enquire. Bill was never one for small talk – cut to the chase, he always said. Okay, here I go with the chase:

'This is about Shelley wanting to go to Cornwall for her birthday, Bill.'

'Yeah, you said. We emailed. I thought we'd agreed. *No.*' There's the sound of a door shutting far away in the place where he is, as Nikolai's high-pitched screaming blocks out all else for an instant. 'Sorry, he's teething. It's a bit noisy here.'

Teething, yeah, right.

'Bill, Shelley really wants to go to Summer Bay for her birthday.'

'Look, things are kind of difficult here at the moment.' I can just feel his eyebrows lifting. 'Anyway, what on earth does she want to go *for*?' He sounds preoccupied. He sounds as if he hasn't slept in weeks. Nikolai probably

70

makes sure of that. 'It's a bit far away, isn't it?' He is thinking about the long drive down there; what it will mean to squeeze it in between a late finish on a Friday and an early start on a Monday morning.

'You don't have to come, Bill. In fact, she doesn't really want a crowd. She's been quite clear about that. She just wants some girl-time.'

He doesn't seem to be listening. He's got the desk diary in front of him, I can hear him turning over the pages, flick, flick, till he arrives at the week at the end of May.

'Not possible, I'm afraid. I've got a meeting first thing on that Saturday morning which won't finish till about one. Nope. No can do, Rachel.'

'That's all right, Bill,' I explain patiently. 'She just wants me and her to go. You don't have to be there.'

There is a silence at the other end while he takes that in.

'We can do all the tea and cakes and presents bit when we get back,' I offer.

'No, we can't.' He sounds petulant. 'It's Stella and my anniversary. When my meeting finishes on Saturday I was planning to take her away for a few days. In fact, there was something I was hoping to run past you regarding that. We were sort of hoping you might have Nikolai for us; just for a few days?'

I am stunned into silence for a minute; astounded really that he can even think of asking me. Okay, so we keep up a good front for the kids' sake but Bill and I hadn't exactly parted best of friends. I glance up as Sol taps gently on the kitchen door and lets himself in. I can see the darker patches on the bottoms of his socks where

71

they are soaking wet. I watch him sit down at my kitchen table and peel them off.

'The conversation we need to have at the moment is about Shelley's birthday,' I remind Bill, 'not your anniversary. Perhaps we can discuss that another time?' I don't know why I say that. There is no question of me ever taking Nikolai off their hands – not even for a couple of hours, let alone a couple of days. I have my own hands full enough as it is. Why the hell do I find it so difficult to just say NO?

'Can't do it, Rachel. Anyway, weren't the kids due to come to me for that Saturday? I was going to take them all out to the park and then on for a burger. That way Nikolai can come too.'

Hmm, and maybe you can then palm Nikolai off onto me later?

'The *park*?' I say. Sol chuckles into his hands at that. He knows who I'm talking to and what we are talking about. 'I think you'll find it's the week after that they're due to come to yours, Bill. I've just checked. The Summer Bay thing is just for Shelley and me, as I've said. It's what she's asked me for . . .'

And she so seldom ever asks me for anything. If only he could see that and break away from his enclosed little Bill–Stella–Nikolai world for a minute.

Had we ever been like that? I wondered now. A little self-contained, totally enclosed unit; a bubble of a family, where inside the fold everyone is totally 'right' and outside it you are likely to be considered completely in the wrong?

'I'll just check on that with Stella. I'm sure you're

wrong there.' Bill's tone is defensive now. I hear him put the receiver down and go out and close the door to talk to Stella.

Were we? Were we ever like that together, Bill and I?

I close my eyes for a minute. I count to ten. Once, a lifetime ago, lying under the canopy of an oak tree on Hampstead Heath:

'I want to know why it is you love me.' Bill had been lying flat on his back, hogging the lion's share of the shade.

'Because you're . . . you're *wonderful*!' I'd told him enthusiastically.

'No, I mean precisely why. Tell me the reasons.' His eyes had opened, caught me laughing, then, while he'd been dead serious.

'I just do,' I'd said helplessly. 'Because you love me. Because you accept me as I am. Because you believe in my dreams. Because when I'm in your arms I feel, oh, I feel I could conquer the whole world, but even better than that, I feel I don't need to . . .'

'The real reason,' he'd rolled over, businesslike, 'is that you know that with me, you're going to be going places, right?'

I didn't know what he meant at the time. Some little village on the outskirts of Mumbai? To Turkey; to Greece, where we could look up the lost city of Troy?

'Women need to know they've got someone to look after them, that's all. You're right, Rachel. Stick with me and you won't need to conquer the world. That's because I'll do it for you.' He'd been so sure of himself. I'd been so besotted with him. He'd meant he'd look after me

73

materially. I thought he'd meant in all the other ways that count.

'Any luck?' Sol glances up at me from the papers he's been scanning.

'You know Bill,' I mouth. 'He's never going to make this easy.'

Sol does know Bill. He and Adam were our neighbours for four years before their business took off and they were able to afford pastures greener. I sit down beside my one-time neighbour and sometime employer and prop my face in my hands.

'Never mind him, though. What interesting work have you got lined up for me today?'

Sol pulls a face, then straightens it immediately. 'Wrinkles,' he tells me, 'I must remember not to do that. Anyway, I've got a pile of typing for you, darling. I think most of it is legible. Let me know what you think of the hero.' He sits back, his white linen shirt half-open, showing off his all-year tan to good effect. He is gorgeous, actually – the thought pops irrelevantly into my head. No wonder Adam was heartbroken when they split up. Annie-Jo has a point. Why do I never notice men at all these days – even the gay ones?

'The hero? Oh, it's your novel then? Not the new brochure for the shop?'

'Justin's doing the brochure.' Sol waves a hand airily. 'He understands the new publishing program better than anyone. He's a whiz-kid. He's young. They're all whiz-kids.' He looks a bit tragic as he says this.

'Adam had a pretty good handle on that side of things . . .'

'Adam was a dinosaur, Rachel. Old-fashioned in the extreme. In *all* his ways.' He gives me a significant look. 'Life's an adventure to be tasted, isn't it, sweetie?'

'So, the whiz-kid is helping you with the brochure?'

'Actually, he's being such a *bitch* about it I told him he could bloody well do it himself.' His voice is blasé, but the pain in his eyes when he mentions Justin is etched deep.

'Justin playing up again?' Uh-oh, trouble at the ranch. I'm still holding the phone to my ear, but there's no sign of Bill coming back just yet. Bill works for a law firm and no doubt he's used to keeping people on hold for great lengths of time, I think. I will hold for exactly two minutes more.

'If I didn't love him so much I would dump him, truly I would. But we're soul mates,' Sol tells me, 'we were destined to be. He's making me suffer to show me what I put him through in our previous existence together.'

'Won't that mean he'll have to come back and suffer the same thing again himself?' I swap the phone over to my other ear, and hand Sol the corkscrew and a bottle of cabernet sauvignon.

'I don't know. Good point. I shall put that to him. He won't care, though, that's the thing. He's a Gemini, isn't he? I was warned. Aquarius rising, too; he won't be tied down.' He pours out a small amount of wine and swivels it around in the glass, savouring its bouquet.

'I'm sorry,' I say. He never used to look this sad. Or even so *careworn* as he does at the moment. Well, stands to reason really. I know Adam was the one who used to take care of the troublesome things in life, like shop brochures and acquisitions and keeping the website updated. Making sure there was milk in the fridge. In short, all the boring little necessities of life, which allowed everyone else – aka Solly – to go out and be 'carefree'.

'Will he let Shelley go with you?' Sol indicates the phone with his head. 'He should let her do what she wants to, poor darling.' He pours out a large glass and hands it to me.

'I've made up my mind I'm going to take her anyway,' I tell him slowly. 'I might need to ask for your help with some things, though. Hattie, for example, will you look after her for us?'

'The tortoise?' Sol grins amicably. 'Sure.'

'Will you be around the last week in May, though? This is really important, Solly. Are you sure you can do it?'

'Sure thing, honey bunch.' He is still thinking about Justin, I can tell.

'Hello, Rachel?' Bill is back on the phone.

'Hello. All sorted then?'

There is a pause.

'No.' Bill is sounding surprisingly determined. You'd think he'd got enough on his plate with the demon child he and Stella have produced, but no. 'This might be what Shelley's asked you for, Rachel, but there are other people's feelings to be considered here too. She's used to getting too much of her own way, I think. That's the trouble with it. When she comes over to us we stick to a much stricter regime and she has to deal with it. She has to eat whatever Stella puts on her plate for one thing.'

'*Meaning?*' What the hell has that got to do with

anything? The two of them have obviously had a very long conversation while I've been hanging on that damned phone. I can feel my ire rising. Why do I always let him do this to me? I swore that I wouldn't, not today.

'She's as thin as a stick, Rach. She can't eat more than a morsel of food on an ordinary day, be honest now. We weighed her when she came to us for that week over Christmas, at the beginning, and then again at the end.' I can hear him sounding a little bit sheepish as he realises what he is admitting to but he ploughs on with it anyway. 'And she'd put on five pounds at the end.' Sheepish, but triumphant nonetheless.

'Now you're telling me that I don't feed her?'

'Stella said when she handed her the bath towel she could see her ribs sticking out. You've got to be aware of this, surely? I have to say it, even if it hurts you to hear it.'

'If you think you could do a better job then we could talk about options here. I'm worn out myself, with being her carer. I love her, but I'm worn out. Maybe you're right. You two might be able to do a much better job than I can manage these days.' My voice is surprisingly calm. A year before I might have made that as a throw-away comment in temper, knowing full well he would never agree to take me up on it. I wouldn't have wanted him to, anyway. But this time I really mean it.

Sol's face is a picture. I cover the phone with my hands while Bill relays what I've just said to his wife. 'He won't take me up on it, of course. There is no way they could hack it. They are both stressed up to the eyeballs with their own child as it is. And,' I turn my face away from the phone to make doubly sure they won't overhear, 'to tell you the truth I think there is *nothing* wrong with little Nikolai, not at all. It's just that some two-year-olds don't want to learn the violin and take French language lessons and gymnastics classes every week. They get tantrummy about it. It is all very well to keep up a military regime for one or two days every couple of weeks but it's not so easy when the child is resisting you all the way, on a day in, day out basis. Shelley won't eat much because the tablets she has to take with her food sit like a pile of gravel in her belly and they ruin her appetite. She copes at her dad's because she just doesn't take the tablets for those days, just so as not to make a fuss.'

Sol nods sympathetically.

I *know* she's too thin. I'd like her to be a lot heavier. I'd like a lot of things that just aren't going to happen.

'Let's not argue over this.' Bill is back and has gone into reasonable mode. 'You know that suggestion isn't practicable.'

'I thought not.'

'But to get back to my previous point, there *are* certain procedures you could put in place . . .'

'Save it.' I am the one feeling tetchy now. 'Save your parenting theories for the one you have to deal with, will you? And let's keep *our* conversation to the birthday plans. That's what I rang about, and I too have a schedule to keep to this afternoon.'

I have to ring the surgery after speaking to Bill and ask why they'd only given me one month's supply of Shelley's tablets again. They used to give me six months, then it went down to three months, and then it became a ridiculous one month's supply! I can't spend my life going up and down putting in repeat prescriptions every four weeks. Everything takes up so much time. Bill doesn't have to deal with any of that, and so he can't possibly know what it is like.

'I want to spend time with her on her birthday too.' He is sad. I can hear it in his voice, and I wish now I had been kinder to him. Why do we always do this? Why can't we just be civil to each other? I can't bear to hear him feeling sad. It reminds me of that small battered place in my heart where I keep all the cherished memories of what we used to mean to each other.

'We don't know if she'll *have* any more birthdays.' His voice breaks here and I just cave in. It is true. He is right. I don't want to be unfair about this.

'Look, we can work something out. Perhaps you can come down and spend the Saturday with us down there then? She specifically asked to be in Summer Bay for her birthday. And she wanted some time alone with me. But if you could make it down for the Saturday, that would be a lovely surprise. We could throw her a party – organise something that she'd never even suspect. You can bring Daniel and Nikolai too. And Stella, of course.'

'It'll be a long drive,' Bill grumbles, but he is caving, I can tell. 'Just for the one day.'

'Stay for the long weekend then. Make it worth your while.'

'Maybe,' Bill concedes. 'I'd have to discuss this more with Stella.'

'Do it then. I know Shelley would love to see you on her birthday.'

'Don't make any plans,' he warns me, 'not just yet. There's a lot we've got to think about here. I'll get back to you about it within the next couple of weeks.'

The next couple of weeks, I know, will be too late. I have a letter, still on the kitchen table, that I received this morning from Maggie at the bed and breakfast; we have to confirm straight away or the last two spaces will be taken.

'We'll talk about this again,' he tells me.

'Sure,' I say, and I remember all over again just what he is like. I know I am never going to get anywhere with him. Bill isn't the reasonable sort. 'We'll talk about it soon.'

Deceit, I think now. This isn't like me at all. This is another one of Pandora's vices. Oh well. Looks as though they're thrumming through the air at a rate of knots at the moment, just waiting to home in on us at any opportunity.

'Who are you ringing now?' Solly watches me curiously as I punch the next number into the phone. 'All sorted, is it?'

'All sorted,' I tell him. 'I'm booking Maggie's place for Shelley and me for the last week in May, just like she wanted.'

10

Shelley

Mum's gone out, thank god. I thought she never would. I've had this paper with Kieran's telephone number on it in my hand since breakfast time when Surinda phoned me. It's gone all crumpled and hot because I've had to wait so long. I probably won't even be able to read my own handwriting now.

To be honest, I've waited so long I've gone off the boil with the whole idea. He would probably be horrified if I tried to ring him anyway. In fact, I'm sure he would.

I'm not going to do it.

I'm going to read a bit more of Mum's diary instead. That's another thing that I can't do when she's around. I shouldn't be peeking in Mum's old diary, I know. It might all be ancient history now but it's still private and she has a right to privacy, but I . . . I just want to know what it used to be like for her.

Her writing was a bit smaller in those days. It was a lot neater too. Her diary has a pale pink plastic cover and she's drawn lots of hearts and loopy-petalled flowers in biro all the way around some of the entries. I can't believe she did that. Ohmigod, it's just what *I* do when

I'm daydreaming. I wonder if that kind of stuff can be inherited? That's just *weird*, man.

It's real funny, thinking about her being a girl my age, having so much stuff to say and the only one she has to say it to is her diary. Just like Anne Frank, when you think about it. God, how sad is that? We all just email each other these days but they had to make do with diaries, I guess. I wonder if people read each other's diaries after they'd written them? What would be the point of it otherwise?

20 October 1978
We have to be careful. I've told Gordon that my dad won't let us have boyfriends and he accepts that. So we take whatever snatched time we can get. It helps that Legrange Studios are having a big refit at the moment. It means everything's a bit chaotic so a lot of the time people are coming and going from all sorts of places where they wouldn't normally be.

Mr Legrange nearly caught me out today. I took a short-cut coming in from the courtyard after seeing Gordon. I ran across the new stage area where none of us are allowed to go, yet. It was the quickest route but Mr Legrange caught me and it was the nearest I've come to being rumbled so far. It reminds me that I mustn't get careless. He gave me that look adults give kids when they catch them doing what they're not supposed to. Luckily, I've got a good reputation. I could see him waiting for an explanation so I told him one of the planks on stage was loose and I'd come back in especially to tell him that. He said which

*plank, and I pointed to one, and he went and jumped
up and down on it a few times. He said he'd have it
checked out and he let me go, thank god.*

*Lily is getting suspicious, too. She's wondering why
I keep finding excuses to go back inside the studio
once we've already come out. By the time I got through
Mr Legrange, I found her waiting, arms folded and
looking fed up, by the toilets. I told her I had to use
the ones usually reserved for the adults but I don't
think she believed me. God, why can't she just leave
me in peace for once?*

God, they were all at it in those days, weren't they?
Sneaking round behind each other's backs like there was
no tomorrow.

Why *shouldn't* I ring Kieran, come to think of it? So
what if Mum won't like it? She's had her moments,
'snatching whatever time she can get', hasn't she? Hell,
I'm just doing it. I'm ringing him now before she gets
back and that's an end of it.

I mean, Krok might not even be there. *Kieran.* I must
remember to ask for Kieran. He doesn't work there
every day. I *hope* he's there. I'm not actually sure if I've
rung the right number. It's been ringing a while. Maybe
they're busy. Maybe I'll ring back later. Maybe I just
won't bother . . .

'Hello?' It's a woman. She sounds middle-aged.
'David's DVDs. Can I help you?'

'Yeah. Er . . . is . . . er, is Krok, I mean *Kieran*, there?'

'Who's speaking please?'

'Tell him it's Shelley.'

She half-covers the mouthpiece with her hand but I can hear her calling out, '*Kie*-ran. Someone on the *pho*-one for you.' She sounds vaguely amused.

'Hey, man.' Kieran's voice is curt, abrupt; it gives me a shock and I want to put the phone down and just run away. He'll think I'm a complete nerd.

'It's Shelley,' I say stupidly. 'You know – ShelleyPixie.'

'Oh my god.' He seems to gasp a bit; I can't quite make out why. There's this silence. It stretches on forever. 'Hey, Shelley,' he says at last. His voice is soft now, I can make out the echo of an Irish lilt. 'How come you're ringing me? Nothing's wrong, is it?'

'No.' I'm staring at the symbols I etched into my desk with the sharp end of my school compass: 'K4S'. I did that the other night when I was on the phone to Surinda and she was waxing lyrical about Jallal. Now I'm feeling embarrassed about it, to be honest, so I've covered it up with my mouse mat. 'I just wanted to say hi.' I feel like a complete fool. A complete and utter fool. Just thank god that he can't see me because my face must look like a beetroot. I clear my throat. 'You haven't been online lately. I wondered if everything was okay? I . . . I . . .' I was going to say 'I missed you'. But that's so much easier to type on a screen than it is to say over the phone. He's a stranger, after all, I'm thinking. What do I *really* know about this guy, other than what he wants me to believe?

And we aren't supposed to contact strangers we meet over the Internet. Everybody drums that into you. All the time. Especially if you're kind of fragile, like me. At least he sounds . . . he sounds like he looks: young and kind and gentle.

'I've missed you,' he says it for me. His voice has gone real low. 'There's been so much going on. Granddad's been ill. And then there's been this game-show thing . . .'

'I heard. Sorry about your granddad,' I remember to say.

'I got you those tickets,' he tells me, 'I didn't forget you were after them. The next filming date is in a week or so. Or you could use them for the final.'

'Did you?' I can't believe he did that. He really did it.

'They're screening the first episode tonight.'

'Yeah, I know.' My voice has gone kind of funny. It's because my mouth has gone all dry, speaking to him. 'I'm going to watch it, for sure.'

'I'm counting on it. You can tell me if I look like an *ee-jut*.' He says *ee-jut* for idiot. I can feel him grinning. He sounds pleased. If they've filmed several at once and he's still going back then he must have done well and got through to the next round.

'I hope this isn't a bad time?' I say after a bit. He's gone quiet on the other end. I think maybe he's just as shy as me? I can't think of anything else to say. Why is this happening? When we talk online my fingers fly over the keys. He makes jokes and I laugh and laugh; he's so witty and funny and fast. I can hear the front door opening now and I hope it's just Daniel back from his bike ride, I don't want it to be Mum back already. I hope if it's Daniel he doesn't come in here looking for me.

'Not in the least. We're never that busy in the morning,' Kieran is saying. 'But, Shelley, now that you're here. I've got those tickets for you, like I said. Would you like me to bring them over to you sometime?'

'No!' My dad would kill me, and Mum, she would *really* kill me if she even knew I was talking to this man. 'I mean, my parents . . .' I trail off.

'Of course. I understand completely. Never give out your address to someone from the Internet, right?'

Kieran doesn't feel like a stranger, though. He's got a nice voice; it's everything I thought it would be. I think of Surinda, talking to Jallal for the first time, and I can't help smiling. She's right. You can fall in love over the phone. Just a little bit.

'Perhaps we could meet somewhere public, though?' I don't want to put him off. This might be the one and only chance I get, and a great wave of bravery lifts me up.

'There's a fair up on Blackberry Common at the weekend. My mates are doing a mini-gig up there. Do you think you could make it?'

'If I can get someone to help me with the wheelchair,' I remind him. He hasn't forgotten, has he? He does still remember that I'm in a wheelchair?

'I'd help you myself but I know you don't want to meet me alone. And you shouldn't. You're sensible to insist on that.'

'How will you find me?' I ask him. 'Even if we agree a specific place . . . how will you know it's me?' My heart is hammering in my mouth. I'm actually arranging to meet Kieran! I still can't believe I'm doing this.

'*Shell*-ey!' Daniel has just discovered that Mum is out. And he's probably found that there aren't any biscuits left. It'll be something like that.

'I'm here. Where *would* I be?' I yell back.

My brother's face is red and flushed as he pokes his head round my bedroom door.

'We're out of squash,' he informs me.

'I know.' I wave the phone at him. 'Drink water instead. I'm busy right now.'

'Is that Mum?' He eyes the phone suspiciously. I don't talk to my friends all that often. I shake my head at him.

'Who is it?'

'It's Kieran. A friend. Now scoot.' My brother darts out the door again.

'I'll know it's you because you are going to send me that photo of yourself that you keep promising me, right?' Kieran's voice is soft and coaxing. I get a crazy thought: maybe he thinks he's falling for me too?

'Right,' my mouth says before my brain screams *No!* Too late.

'Email me your mobile number, Pixie. We'll firm up the times a little later. Okay?'

'Okay.'

'Thank you for your call,' he says before he hangs up. *Thank you for your call.* As if I were a business associate. But he sounded as if he really meant it, though.

I've got a date. Ohmigod. Who shall I tell? Surinda, of course, because I've only got a date if she'll take me to it.

And she will if she wants those *Beat the Bank* tickets.

When I phone her, my fingers still trembling and sweaty on the keypad, her mum tells me that she isn't there. Surinda is at school, she says. I don't know about that, but I'll have to call back later. Her voice sounds a little arch, as if she's wondering why I'm not in school, too.

Stuck on the back of my bedroom door there is an old, gilt-edged mirror. It used to be Mum's. It came from the old house and she didn't have anywhere else to put it. Maybe she didn't want to be reminded, either, of the days when our whole world felt so much bigger – and so much more capable of expanding – than it is now. They were talking of moving to a bigger house in the countryside one time. That's what Dad ended up with. We got Fetherby Road.

This used to be my 'dressing-up' mirror. I used to put on Mum's scarves and her high heels and her lipstick. Oh yes I did! I can't believe it now but I used to twirl around like a princess. What a twit.

I don't think Mum even owns a pair of shoes any more that aren't flats. She used to have some velvet-black stilettos that I loved, and a silver pashmina that she'd throw over her evening dresses (I *loved* that shawl, I think I've still got it stowed away in the back of a drawer somewhere, I saved it from the Oxfam bag). She used to wear a lot of emerald greens to show up the auburn in her hair, and dark russet-reds that showed up her real beauty. That's a pity because she used to look so glam going out to Dad's 'corporate dinners', as they called them. She told me they were very boring, really; it was only the chance to dress up that she liked!

Well, this mirror. I never look at myself in it. Why would I want to see what I've come to look like now? But once I put the phone down I suddenly get the urge to look at myself. I close the door and take a deep breath. Then I peer at what I can see in the half-light.

My arms are skinnier than I remember them. I look

88

like a thin weed, struggling through a shady copse of bushes, all gangly and spindly and droopy in my chair. My face looks too pale. I could look a lot better than this if I took some trouble over it. I know this because everyone says I look so much like my Aunt Lily, and she was a beauty when she was my age. Naff fashion sense, admittedly, but you could see she had something when you look at her pictures. Perhaps I should send him a picture of her? Lol. Nah, not really; I just need to do myself up a bit.

I wonder what I would look like standing up? I'm so *sick* of sitting in this hunk of metal. I haven't stood up by myself for such a very long time. They tell me I mustn't put any pressure on the bones of my legs. That's why they gave me Bessie so long ago, even when I was well capable of walking by myself. I *could* walk, but they didn't want me fracturing the bones in my legs.

Now I've got this overwhelming urge to try standing up on my own two feet. I want to know what I would look like standing up, by myself, without anyone else there to hold me.

Grabbing hold of the knobs on the chest of drawers near the door I pull myself up. It's damn hard. My arms are so much weaker than I thought. Inch by inch I do it, gritting my teeth, gingerly feeling the weight resting on my legs. The effort is huge. The effort is Mount Everest to a crawling baby. For a second, just a brief second, I see what I might look like if I were normal. I'm not as tall as I thought I was. It's just the stick-thinness of me that gives the impression of height. Yuk. I have dark circles around my eyes that most girls of my age would not have. My mouth droops down a bit at the edges. My complexion is a bit grey. My hair is okay-ish. I'm going to get Surinda to cut out the black bit that I dyed into my blonde fringe. Or else she can dye it back to blonde. What will he think if he sees me, looking as I do?

Maybe he won't notice anything but my eyes. My eyes are looking different today; talking to him has put a new light into them. He's made me remember what it feels like to be alive.

My legs give way just then and I collapse back into Bessie again, feeling every limb trembling with a strange fear and excitement and pleasure at the same time. I shouldn't have done that, but it feels good that I did. It makes me think that there are other, unthinkable things that I still might be able to do.

Just like Mum, really. She had to move beyond what was permissible or possible in order to get what she dreamed of.

27 October 1978
In the car on the way home tonight Dad said some-thing that made me sit up. He's heard that Gordon – that Ilkeley chap, he called him – is going to be needing a new partner soon. Amelie's leaving, apparently. Dad said, perhaps we should ask his parents to take a look at what you two are capable of, eh? And he glanced at me in his rear-view mirror when he said it.

Could it be true that they would consider it? I knew about Amelie leaving, of course, from Gordon, but even though we've talked about it secretly, what it would be like if we could dance together, I never in a million years dreamed that it might possibly come true. Mum and Dad have always been so strict about me and Lily sticking together; they never would have even considered anything like this before.

Oh god, if it could happen, though, I would surely be the happiest girl in the whole wide world!

I like the thought of that: my mum being young and having dreams and being happy. Once upon a time, when I was still a princess, twirling in my mum's high heels in front of this mirror, my dad caught me in his arms and told me: *'One of these days I'm going to make all your dreams come true, princess, you just see if I don't.'* That's the kind of sugar-coated person my dad is, really. He might be a corporate hot-shot and all that, doing law for the stock exchange, dealing in 'futures' as Mum once told me, but one thing I do know is he can't deal with 'futures' that look less rosy than he wants them to be.

Still, I remember him saying that now. Not because he stuck with us for long enough to ever find out what my dreams might be. Not because of that. But because, in some way I really can't explain, him saying that made me believe that there were certain doors that one day might be opened. Even if it's me who has to open them for myself, and not him that does it. And I've just got myself a date with Kieran O'Keefe, haven't I? So *something's* going right . . .

11

Shelley

Surinda is coming round after school, she said. She's suddenly become interested in schoolwork whereas she never was before. 'I've got to get my exams, haven't I? I've got to *do* something with my life. Jallal will expect me to work.' This coming on top of a year in which she's spent the best part of each term off playing hooky.

I'm not even sure I want her around today. Not if she's going to be as narky as she was to me on the phone last night. I told her I'd got the *Beat the Bank* tickets and that's why she's coming, but you'd think she's the one doing me a favour and not the other way round. Ever since this Jallal business she's become a very different person, I think.

It's only 3.30 p.m. so it'll be a little while before she shows; this afternoon is dragging on forever. I've tidied the place up a bit. This room is not huge so I had to. By the time you take into account the bed, the wardrobe, the desk with the keyboard and Bessie, there isn't enough room left to swing a cat. She'll have to sit on the end of the mattress, that's all.

I don't suppose she'll be staying that long. Just as

long as she agrees to take me to Blackberry Common I don't care how long she stays. My stomach's all in a knot over it.

If she says no I don't think I'll ever speak to her again. She'll have to be prepared to help me get onto the bus. She won't like that. Surinda isn't known for her patience. She's meeting Jallal the week after next, and she's angry because they've had to put it off a few days. It seems he couldn't get an earlier flight out from Jakarta. I pointed out that gives her a few extra days to drop those ten pounds she's on about losing before she meets the bridegroom but that didn't cheer her up any.

Anyway, the bus. I haven't been on one for a very long time. Daniel gets on one sometimes and he says they're often empty. I wanted to ask him this morning if he's ever seen anyone get on it in a wheelchair but I don't want to arouse his suspicions.

He's back from school now, I heard him rooting around in the kitchen a minute ago, getting himself a drink.

'Shell?' Talk of the devil.

'Yeah?'

'Your room looks different.' He's standing at the door, looking puzzled. He's probably wondering why there aren't any papers or clothes on the floor.

'I've tidied it, dunderhead. You should do yours more often too.'

'Oh.' My brother stands there for a moment, flummoxed. His face is red, his hair all sticky-up and sweaty because it's hot outside and he's just got back from school. 'I'm going out on my bike,' he says shortly. 'Tell Mum.'

'You've just come *in*,' I say. I return my attention to the nail varnish I was applying just a moment before. He's just come in and now he's going out again. And why? Because he *can*. My heart sinks a little. I remember the times when we used to go out on our bikes together. I was the one who used to encourage him to ride. He was so scared. He would never have done anything at all if it weren't for me. I wonder if he's still got those stabilisers on. In a minute I will hear him practising, round and round the drive up front.

Sometimes lately the sounds outside go quiet and I know he's gone a little way up the road to his friend's house. His world is expanding. That's good; that's the way it should be. I envy my brother that.

When I look at the light brown side-panel of my wardrobe and the jutting-out edge of my computer desk, my world feels as if it's shrinking, even though I've just picked up all the crap off the floor.

I want to see something different. A different view; different faces. I want to be somewhere else.

I wheel myself over to the window and take a look at the view from there. We have a little garden. Just in front of my window there's a tiny azalea bush just coming into pink bloom. It's the same colour as my nail varnish, I realise now. The bird feeder that Daniel hung from the washing line is empty again. The garden is very green. It wasn't a couple of weeks ago, but now we've entered May the whole earth seems to have woken up with a flourish.

I wish my room were a tiny bit bigger. I wish I could get in and out of it a bit more easily. I feel so stuck. Deep in the pit of my stomach there's this feeling of stuck-ness. I'm like a rat in a cage. I've got to get out of this place, I've *got* to. I'm withering away.

And with a sinking feeling I realise that it's already begun, the shrivelling that happened to Miriam; it's happening to *me*! Not in my body, not yet, but it's happening in my heart.

The knock on my bedroom door, when it comes, is so loud that it really startles me.

'You in there?' Surinda is standing in the doorway, her schoolbag placed primly in front of her. It doesn't look very full.

'Your front door was just . . . wide *open*, man.' Her kohl-lined eyes take in my little bedroom in one quick sweep. She looks at me, smiling. I get the feeling my place is smaller than she imagined. 'So, you got those tickets, Shell?' Surinda doesn't sit down. Does she think I'm going to hand over the precious tickets just like that so she can make her excuses and be gone? 'Because I've got to get back,' she's saying, 'me mam's taking me shopping for Jallal-clothes.'

'Great,' I say. 'Jallal-clothes. Look, Surinda, you'd better sit down because there's something I've got to explain about the tickets.'

She perches obediently on the edge of my bed and I try to figure out what it is that is different about her. Something is. Her hair is slicked back and held in a pink rosette in the middle so you can see her dangly golden earrings. Her skin is dark, a little more greasy, with dark spots over her forehead. She has dark circles under her eyes. She used to look better than this, I think. But that isn't what's changed; it's something else. She's got a bit more confidence about her, that's what it is. Like she's been places and done some things. She's had a little experience of the world. And me, stuck here, I'm feeling at a distinct disadvantage: I've had none.

'Go on,' she says. She's picked up my nail-varnish bottle and is looking at the label.

'Those tickets that we're after, we've got to go down to Blackberry Common this Saturday and collect them.'

'What?' She's frowning in annoyance now. 'I've got things planned for this weekend, girl. My hair, for one.'

'If you want the tickets . . .' I say.

'Why can't they just be posted?' She puts the nail-polish bottle down on my bed. 'You ring them and tell them that you want those tickets posted.'

'Ring who?' Surinda is looking cross now. I thought she was desperate for those tickets. This whole Jallal business is ruining everything. 'We can't ring anyone. We've got to go in person.'

'I don't think I can help you.' She's shaking her head in a vague kind of way. 'My time's all taken up now. Things aren't turning out exactly how we'd like them, either.'

'What things?' My heart is thumping again. If Surinda won't take me to meet Kieran, then who will? Daniel is too young to be of any use. Solly would never approve of me meeting an Internet bloke – and he'd be sure to tell my mum. And she can't know. She'd tell Dad and he'd never have any of it. They'll ruin everything for me if they know. Surinda is the only one who I can trust with this; she *has* to do it.

'Jallal's dad, it turns out, doesn't actually own the factory in Jakarta that we were told he did.'

'*What* factory?'

'The condom factory!' She gives me a look that suggests I must be a total imbecile. 'The one my family were told he owns. It turns out he's just the manager.'

'And this matters because . . . ?'

'Because it means they aren't so rich, of course. Why else would it matter?'

'Why indeed?' I'm getting this incredibly strong urge to giggle but I have a feeling it might not do my case any good so I try my best to stifle it by coughing into my hand.

'I'm still marrying him, though,' she says decisively. 'Mum and Dad still reckon he's a good catch. He has a third cousin who's very high up in the government, they say.'

Well, if he doesn't make the condom-factory-owner grade there's always the third cousin to fall back on, I think.

'Always useful to have,' I agree.

'I don't think you're quite getting this, are you?' She takes her chewing-gum in between her fingers and looks around for somewhere to deposit it. 'This is serious,' she tells me heatedly. 'This is my life we're talking about here. It matters very much.'

'I'm sorry. I *am* taking it seriously. Look, can't you think of something to put off the hair appointment? Have it done the day before you see him. It'll keep better. Krok will be *so* disappointed if we don't go to Blackberry Common.' I don't know if that last bit is true, but it sounds good. 'And what if Jallal is the possessive type and he never lets you out of the house once you're his wife? Won't you regret it then?'

There is a stunned silence for a minute. Then, failing to find any bin in my room, she pops the stale chewing-gum back into her mouth.

'Kieran . . . will be there? You mean we're picking up the tickets from him, *himself*?' Surinda sounds a little too enthusiastic for my liking, all of a sudden, and why does she call him *Kieran*? 'Well why didn't you say so before?' She stands up and looks at herself in the mirror behind my bedroom door. 'Oh god, Shell, you should have said. Of course I'll come.'

'We'll have to take the bus,' I warn her.

'The bus. Right.' Her eyes have gone a moist, glowing shade of black. She fancies him. I can't believe it. She fancies my Kieran. 'There was a lovely picture of him in this week's *Telly Stars* magazine.'

Was there?

'He's only a contestant on a game show,' I tell her shortly. 'Are you *sure* it was Kieran? He isn't actually a telly star, is he?' Surinda's uncle owns a corner shop so she gets to look at all the trashy magazines as soon as they come out.

'He's on the telly. He's drop-dead gorgeous and people have noticed him,' she asserts. 'Someone from *Corrie* has offered to introduce him to her agent, apparently. I think it's them blue eyes, myself.'

Blimey. At this rate the world and his wife will all know about my Kieran. Maybe this *Beat the Bank* show wasn't such a good idea after all? All those beautiful

98

girls out there will see him and then what chance have I got?

'Well anyway, about the tickets, you can't tell anyone,' I warn her. 'My mum must never find out. She'll kill me.'

'Not a soul,' she breathes. 'Not a soul.'

'You can make it then?' I watch anxiously as she smooths down her school skirt over ample hips.

'I've lost weight, haven't I?' She turns to look at me and I nod rapidly in agreement. Who knows if she has or not? Who cares?

'I've not been eating a thing,' she glowers. 'Apart from my food, of course. Ohmigod. Kieran O'Keefe! I'm going to meet Kieran O'Keefe.'

'Well, I am, actually. You're just coming along for the ride,' I remind her sharply. 'You've got Jallal to look forward to.'

'Course I do,' she laughs. 'We'll both be sorted then, won't we?'

I wish I could trust her more, really I do. I don't trust her. But then, what option have I got? There is no one else who I could ask to take me there so it'll have to be her.

'It's going to be *so* hard not to mention it to all them other girls at school, innit?' Her eyes are dark as black-currants. I wish I could see into them. If she tells anyone and word gets back to my mum– which it will, if Michelle gets wind of it – then I'm done for.

'If anyone finds out and my mum stops me going then you won't be going either.'

'If anyone finds out what?' Daniel is standing at the doorway, his skateboard under his arm, looking from Surinda to me and back again.

'Don't you knock on your big sister's door?' Surinda gives him a withering look.

'Mum's gone out,' he says to me.

'I know.'

'Why has she gone? How long will she be?'

I shrug. 'I don't know.' I'm going to leave it at that – I don't want him in here interfering when I'm planning something as important as this. But on the other hand I don't want to be mean to him either. Especially since I don't know how much he's heard.

'She won't be *too* long, I don't think. She's gone to Solly's.'

'I'm going to go to Mote Park,' he says. 'With Lloyd. His mum's taking us. Is that all right?' If he's going with an adult that should be okay, I think. 'They've got a skate-ramp now,' he adds, his eyes gleaming. They didn't when Danny and I used to go there, I think. 'They've got a whole new host of things down there that they never had before. You'd love it, Shell.'

My eyes skim over the skateboard. He hasn't got the best sense of balance, my brother. I hope he's telling the truth about Lloyd's mother. He'll need to have someone there for him if he falls. It should be someone like me, really.

'I guess I would have,' I shrug. 'If I were *your* age. Take my mobile so I can get hold of you, okay?'

That seems to satisfy him. When he turns on his heel and walks out again, his hair looking like a complete scruff at the back, I notice he seems to have got even taller, taller than he was yesterday. My kid brother, how does he do it? He's a pain and it's unbelievable that he's got to come and poke his nose in just when *for once in my life* I've got something confidential going on, but I still feel an ache in my heart every time I look at him because I know I'm going to miss him. Wherever it is that I go to, when I go, I'm going to miss my Danny like crazy.

'Solly's having man troubles.' I roll my eyes at Surinda once Daniel's left.

She giggles. 'Not like *us*, eh?' She pushes her hair back from her face and I see she's been experimenting with her eye-liner. I might just ask her how she gets that kohl-eyed effect, it makes her eyes look less piggy. I don't like to admit it but I feel this little conspiratorial thrill as she leans closer to me, all confidential-like, and says,

'So, what are we both wearing on Saturday? We've got to look the *business*, sister.'

12

Rachel

'So, Darryl turned to me and said – you wouldn't believe what he said to me, Rachel – he said, "If I had a face that was as wrinkled as yours I wouldn't bother with cosmetic surgery, darling, I'd just have my whole head chopped off."'

Cripes.

'You don't need any cosmetic surgery, honestly, Solly!' He doesn't. He's obsessed with the idea that he's getting older and he can't bear it, that's all.

'Now, why don't flowers like this grow in *my* garden?' I'm trying to throw him off the scent of last night's disastrous dinner party. Commenting about his pride and joy of a garden usually does the trick.

'Careful with that. That's Molly the Witch.' He snaps off the delicate stem of a sunshine-petalled flower and holds it up to my nose. 'This one's for you. Direct from the Caucasus mountain range in the wilds of Azerbaijan.'

'What, for *real*? I thought you got it from Nelson's Nurseries.'

'Nelson had to get it from somewhere, didn't he?

Anyway, I was saying – Justin – do you know what he did when Darryl said that to me? He *tittered*.'

I can imagine Justin tittering. I twirl the flower around near my face. Butterscotch, I think, I can catch the faintest whiff.

'Young people can be so thoughtless, can't they?' I'm thinking about Michelle and her blasted party. But I scotch that thought. I've got to let it go, I really have. Shelley was waiting for her friend Surinda today. I wonder if she turned up in the end? I wonder if I should check in with her, just to make sure?

For some reason Solly looks mortified.

'Am *I* thoughtless, do you think? Be honest with me, darling.'

I join him by the *Calendula Officinalis*. We're in the 'orange' section at the moment. Solly orders his garden like his wardrobe: by colours. I have to think about this one. If I say 'yes' – and it's true, sometimes Solly can be thoughtless – then he might get offended. If I say 'no' – does that put him in the bracket of 'old people' (who aren't supposed to be thoughtless) as opposed to the 'young' ones who are?

'Why in heaven's name would you ask me that?' I evade. I rub my hands together and the powdery earth falls like a tiny black dust storm all over his lawn. He'd normally tell me off for that but today he doesn't notice.

'Oh, I don't know,' he says disconsolately. 'Sometimes I just think that I must be. Thoughtless and just too . . . fancy free. You know.'

'Are you regretting your misspent youth now?' I grin.

'Oh no,' he interjects. 'I regret nothing of my misspent

103

youth. I intend to keep on misspending it till it's all used up in fact. What's this?' He picks up a folder that I've brought with me. I found it in the bottom kitchen drawer last night.

'I thought maybe some of that would come in handy. It's bits and pieces, articles I've cut out over the years about garden design. I've never actually got round to implementing any of it in our patch, as you know. But you might do . . .'

'No, *this*.' He pulls out a curling yellow folder that had obviously been stuck in there along with all the other papers aeons ago . . . 'Jewellery design; advanced course. Adult ed?' He shoots me an impressed look. 'I never knew you did all this.' His voice is filled with admiration as he flicks through my folder, not bothering to ask me if that's okay. Hmmm, the answer to the previous question . . .

'My, you're a dark horsey, though, aren't you, Rachel? You did all this and I never knew anything about it. Did you finish it?'

'The jewellery design thing?' I shake my head. 'I was bang in the middle of it when Shelley first got diagnosed. Nobody knew what was wrong with her initially. I thought it would just be a matter of putting it off for a few weeks. Or a term or so – or maybe a year – but well,' I hold my hands open. The rest is history.

'That would have been – what – seven years ago now?'

'About that.'

'Wasn't all that about the time when Bill was talking about moving the whole family to London?'

I laugh dryly. 'You remember that?'

'I do. He kept bugging me to get my brother-in-law,'

he checks himself, 'my *ex*-brother-in-law, to do a house survey for him.' He's referring to Adam's brother, the surveyor. If such a thing had been possible at the time – which it wasn't – Solly probably *would* have married Adam, I think now.

'And what did he want to move to London for? He hadn't got his fancy-woman going at that time, had he?'

I swallow. Solly is not the most tactful person in the whole world. I had a feeling that this conversation was going in a direction that would tie in with his own ongoing concerns sooner or later. He has given up the weeding, thrown himself back onto the lawn, his trowel abandoned. I put down my own trowel. Without his guidance I will probably dig up his half-hardy perennials and water his weeds.

'No, Solly, he hadn't. That was later. And why are you suddenly so interested in what motivated Bill's desire to move to London?'

Solly doesn't reply so I hazard a guess.

'Justin wants to move out, right?'

'Just temporarily, Rachel. It's to do with a job he's been offered in Putney. Arts Council stuff. I trust him, I do. I just wondered . . . you know,' he trails off.

'Well, it was the same with Bill, as you're asking. He wanted us all to move so he could be nearer work. He got offered that promotion, didn't he? He turned it down first time around. It would have meant too much commuting at the time. And being away from here. And with his daughter sick, that wasn't what he wanted to do.'

'I thought he did take that promotion, though?' Solly

105

looks at me curiously now. 'I remember you all having a celebratory party out in your garden. Adam did the cooking on the barbie. I made the punch, remember?'

I laugh.

'Adam was a great cook,' I remind him.

'He wasn't good for my waistline, though, darling,' he says briskly. 'Anyhow, Bill's promotion?'

'He took it the third time they offered it. The idea was, we would all go to London.'

'Hmmm. Persistent. They must have really wanted him.'

'He's a company man, isn't he? He's good at what he does. He *likes* being at work.' I defend Bill. 'And by then it was clear Shelley was only going to get worse. He said we could afford a better house if he took the job, better facilities and treatment for her, if he earned more. I think he felt helpless; okay, when he was working locally he was around more but he wasn't all that useful in truth.'

'No?'

'No. Because it wasn't what he *wanted* to do. He couldn't make her better and he couldn't bear to stay and watch her getting worse. His rationale was that what we needed was more money.' I throw my hands in the air now, remembering how we had fought over that. Money was never going to solve Shelley's problems. Bill and I knew that.

'And did the extra money help?'

'Huh!' I shrug my shoulders. 'Well, we couldn't *all* move to London because it would have meant changing round all her medical care and I just couldn't face it. I fought with him at first. I fought tooth and nail for him not to take that job. I knew it would change everything. But in the end – Solly, in the end I couldn't wait for him to take it just so we didn't have to be sharing living space for those extra hours of the day while he was out at work. He resented the fact that his career was never going to get back on track. He resented the thought that his whole life was going to go down the pan just because our poor daughter was losing hers. And Solly, I can't say I really blame him.'

'So . . . why did you fight him about taking the job?'

Why did I? Good question. And the strange thing was, that was the first and only time we'd ever really fought about anything in our whole marriage. I was usually so easy-going and Bill so determined to get his own way that there was no contest.

'I guess I just felt . . . this was something that really mattered. He needed to be there for her. He should have been there for all of us. And we didn't need the extra money. We needed *him*. The job was only going to take him away from us for longer hours.'

'Yet when he was around he was only being a pain?'

'Exactly.'

Solly laughs. 'My poor dear.'

'I suppose what I'm saying is – I wanted him to change, if I'm honest . . . I wanted him to come to terms with what it was that we all had in front of us. I saw the promotion as just . . . Bill running away.'

'So – you think he'd have stayed closer to home if he'd felt that him being there made a difference?'

'He didn't think it was worthwhile. And he was right. There was no point in the two of us sacrificing our lives.

I could look after her perfectly adequately and he could have the job he wanted. But after that . . .'

Solly looks at me intently but I don't want to go on. After that, things were never the same between us again. It wasn't the decision that Bill made, it was what all the fighting between us had thrown up in the meantime. '*The worm that turned*' Bill had called me. And why? Because I had dared to disagree with him. Because I had for once in my life stood up and found my voice and told him that I thought what he was doing was wrong. It didn't matter if he was *actually* right or wrong, or if I was – it was the fact that he couldn't bear me to contradict him that surfaced with such a vengeance.

It made me furious at the time and still makes me furious to think of it now.

'After that . . . ?' Solly prompts.

'After that, I never finished the jewellery course.' I smile with what I hope passes for nonchalance at Solly, patting the curling yellow folder in his lap. It's easier to talk about that than to talk about what happened between me and Bill. I let the jewellery thing go so very long ago. It hardly matters any more.

'One of these days,' I say, 'I'll pick it up again.'

I will, when . . . when what? A tide of guilt sweeps over me, that I could even *think* of a time when I might ever re-take up my own life.

'Seven years ago,' Solly marvels. '*Tempus fugit.*'

'*E non ritorna più,*' I finish.

Times flies away and it never returns.

'Maybe we are getting old, my darling.' Solly leans over and pats me consolingly on the knee.

Old age, I think. Another one of Pandora's Spites.

I've been too busy to even think of myself as getting older. If it's been happening while I wasn't looking . . . then, hell, what is happening to my *life*? I've been thinking of time as something frozen. Like it's stopped while we've all been waiting for Shelley's drama to play itself out.

But it hasn't stopped at all. It's moved on and moved ever upwards, just like Bill has, and Annie-Jo, and Adam, and even Pandora.

It's only me who's still stuck here, waiting; waiting for the only awful and unbearable resolution that can come and give me back my life.

13

Shelley

I've got a really bad feeling about this. Surinda promised me she'd be here by nine o'clock on the dot. It's now twenty past. I've come out on the front drive so I can nab Surinda as soon as she arrives and be gone. Mum's already asking me a few too many questions, and the more she asks the more I have to make up lies about where we're going and I hate that. I think she suspects something. She's, like, hanging around me this morning. She has absolutely no reason to be out front right now but she's here anyway, picking weeds out of the cracks in between the paving stones.

'She's late?' Mum looks at her watch then back to me.

'Just delayed, that's all. It's not important. I'm sure there'll be stuff going on for *hours* yet.'

I've told Mum we're going to help out at the junior school summer fair over the road from our school. That will account for a good few hours of the day. I'm trying to sound dead cool about it, but the truth is I've agreed to meet Kieran at eleven thirty and I imagine it will take us a good hour to get there. I don't know how long we'll need to wait for the bus but I know that we have to change on the way. I've got the route map in my purse.

'You're looking nice,' Mum smiles appreciatively, 'without the black make-up,' she adds.

'Thanks. Er . . . haven't you got to take Daniel to his Saturday cricket or something?'

Normally they'd be on their way by now.

'Yes, I do.' She looks at her watch again. 'Just thought we'd see you off, but if she's delayed . . .'

'Mum! I'm only going to be away a few hours.' Why does she have to make such a fuss? It infuriates me. Daniel can be away the whole day and she won't fret about him at all.

'I'm not used to you being out,' she apologises. 'So, anyway, Shell, you *sure* you'll be all right if I go back to Solly's to finish off in the garden, after I drop Danny at cricket?'

'I'm not going to be here,' I remind her. *Oh just go away before Surinda arrives and says something stupid and then I have to tell you even more lies!*

At *last* she chivvies Daniel into the car and they go off, waving at me, and it's 9.35 already and there's still no sign of Surinda.

Surinda will be taking her time putting on her make-up, that's what it will be. She'll be curling up her eyelashes with those curly metal implement-of-torture type things. She'll be putting on all her different shoes to see which ones go better with her outfit. She has twenty-one different pairs of shoes, get that! *Twenty-one*. She gets them dirt cheap down Camden Market. She told me all about it. Most of them have killer heels. But I've seen a

111

couple of them, black and strappy and with shiny bits like little beads or glass sequins to catch the sun, and I wish I could wear stuff like that. I only ever get sensible shoes. But I'd look a bit stupid wearing high heels given that I'm never going to stand up in them, wouldn't I?

This top that I'm wearing is a bit out of date. She told me that last time she was here, rummaging through my wardrobe, looking for 'what we would wear'. She said it was the best out of a bad lot and it would have to do but that there was no need for me to 'let myself go' fashion-wise just because I couldn't use my legs. She has a point. Maybe I can persuade her to take me shopping sometime too, if this trip works out? Maybe I can go to Camden Market with her one of these Sundays? I could if Yusef would take me up with them in his car.

I'd love to go to Camden Market. She says they have all *sorts* of cool stuff there. And it's at a fraction of the price you'd get it in the boutiques. And she said something about the air smelling all sweet and cloying and 'funny' the minute you start getting near to the market because 'They're all, like, you know . . .' (giggle, giggle) '*smoking*', standing in the doorways of their shops or stalls or whatever they have and '*smoking*', which is probably what a lot of the girls I used to know at school are experimenting with, for all I know, but I don't even know what that stuff *smells* like.

I've got to get a grip on my nerves this morning. I've got to start using all the breathing techniques I've read about that tell you how to get over nerves. Nerves aren't cool, and Kieran is . . . well, he's dead cool. He's so cool he's probably going to run a mile when he actually sees me. It's not like I slept much last night. It didn't do the dark rings under my eyes any good. And that stuff Surinda lent me the other day to get rid of them – what she uses – it was no good for me because her skin is that much darker than mine. It made me look like a photo of a panda – only the negative. So I had to scrub it all off. And nobody looks cool when they're uptight and worried.

And if we could only get there in good time I wouldn't be so worried. Even if we got there an hour early, I wouldn't mind. I just don't know how long that bus will take, it wasn't really clear, because I'm not sure what stop we need to get off at. Surinda will know. She takes buses all the time. She's a woman of the world. She won't worry that she'll miss her stop and go sailing off onto some other place that's a million miles away, and that she'd have to spend hours and hours and hours trying to get home from . . .

I don't want to hassle her, I know what she's like. She'll be on her way, just taking her own sweet time, that's all. She has to take the bus to get here for starters. It's very good of her really. All that money she's spending on all those bus fares. I just need to know how much longer she's going to be because I'll have to go inside and do another pee if I wait here much longer, I'm so nervous . . .

I punch Surinda's number into my mobile and while it rings I wheel Bessie into a shadier spot under Mum's giant Kerria bush.

'Yeah?' Surinda finally picks up after about twenty rings. She's tense, breathless. I can hear her mother yelling at her in the background.

'Surinda. Where are you? I've been here half an hour already.' No, that can't be her mother! Surinda's on the bus, she's got to be on the bus. She'll be getting off at the next stop. She'll be here in five minutes and I shouldn't have bothered her . . .

'Oh that. Yeah. Um . . . I'm not coming. Sorry. You'll have to get your mum to pop you down there for the tickets after all. I'll come by and pick up my one some-time next week, yeah?'

It takes me a good few seconds to find my voice again and when I do it's just a croak.

'Surinda, we had an *arrangement*. We planned this all week. Everything . . . everything's arranged. You can't just back out of it now. You just can't.'

'I would come,' she wails at me now, 'but Jallal is here. He got on last night's flight and they're on their way over from the airport right now.'

'Oh.'

'So you see, I can't.'

'You could have rung and told me,' I accuse.

'There's so much going on here, Shell, you wouldn't believe. I'm sorry I forgot you were relying on me.' She says it almost defiantly, as if her letting me down is partially my fault because I asked her in the first place. 'You get your mum to take you,' she repeats.

'I can't, Surinda! She's gone now. She's gone out for the morning. If you'd rung me *before* I would have maybe . . . thought of something. I could have got my mum to take me up there, somehow, some way.'

'But Jallal's on his way.' She isn't thinking about me at all. I can hear the jubilation in her voice now. 'You

114

should see the faff my mum and me got into yesterday when we found out about it. She had to go out and get me this turquoise sari to wear. I look the *business*, girl!'

'You mean you knew about this *yesterday*?' I'm trying to get my head round this. She knew she couldn't make our trip a whole twenty-four hours ago and she still didn't think to let me know?

'Which is ridiculous,' she agrees. 'Hardly enough time for us to prepare, I know. My head has been such a whirl. I'm in seventh heaven!'

'And *our* trip?'

There's a short silence at her end as she has to reconnect with what I might be talking about.

'Ring him and tell him you've changed your mind,' she advises me now. 'Tell him something's come up but you might make it next Saturday. After all,' a new thought pops into her head, 'we don't want to lose the chance of those tickets, do we?'

'If Jallal won't be here for a few hours, that's still enough time to get me there, Surinda. You could nip up. I'll get myself back somehow.' I'm grasping at straws, I know, but if a straw is all you've got . . .

I hear a tinkle of laughter at her end, followed by the sound of her mum snapping at her to *get off the phone, you lazy good-for-nothing girl, and come and help me with the rice before the guests arrive.*

'Why doesn't he just bring them to you himself?' she puts in helpfully before she has to ring off.

I hang up without even saying goodbye to her. I can't believe what she's just done to me. She didn't even ring! How could she do that? Doesn't she know what this

115

means to me? Doesn't she know this is going to be my one and only chance *ever*?

Oh, god, I can't believe it!

I hope Jallal is . . . is as ugly as a toad and he has bad breath. And I hope he's fat, and has BO and he's *poor*. I hope he's horrible and then she'll know what it's like to have nothing to look forward to and have a miserable life and be let down by someone . . .

Oh why don't I just *die* already!

14

Rachel

'So you're worried about *what*, exactly?' It's the middle of Saturday morning and he's opening the wine. Solly's a real one-and-only. He's opening the wine and the worst of it is . . . he isn't even drinking any. ('*One hundred calories a glass, sweetie, and I've got to watch my intake.*') But I'm drinking it. He's turning me into a lush. Three glasses and half a box of Kleenex later and now we're onto the hardcore stuff.

'She said she had a girlfriend picking her up this morning but the girl hadn't even arrived before we left. What if she doesn't turn up? I just have a feeling the girl isn't coming. Shelley will be *crushed*. She was so looking forward to going to the jumble sale. She never gets out, you know. I need to ring her and find out what's happening . . .'

'Do you think she'd appreciate that? You checking up on her just as she's about to go out for once? She is nearly fifteen, darling.'

'It's not that I want to go home right now, Solly.' No, I don't. I really don't. I don't get out too much either these days, I realise suddenly. Not even to visit Solly in his garden.

117

And this garden, even though it is mostly running wild, is so very beautiful. I want to just lie here in the sun and ruminate for a while. From this angle, my head lying on my outstretched arms across the smooth wood of Solly's garden table, I can spy the drooping white bells of a cluster of Solomon's Seal under the oak tree, their edges just rimmed with the faintest hues of green. Underneath it, a carpet of sky-blue forget-me-nots puts me in mind of one of the designs I've just spotted in my old jewellery design folder (yes, he's got the folder out again and we've spent more time looking at my designs than we have the gardening articles); I'd roughed out a wedding tiara studded with tiny pearls (*or opals?* I'd scribbled in the margin) and the deepest of blue sapphires. I'd envisaged the earrings I'd drawn to match it to be quietly charming; they'd been shaped just like tubular white flowers of the *polygonatum*, I saw now. I'd imagined the material they'd be made of as something iridescent, like the insides of a mother-of-pearl shell, and they'd each have the tiniest of milky white pearls at the tip . . .

'I think you've had a little too much to drink to drive home just at this moment anyway,' Solly interrupts my reverie.

Oh, crap! I turn my head to face him and the warm edge of the wooden table is soothing against my cheek.

But I'm not really back with Solly. Seeing those designs in that yellow folder has set me off on a train of thought that I never wanted to go back down again. It's stirred up deep yearnings like . . . like the seeds of that desert plant that Solly was telling me about a moment ago when I wasn't really listening to him. The plant – whatever it is – is particular as hell when it comes to 'external conditions', so if the winter's been too hot or the spring has been too cold or the ground has gotten too dry, it doesn't bloom. It might not bloom for – oh, ten or even twenty years, that's how long the seeds can remain dormant; waiting for the right conditions. And when they *do* bloom the whole desert comes out in a sea of colour for a few days and all the photographers from around the world fly out to take pictures of this phenomenon of nature. That's along the lines of what Solly was saying, but the key thing is, when they decide they're going to bloom, when that pent-up *yearning* is unlocked, what force on this planet is ever going to be able to stop them?

Behind Solly, his head framed by a profusion of vermillion dahlias (*Bishop of Llandaff*, he tells me), I am reminded of the deepest hues of almandine garnets; the rhubarb stalks by the compost bin are great nuggets of pink tourmaline, and behind them, straggling in and out among long-deserted flowerbeds, love-in-the-mist sparkling with the morning dew becomes a shimmering of quartz crystals. And it feels as if they're all just waiting, just *dying*, in fact, for me to take up my tools again and fashion them into something beautiful.

I want to start designing things again. I want to start planning my future. I want to . . . oh, I so want to start living.

But I can't.

'*I'll* go and see if Shelley's okay, shall I?' Solly is still talking to me through the haze of too much wine drunk

119

too early in the morning. What the heck did he give it to me for? And why the heck did I accept it?

'Um . . . Yes, actually, that would be . . . very kind of you. If you're sure you don't mind.'

'She wasn't picking up the house phone so I'm sure she's already gone. But I don't want you to worry about her. It'll only take ten minutes.' He snaps his mobile shut and slides it back into his pocket. Did he ring home? I didn't even see him do that.

'I'll get you some coffee before I go,' he observes dryly. 'I think you need to sober up, *Mum*.'

Blooming cheek! He's right, but he's still got a blooming cheek. Ah, but the beauty of too much alcohol is that you realise nothing is quite as important as you thought it was, after all.

I'm trying to figure out if there's anything I should really regret in all of this. If my life's ended up being such a bloody mess then maybe it's because, somewhere along the line, I've made some mightily huge mistakes?

But – here is the strange thing – when I let my mind dig down deep, sink below the substrata of my memories of my marriage, there is *nothing* I can find there to regret. When I trace the roots of my past life back, they don't end in some tangled ball like the clinging hands of a bindweed. They peter out into little hopeful tendrils, each embedded in some happy memory, some dream of the way things might be . . .

I don't know if I'm dreaming now or just remembering. Or maybe it's a bit of both? The sun is so warm across my shoulders and my back. And Bill, he looks so young again. He's just how he was when I saw him the first time. His hair is long, and curly. And there is lots of it. And he's tanned because he's just come back from a gap year in New Zealand. And he's joined the same uni as me as a fresher; I'm doing art and design at Warwick. He's going to be studying law, and his dad's an important solicitor somewhere so he's going to join the firm when he's done, but he wants to do *art*, really, he tells me laughing, he wants to do *'art or some crappy useless subject like that, which will get me nowhere in life except it might just make me happy'*.

And he likes to look at my folders, all my design projects. He likes to run his fingers along the rough edges of the paint and along the smooth surfaces of the ceramics that emerge from pottery class. He likes to look at me and my friends at work after he's released from his lectures on 'Employment law' and 'Contracts'. He marvels at our daring, even as – with the passing of time, and the strengthening of our relationship – he criticises the colours that me and my friends mix, laughing and joking about daring to put so many 'unsuitable' things together, as if colours could kill you, as if there were any way you could really do them wrong.

And now I know I'm dreaming because I'm graduating and he's so happy for me, when I turn around there are tears in his eyes. He wants to fly kites in the park. He wants us to go back to New Zealand so he can show me all the things he discovered out there that made him the person he was when I met him.

But when he graduates, a year after me, there is no more time for 'messing around'. If I'm going to 'throw pots' for a living then I can do that at any time in my life. His career path, however, is far more urgent, far more prescribed. He's got to do what he's got to do or he'll never get on the ladder and all his hard work and slog will have been for nothing . . .

And the roots of my memories go down a little, further down, and I remember how I loved him at the beginning and how when we were together I always felt safe. And I wore the beautiful clothes that I wanted to wear, because he liked me to look nice. He appreciated that I looked nice in them. And all the while there was this sense that my fanciful 'arty' ways were something he aspired to; I was the person he would have liked to have been. He allowed me to be who I wanted to be. At first, he did.

And when I take a sip of Solly's coffee – when did he leave it there, when did *he* leave? – it is lukewarm. The weather is darkening overhead; the sun on my shoulders no longer feels warm. How long have I slept here? How long have I been remembering and dozing, half in and half out of sleep? My mouth tastes strange. Like I've just come out of a stupor. There are darkening spit-spots of rain on the bright yellow of my design folder. I close it up and put it under my arm. Later on, I will go home and put it back where it belongs underneath all the other junk in my bottom kitchen drawer.

And I *will* stick to my own guns and act on what I know to be right. Sod Bill and his controlling ways. I press Bill's house number on my mobile phone. A raindrop lands right on my nose and it is cold. I'm going to tell him that I've booked me and Shelley in for Cornwall. I'm not going to deceive him.

I'm not frightened of him, so why shouldn't I?

'Yes?' His voice, answering so promptly and abruptly in my ear, startles me.

'Hello, Bill, it's Rachel.'

'Yes, Rachel?' I hear his car door shut. He mutters something low. To Stella. I don't hear her reply. I can imagine her, though, the acquiescent nod, the down-turned eyes. She would be pretty if she didn't always look so worried.

'About Cornwall . . .' I catch his impatient intake of breath, the wind whistling through his flared nostrils. The blackness of his mood soaks down the phone like used-up water through a soakaway. Such a short moment's silence. It is nothing. But I sense him closing his eyes, I *sense* it. Underneath the voice that is seldom raised, pure sulphuric acid shimmers and bubbles.

'I have just pranged my car,' he informs me. 'I have just dented the bonnet of my new fifty-five-thousand Volvo, and scratched the paintwork on a seventy-something-thousand BMW.'

There's not a lot I can say to that. Not a lot I dare to, actually.

'So . . . your – your *plans*, are really the smallest, most insignificant and least important thing in my life right now.'

'I see.'

'I need to bloody well get us out of here as soon as possible – no one saw it – and you ring me about some crap. You never *change*, do you? Well, you've got to stop it. Grow up and manage your own anxieties, woman. I've made myself perfectly clear, I hope?'

123

More silence. And the rain drops into the cold coffee, disturbing the milk on the top. I cover the cup with my hand. He's right. I do need to change. I need to stop thinking the way I do. And I *don't* need to tell him about my plans. It isn't a matter of proving that I'm not too scared to do it without his consent. I'm trying to do the honourable thing by letting him know we're going and the only end result will be that he will stop us.

I don't answer him, in the end. I just press the red button and the call is over. My reverie about him, about how he was, how we were, it's over too. 'Reality strikes', as Shelley would say.

Thank goodness I'm not like that desert plant, really. I can put the lid back on my yearnings. I can wait a little longer till it gets to be my time to bloom. I've got to have had *most* of the Spites come out of Pandora's box by now, surely? There can't be many more in there waiting to emerge and sting me?

I'm still waiting for the Hope.

15

Shelley

I'm so mad I don't even notice Solly parking his car on the drive. I don't notice him, in fact, till he's out of it and walking up to me on the drive under the shade of the yellow bush.

'Hello, my darling,' he leans down to me and there's a little rush of air as he kisses both of my cheeks and his aftershave smells of cinnamon. 'Where's your mum?'

'She's taken Danny to the cricket. She was going down to yours after that, wasn't she?'

'Oh.' He looks puzzled. 'She, er . . . changed her mind. She went to someone else's instead. Anyhow, I'm here on tortoise duty.' He gives me a mock-salute. 'I'm to pick up Hattie so you lucky lot can all go off on your holidays.'

'What, today? Why today? We aren't going anywhere for another two weeks. My birthday is at the end of May, remember?'

'You're kidding?'

'No. I think I remember when my birthday is.'

Solly covers his mouth with his hand. 'Oh, Shelley! I've got the date wrong, haven't I? I could have sworn your mum said it was this week. I'm no good with dates. You know I'm no good with dates.'

You never forgot my birthday before, I think. But then maybe it was Adam who remembered all that kind of stuff for him?

He brightens suddenly. 'But you know I love to see you anyway. And I don't often find you out of your cave?'

That's what he calls my room. Because it's so dark and small and dingy.

'Did your mum tell you, I've landed the part of the "handsome prince" in this year's panto?'

I cough out a laugh so he won't see how upset I am.

'Nearly got beaten to it by some spotty sixth-former, but I can do the splits better than he can.'

'I used to be able to do the splits,' I remember suddenly. 'Second grade, ballet school. I was the only one in Miss Townsend's class who could do it. Did Mum say when she'd be back? You've spoken to her, have you?'

'No she didn't er – say. Did you need her for something?'

I shake my head.

'I never knew you could do the splits?' he prompts me.

'Yeah, Miss Townsend reckoned I might turn out to be some great competition-winning dancing person, just like Mum.'

'Is that what your dream was, my love?' He gets tears in his eyes so easily sometimes, dear Solly.

'Not at all. I wanted to be a vet. But then eighty per cent of kids want to be vets, don't they?' I shrug.

'You're clever enough to have been a vet. What is it

126

you'd like to do? There must be something you still want?'
He looks at me curiously.

'I know. But none of it really matters any more, does
it? The fact I could once do the splits. The fact that I
used to be top of my class for just about all the subjects
going. What would I like? Hmmmm. Something simple.
I'd like . . . I'd just like to be able to grow *old*, Solly.'

He looks real strange when I say that. He looks at the
floor as if he can't quite bring himself to make eye contact.

'And if you *could* grow old, what would you like to
do with all that time?'

I shrug. Who knows at fourteen what they really
want to do when they grow up? None of my friends
do. I think for a bit. The sun is so bright. On a day
like today, sitting on the drive, you can see right down
the road to the bend that leads to the river. You can't
see the river from here, but you know that it's there.
I know that it's there. Go down the road long enough
and you get to the traffic lights and there's the arch-
bishop's palace on the left and then that steep,
cobbledy-earthy ramp that goes down, down to the
waterfront, and then . . . if you go right, along the tow
path past all the swans that honk-honk, ignoring all
the floating bits of soggy bread and going under the
bridge, which is part of the overhead roundabout, you
get to the narrow bit of the tow path, surrounded by
trees. It gets so muddy when it rains I can't go there,
I haven't been there in a very long time because my
wheels get stuck and the tree roots stick out from under
the mud and make it even bumpier, but you can see,
if you go there, all the barges sailing up the river, and

the white boats that take people on a twenty-minute trip down to the lock and then set them down at the Malta Inn before they turn round and make the trip back. And I think I want to go . . . further than that. I want to go to the farthest reaches of the earth. I want to explore all the cracks and crannies of places that people never bother to look at.

'I want to get old so I can go very far away,' I say to him at last. 'So then I will have somewhere from which I can make my way back home again.'

'You want to get old, and I . . . I am getting old and I don't want to,' he says at last.

'Ha ha.' I'm trying to keep up my usual sarcastic banter with him because it's what he expects – but now I've got these tears of disappointment welling in my throat and it's really hard.

'What *is* it?' Oh no, not sympathy. I can deal with just about anything else but not that. If he starts being sympathetic towards me I shall break down and cry, and I don't *do* crying any more.

'Nothing. Look, it's nothing.'

'Piffle is it nothing. Tears don't just fall for nothing.' Solly kneels down beside Bessie on the gravel and gives me a hug. The longer he hugs me the more these huge gulping sobs just keep coming up from nowhere and the more worried he gets.

'It isn't *starting*, is it?' He looks at me fearfully and I can see the tears welling up in his own eyes. 'The End. What happened to Miriam?'

I give a huge sigh. How can I tell him? In a way I feel that it is – not in my body, maybe, but in my soul. I seem to be disappearing. I've been in one place for so long I've outgrown who I am and I haven't got any new *me* to be any more. How could anyone understand that?

I shake my head because I can't speak just yet. Solly lets out a long, shuddering sigh to echo my own. His fingers grip mine warmly, urgently, calling me back.

'You haven't forgotten your promise to me, have you, darling?'

I meet his eyes, which are moist and full of sadness. What promise? I frown at him.

'About Suko. *Afterwards*,' he whispers. 'You'll *contact* him, you promise?' Suko is the Japanese guy who always wears that funny turban-looking thing, who comes and reads the tarot cards at all of Solly's parties. I remember now. I'm supposed to contact him once I've 'crossed over' and come through with a message for Solly so he can run back here and tell everyone that I'm all right. I used to think he was nuts for asking me. But it's probably a good idea when I think about it now.

'I haven't forgotten,' I tell him. Then a thought strikes me and I stop crying, thinking about the practicalities of this little arrangement. 'How will you know it's me, though? How will it be provable?'

'We'll have to have a secret sign.' Solly leans in closer. 'Suko will have to be given a code that only you and I know about. Something out of the ordinary that wouldn't happen just by chance.'

'Okay,' I tell him now. 'You decide what it is to be.'

'Give me something of yours,' Solly says suddenly. 'Something personal.'

I reach up to my hair then hand him a hairgrip with

a silver butterfly. Solly hurls it under Mum's Kerria bush so that it disappears from view.

'When that appears again, I'll *know*,' he says. He seems relieved. I'm not sure how any of this helps *me*, though.

'You'll know what?' I liked that butterfly clip! Danny got it for me last Christmas, and I don't really want to lose it like this.

'That everything's okay, of course. That you're – you know – all right.'

'I see.' I'm about to ask him if by 'all right' he actually means 'already dead' when I have an attack of conscience because Solly's all upset about my imminent departure and that wasn't really why I was crying.

'Surinda was supposed to take me to Blackberry Common to meet a friend today,' I confess after a while, 'but she's backed out so now I can't go. That's the reason why I was crying, Solly.'

'Oh dear!' He looks at me in astonishment. 'And Mum can't take you to meet your friend? A little later?'

'No, she can't!' I take the hanky that Solly offers me and blow into it noisily. 'She doesn't know anything about it. Look, Solly, it's a boy I met over the Internet. We met on a bereavement site, when I was trying to get over Miriam, okay?'

'Phew.' Solly gives me a long, hard look. 'So you're not . . . er . . . deteriorating?'

'No,' I say shortly. Then it all comes tumbling out. 'Listen, Solly, Kieran's a *really* nice guy. He is. But you know full well that Mum would never let me meet him. She'd probably only allow it if she could come too . . .'

'Which is wise, considering she cares very deeply about

130

her daughter,' Solly concedes. He's going to take her part in this. I should have known he would. I shouldn't have mentioned anything to him at all.

'But I can see from your point of view that having Mum tag along on a first date would rather – shall we say – defeat the purpose.'

I look at him in surprise.

'Well, yes. Something like that. Not that it's actually a date. And now you'll feel duty bound to tell Mum and I'll get an earful from her when she comes home, on top of everything else.'

Sol laughs dismissively at this.

'I'm not really that bad, am I? I used to be a bit of a rebel in my younger days.' He puffs out his chest without even realising he's doing it.

'You did?'

'I did. *My* parents didn't want me going out meeting any boys either.'

I have to grin at that. 'I can imagine.'

'So I used to sneak out on occasion without them knowing.' His eyes are twinkling. Then he taps my nose with his knuckle like he used to do when I was a kid. 'Not that I'm suggesting you should do that.'

'Like I could.' I look pointedly at my wheelchair.

'But there's nothing stopping *me* from taking you to that fair, is there?'

'You?' I stare at him in surprise. 'You mean you would? You'd do that?'

'We don't have to mention anything to your mum about the . . . er . . . friend, do we?' Solly examines his fingernails, which are perfectly manicured and clean as always. 'This way I can keep an eye on the two of you while keeping a respectful distance. How does that sound to you?'

I laugh. It sounds just like the scenario Surinda has told me about, for when she meets Jallal. They'll be let loose together but they'll be chaperoned in a discreet sort of way.

'It sounds way cool. Oh, Solly, you're the best!' I can't believe the turn my luck has suddenly taken. I don't have to go by bus now, so I'll be there in good time. And as long as he doesn't spill the beans to Mum I'd a million times rather have Solly by my side than Surinda any day.

16

Shelley

At Blackberry Common the crowds are just starting to gather. Unfortunately, so are the clouds. I can't believe that an hour ago I was frying out on the driveway in front of our house and now I'm so chilly my arms have got goose pimples. I don't know why, but I've got the worst feeling about this; it's just making me sick.

He isn't going to show. The weather has gone too bad. Nobody comes out on a day like this unless they really want to, like me.

'Uh-oh.' Solly glances up at the glowering sky overhead. 'It's going to pelt it down, darling.' His face is determined, though, and he manoeuvres me through the throng towards Uncle Bob's Doughnut Stall, which has a wide awning for sheltering under and a growing number of customers as a result. I pull my jacket over myself like a blanket as the first fat raindrops hit our heads. Solly's thin white T-shirt is becoming see-through. I can see the dark hairs on his chest underneath and he must be feeling cold. He doesn't seem to care.

I'm just praying that the rain won't have put Kieran off. And even if it hasn't, how will he ever find me? The umbrellas have all gone up now, blocking every square inch of light as well as everyone's view of everyone else. This all feels like a dream. I haven't been out in the middle of a crowd for such a very long time. I'd forgotten what it was like. I'm at the level of other people's handbags, which move back and forth as they walk, and other people's cigarettes, dangling between their fingers at arm's length. A couple of times the woman in front of me gently flicks her ash backwards, towards me. She's intent on her own progress, trying not to step in the potholes filled with mud; she doesn't even see I'm here. I feel small. I feel, in fact, totally invisible. Not for the first time I'm noticing how, when the day closes down dark and damp like it's doing right now, then the people close down too. They turn inward. A little pile of the woman's ash lands in my lap. 'Hey!' Solly yells at her. When she turns round, her face blank and unapologetic, she just shrugs, but turning round makes her miss her footing and her heels get stuck in a clump of mud. 'Instant karma for you,' my hero hisses at her as we move smartly past.

'Some *people*!' He shakes his head with exaggerated disapproval. I'm beginning to think this really wasn't such a good idea. There's an Indie band playing on a platform nearby and a crowd of onlookers has formed around them, thickening the way ahead of us. Solly keeps pushing me resolutely through and most people are good-natured and part the way when they see Bessie coming.

I'm *so* glad it's Solly with me this morning and not Surinda. She never would have coped with this. Solly is strong and steady and he can manoeuvre Bessie into places that she never could, especially now the field is turning to mud.

Uncle Bob's Doughnut Stall looms up at last. There's a line of people huddling under the awning, buying their bag-o'-six, hot and fresh. The combined smell of hot fat and sugar is magically tempting. It reminds me of summer fairs at school and trips down to the baker's when I was little, so Solly buys me some while we're waiting for the rain to stop. I dip into them nervously. My stomach is a tight cramp. I'm remembering I haven't actually eaten anything since yesterday lunchtime and I swallow two of the doughnuts down, barely chewing at all. That's the kind of thing Daniel would do!

Oh, I wish I could just stand again. It makes all the difference to be able to stand; to be at other people's height. Down here, it's so hard not to feel like a child, small and unimportant and unheeded. I wonder if I practised every day, standing up like I did the other day, if I might get better at it?

I won't, though, because of my bones. Dr Lavelle phoned and left another message on the machine yesterday. He said it was really urgent that we contact him but I don't want to see him any more. I deleted the message, just like I did the last two, before Mum could hear it. What she doesn't know won't hurt her. As for me, I've already got my own plans regarding my future so I don't see why I should waste any more time at the doctor's surgery . . .

'Hi, Shelley?'

Ohmigod, he's here! It's him. Kieran has crouched down beside Bessie so he can say hello on an eye-to-eye

135

level and I . . . I just don't know what to say. His hair is darker than I imagined, and longer. It's a chestnut brown, and curly at the end. He's wearing faded jeans, which have gone darker in patches where the rain has soaked them. His T-shirt is black, with the name of his friend's band on the front, and it's clinging to his skin, drenched through. He's . . . *gorgeous*. Just like his photo. So gorgeous that I'm totally embarrassed that I dared to ring him at all to set this meeting up.

I must look grotesque to him, so emaciated and so . . . *withered*, sitting here on this ugly hunk of metal.

'Hi,' I manage at last. I can't cope with this. I can't even look him in the eye I feel so scared. Is this what Surinda's going to feel like when she meets Jallal? Is she going to turn into a tongue-tied ninny who can barely remember her own name? I know she isn't. She'll probably flutter her eyelashes at him, which I saw her practising in my mirror. Good thing that she isn't here now, though, or she'd be practising on my Kieran.

I look to Solly for help, and he's already stretching out his hand, beaming, saying 'pleased to meet you' in his most charming way. 'I'm your chaperon for the day,' he grins.

'Very wise too,' Kieran is saying. He looks younger than I thought he would. The skin on his face is quite smooth, not like some nineteen-year-olds.

I let the bag of Uncle Bob's doughnuts slip onto the grass beside me. I don't want to look like a child, all sticky-fingered with my hand in a bag of sweets, but Kieran spots them fall and immediately picks them up and pops them back in my lap.

'*They* smell good.'

'Have one,' I offer. He can have the lot. I don't want to hold them any more.

Kieran looks at me for a moment, his bright blue eyes holding mine steadily in a way that reminds me how we speak to each other over the Internet. I remember that he is kind and he is trustworthy. I know him already, don't I, through so many conversations? There are many things we have already spoken about. I know his mind and he knows mine.

'You look even lovelier in real life,' he says softly, low enough for it to be for my ears only.

'I look even lovelier?' I put my head down and look at my hands. Solly has wandered a few feet away out of earshot, apparently scrutinising Uncle Bob's billboard. 'Hot sugared doughnuts; jam-filled 30p extra. Large, medium or small.' I've memorised it already because we've been waiting here fifteen minutes.

What is Kieran on about, anyway? This man has an army of adoring female fans – I know, because Surinda told me – ever since he appeared in 'TV's sexiest' last week.

There are a couple of girls standing not two feet from here who are trying to make up their minds if they recognise him or not. They keep nudging each other and giggling in our direction. It would make their whole lives worthwhile if they could get so much as a single glance from him. I, on the other hand, am an invalid. I have been so for a very long time and I know full well that I am not *that* special to look at.

'Don't tease me, please, Kieran.'

'I'm not teasing.' He touches the ends of my finger-tips, ever so softly. So softly in fact that I want him to touch them again, just to make sure. We both glance in Solly's direction but he isn't looking at us.

'Don't feel bad . . . because of the wheelchair,' he's whispering to me now. 'I don't see that. I see you. I told you, it doesn't matter to me.'

'I fail to see how it can't matter.' My voice comes out cold and hard, like a schoolteacher. That wasn't how I wanted it to sound but I can't help it. I could so easily fall in love with this boy. It was what I wanted to do, wasn't it? I wanted to experience that before the end. But him telling me that he cares about me too, that wasn't in my plan. I can't believe it. I don't. I don't know what his game is, but I'm feeling far too confused at the moment to know what to do about it.

So I change the subject, away from him and me, and onto something safe and distant; like his grandfather.

'How's your granddad?' I ask him, before he can reply to the last thing I said to him, and I hear his long, deep breath out before he answers.

'He's . . . he's still angry.'

'He is?'

That wasn't what I meant. When you ask about someone's sick granddad they're supposed to say, 'Oh, he's doing okay', or, 'He's doing as well as can be expected; holding up, you know.'

'What's he angry about?'

Kieran gives me that look again.

'Same thing as you, I guess. He's angry that he hasn't got that long left. He wants to live but his body is giving up on him, letting him down. He isn't that old, you know. He's got so much more left to give . . .'

'He lived long enough to have his family, though,' I point out. 'He had your father, and then he lived long enough to see you.'

Kieran leans in a little closer. 'That's what I've been telling him, Pixie. He *has* had his time. I've been telling him all about you, and how brave you're being. You've been an inspiration to him, really you have.'

'How could that be?' I'm curious, and my curiosity makes me feel brave. 'I'm not an inspiration to anyone, Kieran. I haven't done anything special.'

'That's just it, though, isn't it? It isn't the things you've *done*. It's the way you are. That's why I love to talk to you online. You brighten up my day. You've been through such a lot of bad stuff in such a short space of years but I never hear you complain. You take every day as it comes.'

I don't answer that and so we're both silent for a while until:

'My mum was in a wheelchair,' he says, ever so softly. 'Did you know that?'

His words hit me like a gust of cold wind blowing suddenly through a window. I didn't know that.

'I thought she died in a car crash at the same time as your dad?'

'She did, but she'd been using a wheelchair on and off for a couple of years beforehand. She had to use it on the days when she was too tired, but otherwise she could walk. She'd been such an active person before – swimming, tennis, you name it.'

I look at him in wonder. He talks to me about his

parents all the time. I thought I already knew most of what there was to know about them. His dad was an ex-boxer who became an arts director at the theatre; his mother developed knitting patterns for kiddies' jumpers and more fancy ones for designer clothing stores. I got the impression she flew all over the world gleaning ideas for her designs.

'She didn't have what you've got – it was never going to kill her. But the funny thing was, it did change her.' Kieran is still playing with the ends of my fingers. He's obviously a tactile person. Solly is keeping a close watch, I can *sense* him. 'That's how come I first noticed you on the "Shared Tears" website,' he confesses now. 'Something about you did remind me of her, I'll admit it. When you said you needed to use Bessie I noticed you, but when we started to really talk I saw something else there, something that was really special about her and you have it too . . .'

What was that? My eyebrows go up curiously.

'. . . It was something about the way you *accepted* your situation. You weren't resigned to it. You were at peace with it. Like she was. That's a very unusual thing, you know.'

'I'm not an angel, Kieran.' I want to say more but my throat just closes up. I'm *not* good and wonderful and brave. I've never pretended that I am. I do complain and moan sometimes. I hate being in this chair. I want to walk. I want to live. I shake my head and say softly, 'I want to do all the things I know I'll never get to do, Kieran, and some days I really feel so sore about that . . .'

'But you're here now, aren't you?' He squeezes my

140

fingertips and I close my eyes. From the tips of his fingers I can feel the whole warmth of his hand, the strength of his arm. He's here. I can feel a damp breeze caressing my skin, and it smells of the faint saline smell of a river; it smells of Uncle Bob's doughnuts and the rain on the grass and the turf that's been kicked up underneath a hundred feet.

I'm here. Far away across the field the rock band has abandoned another set and a collective moan runs through the field. The crowd under the awning is getting thicker as the rain starts pelting down again. The water has cleared the common of the throng of bodies, though.

'Isn't it strange,' I say after a while, 'how we both got to be here? The chain of events that had to happen for us to end up here? I mean, you normally live in Dublin – but it was your granddad getting ill that brought you here to look after him and that's meant we're now close enough to meet.'

'And it took Miriam and my parents to pass away to get us both onto the same website. If you hadn't mentioned how you needed to use Bessie, come to that, I might never have even properly noticed you. We might never have got chatting.'

They say there's always a silver lining, don't they?

'Shall I take you somewhere?' Kieran whispers to me after a while. 'To where it's less crowded. If you don't mind getting wet?'

I don't mind.

The rain doesn't feel cold any more, it just feels fresh on my upturned face. There's the sweet smell of mayflowers in the air as Kieran takes the handlebars of

141

Bessie and directs me out and away from the throng. His hands feel steady and firm at my back. When I glance behind me I see Sol walking a few paces further down, talking animatedly into his mobile phone. He's keeping his eye on us, but he isn't making it obvious, and I'm so grateful for that.

'Where are you taking me?' I smile at Kieran and he smiles broadly back. He's eating my doughnuts and the rain has melted the sugar on them and made them all wet.

'To the edge of forever,' he tells me, and I recognise the lyrics from one of his friend's songs.

Forever doesn't have an edge, I think.

It doesn't have an ending.

Just for today, I'm not going to worry about time and how much of it I still have left and when it will be over. I have to keep looking behind me to convince myself that it really is Kieran at my back, pushing my chair. He said I was lovely. I can still hear his faint Irish lilt, softly in my ear, telling me that. He meant it, too. I don't know how, but he did. So I let him take me out across the common and into a wooded area that turns into a little path through the trees, with Solly trailing a little way behind us.

Just for today I'm going to pretend that I am everything Kieran thinks I am; that I am truly lovely and patient and at peace with my lot. And that because we are together nothing else matters, nothing at all. Not Dr Lavelle's unanswered phone calls; not my mum back in Maidstone fretting about me; not the thing that I have to do in two weeks' time on my birthday. Just for today it doesn't matter, none of it, nothing at all.

142

17

Shelley

'I want you to meet someone, Pixie. Someone very special.' We've left the path in the woods behind now, and have come out onto the back of an estate with its rows of dreary-looking terraced houses. Kieran is fumbling in his wet jeans pockets, looking for his keys, and just for a moment he shivers. I feel so sorry for him it's like my heart's going to break. Because the thing is, Kieran is so strong and so very full of life. He's a man in the prime of his youth, as Solly would say, and yet he has this vulnerability about him. I can't help thinking he's got soaked through just because of me. He's come all the way out here because of this dream, because of this person who he thinks I am – I can't help noticing that he's called me Pixie, my online screen name – several times now. I'm not a *pixie* in real life, that's the thing. I'm a real flesh and blood girl. I still don't know if he sees that.

I want him to, and at the same time I don't. If he sees me as I am – as I *really* am, an emaciated invalid in a chair – then he might not want to know me any more. As it is he thinks I'm some sort of ethereal being, made of glass. He thinks I'm special. He thinks I don't notice the contours of his muscles under his rain-drenched T-shirt, but I do. Oh, I do!

'This person you want me to meet, am I allowed to know who it is?'

He doesn't have to tell me, though, because I can guess. As soon as he opens the door onto the dingily lit narrow corridor of the townhouse, with its yellowing large-flowers wallpaper, I think: It's an old person. It's got to be. That's the kind of yucky wallpaper Mrs Simmonds next door would go for. That's the kind of half-hearted lighting she would choose for her hallway, like she doesn't want to use up too much electricity.

'It's my granddad, Shelley. I hope you don't mind?' Kieran is wiping his muddy boots very thoroughly on the doormat (my mum would *love* that). Then he wipes the raindrops off his face with the back of his arm.

'Are you getting a change of clothes here?' He must be freezing. It's got so cold and there is no heating in this house. Kieran touches the radiator and from his expression I see that it's stone cold.

'Not here, Shelley. I'm okay, really. What about you?' he asks me solicitously. 'Do you need to be getting home?' He glances at Solly who's caught up with us now and I can see that the question is half-aimed at him as well. Solly shakes his head, half-shrugs. I'm just fine, he motions.

'I was under the waterproof,' I point out to Kieran. '*You're* the one who got drenched.'

'Look, I . . . I hope you don't mind,' Kieran says again, 'meeting Granddad?'

'Why would I?'

Kieran shrugs. 'He's . . .' he clears his throat, 'he's got terminal lung cancer, as you know, and he's been sent home from the hospice because there's nothing more they can do for him and it's what he wanted. But he isn't the easiest man in the world.'

Kieran is standing at the foot of the stairwell, his hands in his pockets, and his dark hair has gone all curly with the rain. The nape of his neck is wet. Even his eyelashes are wet. His breathing is uneven as if he's not sure what's coming next, and because I am a girl and not a pixie, I can't help but notice that this is exactly what he must look like when he steps out of the shower in the morning. Minus the clothes, of course. Oh god, what am I thinking? Thank the lord for his granddad's crappy hallway lights that won't reveal that I'm blushing . . .

'So . . . can he come down?' I glance up the steep stairwell.

'He's bedridden. He's got twenty-four-hour care and he doesn't expect to come down these stairs again.' Until he's in his box, I think. God, that's sad.

'The thing is,' I shrug uneasily, 'I don't have wings.' (Not being a pixie.) 'So, how exactly is this meeting going to take place?' I'm so focused on the *how* that I don't even wonder about the *why*.

'You don't look like too much of a heavy weight to me.' Kieran flexes his muscles in a mock show of strength. He *has* got nice biceps. I wish he wouldn't do that. He's got to see my reaction, for sure. And anyway, every time my attention gets drawn to how strong and healthy and *male* he is, I also catch a glimpse of something else; the

145

part of him that's tender and vulnerable and not so strong. He doesn't just want me to go up there and meet his granddad. I can feel it. He wants me to do something for him. Heaven knows what. Perhaps he wants me to be that inspiration he keeps telling me I am; some bullshit like that.

I glance at Solly. Will he go along with this a little bit further?

'Can we go and meet Granddad?' I ask softly. Solly smiles at me. 'Whatever you want, honey bunch', then, 'Oh *hell*' as his ringer goes off again. He fishes his mobile out of his pocket and checks who's calling. I see him stiffen; take in a sharp breath, as if this is the one call he's been waiting for. 'It's Justin. Er . . . you two go on up. I'll be two ticks, no more.' Then he dips out the front again, leaving the door wide open. I can see the rain slanting in through the doorway. It must be wetting the carpet. But Solly isn't leaving me exactly unattended, bless him – I can see the raindrops pelting down onto the back of his black leather coat; he's still got one foot around the door, propping it open.

'Are you up for it?' Kieran leans over me, his hands on Bessie's arm-rests. 'Will you let me carry you upstairs?' His voice is so soft and sweet and . . . well, yes, it's sexy. In another lifetime I will come back and hear this man speak these words again, I promise myself, and it will be in a happier scenario than this. *Will you let me carry you upstairs?*

I lift up my arms to him. Solly still has his back to us, he's hunched over his phone by the door.

For a moment Kieran doesn't move.

146

He just looks at me and his blue eyes are as soft as the morning dew, green as the forest after a rainstorm. I could write a whole book of poems about his eyes.

'You okay?' I smile at him.

'I'm okay.' His voice is hoarse. 'I was just wondering . . .' He comes in a bit closer, so near that I would draw back if I could but I've nowhere to go. When his lips close in on mine it is as if everything else on this earth all falls away and there is only this moment between us. Ohmigod, why does it have to be like this? Why do this man's lips have to taste so good? Better if my first kiss had been naff, horrible, yucky, so that I wouldn't have to know what I'll be missing. His lips are soft at first, and then more urgent, parting gently, engulfing me so sweetly that I wish it would never end.

But it does end, and he lifts his eyes to mine, smiling sheepishly, almost apologetically.

'Sorry,' he says, glancing towards the front door where Solly still has his back to us and is hissing quietly into his phone. 'I couldn't resist. Are you mad at me? You didn't think I was taking unfair advantage, did you?'

I close my eyes as Kieran picks me up and my head leans in against his chest. Just for a minute, I let myself forget how incredibly light I must seem to him, what a pathetic little bag of bones I am underneath all the clothes that I wear to keep me looking as padded out as possible. I can feel the skin of his cheek against my face, just a little bit scratchy but I don't mind. He smells sweet. His arms underneath me are steady and strong but his eyes are unfathomable as he carries me the whole of the way up those dim and airless stairs. Once at the top, he raps against the door with his knuckles without putting me down.

'I'm here. Granddad, it's me.' And I can hear the movements of someone inside, the dragging of a chair's feet against the wooden floor as someone gets out of it to open the bedroom door.

'He's just woken up.' A chubby West Indian nurse opens the door to Kieran and I see her eyes widen in surprise as she sees me in his arms. 'Oh, my! More visitors today,' she beams. Then, looking slyly at her watch, 'You'll be all right with him if I get myself a drink just now, then? I've been on duty here with him since ten last night and I didn't dare to leave him long. He's been in such a foul mood,' she smiles jovially. 'Haven't you, Mr O'Keefe?'

Her bedridden charge just snarls, and I feel myself gripping Kieran's wet T-shirt a little tighter. I could have done with being in a different place to here right now. I've got the taste of Kieran's kiss still on my lips. I'm feeling weak with delight and just all funny inside, oh to be alone with him for just a few more minutes, but instead we're in the old man's bedroom and the place is even darker and more airless than his hallway. The one difference is that the radiator up here is on full blast, the windows closed.

Kieran glances at the drawn curtains.

'He won't let me touch them.' The nurse pouts a little now, following his gaze. 'We gotta have them curtains drawn, all the day and all the night long.'

'Sure, you go and have your drink,' Kieran tells her.

'We'll see to him for a while. Uh – that's our friend by the front door, by the way. He might want to come in now. He can have his conversation in private seeing as we've come upstairs.'

'And who would "we" be?' The rasping breath coming from the bed ceases momentarily as its occupant speaks. Then a long hacking cough follows. It sounds rather angry. The old man clears his throat of phlegm. 'Who've you brought to me now, Kieran? I don't want to be quizzed by any more of those homeopaths or acupuncturists . . .'

'It's Shelley.' Kieran moves closer to the bed with its single yellow bedside lamp. I clutch at him tighter still, looking over my shoulder at the bed's occupant, who is mostly hidden by a mountain of bedclothes and pillows. 'ShelleyPixie, remember?'

I wince at that. Kieran isn't supposed to be sharing my screen name with his granddad, for pete's sake!

The rasping breath from the bed goes quiet for a minute as if the old man is considering before he speaks. When I look back at Kieran, I see his eyes are fixed on his grandfather, compassionate and sorrowful. I feel so sorry for him. But I also feel strange in his arms now, as if I were some sort of offering he's bringing up to appease the old man, ridiculous as that sounds.

I wish Kieran would just put me down. I could sit in that chair the nurse has left. What am I doing here? What am I supposed to say to this old man, anyway?

'ShelleyPixie,' the old voice says at last. 'You came.'

I came?

I look at Kieran.

I was brought, more like!

149

'He's been asking to see you,' Kieran confesses. My heart sinks a little at that. I don't know why. Maybe it's the thought that perhaps *this* is the real reason why Kieran wanted to see me today? 'I've told him all about you.'

'Yeah?' I say. What else is there to say? He's told me a bit about his granddad too. But I never quite pictured this.

'Why do you keep it so dark in here?' I blurt out, because I can't think of anything else, and anyway, this darkness is making me feel uncomfortable.

'I like it that way,' the voice comes back from the bed. 'Put her down, boy, for heaven's sake. I want to see what she looks like.'

Kieran obediently deposits me in the chair. It's so hot in this room, so stifling, I swear I can see little wafts of steam rising off Kieran's clothes as he leans against the thin shaft of light given off by the bedside lamp.

'Kieran, there's a good lad. Will you go over the road and buy me some ciggies while that silly bitch of a nurse is out of the way?'

'Granddad . . .'

'There's no use lecturing me, boy!' The old man may have hardly any breath left in his body but what he does have he uses to very good effect. He's got a will of iron, this old geezer, unbendable, stubborn, not to be crossed. 'I'm on my way out anyway. One or two puffs more won't make any difference now, will it?'

Kieran shrugs, and to my horror he shifts to take himself out of the room, leaving me alone with his smelly granddad. 'I won't be more than ten minutes, Pixie, I

150

promise you. I'll tell Solly to come up after me so you won't be alone.' He makes up for leaving me by planting his soft lips against the crown of my head as a parting gesture.

Now he's leaving, though, and this foul old man who is domineering as hell and likes to dwell in the dark like a toad has me all to himself.

'So, what did he tell you to tell me?'

Now that we're alone together the arrogant tone of his voice doesn't intimidate me so much as bother me. After all, we're both at the same disadvantage here.

I can't move and neither can he.

'Absolutely nothing,' I assert. 'What were you expecting?'

'Hi!' Solly has just bowled up the stairs. He glances into the room and his instant reaction is exactly the same as mine was. *Yuk.* But he recovers quickly, motioning his phone with his free hand. 'Justin's still . . . er . . . talking. You mind if I stay just out here?'

'Sure thing, Solly. You carry on.'

I turn to look the old geezer full in the face. What did he mean by his question to me, I wonder? *What did he tell you to tell me?* Apart from mentioning his granddad was sick, Kieran has barely ever talked about him, and that's the truth. The skin around his eyes has gone a pretty nasty shade of yellow. His upper body is naked underneath the blankets. I can see the tops of his stick-thin arms poking out and he is completely emaciated. I doubt that he's bothered to eat in a while.

'What was I expecting?' A bony finger emerges to point at me with surprising strength. 'What do you think? The boy has lost both his parents just under a year ago. Now he's about to lose his only living relative: me. He imagines you can somehow pep-talk me out of dying.' The breaths in between the words are painful, deliberate. 'But I can see that you understand enough of what I'm going through to not even attempt it.'

'Fair enough,' I concede. He is right. And anyway, I don't want to try making him feel better. 'I imagine it will be a blessed relief.'

'Not where I'm going,' the old man snorts. 'Hell, probably. I'm a Catholic, you know. But never mind that. I've got something I want to tell you.' He tries to lean forward but he doesn't quite make it. I hope the old man isn't going to keel over and die with me here in front of him and no one else. Downstairs I can hear the nurse whistling to herself, bustling about in the kitchen. Solly seems to have wandered away down the stairs a little and no doubt he's still whispering into his phone. I know Solly has left the door open again but that doesn't make me feel any better. Don't die right now, I think.

'Yes?'

'From here on in,' he tells me assertively, 'I want you to promise me that you'll leave my grandson alone.'

'What?' It's more of a command than a request.

'Stay out of his life. Don't call him. Don't email him. Leave him alone.' The puckered mouth purses up and Granddad sinks back onto his pillow. His bony finger is still pointing at me, though, and I have to fight the urge I have to lean forward and snap it off. I may be weak, but I'm still stronger than him.

'It's an ugly sight, isn't it?' he adds, seeing my reaction

to him, 'witnessing somebody else coming to the end of their life like this?'

'I've seen it before.'

'Oh you have, have you? And does it scare you?'

'*You* don't scare me,' I tell him.

'Maybe not. But you're still going to stop seeing my grandson.'

'Says you.' I turn my body away from him and look towards the door. Christ, Solly, hurry up and get off that darn phone, why don't you? And when oh when is Kieran going to get back here? The bad way Kieran's granddad is in should make me feel sorry for him but it doesn't. He makes me feel sick. He reminds me of the way I could end up if I don't watch out. He's reminded me of all the reasons why I made up my mind to do what I have to do. He's made my resolve stronger, so I should be grateful to him for that much.

'What makes you so sure that I'm going to do what you ask, anyway?'

'Oh, you will,' he asserts, sucking in at his tube, hanging on for dear life. 'You will, because you give him hope. And to give him hope is wrong. He's going to lose me. He's going to lose you too, isn't he? Maybe sooner than he thinks?'

I feel a shiver of revulsion run through me at that. Why does he say that? Can he feel the shadow of death hanging over me just as much as I can feel it over him?

'Giving Kieran hope can't be wrong,' I put back to him. 'He's still got his life to live, hasn't he? He can still make good for himself.'

'Yes, you bring him hope. But it's false hope, if you're

153

honest. He won't win the million pounds in the quiz show . . .' His voice deteriorates into a bout of coughing here, he's obviously getting worked up. 'I won't live. You won't. Sooner or later he's going to be let down by all of us, isn't he?'

'I can't help that, though. I can't control what's happening in my life any more than you can control yours. I can't help it if your grandson is going to be let down by life sometimes . . .'

'Look here, young miss.' His dark eyes burn into me like so many fag-ends he's burnt in his life. 'What you can help is what you're doing to him right now. He's coming to rely on you.'

'We've barely met . . .'

'But the way he held you, the way he looked at you when he set you down on that chair . . .' the old man shakes his head, 'oh, he's come to rely on you all right. You might not see much because you're young, but you're a woman and you'll see that much at least. A woman knows when a man has fallen for her.'

I fall quiet for a bit, while I stop and think. If even this old sour puss is so sure that Kieran has fallen for me, then it must be true. He wouldn't tell me these things to flatter me, that's for sure. He doesn't like me and he doesn't want me in Kieran's life; he's made that plain.

'So you really think he's falling in love?'

'He's vulnerable, my lad is. He might be charming and a good-looker but he's independent-minded and that's always made him a loner at heart. He's fallen for you because he sees you're like him in some ways. He could fall in love just as easily with someone else, don't you see that? A woman who is healthy and whole; a woman who can be all the things he wants you to be for him, but you can't.' He's silent for a while, and then, 'You could do him some good, yet, though.'

I draw in a shuddering breath at that. Part of me is feeling stung to the core with what he's just said; all that stuff about Kieran falling for someone who's 'healthy and whole', as if I were just some piece of rubbish to be discarded, useless and worthless, to one side. Then there's that other part of me that's feeling jubilant. If even this old guy thinks Kieran feels so deeply about me – then, maybe it's true?

'*My* feelings don't matter very much to you, do they?'

He shrugs. 'Finer feelings are all very well for those who can afford them. You and me – we can't.'

I really don't like the way he has lumped the two of us in together in that phrase.

'Look, butt out of this, okay? You needn't worry, I shan't be around for too much longer anyhow.'

'Is that what the medics have told you?' His shaggy eyebrows are drawn down and he looks at me with renewed interest.

'No. It's what *I'm* telling *you*. The medics don't know everything. They don't know how long this will go on for. But I'm not planning on . . .' I bite my lip, stopping up the words that I never meant to say to him, things that are no business of his. 'Look, all I'm saying is that I won't be around for too much longer.'

'But you haven't been given any time frame? You don't know how much time you're looking at?'

'Actually, I do.'

'You could keep the boy holding on for months, falling more and more in love with you every day, and then in the end . . . *whoof!* You'll be out of his life in a flash. Just like his parents. Just like me.'

'No.' My voice is sticking in my throat. 'I'm not going to do that to him.'

'No? You're not?'

'Look, I'm not, all right, you ill-tempered old man! How dare you lie there telling me what I can or cannot do with what's left of my own life? I'll see Kieran for as long as I want to and it's none of your affair. But I'd never hurt him in any way, ever. I'll see to it that I don't make him suffer just because *I've* got to. I don't want anyone to suffer because of me, not anyone. Not Kieran, not my mum or dad, not my brother or Solly . . . oh, what would *you* know about anything?' My heart is hammering so loud in my chest now that I can't believe Solly hasn't come rushing in to rescue me. Nasty old man. Horrid old man.

'Oh he'll suffer on your account all right. It'll just be a matter of degree, won't it? If you really *cared* about him you'd leave him now.'

'I *am* leaving him now!' I storm. 'I'm leaving *everyone*, if it's any of your business, because I've already decided it's the best way to do it. It's the only way. It's the fairest thing on everyone. I'm going to do it in a couple of weeks, in fact. So there. You can shut up now and go back to sleep, or whatever it is you do when you don't have anybody come to visit you.'

'Oho.' I can't see it, but I can sense his quiet smile in

the darkness. 'Are you planning on taking your own life, girl?'

I don't answer him and I don't move, but even in that stuffy, overheated, dark and airless room, he reads my mind.

'That will take some courage, I grant you. If you do it, then you have more courage than me. I wish I'd done it while I had the capacity.'

I look at my hands, which are folded in my lap. Right now I can't help but echo his own sentiments.

'What's your plan?' he's asking me now in his cunning old voice. 'How will you do it?'

'I'm going to jump off a rock,' I tell him through gritted teeth. In a strange kind of way I feel I *can* tell him, because he matters nothing to me. And because he won't care, either. 'In two weeks' time. On my birthday, at Summer Bay.'

'That's a good plan,' he says.

You old bastard, I think.

'So I'll be out of both your lives forever. You don't need to worry about me and Kieran now, do you?'

'Not if you leave him alone *now*,' the old man says. 'Make your excuses and leave him in peace. Or else, one way or the other, you'll only break his heart afresh.'

'You're suggesting that I drop all contact with him so he doesn't have to find out about it? So he never knows what I've done?'

'That's the way.'

'And he won't wonder why I'm not contactable any more?'

'No, he won't, because you'll already have made the

break with him beforehand, won't you? Ah, yes now, I see she gets it at last.'

We can both hear the sounds of Kieran's footsteps as he races back up the stairs to us, his face bright and breathless as if he's run every step of the way there and back.

'I wasn't more than ten minutes, was I?' He gives me a quick hug as he drops the ciggies on his granddad's bed.

Ten minutes too late, I think. I'm trembling, churning inside with a rage and a hurt that I didn't think I was capable of feeling any more. Solly reappears then, pocketing his mobile. He looks at me curiously.

'I want to go home now, Solly. Will you take me home now please?'

Kieran looks from his granddad to me and then back again, and I can see he's wondering what on earth has gone on between us, what could we both have said?

'Sure, Pixie,' Kieran says and then he picks me up. I wonder why it is that I get the impression when he takes me through the door, even though I never once look back at the old man, that he thinks he's *won* something, something very important.

18

Rachel

'So, you're coming down this way then?'

With both Shelley and Daniel out I decide this might be a good time to make this phone call to my sister. And I had to take the *bus* home from Solly's, after all . . . he took ages before he rang to tell me that Shelley's friend was a no-show so he'd taken her out for the day instead. I can't decide if my sister Lily sounds more relieved or alarmed at the news.

'Well, Cornwall way. You're in South Devon. But if you want to meet up with us while we're down there it might be easier than coming up here.'

'I suppose it would be easier.' Lily sounds pensive. 'I'll drive over to where you're staying, of course. I wouldn't expect you to travel any more than you have to.'

'That's very kind of you.' I'm aware of how stilted the conversation is between us. I haven't seen my sister for a few years now. We exchange Christmas and birthday cards; that's pretty much it.

Except, since Pandora left the country Lily's phoned me *three* times, no less, saying she wants us to meet up.

'And you've been in touch with Mum?'

159

'Oh yes!' How could you even ask, her tone implies, what dutiful daughter wouldn't? 'Most days, in fact. She asks after you, of course.'

Not that you'd know anything much about what was going on in my life, I think. I bite my lip rather than say it out loud.

The window I'm looking out of as we speak is absolutely filthy, I realise now. How long could it be since I last went out and cleaned it? It wasn't last summer, that's for sure. Good grief. Could it really have been the summer before last? I rub at it with my little finger and a streak of daylight pours through where I've cleaned the dust trail.

'Crikey.'

'What's that?'

'Oh nothing, just the dust on this window . . .' I give a polite laugh. Just as well Lily isn't coming up here, really. 'And Mum's settling in well, is she?'

'It sounds divine out there, Rachel. They have a house overlooking the sea with twenty-two acres attached to it. She's going to take up riding again. I'm going out to join them for the summer as it happens. I might even be tempted to stay.'

'I didn't know you and Guy were thinking of emigrating?'

'Oh I don't know about *him*.' She gives a high laugh and I hear her voice crack. 'I might just leave him to his own devices. Anyway, I know you're busy. You're always busy. So, just give me your mobile and let's pencil in a date for lunch when you're down.'

'Any day will be good for us,' I say to her. 'And Mum

160

sent me a whole box of photos and stuff – you know, dancing memorabilia – that you might like to have a trawl through. I'll bring it down for you, shall I?'

'Sure,' she says. 'Shall we say the Tuesday then? Shall I pencil that in?'

'That'll be good.'

Why are we meeting? I wonder. Why has she phoned me three times to arrange for us to meet when we clearly find it so hard to be in each other's company?

'It'll be nice to see you again, Rachel.' I hear her familiar voice, cool and detached as ever, and I wonder if she really could be missing me so much just because our mum has gone away? 'And there's a little matter that I'd like to talk to you about . . . oh, nothing I want to expand on just now, it can wait till we meet up, nothing crucial, you understand, but just something that needs clearing up once and for all and it'd be easier for us to do it if we're face to face.'

Good grief. I can feel my face flushing from ear to ear, my heart hammering like a blacksmith in my chest when she says those words. She *knows*. After all this time, how could she have found out? How could she? It's impossible, unless . . .

Unless Pandora didn't send me *everything* that was inside that box?

Unless she sent some of it on to me and some to my sister, and now Lily, after all this time, has found out the truth?

19

Shelley

Possibly the last person I expect to be calling me at 7 a.m. on a Sunday morning is Surinda Chellaram.

'Why so early?' I rub my eyes, checking the alarm clock by my bed; it really is 7 a.m.!

'I'm on Yusef's mobile, aren't I?' She sounds irritable. 'It's the only time I can make this call without anyone knowing I'm doing it.'

If she can't sleep, I'm surprised she isn't just texting. In fact, after the way she let me down the last time we spoke I'm surprised she's got the cheek to even contact me at all. What is so urgent?

I've been wide awake myself admittedly, thinking about Kieran since the crack of dawn. I still don't believe all the things that occurred yesterday; it all happened so quickly and unexpectedly. I feel as if my life is trying to take a huge great big U-turn but it can't; it's an enormous armoured truck set on its course and nothing is going to be able to change it now, nothing at all. So why am I spending all this time thinking about him? I can't help it really. It's what I want to do.

She's disturbed me, in fact.

'Why don't you just MSN me later, Surinda?'

'I can't MSN you because they won't let me use the computer, will they?' She's sounding really stressy. When Surinda gets stressed her accent becomes stronger and I find it more difficult to understand what she's saying.

'Look, *who* won't let you use the computer?' I'm up on my elbows now in my bed. The curtains are only half-drawn because I liked the colour of the light coming through the sky last night, all pink and salmon and rose – 'shepherd's delight', my mum would say. I wondered if there were any shepherds out there thinking just the same thing, but it's red sky this morning too ('shepherd's warning'!), so that's confusing. It's like my life at the moment, conflicting signals coming from all over the place.

'*They* won't.' Surinda is hissing back at me and I can hear the tears in her voice. 'My family.'

'You're banned from the computer?' I say, stupidly. Why would she be banned? Sometimes Mum bans Daniel, but only when he's been very naughty or he's been on the GameBoy too much. Surinda is too old for all that.

'Yes, I am banned,' she tells me through gritted teeth, 'and I am not allowed to make contact with anyone, no one at all. Not even you, and my ma thinks you are a good influence. They're afraid that I might try to escape.'

Oh dear, oh bloody hell, she's started to cry really hard now. Then the penny drops.

'This is about Jallal, isn't it?'

He isn't what she expected.

She's got a dud.

163

Uh-oh. I sense trouble brewing here, *big* time.

'He's . . . he's . . .' She's almost choking on her words and I get a momentary flash of guilt because I remember now wishing her a bad 'un. I wished him to be smelly and fat and all sorts, didn't I? Oh shit, I did, on Saturday, when she let me down.

Still, I tell myself, I couldn't have actually wished a horrible Jallal into being for *real*, could I?

'So, he's a toad, is he?'

'Toad . . . doesn't describe it, man.'

'Tell me.' I settle back comfortably with my pillow behind me. It occurs to me that I'm not going to be able to tell her a thing about my own adventure yesterday now. It wouldn't be very kind to rub it in her face like that. I only met Kieran O'Keefe and he kissed me! I can't tell her about how he looked in his T-shirt or that look he gave me when he took me upstairs or the things he said in my ear. I might be able to tell her about the evil granddad; when she's done telling me about *her* troubles, of course.

'Jallal is *not* what he made himself out to be,' she's saying tearfully. 'He is, maybe, fifteen years older than he was in that photo his mother sent to us.'

I remember now how Surinda had asked me how to use Photoshop to disguise some of her facial hair before she sent off *her* photo, but to use a fifteen-year-old one is really below the belt – hell, she would have been a baby in nappies if she'd tried that one on him.

'Whoa, that's *bad*.' A lot can change in fifteen years. 'But what about his voice?' I remind her. 'His voice that was so dark and sexy and stuff? You fell in love with his voice, remember?'

'He doesn't sound the same.' I can pick up a trace of disgust in her own voice now. 'He sounds all high-pitched and squeaky, like he's had his balls pinched off. He's about forty pounds heavier. He's jowly, he's got a bad case of BO, and he looks nothing like Jay Surinham at all.'

Jay Surinham is a Bollywood icon Surinda sometimes talks about. He does nothing for me, but apparently there are about three million ladies on the Indian subcontinent who swoon over him regularly.

'Look, you're not married yet. You can still get yourself out of this.'

'But *how*?' she's wailing at me, forgetting that she's supposed to be quiet and not wake all her family up. 'They aren't going to let me out of their sight. Anyone would think they suspected . . . how . . . angry I am.'

'You mean you haven't said?' I swap my weight over to the other elbow. 'You haven't told, like, your mum or anything?'

'My mum isn't *your* mum, don't forget. She went all funny as soon as they arrived, didn't she? Anyway, it's too late. She and Dad have been won over. His parents came over with some very fine presents. And a signed photo of his cousin who's in the government. I think they've been bought off; bought with the price of my happiness.'

I should think that happens to a lot of girls in her situation; I did try to warn her, but she was so enthusiastic.

'Oh, Surinda.'

'And his mother tells me . . . get this . . . that despite

his shortness in stature *he is a fine big lad*, not to worry!'

'Oh, Surinda!'

'I can't do it, though. I'll hang myself before I get to see how well-hung he is. That is what this really all boils down to, isn't it?' she says to me in disgust.

'What?'

'Breeding. His mum commented on the size of my hips. "Good for child-breeding," she said. And after all my blasted dieting, too . . .'

'I don't think she meant . . .'

'I'm not having his sprogs. I want to be a career girl, don't I? I'm doing my *exams.* But there is no way out of it for me. So I will hang myself. Before they can marry us.'

I go quiet for a bit here. There is no way of telling just how serious she is about this. She can be very impetuous, Surinda. She's the sort who might make a grand gesture like that, if she felt desperate enough. She certainly sounds it at the moment, too. I wonder if I should tell her what's on my mind regarding my birthday plans? As she hasn't even asked me about the *Beat the Bank* tickets, it's probably the one and only thing that we've got in common at the moment.

'So, when are you planning to do it?'

'Sometime soon,' she says ominously. 'As soon as I can get hold of the right sort of rope.'

'I would have thought just about anything might do the trick, if you were really serious about it. Some bed-sheets knotted together, maybe?'

Now it's her turn to go quiet. Does she think I am

166

calling her bluff? Should I be trying to talk her out of it?

'I don't think you realise just how *desperate* I am feeling about this.' Her voice is icy, as if it were somehow all my fault. 'You have no idea what I am going through, the thoughts that have been running through my mind . . .'

'Maybe I do, though. You forget that I am in a similar situation to you: the future ahead looks bleak and with no way I can really change it.'

'I suppose . . . ' she says slowly, 'you *are* in the same situation, aren't you? I'm sorry, I never really saw it from your point of view. You've just always sort of accepted things, haven't you? You're so calm about it. Maybe because you've always known it would be this way.' For once, Surinda is actually making sense.

'Well, yes,' I say.

'But I think you're not desperate,' she adds. 'Not really desperate like me, because you don't have to make this terrible decision that I've got to.'

'Don't talk bollocks,' I say to her at last. She's getting my goat now, I must confess. 'You've got choices, haven't you? Where there's life, there's hope.' That's one of Solly's sayings.

'Not if you've got a family who will track you down and murder you if you don't make the choice that they want you to.'

'Your family wouldn't do that, surely?' I can't believe that. You hear about this kind of thing sometimes in the papers, but no, I can't believe her people would really . . .

'There are people in my extended family who would

be very offended if I tried to run off. They would take it personally. Very personally,' she says with emphasis.

'Well, maybe they would. Then again, maybe they wouldn't. All I know is, you can't even compare yourself with me. You didn't see what happened to my friend Miriam in the end. You didn't see how it was for her. I'm willing to bet she would have married even Jallal if it could have got her out of that end. I'm willing to bet even I would.'

'You have no pride, then!' she scoffs back. 'Why subject yourself to that when there are easier ways to end it?'

So easy to say, I think, when it isn't you that has to do it.

'How do you know I'm not?' I blurt out. 'How do you know anything about what's going on in my head at all? You never shut up long enough about all those bloody pop stars to let me get a word in edgeways.'

'Well . . . *are* you?' she challenges at last.

'I've got my plans,' I tell her. 'I'm not planning to let it run its course to the end like Miriam did, I can tell you that. But if there were any other way out for me – like running away and hiding for the rest of my life if I had to, like you could – you can bet your bottom dollar I would take that option first.'

Now she's crying. Quietly, snivelling into the phone. 'I'm sorry,' she says again, 'I didn't realise it was like that for you. You never let on.'

'What would have been the point? I don't want to go round making the rest of the world miserable.'

'How are you going to . . . you-know-what?' she whispers, almost breathless. I think I have stunned her with

168

what I've just told her. I've probably got her attention properly for the first time since we've known each other. 'You weren't going to tell me?' she accuses. 'All this time we been mates and I never even knew what you been planning . . .'

'Look, I'm going to jump off a high place. Okay?' I forget for one minute that we aren't really mates, not like me and Miriam were. Miriam was different. Even Kieran is different. I trust him. I know I can't really trust Surinda; nothing personal, but that's just the way she is.

'When?' she demands to know.

'On my birthday.'

'Where?'

I sigh. I shouldn't have got into this, I really never should have.

'We're going to Cornwall, okay? I'm going to do it there. Do you want to join me?' It's wicked of me to offer, I know, but I don't really believe what she's telling me about her topping herself, too. She hasn't got the guts for it. Maybe I haven't got the guts either, if that's the right word for it.

'How are you going to get up there?'

'Mum's taking me.'

She gasps. 'What, up somewhere high so you can jump off? Bloody hell.'

'Of course not! She wouldn't do that in a million years, would she? She's taking me to Cornwall, I meant.'

'And who's taking you up to the . . . high place, so you can . . .'

'Details, details.'

169

'Well, if you really meant what you said about joining you, how about me?'

'You'll take me up a cliff?'

'You wouldn't want to be there alone at the end, would you? Besides, those hills are steep. You'd never manage it by yourself.'

'Do you realise what you're saying, Surinda?'

'It would be the act of a true friend, wouldn't it?' she tells me solicitously. 'You've suffered enough. You don't want it to be like Miriam. You said it. And there is no way out for you. I will do what I can to help you, if you let me.'

'The thing is, I don't feel good about you jumping with me, Surinda. There really is no need. There must be some other way out of the dilemma for you.'

'Who said anything about me jumping? I only ask that you take me to Cornwall with you. And that you give me whatever possessions you have that are of any value that I might be able to hock or use myself in my new life.'

Okay, that one really took my breath away. When it comes down to it, I think there's not really a lot to choose from between Surinda and Kieran's granddad. Both of them are quite happy to see the end of me if it suits their own purposes . . . as far as they're concerned it isn't bad to think that way because my end is assured anyway, it's just a matter of timing.

The worst of it, of course, is they're bloody right!

20

Shelley

One week to go . . .

I've been sorting out my things: everything I've got in my drawers, all my papers and stuff, Miriam's emails. I haven't read any of those in a long time. The garden is hot this morning. There are fat bees buzzing all around the peony bushes. I've got a black rubbish bag to one side of me and Bessie behind me and I'm sitting on the grass, which is short and stubbly and going all yellow and it feels a little bit prickly on my legs. I don't mind, though. I like it here. I can hear the blackbirds singing and squabbling and there's a breeze blowing through my hair.

I'm not sure I really want to look at Miriam's emails but I can't rip them up unless I read them again, and there's no way I'm leaving any 'Pandora's box' type of legacy with all my personal stuff for people to go through once I'm gone. So, it's got to be done.

From: **Miriam Marshall**
To: **Shelley Wetherby**
Subject: **RE: Weds**
10 February
Hiya, Shell, sorry I didn't answer you yesterday. We had another uber-urgent trip to see Dr Gee-Gee as he wanted to screen my bloods again. Ari Lavelle was in there, clucking over everything like a chicken as usual. Clinic people getting all panicky; don't know why. I was fine last week; they gave me the usual 'all clear'. They've been doing different tests from what we normally get. Must admit, feeling a bit wonky this morning so maybe they're right to look into it (or maybe it's the effect of yesterday's tests).

Mum says can you still do Weds?
Love M

I thought today would be a good day to do this, because I've got Kieran to look forward to this afternoon. A miracle has happened. Mum and I have been invited around to Solly's and he's organised to have Kieran there too. I have to keep pinching myself to believe it. Mum doesn't know anything about Kieran, and now she doesn't have to. As far as she's concerned, he'll just be one of Solly's friends who's more or less my age, so while they drink wine and do their gossiping together, I get to spend time with Kieran in Solly's beautiful garden, just the two of us, all by ourselves. The thought makes me so happy I feel strong enough to get through this paperwork. Papers, that's all they are, after all. Oh I *so* wish Miriam were still here so I could tell her about Kieran . . .

From: **Miriam Marshall**
To: **Shelley Wetherby**
Subject: **RE: Weds**
2 February

Hiya S. Can't do Weds now as the medics want me in again. Not Gee-Gee because he's gone and his lovely smiling face has been replaced by that sour old goat Ari Lavelle. I'm so cross Gee-Gee has been replaced. Mum says that's typical, though, and we should just count ourselves lucky that we had him for as long as we did. It seems now a new department has got the funding for doing the research on our condition so other people have got to be in charge of us. Something like that, anyway. But I will miss him so much.Had a headache for two days now and my breathing is difficult. Mum says it could be these new tablets they put me on. Or maybe I got a virus? Will let you know. How about next Mon? M xxxx

From: **Miriam Marshall**
To: **Shelley Wetherby**
Subject: **RE: Flowers**
20 February, 10 a.m.

Thanks for your phone call, Shell, and the pink flowers from you and your mum are so lovely, I've made them put them in a vase here by my bed. I didn't know once they got me into hospital that they weren't going to let me go for a while! I can have visitors now and Mum has brought in the laptop so I can email again too. Look forward to being able to CU later. M xxxx

From: **Miriam Marshall**
To: **Shelley Wetherby**
Subject: **RE: Earlier**
20 February, 6 p.m.
Shell, it was so good to see you. I cried when you left, selfishly, because now you're going away with your family for a couple of weeks and I won't see you. I'll probably be out by the time you get back so please come and tell me everything then.

These yucky tablets are making me so weak. At least the painkillers are stopping the leg cramps and all that. But they make me sleepy too. Missing you already. Don't forget to send lots of postcards.
M xxxx

Kieran doesn't know it yet, and neither does Solly, but this afternoon may well be the last time we ever meet. I wonder if Miriam had any idea how close to her end she was when she wrote me those words? In her heart of hearts, I mean; I wonder if she even had an inkling?

Maybe I'm lucky that I *do* know. In a week's time I'll be off to Summer Bay and then . . . that will be that. I don't know what I'm going to tell Kieran when I see him today. I still don't know if I'm going to split with him because that's the kinder thing to do. I just . . . can't think about that. I don't want to think about it. I'm just going to wait and do whatever feels right when the time comes.

It's getting really hot out here now. I'm going to have to bottom-shuffle away from here and into the cool, *and* drag these papers along with me at the same time.

The phone is ringing inside. Danny has gone out the

front, practising his bike again, and there's no way he's going to hear it. That means Mum is going to get it and I don't want her to. I get a small tight feeling of panic in my chest these days every time the naff thing rings because I keep thinking it's going to be Dr Lavelle again. He tried to get through once already yesterday. I notice it's him ringing now, and not one of his staff.

Why can't he just leave me *alone*?

If he thinks I'm going to go into the clinic and it's all going to happen to me just like it did to Miriam, then he can think again. What's the point, anyway? It's not as if the doctors can do anything, it's not even as if they know that much about this disease – they didn't do anything for Miriam, did they?

Mum is coming out now. She's got the phone in her hand. Her face is closed, deadpan. I can't tell if it's the clinic or if it's not but she's coming out to me anyway.

'It's for you.' She hands the phone over and I get a moment of panic – god, it's not Kieran, is it?

'Hello, Shell?' The familiar voice at the other end is friendly and rather more relaxed than it was the last time I heard it.

'Hi, Surinda.' I watch as Mum wordlessly picks up my bags of paper and drops them down nearer to where I'm now sitting. She always does that; she reads my mind; she predicts my every need. The last thing she picks up is the black bin liner that I've already half-filled with the ripped-up bits and it's heavy. Mum pulls a face at the weight and I watch as a few bits of white paper float down onto the short dry grass. One of them is part of Miriam's last, desperate email. *Missing you already.* The

175

little papers lie there like so many bits of confetti on the day after a wedding.

'Okay?' SugarShuli sounds as if she really cares about me today.

'Yeah. You?'

'I've been very good.' Her voice goes down a notch or two now. 'And they're loosening off the noose a bit now. That's why I can ring you. I've told them that I'm in love with Jallal and . . . I think they believe me.'

'Good.'

Mum smiles at me and pads back towards the kitchen. Her slippers – they're mules – are all worn at the back with little bits of stuffing coming out and for some reason that makes me so sad I just want to cry. If I could jump up and run after her and give her a big hug, I would. I don't know why her worn slippers should make me feel like that, but they do.

'So, anyway, have you asked her yet?'

'Have I asked *who*, *what*?' The plastic of the phone handset is already feeling warm in my hand. I'm having to concentrate hard to stay with Surinda at the moment, my mind keeps wandering.

'Your mum. Have you told her that you want me to come with you to Cornwall?'

Oh shit. No, I haven't. I haven't even thought about it.

'It slipped my mind,' I tell her. 'I'm going to, though.'

'Do it now,' Surinda hisses, 'while you're thinking about it. I need to know, man.'

'Yeah. Course you do. Hold on a minute.' I cover the handset and yell down to Mum, who's about to disappear through into the kitchen. 'It's Surinda. She wants to know if she can come to Cornwall with us? It'd be real cool if she could,' I add, as Mum comes back up the path, a puzzled frown on her face. 'You're always telling me I need to make more friends. Surinda is my friend now. Can she come?'

'Well,' Mum hesitates, 'no, darling, she can't. Maybe if you'd warned me a little sooner . . . but these things have to be planned. Maggie only had two spaces left at her place and I booked us in weeks ago.'

'Are you *sure*?'

Mum shakes her head in a very definite way and, although this scuppers my plans somewhat, I don't really feel sorry about it. No more sorry than I was when Surinda couldn't come to Blackberry Common.

'Sorry, no can do,' I tell Surinda once Mum has gone in, 'she says everything's booked already and there aren't any more spaces.'

There's this huge long silence at the other end while Surinda takes this in.

'Who's going to push you off the cliff, then?' she demands.

I shrug, even though she can't see me. Actually, she's pissing me off now. I don't want someone like her to do it. It's got to be someone who does it out of love, not out of self-interest. Silly bloody cow.

'Someone will. Or I'll manage it myself. Don't worry.'

'What about me, though?'

'What about you?'

'You were going to help me . . . to get away from here.'

'I'm sorry, Surinda. I would have helped you if I could but . . . Mum says no and she's the boss. You'll have to

177

find some other way out of it. I'm sure you will. Don't worry.'

'You've, like, got to be kidding?'

I don't like the tone of her voice. I really don't. It's not as though I *owe* her anything.

'I'm not kidding you, Surinda. That's just how it has got to be.'

I want to go. I really don't want to talk to her any more.

'And *Kieran*,' she says now, 'does he know what it is you are planning to do? You never said anything about that meeting you had with him the other day, did you? It seems you made quite an impression on the boy, after all.'

'How would you know?' My blood freezes. How could she possibly know anything about my meeting at all, unless . . .

'I emailed him, didn't I? He already knows me as your friend or I don't suppose he would have answered, but you introduced us the other night, remember? He told me he had given you the tickets for us both.'

'What did he say?'

He didn't say that about the tickets, I think. I know he didn't because he'd forgotten to give them to me at all.

'He said you took my ticket.' God, she's a liar.

'About *me*, I mean. He forgot to give me any tickets, Surinda.'

'He said you two got on very well.' She sounds tight-lipped.

'Send me a copy of what he said to you.'

178

She laughs. 'No chance. Not if you won't take me to Cornwall.'

'Sod it then. Don't. I don't need you anyway.'

'Does he know, though? You didn't answer me that, did you? Have you told him what you're planning?'

'NOYB, Surinda. Drop it, okay? I've changed my mind anyway. I'm not going to do it if you can't come with me. I've changed my mind, just like you did.'

'*Meaning?*'

'You were going to go looking for a "suitable rope", remember? The day after you met Jallal for the first time.'

'I don't remember. I don't think I actually said . . .' She dismisses that thought casually. 'Anyway, I hope you can live with what you're doing.'

She said that, she actually said it. I can't believe she's so thick she can't see the irony in it!

'I've got to go, Surinda.'

'Be like that, then.'

'I'm sorry,' I say, before she slams the phone down on me. Fair enough, I guess. I've let her down badly and I slammed the phone down on her the other day. Tit for tat.

Oh god, what a mess. If it wasn't for the fact that I'm seeing Kieran later on I'd be completely in tatters.

I wanted to leave everything behind in good order. I wanted to sort out all my worldly affairs, as Solly would say, but it looks as if some of my worldly affairs are going to stay messy and unsorted, no matter what I try to do now.

Oh well.

Surinda never really was such a good friend, after all.

It's people like Danny and Solly and Mum and Kieran that I need to say my goodbyes to.

Talk of the devil, because here's Danny-boy now, dragging his bike along behind him with blood pouring out of his left knee and a bruise on his face that's going to come up as big as an egg in a minute. And he's smiling!

'I did it,' he says, and his voice is gruff and low and *proud* and I can tell that the smile inside his heart is even bigger than the one on his face.

'You did it,' I echo back to him. Okay, I'm confused, but I'm sure he's going to tell me in a minute just exactly what it is he's done. And then I see the stabilisers are in his hand, not on the bike any more. I nod at him, and laugh.

'All the way to Lucian Baldwin's house,' he adds, and my heart soars for him because I know what this means to my little brother. It means he's broken the chains that were binding him to this house, to the gravel path out front, to our mother's apron strings and me. It means that now he's free! And while there's still a little bit of me that is longing and yearning to have that freedom for myself, and envies him because he's got it ahead of me, it still occurs to me that Danny-boy's only got it because he was prepared to pay the price. He mops up the blood with a tea-towel that he's pulled down off the washing line. I lean over and give him a hand as best I can. I think he's got a bit of his front tooth chipped as well.

'And was it worth it?' I nod towards his knee. Mum's coming out of the kitchen, frowning, and I hear her sharp intake of breath when she sees what he's done to himself, but:

180

'Worth it? Every *bit* of it!' He doesn't have to tell me, really.

'You're a brave lad, well done,' I say to him, and I watch as a little scrap of paper on the lawn is picked up and rolled over and over by the breeze till it lands in my lap. *Missing you already*, says Miriam. Missing you too, I think. Not so long to go now; only days left, really; days that can easily be converted to hours, and hours into minutes and seconds; that's how long to go before I gain my own freedom.

From: **David Marshall**
To: **Shelley Wetherby**
Subject: **Miriam**
21 May
Hi, this is Miriam's dad, David. Sorry I don't know all of you, but you were on Miriam's system so I take it that you know my daughter. Those of you who know the family well will already have received a phone call, and I apologise to all those who have not. It is with great sadness that I write to let you know that at 4.30 a.m. this morning our beloved daughter Miriam passed away after a protracted downturn in the illness that has dogged her for so many years. We are all devastated by our loss. Forgive the brevity of this communication, but details of any donations for flowers/charities will follow. Thanking all of you who have already expressed your condolences, I remain, yours sincerely, David Marshall.

21

Shelley

The time is going so quickly now. It's quarter to two. I thought I'd have more time left than this. I've barely worked halfway through the things I wanted to sort out and I've got to go back into my bedroom to change this top. It's too dull. I don't like it.

Why haven't I got any clothes that aren't *black*?

'You okay in there?' Mum pops her head round my door. 'Did you sort out everything that you wanted to?'

'Nearly everything.' I take in the surprise on her face as she sees all my drawers open, all the discarded black T-shirts littering the floor. 'Have I still got that pink top that I used to wear?' Her surprise deepens, but she puts her hand over her mouth in a pretend yawn to disguise it. 'I'm just bored of black,' I tell her, like I really don't have a care in the world. She mustn't know what I'm feeling. She mustn't guess.

'I don't suppose Solly will mind,' she says. 'He's used to seeing you in black, isn't he?'

'This isn't about him, though.' Hell, she doesn't think I'm in love with Solly now, does she? 'It's about me. I'm bored of black, that's all.'

Mum smiles. Oh, what the heck, I'll wear a black one. I suppose I'll look like a Turkish widow in mourning but I don't imagine anybody cares. I don't know if Kieran will care.

Maybe he won't care after what I have to tell him today. Maybe it'll make it easier on him if I make myself look as dowdy as I can. His granddad was right. Telling Kieran that I'm finishing with him is the only honourable thing to do. It's the only kind thing to do. Sometimes you have to be cruel to be kind.

Solly's garden on Strawberry Crescent smells like what I imagine an old-fashioned garden must have smelled like: all blackcurrants and lavender and huge overblown roses drifting in and out of straggling flowerbeds, spilling outwards onto the grass. Five years ago, Danny and I used to play 'Getting Lost in the Jungle' here. Today I'm planning to get lost – well, out of Mum's sight anyway – with Kieran.

She kept asking me this morning if I was sure I wanted to come, and didn't I think that maybe I might get a little *bored*? She wants to talk to Solly in peace, that must be it. She's got something on her mind, I can tell. But she needn't worry that I'm going to be hanging around, bothering her. I've got plans of my own today.

He isn't in the garden yet.

He's going to be out here doing some 'gardening' for Solly, that's the plan. And I'll be out here too, and that's how we'll 'meet', here by the swings at the end of the overgrown jungle.

Nobody has been on these swings for years. Not since

183

Danny and I used to go on them, I'll bet. If I close my eyes I can picture us both as we were, sitting on these wooden swing seats, competing to see which one of us could go higher. I used to let him win sometimes. The wooden part of the seats is all cracked and flaking off now, and those ropes that we used to hang on to for dear life are all frayed and worn, reminding me – as if I needed reminding – that everything changes; nothing stays the same. Even the garden equipment moves on and gets used up, it's not just people. Everything has its day. I know this; I've known it for such a very long time that I can't understand why it feels such a huge shock to find the bottom of the garden so ruined from when I last left it.

'Penny for your thoughts.'

I didn't hear his feet rustling on the grass, coming up behind me. 'Kieran's "gardening services" at your disposal, madam. Where would you like me to start?' He turns Bessie round so that I'm facing him and his lips close in on mine in a greeting that transports me back to last Saturday in an instant. And I reach out and pull him closer to me because I haven't got the time left to worry about whether doing that makes me seem too eager or not. I don't have any time. I only have now.

'Wow,' he says, when we pull apart at last. 'Looks like you missed me after all?'

'I missed you,' I agree. 'Never one single minute went by when I didn't think about you.' It's true. It didn't.

He's wearing a light blue T-shirt today. His jeans look different, too. They look new. He's shaved and his hair looks fresh and shining. He's made an effort. For me?

184

I can't believe it, but he's looking bashful, like it really matters to him that I think about him so much.

'I've been thinking about you too, Pixie.' He picks up my fingers and kisses them, one by one. Then he kisses the palm of my hand and as he does so he closes his eyes; that one gesture makes a shiver go through my whole body.

'Would you like me to push you on the swing?'

'I'd like that.' I'd *love* that actually. It'd make me feel more normal. I wonder if I could ask him to push Bessie right to the back of that blackberry bush so that I don't have to look at her any more, so I can pretend that I don't even need her. Would that make me sound just too weird?

When he picks me up he feels so strong, his arms rock solid beneath my body, and I feel him push Bessie away with his foot. Then he just stands there for a minute, holding me, and we both laugh. I don't know why we start laughing but it turns all the sickly butterflies in my stomach into a feeling of something else: pure happiness.

'Just keep holding me forever,' I say to him, and for some reason I don't even feel embarrassed when I say it or when he bends his head to mine so that our lips meet again.

It's like today I've left embarrassment behind. I've left all my awkwardness behind. I don't know where. I feel *powerful*. I feel as powerful as Kieran's strong arms underneath me, as if he could set me down right here on the grass and I'd be able to stand beside him all right, as if everything would be okay.

'Oh god,' he says, when he lowers me onto the swing at last, 'you do something to me, girl, you know that?' And I can't help seeing that there is pain in the depths of his eyes as well as joy. I don't want to see it but I can't help it, I do see it. Maybe he sees the same thing in my eyes, too?

'What do I do to you?' The old frayed rope swing feels rough against my fingers but I'm holding on to it tight. The wooden seat swings gently back and forth, taking me with it. Kieran's hand goes up to the back of his neck and he gives me that look again; half pure love and half pain.

'You make me feel that it's all *for* something, you know.'

'That would be true, Kieran, even if I weren't here. It will *still* be true, even when I'm not.'

'Don't talk about that,' he commands me. For a split second I see a trace of his grandfather in him, the steel will that is capable of seeing only what it wants to see. But it vanishes rapidly when his hand touches mine, pushing me gently backwards on the swing. 'Ever since . . . Mum and Dad died, I've really struggled to . . .' he swallows hard '. . . but I'm better now, so much better since I met you, my love.' Behind him a frilly-edged bunch of pink columbines sway, ladylike, in the breeze and I watch them, helplessly.

Don't talk about it, he said. I don't want to talk about it, either.

But won't it be worse if we *pretend*?

We can't make out that our relationship has got any future when we both know very clearly that it hasn't.

186

'Kieran, that thing you don't want to discuss, *I* want to talk about it.' I put my foot down and the swing comes to a bumpy halt, my knees bumping up against his legs as he stands right in front of me.

'Not today.' He's stroking my hair now, so lovingly that I could believe I really am the only girl in the world for him. That hurts so hard that it brings tears to my eyes and he leaves my hair to brush away the tears instead.

'Please,' he whispers, 'not today.'

'Oh Kieran, I have to. I have to talk to you today. What if . . . what if there is never any other day?'

'What do you mean?' God, he's not making this any easier for me, is he?

'I mean, I think I mean . . . I really don't feel that it's a good idea for you to fall in love with me. Not under the circumstances.' I say that, and all the while it's like I'm crushing my heart through a meat grinder. Of *course* I want him to fall in love with me. He knows it, too.

'Don't you think it's a little late for that, sweetheart?'

'Whatever,' I say desperately. 'You've got to understand . . . please, please, Kieran, try to understand. I'm here on borrowed time, aren't I? I can't . . . I can't be the anchor that you need. You and me . . . we're all wrong.'

'We're all *right*,' he corrects me. 'I love you, Shelley. You might not want me to, but I do.'

'You don't know that,' I spurn. 'What do you really know about me, after all? We've only ever met twice!'

'You know that isn't relevant. You know it. Not with us, it isn't. I can see it in your face.'

'Okay,' I have to concede. 'Well, even if we do love

each other, the reason I came here to speak to you today is because I wanted you to know . . . it's got to stop.'

'Liar.' His thumb brushes over my lips now, teasing me, making me want him again and he's confident of that, oh, he knows it.

'I'm not lying. It has got to stop. I love you too, Kieran. That's why I . . . can't see you any more.'

'Nonsense. That isn't how you really feel, Shelley. You're trembling, look at you. You're the one who called me up, remember? You initiated this – this physical part of our relationship.'

'I didn't realise that it would feel like this, though. I didn't know that *you* would feel so good.'

'You were hoping for something else?' He kisses my lips gently again and I know that if I don't stand firm now then I'm a goner.

'God, Kieran. Don't do this to me. We have to end it here. We have to, don't you see, before this goes any further? I can't become this important to you because . . . I'm not going to be around. It's simple, isn't it? What's so complicated about it?'

'Nothing is complicated. Don't let it be. Let's just enjoy what time we have left, that's all. It could be months. It could be years . . .'

'What if it isn't, though? What if it's . . . what if it's just till, say, next week?'

'What are you trying to say, Shelley? Is there something that you haven't told me?' He's cupping my face in his hands now, looking deeply into my eyes where he knows, even out here in Solly's 'darkest jungle', I have no place to hide.

'Nothing,' I lie, and I know that he sees my lie. I bite my lip.

'Don't keep secrets from me, Shelley, please, for the mother of God, don't do that to me now. What aren't you saying?'

'Nothing,' I croak. 'Just let me go, Kieran. If you love me, let me go. I don't want you to see me like Miriam was,' I add, as his eyes seem hooded now, darker than they were before. Part of him has drawn back from me, and I can't bear it. 'She died . . . in a really horrible way. I don't want you to see that happen to me. I can't let you see it. I've had enough already. I've shrunk up enough as it is. Call it vanity, if you like; call it pride. I don't know what it is. Just let me keep my last little bit of dignity.'

'Is that it?' He laughs in relief and the compassion that comes flooding back into his eyes makes me want to weep.

'I won't let you see me like that, Kieran.' I take his hands and push them firmly away from me. 'And . . . you need someone who's going to be there for you. You've been through enough already, losing your parents the way you did. I can't let you go through that again; I won't.'

'Don't you see, my foolish girl, that your selflessness only makes me love you all the more?' He sits himself down on the swing beside me and he's rocking the wooden seat to and fro, bumping against me teasingly, loving me even though I'm trying my hardest to reject him.

'I want you to put me back in Bessie so that I can tell my mother I want to go home.'

'No,' he says firmly, 'not until we've sorted this out properly. You're not going anywhere, my love.' He pulls my swing closer to his and I can see the movement of his muscles underneath his T-shirt as he leans forward to lift me up and deposit me, whether I will or no, onto his lap. I tried my best, but I have to surrender because I have no power to do anything else. He pulls me closer to him, his hungry lips about to close in on mine when I hear my mum calling.

'Shell-ey! Where are you? We have to go. Daniel's knee has opened up again and I'm going to have to take him down to casualty. Come *on*!' Her voice sounds strained and sad. Something of her heaviness filters through to the way I really feel inside and this intrusion of reality gives me the excuse I don't want, to do what I know I have to do.

'Sorry, Kieran,' I say to him lightly. 'Looks like you'll have to let your prisoner go for now.'

'Just for now,' he warns me, smiling.

I can't find any energy to smile back at him, and maybe he thinks it's because I'm worried about my brother but it isn't. It's because this is the last time I will ever see my beloved Kieran. Oh god. I will never see him again.

I'll email him and confirm it to him later. It's over.

22

Rachel

'It is *very* important that you make an appointment to see Doctor Lavelle, Mrs Wetherby. He's left a note on your daughter's file, asking that we get the two of you in together just as soon as possible.'

'But why? She's not due in yet.' I glance at the dates marked out on the kitchen calendar. Shelley was already seen earlier in the month. Nothing has changed, has it?

'Is something the matter?' I ask. 'We're due to go away soon.' I've only rung to ask for a decent supply of Shelley's tablets. Now I've got the practice manager on the phone and – for no reason she is prepared to give – it seems we are needed down there *desperately*.

'Can we see him today?' I glance at my watch: 10.15 a.m. It is Saturday so the surgery will close at midday. Sol is due here any minute – he is picking up Hattie – and then there are still Daniel's last-minute bits and pieces to be sorted out. He is due at the scout hut at 2 p.m., to pick up the coach that will take them the rest of the way.

Drat. What is up now? I can hear her shuffling away on her end of the phone, speaking to her colleagues. At last, slightly breathless.

'Doctor isn't available now till Monday I'm afraid, but if you don't mind a wait I can squeeze you in at the end of his session.'

'Not Monday,' I tell her. I've taken the call up to my bedroom to escape from the noise of the PlayStation downstairs. From my bedroom window I can see the whole of the sky has been whitewashed with an all-covering splodge of white-grey clouds. I fervently hope that things are looking better in the west. I want some sunshine. I *need* some sunshine. I want to push Shelley along the beachfront and feel the heat beating down on my shoulders. I want us to be able to sit on the sand and read our books and just bask . . .

'I can fit you in on Tuesday then, at five thirty.' The practice manager has taken on an arch tone. She is beginning to get the hint that I'm not as interested as she feels I should be. 'But there may be a wait,' she adds ominously.

'We're away all of next week,' I put in before she offers me Wednesday. 'If you could just tell me why she needs to be seen so urgently, I might be able to work around it.' There won't be any reason, I think. It will just be one of those things. Shelley had her routine tests done two weeks ago and nothing had shown up any problems. I lean out of the window to see, if I look far away enough, if I can find any patch of blue at all in among the dirty white palette of the sky.

'You're away?' She sucks in her teeth. 'Well, if you're sure you can't cancel the holiday, Mrs Wetherby.'

'Not at this late stage, I'm afraid.' Not after all the wheeling and dealing I've had to do to make this happen, I think. I might not get another chance. 'No. I'll just pick up the prescription I put in for earlier this week . . .'

'That's just it, Mrs Wetherby; Doctor's put a block on that for some reason. I think you really do need to come in and see him.'

'And I've just explained to you that we can't. In the meantime, are you suggesting that we stop the tablets altogether, seeing as she won't have enough to take away with her?' This isn't strictly true, of course, I do have some spare, enough to see us through the week, anyway. But I'm not going to let her know that.

The sky has gotten darker even as we are speaking. Daniel is going to be camping out tonight, I remember, in a field not ten miles from here. I hope it isn't going to bucket down on him. He's been *so* excited about going to the camp, but – just in the last twenty-four hours – I've detected a waning in his interest.

'I'm sorry. There's nothing I can do. You'll just have to make your way in as soon as you can. You missed the last appointment, didn't you?'

'We've been busy,' I tell the woman at the other end of the phone. There is a short silence.

'And you're busy next week?' she says at last.

'Yes, we are. And am I clear in thinking that the doctor's stopping all medication forthwith, without even seeing her first?'

'He *would* like to see her, Mrs Wetherby. Are you sure you can't delay the holiday by a few days?'

Why won't she just *tell* me what the reason is?

The door of my bedroom opens then.

'I can't find my sleeping bag.' Daniel's face is disconsolate. 'And it's going to be *cold*.' He rubs his arms with his hands and shivers, just to prove the point. We both look out of the window as, just on cue, there comes a sudden downpour of sleet. '*And* I'm going to get wet.'

I put my finger to my mouth for a moment.

'I think you really need to speak to Doctor,' the woman on the other end repeats.

I count to ten. I let out a breath.

'Okay,' I say, 'make us an appointment for when we get back, the week after next.'

'You'll have to ring us when you get back then,' she answers stiffly. The phone clicks at the other end. I look at Daniel.

'I am going to get wet,' he repeats. 'And I have no sleeping bag.'

'Of course you have a sleeping bag. I put it downstairs last night, along with the other bits for you.'

'I used it this morning!' His eyes light up all of a sudden, remembering. 'It's in the treehouse.' We both look out across the sopping wet garden as the sleety rain lashes the roof of his treehouse. I fervently hope that Sol's repairs to the leaky roof have been effective.

Whoops.

'Don't worry about getting wet.' I turn to look at my son. 'Everyone will get wet. You'll all have *fun*.' When he doesn't answer, I sit him on the little chair where I usually drape my clothes and take a long, hard look at my son. He has dark circles under his eyes that I don't recall being there before. Maybe I just haven't noticed? I *should* have noticed though. If it had been Shelley looking peaky I

194

definitely would have noticed and that's so unfair. *I never meant it to be like this, Daniel. This isn't how I would have planned for things to be, either.*

'You've been looking forward to this for such a long time,' I say gently. 'What's changed?' A little bit of rain wouldn't have put him off a week ago.

'Nothing.' Dan sticks his hands stubbornly in his pockets. He has that old familiar look on his face. He reminds me so much of *me*. 'I've just changed my mind.'

'You can't,' I tell him softly, even though my heart is saying different. 'I've paid all that money now and it was booked up weeks ago.'

Daniel looks at his hands.

'What about Josh?' I cajole. 'He's expecting you. You're both sharing a tent, aren't you? You can't let him down like that. It isn't done.'

'Isn't it done?' He looks at me sideways.

'What do you mean?' I turn to a pile of unfolded clothes that I've brought up to pack for his sister and myself, later. Kneeling by the pile I suddenly get this huge, overwhelming feeling. I still have all our things to pack. But I can't do it in front of Danny because I haven't told Danny where we are going. I've just said we are visiting my sister's for a couple of days – something he won't feel he is missing out on. I wish now that I'd told him the truth.

'Josh said he isn't sharing with me any more. He's switched to be with that new boy. I'm going to be on my own now.'

'No you are not!' I flare at him. What the heck was Arkaela thinking of? 'Look, I'll speak to Arkaela. I'm sure she won't let Josh do that, it wouldn't be fair on you.'

195

'Will you?' He looks at me dubiously. 'I still haven't got a dry sleeping bag, have I? And who's looking after Hattie while you and Shell go to Aunt Lily's?'

'Hattie will be fine.' I shake out some towels, folding out the creases neatly.

'Look, I'll speak to Arkaela about the tents. Sol's looking after Hattie, I already told you.'

'You said he would be here first thing, though. Why hasn't he come?'

'Just been a bit delayed, that's all. You know Sol. It'll all be fine. You mustn't get cold feet now.'

I push our swimming costumes under the duvet where Danny won't see them and start asking questions.

'I suppose so.' He sighs heavily, which isn't like him. 'Something just doesn't feel right, though,' he asserts. 'I'll go, but only if Sol comes for Hattie. I'm not having Mrs Simmonds take her. She won't look after her properly.'

Mrs Simmonds is the old dear who moved in after Sol sold up four years back. She is very kind and obliging, but absent-minded with it. I can see why Daniel doesn't trust her with his precious Hattie.

'I'll ring Sol now,' I offer. It is gone eleven already and the day is hastening on without me seeming to get much done.

Sol isn't in when I call and I tell Daniel another lie. Sol is coming over later, I say; he promised that he would. Well, there is no point in Daniel going off fretting about the beast, is there? He has enough worrying him as it is. I'm not happy about it. This lying business is becoming something of a habit with me. All for the greater good,

196

I tell myself. I want to give Shelley the birthday she dreams of. But I still don't like telling fibs.

Half an hour later I've retrieved the sleeping bag from the treehouse, soaked through and smelling of mildew. I figure I've just got time to put it through the wash and the tumble-drier before we leave. Then we go through Danny's list, ticking off the things that he is down to bring, like instant mashed potatoes and 'a powerful torch-light' for the woodland walk and lots of warm spare socks. It is 1.30 p.m. and I've just got Dan in the car (where Shelley is sending him off with dire warnings about camping trips in the rain), when Sol rings at last, answering the three messages I'd left earlier.

'Justin's left me.' His voice is shell-shocked, barely audible down the phone line.

'I have to go to Paris.'

'Look, wait. Stop. Don't . . . don't do this, Solly. Don't run after him.'

'Why?' he sobs. 'Whatever do you mean? I've got to try. Justin is the love of my life.'

Justin is a spoiled, poncey, stuck-up brat who's only using you because your face fits and you can open doors for him. Adam's the only boyfriend you've had who truly loved you. I swallow that thought.

'Justin is little more than a . . . a lad.' I don't want to say 'boy' because it emphasises the age gap and Solly doesn't like to be reminded.

'He makes me feel like a lad, though,' Solly confesses. 'I was so stuck in a rut. I was feeling so stale. Everyone says how much more energised I am nowadays . . .'

'He runs you ragged,' I point out. 'Look how he's let

197

you down over that brochure. Did you get Adam to sort it out in the end?'

'I'm not on the best of terms with Adam, as you know.'

'Oh Solly! For heaven's sake, sort it out.' I haven't got time for this now, I realise. I haven't got time for this silly histrionic nonsense. I've got too much of my own life digging uncomfortably into my ribs at the moment.

'He's gone to Paris for the weekend with Darryl.' Sol hasn't heard a word I've just said to him. 'They *say* it's business, but we all know what that means.' The misery in his voice is palpable. 'I've got to go after them. I can't just leave things like this.'

'You can't go to Paris. You promised you'd look after Hattie for Daniel.'

'Who?' Sol hasn't a clue what I'm on about, clearly. I might be talking about a broken fingernail while he is suffering from a bereavement.

'Daniel's tortoise. You promised to look after her while we were away, remember?'

'Hattie, of course. But Justin has left me,' he sobs. 'I'll come and get the beast after the weekend. Tell Dan I'm sorry.'

'Sure.' I can feel my spirits dropping lower with every passing minute. I have no intention of telling Dan anything whatsoever. Not at this late stage. He is already wobbling enough about going away himself as it is.

'Shall I tell Mrs Simmonds you'll pick it up from her on Monday?' Daisy Simmonds will do it, I know, not least because it will give her the chance of spending some time with Sol again. She never stops talking about him.

198

Apparently he reminds her of a beau she had once had, before the war.

'Fine. Monday. Oh, and Rachel?'

'Yes?'

'I've decided, seeing that Darryl won't be doing that graphics job for the brochure for me, I want you to do it instead.'

'The shop brochure?' Suddenly, my spirits lift immeasurably. I've been wanting a break like this to happen to me for ages. This will not only be good money – at least three days' work – it will be a lead in to other work. I've been pestering Sol to give me a break for ages, except Justin knows so many people in the same business that I've never before got a look in.

'That's right. He's left it behind, half undone, and I'm all in a flap. I'll bring you the specs around later. I'll need everything by next Wednesday, though, that's the only catch.'

The solitary ray of sunshine, which has momentarily injected itself into my day, vanishes as soon as it has come.

'I'm away this week, Sol. Cornwall, remember? That's why you were having Hattie for us.' Sometimes I wonder if Sol ever listens to a single word I say to him.

'Oh hell!' The penny drops. 'Shelley's birthday trip, of course! How could I be so insensitive? And it's such a shame about the work – it could have opened some doors for you . . .'

I'm only too well aware.

'Can't you take it with you?' he pleads.

I actually consider his proposal for a second. Then I remember that Annie-Jo is sending her calligraphy work through to Shelley on her laptop and I've promised to do that while I'm away, too!

Why does everything always have to happen at once?

If only we didn't have to be away this week. I could take Shelley to the doctor and find out what it is he so urgently wants. I could take on these two bits of coveted work – work I would so much more enjoy doing than those endless bits of typing for Sol. And I could look after Hattie. Cornwall is going to be a wash-out anyway. It is going to be grey and cold and we are going to freeze on the beachfront. We'll probably spend most of it hiring out DVDs and watching them in Maggie's B and B. Why am I putting myself through this?

I say goodbye to Sol and pick up my house keys. At the door I stand watching Shelley give her brother the biggest hug I have seen her give him for a very long time. You would think she's never expecting to see him again. When she thinks he isn't looking, I even see her wipe a tear away from her eye. She is going to miss him. Has she changed her mind, and now she wishes he was coming with us after all?

But it's too late for changing things now. We are all set on our courses. Too many things have been organised. Danny is expected elsewhere. And he needs to go on this trip with his mates. It will be good for his independence.

And Shelley has begged to have this time alone with me. I have bent over backwards trying to organise this for her, and I have been so looking forward to it, too.

So if I am doing the right thing, I wonder, as I walk towards the car at last, my keys jangling from my finger-tips, why is it that everything still feels so *wrong*?

23

Rachel

By eight o'clock the light is waning and, along with it, my energy. I've already set the alarm for 5 a.m. – I figure if Shelley and I can put in an early start we'll hit clear roads most of the way down. There are only the two suitcases to load into the trunk of the car and then I've promised myself an hour's feet up with a glass of wine before an early bedtime.

I'm just turning the car round so the boot will face the house when Shelley notices the problem with the nearside brake light. I feel my heart sinking. The nearest garage is closed, I know, and I haven't the energy left to embark on a ten-mile trip to Green's, which is the next one. Sol could fix it – except that he'll have gone to Paris by now. I'm in the middle of debating who on earth I can call to sort this out for me, when I make out Shelley calling excitedly to me from the window. She's waving the telephone.

What *now*? Not some problem with Danny at scout camp, for heaven's sake! Please don't let it be that. Already I feel I've barely the energy left to crawl up to bed, let alone deal with any more crises. It's at this kind of juncture that I wish – I really wish – Bill would step in a bit more often and help out with his kids. Oh he does the 'every other weekend' thing, but – bottom line is – if there's ever anything out of the ordinary to deal with, Mum's the one responsible. One of these days I think I'm going to run away, I do.

'Who is it?' I hiss at her, covering the mouthpiece as she meets me in the hallway. I don't want to talk to anyone. I really don't.

'It's Dad.'

My eyes roll up to the ceiling. I just wished for him to be available, didn't I?

'Why?'

'He says he's on his way over. He'll be here in about fifteen or so minutes.'

'He'll what? Whatever *for*?' I look at her in horror. Bill and I don't do that 'just dropping round' thing with each other. Our meeting times are always carefully planned well in advance, to avoid awkwardness. What on earth can be up?

'Hello Bill?'

'Rachel. We're about twelve minutes away now. Just to let you know. I never realised you and Stella's brother lived so near to each other.'

'Okay,' I say cautiously. Is that it? He's suddenly realised how near we live to his brother-in-law? He sounds very cool and collected, not as if there is any kind of emergency going on. The fact that he's just been over to his new brother-in-law also rules out my first crazy thought, which was that he's had some sort of upset with Stella and he needs someone he can go over things with. I wouldn't have been that person on any day of the week, but especially not today.

'Is there . . . any particular reason *why*?' I might be frowning into the phone but I keep my voice level. I shoot a glance at Shelley, her face half-hidden in the dim light of the hallway. She has gone very quiet.

'Shelley rang me on my mobile. Well, she rang Stella actually, mine was switched off. We'd just left Stella's brother and as that wasn't more than half an hour away from you, Shelley suggested we come over for a quick catch-up. Nikolai's been asleep the whole afternoon and he won't crash till midnight now so we thought – what the heck!'

I clear my throat. I've had one hell of a day. I am exhausted, and I am going to have to get up at the crack of dawn tomorrow, none of which I can explain to Bill.

'Shelley didn't actually mention any of this to me, Bill.' I look daggers at her. Why has she done it? By the sounds of it, she's only just contacted them too, so she already knows what kind of state I am in.

'Uh?' I can hear the satellite navigation system in his car, directing him.

'I'm . . . I'm pretty pooped tonight, Bill. Can we do this another time, maybe?'

'I've already taken the motorway turn-off, Rachel. Nikolai wants to use the bathroom. And *Shelley* sounded pretty keen to see us. Look,' his tone lowers, conciliatory, 'I'm feeling pretty guilty about not getting back to you sooner after I promised I would. About next week, Shelley's birthday. We were going to discuss things and I never phoned, did I?'

No. you bloody well didn't, I remember now. But you gave me a hell of a lot of crap over that BMW you'd just pranged and were trying to get away from. I haven't forgotten that, either. I wait, silently, for him to continue.

'I thought this might be the perfect opportunity to sort it out,' he continues sheepishly.

'So – you're coming here now?'

'Uh-huh. According to this route finder we'll be with you in just a few minutes.' He sounds triumphant, delighted that his technological gadgetry has allowed him to cut his ETA so drastically. My eyes suddenly alight on the two suitcases in the hallway, still waiting at the bottom of the stairs.

'Okay. See you then.' I crash the phone back in its cradle. 'Why the *hell* did you call them, Shelley? I'm pooped. We're away at the crack of dawn. Frankly, they are the LAST people I want to see right now. I really wish you had cleared this with me first.'

'I'm sorry, Mum.' Shelley is unaccustomedly quiet. I could swear there are tears in her voice. Am I being over-harsh?

'I just . . . I just really, *really* wanted to see Dad.'

'You'll be seeing him sometime after we get back, won't you?'

We haven't sorted out exactly when. Maybe this is what Bill's coming over to firm up? I have the suitcases by their handles, pulling them as fast as I can into the space in the cupboard under the stairs. The Hoover is taking up all the space in there so I take it out.

'What are you doing, Mum?' Shelley frowns at me, puzzled. 'Aren't those suitcases supposed to go in the car?'

'Haven't time,' I tell her. 'I have to get them out of sight before they arrive. And . . .' I suddenly remember, 'you can't say anything. About Cornwall, I mean. You mustn't.'

'Why ever not? They already *know*, don't they?' My daughter looks at me as if I've gone mad.

'You haven't said anything, have you?' I turn my head to stare at her, horrified at the thought. 'Just now, when you spoke to Stella, you didn't mention it?'

'No.' Shelley rubs her arms uncomfortably. I can't swear she is telling me the truth at this moment. She looks pale, sallow somehow. Maybe it is just the hall light?

'I didn't have time to talk about that,' she's telling me now. 'I just said – as they were so near – why didn't they pop over? As Nikolai is still so bouncy, they seemed quite keen.'

I close my eyes for a moment. The thought of a bouncy Nikolai popping over for a social visit when I am this frazzled doesn't bear thinking about. I am just going to have to get rid of them as quickly as I can.

'Look,' I pull the Hoover over to stand in front of the under-stairs cupboard door – the door has an unfortunate way of leaning open that might just give things away. 'Just don't say anything about us leaving tomorrow. Not a word, do you understand?'

'Okay, if you say so.' She gives me a worried look.

'It's just that . . . Stella doesn't know anything. Well, not yet.' I think quickly. 'Your dad wanted the trip down there next week to be . . . a surprise. For their anniversary, seeing as the date is so close to your birthday. A sort of joint celebration.'

'Oh! Dad's going to come down too?' If Shelley isn't too thrilled at the thought of her birthday being hijacked, she doesn't say. 'I thought you were going to tell me Dad doesn't know either! I'm such a fool.' She smiles at me slowly now. 'He *does* know, doesn't he, Mum? He's okay with it?'

'Of course,' I mutter through gritted teeth, 'but please don't bring it up with Dad either. You know how sound travels in this house. It would ruin things for him if she were to somehow find out ahead of time.'

'Of course I won't ruin his surprise. When is he planning for them to join us?' Her voice sounds strangled, caught up in her throat somehow. I wonder why.

'I'm not sure. And in fact, it may not even materialise yet. It depends on if he can get it organised. Just keep schtum for me, all right? I wasn't supposed to tell you either,' I add for good measure. 'So Dad doesn't know that you know.'

That last one is a master-stroke, I think.

Shelley nods conspiratorially.

'I get it. We'll mention nothing about Cornwall at all.'

My heart is thumping in my chest. I *hate* lying to her, but what else is there for me to do? And Bill, he'd sounded cool enough over the phone, but what if he had somehow found out about our plans? He *never* comes over like this, on such a whim. If he is coming here to confront me I am going to look like a damn fool in front of our daughter. I'm not used to lying to people, that is the problem. I never wanted to go behind his back. Not that he worried about doing that to me. If he hadn't been so unreasonable about everything in the first place . . .

'They're here.'

The peace in the hallway is shattered by Nikolai's almighty shriek on the doorstep; Shelley is merely stating the obvious. This is accompanied a few minutes later by the thundering of tiny fists on the door. Where are his parents? Okay, Stella will be struggling, pale-faced, out of the car right now. I can imagine it. She will have opened the door at the child's insistence and he will have run out ahead of her. But what about Bill? Can he really be the same father who had tolerated absolutely *nothing* from his first two children? The thought riles me. Not just Nikolai's behaviour – that is only what his parents allow him to get away with – but the fact that Bill seems so wilfully blind to all of it.

Shelley giggles. For a few moments her face lights up, and I remember what it is I am putting myself through all this for in the first place: it is all for her. If having them around right now makes her happy then I'll put up with that too. I paste on a smile and let them in.

'Hi all.' Bill gives me a brief hug and kisses the air on one side of me. Stella follows him nervously through the door while Nikolai jumps onto the top of Shelley's wheelchair. Shelley laughs at his antics. For some unknown reason she is very fond of little Nikolai.

'What, no Danny-boy?' Bill's voice booms.

'Danny-boy's at scout camp,' I remind him sharply. Then I bite my tongue. This isn't going to do.

'Of course!' Bill hits his head with his hand. 'Of course he is.' He sounds remarkably jovial. I can't help wondering if he's downed a few beers at the brother-in-law's before setting out tonight.

'What's your car doing backed up on the drive like that, Rachel? Not having car trouble, are you?'

'Nope,' I say.

'One of Mum's brake lights has gone,' Shelley tells him as he bends to hug her tight. 'She's going to need that tomorrow. Could you put a new one in for her, Dad?'

'No problem.' He turns to me stiffly. 'Do you keep any spare bulbs in the shed?'

'In the blue box as you go in,' I tell him. The blue box that used to belong to him, when he was in charge of such things. 'Thanks.' At least that is one of my problems solved.

'Hi.' Stella smiles shyly at me once he's gone back out again and I realise that we haven't even greeted each other yet.

'Can I get you some tea?'

'Yes please.' Stella gives me a little smile as we troop through to the kitchen. We can hear Shelley taking Nikolai to the toilet in the hallway, saying, 'No, Nikolai, leave the Hoover alone. It isn't for you to play with.'

'He likes to help around the house,' Stella smiles vaguely. 'It might be easier just to let him play with it for a bit.'

'No, he can't,' I say. I remember the Hoover is propping the door closed and the suitcases are in the cupboard. 'I can't afford to have it break. Besides, I've got a bit of a splitting headache this evening. I was just going to get myself an aspirin.'

'Could I have one too?' she begs.

'Of course.'

'He's a bit of a handful, at times,' she confesses. 'I'm told it's because he's so *bright*. I really don't know how people ever manage to have more than one. I admire you, Rachel.' She looks at me candidly as I hand her the tablets. 'You are such a . . . a *coper*.' She swallows the aspirins without water as if with habitual ease. 'You always appear so unruffled. No matter what. And you have such tremendous odds to cope with all the time. I don't know how you do it.'

'Well, thanks.' I'm not sure how to hide my surprise at her praise. 'I have to get on with it, I guess.'

'If I had a sick child to cope with all the time, like you do . . .' She shakes her head wonderingly, at a loss to continue. 'And the thought that she is *dying*,' she says at last. 'Well, that would just about finish me off.'

Okay, you could have left that bit out, I think. I bite my lip. Outside all has gone quiet in the hallway. Shelley must have taken Nikolai to her room because we are alone.

'Look,' Stella leans forward suddenly, her voice low. 'While Bill's out at the car, Rachel, I just wanted to tell you that . . . I think it's great, what you're doing.'

'Yes?' I turn my back to her, pulling out some mugs from the cupboard, filling up the kettle from the tap. What does she mean, *while Bill's out at the car*?

'What you and Shelley have got planned,' she continues, 'I know all about it. I know what's happening. I think it's really . . .' She smiles coyly here. 'I think it's *great*. And don't worry,' she puts a conspiratorial finger to her lips as the front door closes and Bill lets himself back into the house again, 'I shan't breathe a single word about it to Bill.'

24

Rachel

By 6 a.m. on Monday morning I've finally managed to get us both in the car, even though I had meant us to leave by five. There was a delay when Mrs Simmonds had come over as soon as our lights went on at 4.30 a.m., fussing over what it was we required her to do with Hattie.

'I haven't been able to sleep a wink,' she told me, 'with thinking about the tortoise. It's such a responsibility for me, really.' I'd given her the number of where we were going to be in Trefolgew, and a cup of tea, *and* a listening ear for half an hour, even though it was practically the middle of the night.

Shelley had been sulky, diffident. She didn't get up straight away when I asked her to, and took up far too much time afterwards in the bathroom. I kept wondering: why am I doing this? It all seems too difficult. It all just seems *wrong*.

By the time we leave it is raining, gently but steadily. I keep my windscreen wipers on half-mode. The morning is grey. For some reason I can't stop thinking about my Danny in his tent. I wonder if it has leaked and he has woken up wet; I wonder if he has had to spend the night by himself, after all.

I keep thinking, the farther west we go, the more out into the open countryside and away from the familiar sights and sounds of our locality, the better things will look. Shelley will perk up. This is *her* treat, after all. The sun will come out. Think positive: I won't have to clean the house for a week. I won't cook. I won't have to run any errands or do any typing for Sol or drop Danny off anywhere. I won't have a phone to answer and I can wake up whatever time of day I want to.

We stop for coffee at Salisbury, and again on the motorway stop near Tiverton, more for me than for her, because my head is full of clouds. I keep trying to forget Bill's face last night when I'd told him, in no uncertain terms, that I wouldn't be having Nikolai for them next weekend. He'd got it all planned out, he told me, the quiet romantic weekend just for him and Stella in Paris. He'd *booked* everything already. He thought (somehow) that we'd already agreed to this. Didn't I realise just how much he was counting on me to help him out here? He wouldn't have asked, of course, if Stella's mother hadn't been going through a difficult patch of her own right now. So much for Bill feeling guilty about not being around for Shelley's birthday. *That* had been relegated to 'popping round for a couple of hours after we get back on Sunday evening'. He'd cornered me alone in the kitchen after he'd come in from sorting out my car-light and it had occurred to me then; this was Bill's *real* reason for coming round to see us Sunday night. Not because Nikolai needed the toilet, and not because he wanted to discuss Shelley's birthday, but because his mother-in-law wasn't going to be able to take over so he and Stella could get away for the planned weekend to Paris.

And I remember now what a bully Bill used to be when he didn't get his way over the slightest thing; what a spoiled bully of a golden boy he was and how much better off I was without him. I flick the radio from station to station, trying to find some music instead of the inevitable chat. I have to laugh. First of all, there's a woman singing 'I'll survive, I will survive . . .' (which of course I have) and then there's a song about 'sisters doing it for themselves' – hell, it all makes sense to me now. The only thing I don't know is why it's taken me so long.

Shelley remains sulky and quiet. She mutters something about not being able to get hold of a friend of hers last night, someone she'd been hoping to talk to over the Internet. It seems to have upset her. It's really ruined her mood. When I look in the rear-view mirror one time I catch her silently crying, surreptitiously wiping great tears away with her hand.

I want to ask her why, but I can't. I fear she will snap my head off like she always does if I try to get too close, if I start 'prying', as she puts it. It was probably about the friend, though; the one she hasn't been able to contact. No doubt she will 'speak' to him or her later and then all will be smiles again.

By the time we get to Somerset, passing Stonehenge, a beautiful late morning is opening up, bright shafts of sunlight piercing through the remaining clouds. I watch Stonehenge from the motorway for far longer than I should. Those ancient monuments have always been, for me, a landmark marking all places out to the 'west'. By the time I get past that I am 'somewhere else'; I am in a magical country far away from home.

But it is 3 p.m. before we roll into the courtyard at Crouch's End, Maggie's crumbling Queen Anne house set at the end of a winding Cornish lane amid a valley of alder and hawthorn trees. Nothing much has changed. The two fluted columns on either side of the entrance door still take my breath away. The gravelled pathways down the middle and to either side of the house are still flanked by huge flowering beds, currently sporting the first swathes of the season's dahlias. The scents of the earth and the glistening leaves betray the fact that here, too, it has been raining earlier on.

I open the car door and welcome the air in, refreshing my muzzy head. My legs feel wobbly. But I am so glad to be here. After the long drive, the familiar and beautiful old place welcomes me like a second home.

We are still sitting in the car, on the drive, when Maggie hears us and comes out from round the back, an armful of cuttings on one side and her basset hound Bally on the other. She waves cheerily as soon as she sees us, and I recall that particular non-obtrusive brand of friendliness that she has, which never borders on the familiar. She will welcome us graciously as her house guests for the week but I know I will never be subjected to a barrage of questions about where Bill is – she won't be aware yet that we are separated – or even why Danny isn't with us this time. She won't ask me about anything at all, in fact, that I don't bring up first myself.

'Hello, my dears.' Maggie gives me a warm embrace, and I see her gaze wander to the back of the car where Shelley is still waiting to be helped out. Her eyes soften then, and she gives her a little wave. I wonder if she remembers my daughter as the bright bouncy tearaway that she had once been. 'No better, I see?' She nods quietly at me. I shake my head.

'Reg will take your bags down for you.' She beckons her ancient gardener who's been hovering with a pair of secateurs over a nearby juniper bush. 'And you can help Shelley out. My, how you have grown,' she exclaims softly as I open the back door. Maggie stands to one side then as Bally scrabbles up onto the back seat of the car in excitement, making Shelley laugh. It is the first time I've heard her laugh all day and my spirits rise a little.

'They're staying in the main house, Reg.' Maggie frowns as Reg stands there, unmoving. He's got the boot of the car up, but he isn't doing anything.

'Well, the ladies may be staying in the main house, Mrs H, but their bags ain't in here, that's for sure. Unless they're in this old cardboard box?'

No, they aren't. That's just Pandora's box, brought down to give to Lily.

Oh god, no, I know where our bags are. I can feel the blood draining from my face as I look at Shelley.

'They're still in the cupboard under the stairs, aren't they, Mum? The only thing we've actually *brought* with us is my laptop, which I was carrying with me!'

I bite my lip, unfolding her wheelchair. I can't believe it. How the hell have I done that? How? If only Bill hadn't

214

turned up with his crew just at the wrong moment last night I wouldn't have had to hide our bags. Or maybe if Sol had taken Hattie yesterday then Mrs Simmonds wouldn't have had an excuse to come over and drink tea at 5 a.m. when I should have been doing my last-minute things.

'Oh, hell! All our clothes are in there. Everything. We've only got the clothes on our backs.' And I don't have the money to buy any more. I really don't.

'We only need a couple of T-shirts each, Mum. And maybe some shorts. We can go and look in a charity shop.'

No, we can't, I think. I'm due to meet up with Lily on Monday afternoon and there is no way I am walking into the lounge of the Royal Star Hotel looking like a bag lady. How on earth is it I managed to bring with me the only thing I really didn't want – Pandora's box?

'Sounds as if you two could use a decent cup of tea and a slice of homemade cake,' Maggie observes. 'Just put the box in the blue room for them, Reg. That'll do.'

Maggie makes it sound as if it isn't a problem at all. No clothes, for a whole week! She probably doesn't realise that I can't afford to buy any more.

'What size are you?' Maggie glances at me briefly. 'Twelve, fourteen?'

'Fourteen mostly.' And sometimes more than that. Is Maggie going to offer me something of hers?

'I sell a lot of Indian prints and cotton tops down here in the summer. I've got a bargain rail due to go up next week, mostly with other stuff, more classic. It's vintage – second-hand, and some of it lovely stuff, but the person it belonged to has no need of it any more. I think you could find one or two things you'd like in there. Everything's still at the house so we'll go through it after tea.'

'What about me?' Shelley puts in.

'My granddaughter Ellen is about your size. She's very trendy, forever buying clothes – I'm sure she'd be prepared to loan you some for a few days.'

'It looks like we're sorted then.' I smile a bright smile that I really don't feel and suddenly feel a tidal wave of tiredness hit me. 'Thank you so much for your kindness, Maggie,' I remember to say. She's just averted a major disaster for me. Shelley is trying to be upbeat and positive; the weather forecast for tomorrow is plenty of heat so it all looks rosy, but I *still* can't shake off this bad feeling that something terrible is waiting to happen. Just around the corner.

25

Rachel

'*Cool*,' Shelley is looking around in pleasure, 'this place is *way* cool . . .'

We're upstairs in a dusty stockroom-cum-storeroom where Maggie has told us we'll find her 'bargain rail'. I was expecting the fusty smell of a charity shop; a stark room lined with cardboard boxes, maybe, filled with miscellaneous odds and ends. What we've found instead is more akin to Aladdin's cave: wooden crates, packed with crystals and semi-precious gems, take up most of the floor space. Against the wall I can see shelves stacked with scented candles, wind-chimes, Native American goods, necklaces of coloured beads, esoteric books. Right at the back, near the window, I espy a rail full of what must be Maggie's vintage clothes selection.

'I want to come right in. I want to *see*,' Shelley is protesting. I've left her sitting on a wooden crate by the door as I thread my way across the floor. The wheelchair is downstairs in the hallway so until I help her she is basically stranded.

'Just a second . . .' I look around for a spot where I can sit her, taking in the room as I do so. I love the way

Maggie has painted the walls a delicate duck-egg blue. The windows are curtainless, facing out towards the back so not overlooked but letting in the maximum amount of light. When I glance out of them, the garden beyond is a wilderness of deeply-hued peonies and roses and rustic benches hidden away inside little arbours. Everything outside is wet but gleaming in the sunshine. Motes of dust float on a beam of light that shines through onto the storeroom floor, lighting it magically. 'Come and sit over here,' I tell her gently, and together we get her in and seated on a cardboard box where she follows my lead and peers out of the window.

'*So* cool,' she repeats.

'My artist's eye says this would make the perfect painting room. What do you think?' For a moment I feel a deep stirring, a long-forgotten yearning in my heart, that I might one day have a place like this for my own use. I *want* it. I want this room and everything in it. I want Maggie's whole house, in fact.

'I think you're right,' Shelley grins at me, her eyes bright and interested for once. I get the feeling she knows exactly what's running through my head. 'Do you think we could persuade some rich sugar-daddy to buy it for you?'

I snort in response.

'Maybe I'll buy it myself, thank you very much,' I tell her shortly, 'one of these days.'

'You know, most of these look new, Mum.' Shelley changes the subject, running her hand along the clothes on the rail. 'Wow, Stella McCartney, Chloé . . . Mum, these things are quality.'

'This can't be the bargain rail then.' I scan the room for something else – maybe the clothes I am looking for will be in a crumpled heap at the bottom of the clothes rail? 'There is no way these clothes have ever been worn by anyone else.'

'They were, though. Some of them have got name-labels in, Mum, like the ones you've just sewn in for Danny.' Shelley points out the waistband of a deep lilac skirt. It says, simply, 'Esme'. I pick the skirt off the rail. It is my size. It is *my* colour. I feel the sudden deep yearning to have it that I'd experienced a moment before, seeing the colours of the room. I love the way it swirls out gently at the bottom; I love the pretty green and purple flowers that have been sewn laboriously onto the panels. It screams quality. I *want* it.

'And this is Esme's blouse, look. And her green Chloé jacket.' Shelley looks at me in wonder. 'These things are great, Mum. She can't be that old, whoever she is. I wonder if she's dead?' Her eyes widen melodramatically.

'Or just moved on to next season's fashions, or having a baby?' I suggest. 'You're right, though, they are so beautiful – oh, Shelley, I just wish they'd been in your size instead of mine . . .'

'I won't need them.' Shelley shakes her head decisively. 'And I'm glad you're going to look great for Aunt Lily tomorrow. I just wish I could see her face when you turn up in all your finery.'

'Won't you be coming?' I'm lost in a rail full of white silk blouses and satin slips and dark velvet jackets. They are all in my colours too! I want to own the lot. 'How much will Maggie want for these do you think?' I want

219

to throw caution to the wind but I know that I cannot. I will pick out an outfit to wear for meeting Lily, just one outfit. I can't go back to the days when I dressed for the sheer pleasure of it, and to hell with practicalities. But, just for one day, for tomorrow, I will.

'She said fifty pence an item, didn't she?'

I laugh. 'She must have been joking. Seriously.'

'I don't think she was.'

Hmm. I might be tempted to take a couple more items, then.

'Don't you want to come, tomorrow?' I put down the dark red dress with the cross-over panel that I'd been admiring. 'I'm sure Aunt Lily wants to see you too . . .'

'Well, she will see me, of course,' Shelley shoots me a loaded glance. 'It's just that you'll probably do better meeting her alone. *Without* me being there.' She takes the red dress from me and starts to deliberately undo the buttons. 'You should try this one on.'

'I will. Later. What do you mean I'd do better to meet with her alone?' I drape a turquoise Hermès scarf around my neck, enjoying the feel of the silk. Perhaps there is a mirror in here somewhere?

'You should,' my daughter tells me seriously. 'You two need to talk. You need to connect. You said you were close, once.'

'Well, we were. People drift apart, though. It happens.'

'Why does it happen?'

'Because everyone changes. *I* changed. I guess . . . I guess I just got fed up of feeling so responsible for her all the time. Lily is just so *fragile*. She's always been so delicate.' I pull the scarf off sharply. I don't know where

I'm going with this conversation, really. What am I bringing all this up for?

'You, responsible for Lily?' Shelley laughs but her eyes regard me curiously. 'She's done all right for herself, though, hasn't she? She's a darn sight better off than you are, that's for sure. Maybe she's the one who should be feeling a little responsibility towards you. After all, in your situation you need all the help you can get.'

'Well, *thanks*!' I frown at my reflection in the mirror. I need all the help I can get, do I? Is that how Shelley sees me? Is that how Maggie sees me? I place the beautiful scarf carefully on the rail. Maybe they're right, though. I *do* need all the help I can get. Why does it rankle so much to have to admit to that, though?

'Do you think I'm looking old, Shell?'

My daughter pulls a face at me. She's too tactful to tell me the truth. 'You've got Granny Panny's genes, haven't you? You're always going to look gorgeous, no matter how old you get.' She grins wickedly. 'You're worried that you're going to look like an ugly duckling tomorrow, next to your glamorous older sister, aren't you?'

'No, I'm . . .'

'So, why *is* she coming down to see us tomorrow?' Shelley cuts right through my thoughts. 'It's not as if she lives nearby.' She gets to the last button of the dress and hands it back to me. 'It's got to be . . . what . . . three years since we last saw her?' Shelley looks at me curiously.

'There is a matter that we need to settle up between us,' I concede at last. 'It isn't purely a social visit, you're right.'

'A *personal* matter?' Another time I might have told my teenage daughter to get off my back, but this time I don't. Looking at her sitting opposite me, shrewd eyes narrowed, she could be a colleague or a friend, a person I could confide in. She must have metamorphosed into such a person when I wasn't looking. Maybe that's what all those days and nights hunched over her computer in her darkened room have been about?

'Yes and no,' I tell her reluctantly. 'It's just some matter that's come about as a result of your granny leaving.'

'Something that's come out of Pandora's box?' My daughter leans forward intently. 'That box of stuff she sent you, that you've brought down here to give to Aunt Lily?'

'Heavens, no!' I laugh. 'There's nothing in there that's really of any interest to anyone at all now; just some old photos and a few championship rosettes. Lily might want those.'

'Well, *I* found a couple of nice pictures in there. I took them out, just so you know. I don't see why she should get the whole lot. You should keep some for yourself too.'

I hang the dress back on the rail reluctantly. Even looking at these things is silly. These can't be the items that Maggie had meant. There is no point even taking anything to try on.

'Maybe I don't want to remember that particular chapter of my past,' I offer. 'All that dancing malarkey, it meant so much more to Lily than it did to me. No, we aren't meeting up to talk about that. There's an old ramshackle property – little more than a tumbledown shed really – that belonged to my granddad's side of the

222

family. When he died it went to my mum, but the deal was that if she ever left the country it would go to Lily and me.' I've just made that bit up. I mean, it's true, but it isn't the real reason that Lily wants to see me.

Unless – now I think about it – maybe it is? Hey – maybe I've been panicking like mad for nothing and all Lily wants to settle is what we do with the old shack?

'You mean we own some *property* in Cornwall?' Shelley's eyes light up.

'I just described it as a tumbledown shed, didn't I? And that was back in the days when somebody actually lived in it. Lily said something about selling it to the guy next door so he could extend his garage or something. She's going to deal with it. I've got more than enough on my plate.'

'Well, it's a pity it takes something like that coming up before she'll agree to meet up with you.' Shelley flicks back her hair. . 'She could come down to see us anytime. I mean, what does she *do*?'

'It can be hard work being a lady of leisure.' I lean over and ruffle her hair and for once she doesn't shrug me off.

'Well, I think people should make *time* for each other.' Shelley turns to look out of the window and as the afternoon light shines on her face I marvel at how someone can look so old and so young both at the same time. 'I mean, time to talk. To say the things that they need to say, before it's too late.'

'Is there . . . is there something that you want to talk to me about, Shelley?'

'Yeah.' Her voice is a mere breath, almost lost in the

burst of birdsong that streams through the window. She is peering down into the garden, but she seems to be looking at the floor. 'We've got to talk.' She turns back to me, her face bright but somehow closed. 'But not now, Mum. You're Cinderella getting ready for the ball. Let's check out with Maggie if this is the right stuff and then find you something special to wear.'

'As I recall, Cinders had a date with a handsome prince, not just her sister,' I remind her, and for one crazy, self-pitying moment I wish that I did, too. I lighten my tone, smiling at her. 'Where are all the handsome princes when you need one?'

'Maybe they're like buses,' Shelley offers, 'and some-time soon two are going to come along at once.'

'I should be so lucky!' God, what am I *saying*? Am I really that lonely? If I am, I've never noticed it before. I shrug off the thought.

'Okay, I'll go and ask Maggie if we've got the right "bargain rail". You mind you don't lean too far out there.' She is leaning out over the window ledge again, looking at the grass below intently.

'*Mu*-um!' Her voice has regained its usual teenage edge of sarcasm. *As if.* She is far too old for me to be treating her like an infant, and I bite my lip, cringing at how automatically I do it. We need to cut the apron strings, Shelley and I.

I need to let her grow up. I need to let her go.

26

Rachel

Tuesday morning

It's early morning, far too early for my liking, around 7.30 a.m. There's a certain beach-washed quietness hanging over Trefolgew at this point in the day. The sky is bright, but not yet hot. The air has that peculiar fresh-fish ocean breeze tang about it that makes me want to breathe in deeply and fully, even as I'm debating whether to cancel my plans to go and say hi to Maggie at her shop or just go back to bed.

But going back to bed seems such a waste now that I'm up and, I realise with a flutter of excitement, I'm *free*. Getting up at the crack of dawn so that Maggie's teenage grandchildren – twins, Ellen and Jazzy – can take Shelley on a boat-trip to some cove somewhere has awarded me at least the first half of the day to do exactly as I please with. At first I was a little put out – wasn't this time meant to be for me and Shelley? But now I've got over that I'm feeling quite excited that they didn't want me to come. The twins have promised to take Shelley for breakfast in a café later and they should be back by early afternoon.

So, I'm free.

Without thinking, my brain in early-morning slow-mo gear, I've stopped the car in the lay-by at the head of the beach. I might as well go down to Maggie and take her my jewellery designs now. She promised me that there would be nobody else around at this time of day, only us. We'll have a coffee and she can look at what I've brought along and see if there's anything she could get her friend to make up for the shop.

Once out of the car, I just stand there for a moment with the early sun on my face, my eyes closed, relishing the solitude. The day is a bright screen of orange behind my closed lids. Every so often a gull flies in front of me, darkening the brightness. I can hear them swooping, looking for landing places, scanning for fish. Even up here, I swear, the air carries a hint of the sea-salt spray that makes you want to lick your lips and go looking for a drink. When I stretch out my open hands, I imagine I can feel the sea-dampness on the breeze that caresses my fingertips. We used to do this all the time; I have a sudden flash of memory. When the kids were little they used to get up so early on their holidays and race down to the beach and we always used to do *this*, 'feeling the morning' Shelley used to call it.

What does this morning feel like?

It feels exciting and it feels scary at the same time. The sea isn't rough but there's a stiff breeze far out whipping the edges of the waves up into little meringue peaks. The water looks inviting, but you just know it will be damn cold. The sun is bright, glinting off distant cliff-tops. The gulls are loud, but most of them are far away.

226

The morning feels like it might be on the brink of something. Like me, standing at the head of the beach by the lay-by up here on the hill. I'm on the brink of something but I don't know what.

I'm feeling more nervous than I care to admit. I haven't done any drawings or shown anyone my designs for such a long time. 'Rachel the artist' feels like an alter-ego that I abandoned half a lifetime ago. Who am I kidding, thinking that anyone will still like my work? And even if Maggie does like it, how do I know that I can still do this? Maybe I've lost the knack; I haven't done any for so long. Surely there are hundreds of talented young things who have crept up behind me with newer, better ideas, using more modern materials and techniques that I couldn't even dream of . . .

The pebbly hill down to Maggie's shop is a steep one. I can feel my mules slipping; they hardly want to grip the road at all. I'm just thinking, thank god there is nobody to see me if I slip and end up crashing in an ungainly heap with Maggie's 'bargain rail' lilac skirt a dishevelled parachute over my head, when I catch sight of him. A lone man, dressed like a hiker, sitting on a clump of grass with his back against a smooth granite stone.

I don't know why seeing him has made me stop. He hasn't even seen me yet. He's got his head down and a pencil in his hand and he's concentrating on the sketch pad balanced on his knees. He's got short, almost spiky straight hair I can see from here, sandy-coloured. I can't make out his age. But he's not old. I can tell that from the way his muscles move underneath his T-shirt; he's not an old man. But, my artist's eye judges him, he's solid enough not to be a youth either.

But I have stopped for too long, stared at him for too long, and he has sensed me and now he's turned and looked up the hill. Of course, the sound of my footfall against the gravel has suddenly halted and that must have alerted him. Above the gentle crash and ebb of the waves and the distant cries of seagulls, there is no other sound. His eyes are light grey-brown and they narrow as he catches sight of me. There is a wariness in his eyes, an alertness, and I do not know why. But he nods towards me in friendly acknowledgement nonetheless. I think I nod back. I'm not sure. Somehow, I don't know why, this stranger has taken my breath away.

I don't know him, it's true. He is a stranger. But just for a second there I felt such a powerful feeling of recognition that it's left me feeling quite wobbly. I am quite sure we have never actually met. I grip my sketch pad tighter. I can see that he's spotted it, just as I have seen his.

When I put my head down, my face suddenly feeling pink and hot, I can feel the breeze cooling my skin as I resume my descent of the gravel hill. For once I'm glad of my unruly hair that blows everywhere, covering up my face. He isn't even looking at me any more. I can sense that, even though I'm not looking at him. I won't, either. I have to pass him to go into Maggie's shop but we've already acknowledged each other in the vague way that is appropriate for us to have done, strangers on a deserted early-morning beach. If Maggie's shop isn't open I am just going to *die*.

228

What's wrong with me? I think he said good morning but I didn't answer. Poor man. He must think there is something wrong with me now, either that or I'm just plain rude.

Maggie isn't here. Both the shop doors at the front and back are open, though. A gentle breeze is flowing deliciously through the shop, tinkling the wind-chimes that cascade from the rafters at the front.

He's waiting for someone, that's it. He has probably got a wife or a girlfriend using the toilet facilities in here. He didn't sound English. His voice was deep and a little gruff and . . . American maybe? Canadian? I should have answered him, said good morning or something myself. Then he might have said some more and I would have been able to place his accent. But what do I care? His other half will probably appear from the Ladies any minute and his wait will be over. They'll go off into the sunset together and I will never see him again.

Calm yourself down, Rachel, I tell myself – this isn't like you at all!

I'm nervous because of the designs, that's the real truth. Showing them to a potential buyer after so long makes me feel vulnerable and exposed. I was looking at them last night – thank goodness they got left in the car after I took them to Solly's – and some of them didn't seem too bad, but what do I know?

Maggie has some incense burning in a little pot on the counter. It smells pungent but really quite nice. It reminds me of going to church when I was a kid. The open bag beside the pot is full of little granules, and is labelled 'Frankincense and Myrrh' – three pounds fifty.

Not bad really. Two out of the three wise men must have got themselves a bargain gift for baby Jesus.

I like this place so much. Pottering around in here, touching Maggie's artfully arranged amethysts and rose quartz pieces, I remember that I need to get a little something to take back to Sol before we leave. He loves all this New Age stuff. He'll have to come here with Justin – when they've made up – and walk along the beach one morning when the sand is so flat and unspoiled, just like it is right now. What could be more romantic than that?

Oh no, I've just spotted him again.

The man, sitting against the stone with his sketch pad. I just caught him looking in at me, pottering around in here thinking my silly thoughts. I'm going to duck out of sight.

The bathroom in here is cool and shady and the mirror looks like something that Maggie might have on sale outside, the frame all embellished with little shells and mother of pearl and tiny sea-horses. My face, when I look into it, appears flushed, even in this dim light.

I'm going to reapply my lipstick and just bide my time a bit. I can't hear any footsteps outside just yet so no sign of Maggie. Nobody has come into the shop. Is he still out there waiting, I wonder?

I'm feeling calmer now. It would be stupid for me to hide out here for too long when I could be browsing through all those pretty trinkets. Besides, I've left my sketches out there. On the counter, I think. I can't leave them there for anybody to wander in and look through, I'm going back out.

Oh heck. He's in the shop now.

He's got a bottle of water out of her fridge and while he's waiting he's – oh my god, he's *looking through my yellow folder*! I can see him, I'm sure that's what he's doing, casual as you like. Cheeky bugger! People shouldn't just – just look at documents that are left on the counter while they're waiting to pay for their water (it's in a folder with my name on it, I mean it looks private enough). What on earth does he think he's doing? That's *mine*.

I should say something, I know.

But I don't want to talk to him. And anyway he seems so engrossed in looking at the designs I'm kind of curious to see his reaction.

For the moment, just to look like I've got something to do, I pick up a set of 'Angel' cards. By my watch it's now nearly eight o'clock. Maggie should be back soon, surely? The cards fall out of their pack easily and I can see that they're worn and used. Maybe this is the sample pack? The pictures are so pretty. They seem to be of Celtic angels with faintly luminescent wings; they look more like faeries to me. I pull one out at random; 'Be at peace with your time. Know that nothing is ever wasted.'

The man at the counter has stopped at one of my designs now and he's . . . he's actually copying it into his sketchbook. No, I don't believe it – he couldn't be doing that, surely? I can see his hand moving though, I can hear the scratch of his pencil, he *is* doing it!

How could he do that? Those designs are mine. He shouldn't even be looking at that folder.

I cough loudly so that he looks up and catches my

eye and he knows that I've spotted him. He doesn't seem embarrassed in the slightest, though, he just smiles at me and carries on.

'The owner will be back soon,' I tell him, warningly.

'I hope so.' He takes a swig out of his water (*and he hasn't even paid for it yet!*). 'I want to see her. Do you know where she's at?'

I shake my head.

'But I'm sure she will be back *any moment.*' I look at the yellow folder pointedly. 'Do you really think you should be looking through those?' my voice is shaky, 'or even taking notes from it? I mean, it's private property isn't it? The person who drew those things spent a long time thinking them up. You can't just copy down things that you fancy.'

'I didn't realise I was doing anything wrong.' He snaps it shut, turning to give me his full attention. His eyes are a light grey-brown I see now. 'Well, actually, all I was copying down was . . .'

Didn't realise he was doing anything wrong?

'It's infringement of copyright, it's unfair, it's . . . it's immoral.'

'Well I wouldn't want to upset you. I won't copy down anything more.' He looks, my god he actually looks *amused*. 'Are you the artist, by any chance?'

'Why do you think that? I'd be saying this whoever's work I caught you trying to pilfer.'

'Pilfer?' He doesn't know the word, obviously. 'I thought you might be the designer. You've got good colour sense. I like your skirt, for example,' he adds. 'Those colours look really pretty on you.'

He's trying to distract me from what he was doing. Flattering me isn't going to work. No, it isn't.

Shit, I'm blushing again.

For a moment I do something that the lady ay my old aerobics class used to close each session with. I just stop all other thoughts and breathe in deeply. In that breath there is frankincense and myrrh and ozone and wet sand and the deep faraway smell of salt water and many silver swimming fish. And him. I realise now that I caught the scent of his aftershave as I scurried past, just a hint, just the briefest note of it, but it comes back to me now like a cherished memory.

'Good morning!' Maggie's husky voice brings me out of my reverie. She's wearing some sort of beach wrap and her beautifully-cut silver hair looks damp, her face flushed with the exercise. She shakes out her hair with her fingers. She is sixty-eight, I recall now but she could pass for a good ten years younger. She's the same age as Pandora. And, like Pandora, she is determined to make every moment count. Maybe I should take a hint from the pair of them?

'Hiya, Maggie.' The guy at the counter smiles sweetly at her. He's got my folder open again – the cheek of it! He doesn't even care if she sees him – and his pencil is even poised at the ready to copy down some more.

'Hello darling. I'll be with you in a minute.' She turns back to me. 'Have you and Frank introduced yourselves yet?' She pauses with her hand on the door to the back room.

'Who?'

'His name is Frank Dwight,' she smiles disarmingly.

'I told him to be here early as I knew you were coming. I think he's been waiting here a while.'

'Um, I haven't met anyone yet.' I slip the Angel cards back into their box.

Frank. Is that his name? That cheeky so and so who's been copying all my designs?

'Who is he? Why do you want us to meet?'

'Because he's lonely,' she says, and pulls me just inside the inner door, her voice low. 'I know you aren't looking for a man at the moment, you made that perfectly clear when you told me all about you and Bill last night, dear,' she lays a comforting hand on my arm, 'and with the way things are for you at home that's hardly a wonder. But Frank could do with some female company, and you would be doing me a great favour if you let him take you out for a walk and pretend that it's *you* who needs looking after.'

Ha, if she thinks she's on a match-making mission Maggie's got another think coming. Just because I opened up and spoke to Mags last night about the situation with me and Bill doesn't mean I'm giving her the green light to go ahead and drum up a fella for me!

'You know I respect your privacy and I'm well aware that you need some space, so don't think I'm match-making,' she adds, reading my thoughts, 'it isn't like that at all, I promise you.'

'No.' I find my voice at last, even if it is just a whisper.

Maggie just stands there and looks at me for a moment, her eyes dark and unfathomable. 'Why ever not?' she says at last. 'I thought you two might have things in common. His sister back in the States owns a jewellery outlet and

234

she's always looking for unusual, Celtic-based designs. I asked Frank to look at yours. He seemed quite interested in them, from what I could see.'

'Oh. You mean *he's* the person you were talking about who . . .' Maggie gives me a puzzled look.

'I'll be out in a tick,' she says. She needs to get into something dry. Oh what a fool, what an *idiot*, I've been. My face is flaming like a beetroot. He's the one she wanted me to talk to; he's my possible avenue of hope for selling my sketches and I've just been so rude to him that the guy will never want to deal with me again. I've got to apologise to that poor man. He shouldn't have been copying down my stuff though, I tell myself. If he hadn't been doing that I wouldn't have got so riled with him. I'll explain that. I would never have reacted as I had.

When I dip back into the shop, he's disappeared. He's left his sketch pad on the counter though, beside my folder, and all I can see written on it, in pencil, is my name and my telephone number.

No pilfered sketches at all!

27

Rachel

'Nonsense,' Maggie snorts, 'you've got ages yet. Please don't argue with me. I'm freezing.'

'I can't go,' I begin, my voice suddenly going up a pitch, when he walks in through the shop door and catches my eye and holds it. For one long, warm moment he just holds me there, my heart pounding so loud I cannot see how they can fail to hear it. Then his eyes slide gently down me, taking in first my blouse (open at the top button because it is warm), then the pretty lilac skirt that Maggie sold me – he lingers over that – and then at last comes to rest on my unsuitable walking shoes. He seems to approve of what he sees; I don't know, though, as he doesn't say anything. I offer up a silent prayer of thanks to Lily because if it weren't for the fact that I'm meeting her later I would never have acquired this outfit.

I realise, all of a sudden, that I've been holding my breath as we stand there. What if this is my one and only chance to get someone interested in my designs?

'I'll go,' I say to Maggie at last, 'if you like.'

'Rachel, this is Frank Dwight.' She turns a goose-pimpled arm towards him and then in quick succession

236

towards me. 'Frank, your lady awaits. Hell, I'm still freezing. I'm going to have to get another top on. Have fun, you two.' Then she disappears behind the beaded curtains at the back of her shop.

Your lady awaits, indeed! Hasn't she just told me very clearly that he isn't looking for anyone? She isn't match-making, she says. What *is* she doing then?

'Hi, Rachel.' Frank steps forward and offers me his hand with a shy smile. His grip is firm but gentle; his hand is warm, I notice, but not sweaty. As he leans in to me there is that lingering scent of his aftershave again, I catch the faintest trace of it, sweet and sunny and intriguing and dangerous all at the same time.

'Frank,' I cough, covering up my embarrassment, trying to get my voice back because it seems to have got strangled in my throat. 'I'm sorry if we got off on the wrong foot back there. I didn't realise you knew Maggie . . .'

'It's okay.' He dismisses my apology with a shrug. 'I . . . er . . . couldn't help but notice your shoes. If you're coming walking we'll have to borrow some off Maggie. You've only got little feet. Hopefully you should be about the same size.' Frank dips behind the counter and brings out a pair of well-used women's walking boots. I notice he doesn't feel the need to wait and ask Maggie about it. It makes me wonder what his relationship to her can be. Is Frank her son, maybe – her nephew? I'd ask her but I know how private she is, and if she doesn't actually offer the information I'm loath to ask.

Outside, feeling the sun on my neck as I stoop to do up the laces, I am aware of him bending easily to pick

237

up his rucksack, stuffing his jacket into one of the side compartments.

'Don't worry about ignoring me before,' he's telling me, 'we can start again, right?'

I laugh self-consciously, still embarrassed, but more at my reaction to this man than at anything else.

'I'd like that. Thank you for offering to take me out this morning.'

He laughs then, and I see that sweet, shy look again.

'From what I could gather Mags had to pretty much twist your arm to persuade you to come out with me.'

'Not true,' I defend myself. 'Besides this isn't exactly a date is it? She made that perfectly clear. It's just a walk.' He could hook his own fish, I was sure, if he had a mind to do so.

'Well, I appreciate you coming, Rachel,' he grins suddenly, 'and you're right, Maggie is rather protective of me. She knows I'm a bit . . . fragile, right now. I couldn't cope with any hard-hitting broad and maybe she thought you – someone like you – would be better company for me. Do you mind?'

I let out a breath. 'Not at all.' We are climbing back up the gravel path towards the car park. The breeze is already getting warmer and it can't even be eight thirty yet. Maggie is right, today is going to be a scorcher.

'Are you two related, then?' I look at him curiously. I don't want to appear too vulgarly interested. If he is lonely, then it is none of my business, is it?

'Mags and I have interests in common,' he tells me noncommittally, but he doesn't expand on that. 'We've known each other for many years.'

We watch then, as three noisy kids hurl themselves down the path towards us, arms flailing free as their middle-aged parents bring up the rear, burdened down with beach gear that their offspring would no doubt later enjoy. Frank watches them more closely than I, smiling at the children's antics, but I think I glimpse a taut sadness in his eyes. I remember a time when I had felt like that, too. A time when I'd been away for just a few short days when the children were very little, catching sight of another couple with their toddlers had filled me with a yearning to be back home with my own.

I want to ask him if he has children of his own but I can't. I know, in the way you instinctively do with strangers, what the topics of conversation are that need to be avoided. It makes me burn to ask him about precisely *that*, of course. But I don't.

'Do you live locally, Frank?' I really want to ask him if he has any kids. I want to ask him other things too, like *how* many years he's known Maggie – Mags – and in what capacity. If they aren't related, but he still feels comfortable enough to borrow her boots for me without asking, then what kind of association do they have? Are they business partners? Ex-lovers, even? I glance at him covertly from behind my sunglasses. He would be a good deal younger than her, I judge, more my age than hers.

He is in better physical condition than me, though. I don't get as much exercise as I should, and I am, much to my mortification, already panting a little. The hill has presented him, on the other hand, with no challenge at all.

Frank shakes his head, gallantly slowing down his pace to allow me to catch my breath a little.

'I'm based abroad – Toronto – but I come here regularly. I have . . . a particular fondness for this place.' We've reached the car park and we both stand surveying the view for a few moments. The beach is no longer so deserted. Apart from the family who passed us (now setting up station on a favourable spot near the shoreline), several surfers are starting to emerge from campervans parked further up on the road.

'They won't get much surfing done here today.' He indicates them with his head. 'It's much too calm. If they go on a few miles further up the coast they might have better luck.'

'Do you surf?'

'Back home. Less now than I used to.' He gives a dry laugh, hinting at former halcyon days, but he looks like a man still in his prime to me.

'How about you?' I get a direct look from those grey-brown eyes again.

'I don't surf.' I shake my head and his face crinkles with amusement.

'Where do you come from? I mean, I saw you in town yesterday, with your daughter.'

'You did?' And he *remembers*? My heart is beginning to race again. How many strangers might we all pass in a busy shopping mall on any given day? How many of them would we actually remember if we saw them again?

'She's in a wheelchair, isn't she?' We have passed the car park now and taken a narrow dirt path that seems to lead out towards a grass cliff-top walk. The air smells warm and of the ocean spray, even up so high.

'I wonder that you noticed the two of us,' I tell him, trying to mask my disappointment. 'We're not local, as you know, we're staying with Maggie. We only arrived yesterday, in fact, and we weren't at the shopping centre for long, just picking up some provisions.' Did we stand out that much, Shelley and I? I tried to recall if we'd had an argument at all . . . Shelley is a great one for being stubborn in public places and kicking up a scene in a teenagery sort of way. I didn't think we had.

'It was your daughter I noticed first.' Now it's Frank's turn to sound embarrassed. 'Something about her . . . she had a certain look on her face.' He looks at the road. 'She must have reminded me of someone, I guess.'

'Shelley did?' I stop to redo the laces on Maggie's boots, lingering over them to give him time to answer me. 'Who?'

Frank doesn't answer me. He just stands there, waiting patiently for me to finish with my laces. 'You have a daughter?' I probe, unable to stop myself.

He shakes his head. 'Can you hear that?' he says at last.

I listen, crouching down still over my boots. There is the breeze rustling through the sea-grasses and the faint, faraway shouts of children on the shore. The sea; waves gently breaking, rolling back down. There is the drone of one or two cars on the road above the beach. The calling of some gulls.

I look at him. Frank puts his hand to his ear, cocks his head to one side.

'Listen,' he coaxes me, and I listen again. Does he mean the birds? Somewhere close by, the high tinny sound of a young bird calls out repeatedly to its parents. That must be them, the two birds circling close to the cliff's edge, just by where we are walking. 'They must have their nest close by.' Frank drops onto his hands and knees then and peers round over the edge; it looks like a pretty sheer drop from where I'm standing. 'Ah, I thought so. The little fella has fallen out.'

'Fallen *out*?' I edge a bit closer but it looks like a long way down and I immediately want to step back. 'Where?'

'There's a little ledge there, just under the precipice, can you see it?'

'I'll take your word for it.'

'If I could just get close enough I could slide him back into the nest. He's going to fall, otherwise. His wings aren't well-developed enough yet to fly, poor little critter.'

'How are you going to get close enough?' There is no *way*, I think now, peering over at the ledge he's just referred to, that he can get near enough without putting himself at great risk. The cliff-face juts out and over, proud of the cliff, which makes it all the more difficult a task.

'There's a foothold there, right there, do you see?' He isn't actually talking to me any more; he is intently calculating how he is going to get that bird back.

'Frank, please, I really don't think you should . . .' But he's already walking a little further back the way we've come, judging the angle, trying to get a better view of it.

'There's a clump of grass on the left, and a space big enough for me to stand,' he is saying.

'Not exactly big enough to *stand*,' I correct him. 'You might get a toe-hold . . .'

'A toe-hold is all I need, then.' He slides his backpack off his shoulders and I watch it slump to the ground. Above us the parent-birds are still calling, still fretting. He glances at them, a sheen of sweat beginning to appear on his forehead, and I feel a horrible band of fear constrict around my chest.

'Please don't do it.' My voice is hoarse. But I can't exactly throw myself on him and beg him not to take the risk. 'If you fall,' I say, 'it is an awfully long way down.'

'I know,' he tells me steadily, 'I'm just going to have to make sure that I don't, aren't I?'

I step back then, my arms folded across my chest. I'm not going to be able to stop him, no matter what I say. But I don't have to stand here and watch him, either. There must be hundreds of baby birds falling out of their nests every day, I think; what bad luck that we have to chance upon one in such a precarious position. What bad luck that the first guy I've met in *years* who really engages my interest . . . has to have such misplaced hero tendencies. 'Look, I'm sorry; I really can't bear to watch you do this. Can't we wait and get a rope or something? Wouldn't that make more sense?'

'I don't think we've got time. He's edging over to the ledge even as we speak.'

Damn it, then! I think. Just leave the thing. Don't *do* this. For an instant I turn my back on him, feeling a sick fear in the pit of my stomach, knowing that I can't stop him, angry at him for making me feel this way. Doesn't he have any consideration for *my* feelings? I've got this thing about heights. I can't bear anyone I care about being near a dangerous drop, it just makes me ill.

Of course he can't possibly know what my feelings are, I grudgingly admit to myself after a bit. We are just polite strangers who have barely learned each other's names as far as he is concerned. I keep my back to him for as long as I can bear. All is very quiet behind me. Even the parent-birds have gone quiet. They must have flown off. See, even they aren't that bothered, I think tensely. They aren't going to put their lives at risk.

I look at my watch, tracing the second hand as it sweeps around the dial. I will wait two . . . no, three minutes before I go back and look. Maybe I should wait five? How long will it take? If I wait too long might I miss it if Frank falls and then risk a delay of precious minutes when I could have been getting help?

This isn't fair. I'm supposed to be having time off this morning. I'm supposed to be free from all responsibilities and troubles for these few precious hours.

I just won't think about him, that's all. He'll probably be fine, maybe he does this kind of thing all the time, maybe he is a fireman or an athlete or a stunt coordinator?

Down on the beach the three kids have been joined by another two and their dads have joined them. They are planning on making a sandcastle that looks – by the proportions of the lines they have drawn on the shore – as if it might take up every grain of sand on the beach. The mothers are chatting and laughing and they keep looking up in my direction. I want to lose myself in the detail, take my mind off what Frank is up to, so I notice how the women are wearing almost identical beach-wraps, and pretty pink bathing suits underneath them. They must be the kind of friends who go shopping together, arm in arm, scouring the same boutiques for pretty, coordinating clothes. Maybe they are sisters?

That makes me think about Lily, of course. I suddenly become aware of a tightness in my stomach. Okay, maybe Shelley is right. Maybe I *am* nervous about meeting up with my sister again after three years. I look at the women and try to imagine myself and Lily, down on that same beach later on, laughing and chatting and pointing at the things that catch our interest. I can't do it. All I can manage is the two of us as children, me with my big green net, scrambling over the rock pools, and Lily sitting delicately on the edge of a mossy boulder, her arms flung backwards like some Hollywood starlet, her face tilted up towards the sun.

I know that we won't be coming to this beach together, of course. That is just a pretty fantasy to take my mind off Frank dangling off the cliff edge just a few feet away from me . . .

No, my darling sister Lily would doubtless not move herself more than two feet away from the hotel swimming pool if she could help it. And Lily and I never went anywhere in matching clothes, then or now. I wish! Her couture is a little beyond my pocket. Maybe the heavy lump that feels like a bag of sand in my stomach is about Lily, and not Frank, after all.

I can see the women, even though they are so far away, their bodies facing towards me, arms folded across their chests. They call their loved ones and then the children all start pointing.

245

They are looking at Frank, of course! I force myself to look at my watch. It has been six minutes already. If I don't go back to him now I feel as if I am going to burst.

'Frank?' I call to him but the breeze lifts my voice and takes it away somewhere else. I have to go back to the cliff edge. 'Are you all right, Frank?'

'I'm nearly there now.'

'Can you come up now please, Frank, you're giving me a heart attack.'

A moment later his left hand appears, waving, over the top. Just what his feet are being supported on, I can't begin to guess.

At first I think he is just letting me know he is still here, but then I see he is scrabbling about blindly, looking for a clump of grass or a crevice to get a hand-hold on.

I kneel on the dry sand at the top of the cliff. It is peppered with tiny pebbles that sink into my knees painfully but they don't matter. All I can focus on is his hand. I take in his palm, which looks broad and strong; dependable. I take in the short, close-bitten nails and I wonder what it is that has troubled him so, that he should bite them down to the quick like that. I take in the tiny bleached hairs on the backs of his square fingers. And then, without even wanting to, I notice that he wears no ring on his third finger.

'Frank?' I call out softly. '*Frank?*' His fingers suddenly reach, outstretched, towards me.

'Could you give me a hand, Rachel?' He must be in trouble.

Instinctively, I grab hold of him. His palm is not sticky

with sweat where I grip it, but cool and firm, responsive to my touch.

'I don't think I can haul you up,' I croak. He's twice the size of me and, even with lifting Shelley and wheeling her around so much, I'm not that strong.

'You don't have to, Rachel.' I marvel that his voice can remain so sure and level. 'Just anchor your feet in the sand as best you can and push your weight backwards. I'll do the rest.'

I do as he says, digging the heels of the walking boots into the soil on the cliff edge as far as they will go.

It can only be a moment. No more than a moment, and yet the whole world seems to stand still, not breathing. I cannot hear them any more, the people on the beach. I can't hear the children who have been laughing and playing, or the waves that have been rolling onto the shore. There is just this gap in time while I hold on to his hand in terror, knowing full well I can never pull him up and wondering how on earth this can end. Maybe the people on the beach, or the coastguard, they'll see he's in trouble and they'll come? I can feel him tugging on my hand as he searches for a way to haul himself back up. How crazy is this? All just for one tiny bird who might decide to do the whole thing all over again as soon as we walk away!

I could walk away from the bird, but there is no way I am going to leave Frank now until he gets back up. Even if my feet *are* sliding on that dusty sand towards the edge. I'll never let him go; I'll go over with him first.

'Oh god, Frank, Frank, I don't think I can *do* this.' I can feel tears of desperation rolling down my cheeks.

247

From my faraway place I can just make out his voice, calling me. 'I'm up. I'm nearly at the top.' His arms are straining, pulling himself over.

He is lithe, and once he finds the hand-hold he needs, he is over the top instantly.

I wipe the wetness off my face. I am sweating profusely, shaking, even. *God*, I want to go home!

Frank just stands there for a second, then he hugs me tightly, a big bear-hug. 'I'm so sorry, Rachel. I didn't mean to scare you like that. That was so *thoughtless*.'

'You didn't know.' I'm trying to laugh it off, though I am still shaking. 'You couldn't have guessed what a wuss I am when it comes to heights.' He is still holding on to me, gently, like a concerned friend might; he has his arms around my shoulders, his fingers just under the hair at the nape of my neck. He can't guess what effect his touch is having on me just at this moment, either. And I don't want him to. I inch myself back out of his reach, ever so slowly, and he drops his arms in response. I hang my head then, coward that I am, because I don't want him to see what is going on inside me. It's all too sudden. You can't develop feelings like that for a person in the short space of time that I have known this man. It isn't possible. No, it just isn't. It's the drama of what just occurred, the life and death scenario, the fragility of our existence.

He is a genuine, friendly guy, that is all. Sol would have hugged me like that, under similar circumstances. There really is nothing to it. Only I know, if I am honest, that I wouldn't respond to Sol in the same way. Not in a million years.

Far away on the beach the sandcastle families suddenly give up a loud cheer, breaking the awkward moment between us. He turns to wave at them for a minute, grinning in acknowledgement, and then he turns back to me. 'Sorry if I scared you, Rachel. I couldn't just leave it there. I'm sorry.'

He dusts himself down then, bends to pick up his canvas bag and pulls out a bottle of water.

'Have some water, you've had a shock.'

'No, thanks.' I shake my head. 'I mean, yes, I will, but please, you go first. That must have taken some guts.' I glance back over the cliff edge. 'Is he all right?'

'He's back where he's meant to be. With his parents.' Frank ignores my suggestion that he should drink first and places his water bottle in my hands. I wet my lips gratefully.

'Thanks, Frank.' I laugh shortly, trying to get my composure back because he is still looking at me in a way that sends my pulse racing. 'You handled that like a pro. Do you rescue people for a living?'

'Not as a rule.'

'What do you do then?'

'I run my own production company.'

'Oh,' I say, 'you make films?'

'Documentaries, mainly, though we've been moving into the docu-drama arena lately.'

'Ah.' I hand him back the water bottle. 'Is that what your connection with Maggie is?' I am back interrogating him, I just can't help myself. I know that is what I am doing even though I am trying to make it sound like casual conversation.

249

'No,' he says at last. 'My association with Maggie is personal.'

'I see.' I want to add, 'and it's clearly a state secret exactly what that personal association is because you've done everything but tell me . . .' but I resist the temptation. Any more along those lines and he will surely rumble that my own interest is far stronger than it should be.

'So, anyway, you were telling me about Shelley,' I prompt him. 'You were telling me that she reminded you of someone and that's why you remembered seeing us out shopping yesterday?'

Frank shakes his head, then looks away before looking back at me with those oh-so-direct eyes.

'I'm sorry, I didn't mean to embarrass you, Rachel. I shouldn't have mentioned anything.'

Why should I feel embarrassed? He isn't being very clear. 'What do you mean?' I persist.

'She looked . . . sad, I guess. She looked spaced-out and scared and somehow very sad.'

'You're an observant man,' I tell him. We are on safer ground here. I can talk about my daughter for hours. 'I think Shelley *is* sad. We used to come down here when she was a child. She could walk then. It must have brought back memories for her. It was her idea to come here, though, for her fifteenth birthday.

'What happened to her?' Frank's voice has gone very low. He is listening intently. He has dusted himself down and picked up his bag again. We saunter along together in silence for a bit while I try to figure out how to explain it all to him.

'Did she have an accident? A car crash?'

'No, not that. It was something that just developed. A motor neurone disease that apparently has a genetic basis. It's so rare they haven't even decided what to call it yet! Some people develop worse symptoms than others. Some people can carry the gene and never develop anything at all. It depends on other genetic factors, it seems. In the most severe cases it is fatal. Shelley *is* depressed. Her closest friend, Miriam, who was diagnosed around the same time, passed away a year ago. And it isn't just that she's lost her closest friend. The end wasn't pretty. Miriam had a really hard time of it. I think that's scared my daughter witless because we've always been told that Shelley has a worse form of the disease; Miriam's was supposed to be quite mild by comparison.'

'I'm so sorry.' He turns his head away from me for a moment, and I could swear he wipes his eyes with the back of his hand. When he looks back at me again he seems more distant, though, as if something has closed down in him. One minute he is an open door I am about to walk through; the next moment he just shuts me off.

'Look, it's ten o'clock.' He glances at his watch. 'You said something to Maggie about having to get back for Shelley? I mean, I wouldn't want to keep you from this time you're supposed to be spending with your daughter . . .'

'Well,' I hesitate, 'I'm sure we've got plenty of time yet.' I should ring her, I suppose. Heck, Shelley's the one I'm supposed to be here for. But I haven't felt so free in such a long time. And I haven't been in the company of a man who looks at me the way Frank does, for even longer . . .

251

'It'll take at least half an hour to get back to the car park,' he tells me. 'Then you've got to drive back through town.'

'If you think we should be getting back . . . ?' I offer. Maybe he's had enough of me. I wasn't exactly stalwart a moment ago when he rescued that bird.

'It might be best, Rachel. I'm not much company at the moment and I don't think . . . well, maybe this wasn't such a good idea after all.'

'The walk?' I look at him brightly. I have no intention of showing him what I am feeling.

'*Us* walking. You and me. I've got a lot of heavy things going on at the moment and I can't be myself. So it isn't fair. Do you understand?'

'Nope,' I tell him. 'Well, I understand that you're saying we should both get back and you've got a lot on your mind, and you don't really want to talk about any of it . . .'

'That's pretty much all you need to understand, Rachel.'

'Okay then. I get it.' I don't get it. I don't get any of it at all. I don't understand what is going on with him – though I know I have no right to that information either – and I don't understand why he affects me the way he does. Or why he is so tender and caring one moment and the next he is being so distant that he can't get rid of me quick enough.

The breeze is trying to lift up the ruffles on my skirt and I have to hug it hard with my hands, close to my hips. 'I know my own way back,' I tell him. 'Please don't feel that we're tied at the hip.'

252

'Of course not. Look. I'm going to make my way back via the south beach. I've got a friend I need to stop off at on the way. If you're sure you'll be okay . . . ?' He takes a few steps from me then, ready to go on his way, already taking his leave.

What if I had just said, *No, I won't be okay, I'll get lost and nobody will ever find me again.* I know full well my sister Lily wouldn't have thought twice about playing the damsel-in-distress card. And if I did, I know full well he'd walk back with me, take me to Maggie's or to my car. And maybe as we walked we might talk some more and I might find out what it is that is bugging him; what the thing is that is really eating away at Frank Dwight.

But I am too full of a stupid hurt pride. If he doesn't require my company any more then the last thing I'm going to do is let him see that I care!

However, by the time I've found my way back to Maggie's, my feet rubbed raw and sweating inside her slightly-too-big boots, all I can think of is that he hasn't asked to see me again. He clearly isn't interested.

Oh, I'm past all this 'dating' stuff!

I don't know how people are supposed to do this, any more, I don't know what the etiquette is, or what I'm supposed to be looking out for. I know this wasn't a proper date – we were both quite clear on that – but what he *said* and the way he kept on looking at me didn't quite add up.

I'm confused. Does Frank like me, or doesn't he? Do I even like him? I don't want to, but I'm very much afraid that I do.

I know what it is that did it. It was when I told him about how bad things are with *Shelley* that he suddenly backed off – that's what it was, I remember now! Of course, how could I have been so blind? I've encountered that reaction on more than one occasion before; a man shows some interest in me, then cools off when he realises what it is that I come with.

I should have known that it would be like that.

As I kick off Maggie's shoes I remember that I've left my own, familiar mules back at her shop. I take off the lilac skirt that Frank so admired and put that away in the wardrobe. I've had enough at playing that I'm living someone else's life, for today. What's the point? At the end of it I always come back to my own life and that doesn't change, does it? Not ever.

28

Shelley

Tuesday morning

Mum's in love with this place, you can tell it from her face. I think it makes her sad as well, though. I think staying here with Maggie brings back memories of the time when me and Danny were little and she used to come here with Dad, when we were still all one family. Before I got sick.

Anyway, she cheered up well enough yesterday night when Maggie told her that those clothes on the bargain rail really were all just fifty pence! Fifty pence, I ask you. That's just crazy, they're worth a darn sight more than that and Maggie's got to know it. You'd think if she was just being charitable she'd say a fiver each or something, so Mum wouldn't feel like she's giving them away. Mum's like me; she's got her pride. So she took about three items in the end, but no more. She didn't want to take advantage.

Helping Mum choose the clothes and having tea and cake with Maggie took up a whole bunch of time, and then afterwards I helped Mags prepare the salad things for tea and that took up a bit more time. So I wasn't tempted to look at my emails last night. This morning

I've been on the boat with the twins, Ellen and Jazzy, Maggie's grandkids. Ellen is really nice. She came round here with her brother last night and brought me some things to borrow for the week and then suggested I go out on their boat-trip with them, just like that. It was really good fun. I never imagined it could be that good, going out on a boat. But it was. They put a life-jacket on me, which meant that the skipper (a guy of about twenty, but an experienced sailor) didn't get one because there weren't enough to go round. They kept joking with me, saying that if he went into the drink I'd have to be the one to man the boat because I'd taken his jacket. But I felt good. I felt really included, for once. After we went round the cove we stopped to have sandwiches on the beach and then they brought me back here, but they promised me I could go out with them again another time. I was so happy, I forgot all about my laptop and the emails that might still be waiting for me to reply to them.

I've managed to resist looking at emails ever since Saturday when I sent Kieran that terrible message. It's really bugging me, not checking the laptop to see if he's replied, but if I check and he's sent me something heart-breaking in return then I'll have to cope with that as well.

So I won't look.

I'll just keep myself busy, busy, busy. I should be tired after that trip out on the boat so early this morning but I'm not. I feel alert and totally awake and ready for anything. Mum's still out having lunch with Lily, I suppose. There's no sign of her here. It's totally quiet and peaceful.

I've been looking through Pandora's box and I found

Mum's old diary again; I kept wondering what happened to her and Gordon in the end so I've been thumbing through it.

The pages of her little book are thin and yellowing now. She has written so much! I don't even know where to begin. I feel guilty as hell, actually.

Oh god, just open it on one page, Shelley, any old page. Deep breath in and here I go.

November 5th. That sounds like a good date.

5 November 1978

Something's up; I know it is. I just don't know what. I saw Mum hiding something this morning. I could have sworn it was a letter addressed to Dad because I saw the postman bring it, but Mum didn't hand it to Dad like she normally would, at breakfast. I can't help wondering if it's a letter from Gordon's parents. They said they would write. They've already auditioned Lily and myself, along with a whole load of other girls all hoping to take over Amelie's place when she leaves. But we haven't heard anything from them yet. Whatever it is, why doesn't she just give Dad the mail that comes in for him? What is she up to?

12 November 1978

Gordon swears he doesn't know. He tells me his parents won't let on who his new partner will be till they get an answer back from her parents, agreeing to their offer. I caught him smoking yesterday, behind Legrange's studio, with the other lads. He offered me a puff but I didn't want one. Lily came up behind

*me just then and said she'd take one if it was on offer.
I don't know where she came from; I could have sworn
I'd given her the slip. She gave Gordon that look she
sometimes gives boys. God, I hate her at times! She
knows, now, how I feel about him, that we've got this
thing going between us; I had to tell her about Gordon
because she wouldn't stop bugging me. Now I have
this horrible feeling that she's trying to flirt with him
herself. She doesn't do it obviously, but it doesn't have
to be obvious with boys, does it? They'll take the
slightest hint. They know what they're looking for.
Like the way she rolled her lips around his cigarette
when he held it out to her, making a big pouting
shape with her mouth. What does she think she's
playing at? I'd have a go at her but I can't. She knows
my secret now so I have to put up with her.*

Whoa! Sounds like Mum and Lily had a little bit of sibling
rivalry going on there. I know about that. We did it at
school. I have it with Danny a little bit sometimes, only
it isn't as bad between him and me as it is between some
of the girls and their sisters at school. Sisters must be a
lot worse than brothers, I reckon. Brothers just try to
wrestle each other to the ground and beat the shit out
of each other, but sisters do all sorts of sneaky things,
play psychological games with each other. That's the
conclusion my social studies group all came to at school,
anyway.

Hmm. I wonder what did happen with Mum and
Gordon in the end?

29

Rachel

Tuesday, midday
The Royal Star Hotel is located in the better part of the town, its shining façade announcing that you needn't come in here if you're looking for anything below five-star ratings. Typical Lily! She's always had to have the very best of everything. She wouldn't know how to cope with anything less.

In that split second that I see her before she sees me, I get a snapshot of my sister Lily that I know I will frame in my heart.

A golden shaft of sunlight, beaming through the great west window, is framing her blonde head. She has her face angled only slightly away from me, her aqua-green eyes looking into some undefined space in front of her. At first I think: Lily, she doesn't change. She never changes. She's nearly forty-five years old and she could still pass for a woman in her late twenties. And then she moves her head slightly and the sun catches the small tired lines around her eyes; it catches the yellow brittleness and the harsher tones around the roots of her hair. She looks older, harder, yet curiously more vulnerable.

Her shoulders are still slim, dainty in her Jaeger jacket, but no longer as proud as they once were.

All at once, in that one glance, I catch the slender lines of her arms draped along the length of the white hotel sofa, and I see how limply her wrists hang down at the end. Something has gone out of her, my Lily, something I can't yet define, which pulls me up short nonetheless. It is as if the perfect, pale white flower that she was has started to wilt.

'Rachel!' I hear the bright melody of her voice calling out to me, I see her whole face light up as I catch her eye. 'Where have you been? I've been here over half an hour already. Shelley picked up your mobile when I called; she told me you'd both gone your separate ways today?'

'I'm sorry, sis.' My voice gets muffled in a hug and I catch the familiar scent of her hairspray laced with an expensive perfume. 'I got caught up.'

Lily tut-tuts and shakes her head in mock disapproval but she isn't really cross. I doubt that she's been waiting for half an hour. That would have made her actually on time for once, which would have been a first. The truth is, I fell asleep after I got back from Summer Bay. I hadn't meant to fall asleep. I had just lain down on the cool sheets and the peaceful quiet of the late morning with everyone else out had been blissful. My head had been full of Frank.

'My, but you're looking well, though.' Lily looks me up and down, scrutinising me briefly. Then she smiles at a hovering waiter who swans over and takes her order for a mint julep and a G and T with ice. 'In fact you look a damn sight better than you did when we last met.'

She takes in my lilac skirt and my elegant cotton blouse. Mentally, I offer up another prayer of thanks for Maggie's bargain rail. I must be looking positively well-to-do, in Lily's eyes.

'Thanks,' I breathe. Then I see her eyes go to my handbag, which is my own, and not in the same league as the rest of the clothes. I discreetly kick it out of sight under the table with my foot.

'So, how's my favourite niece? She sounded happy over the phone.'

'Did she?' I look at her, suddenly anxious. 'I'm so glad to hear that. She's been a bit down recently. That's why we're here, in fact.'

'It must be so hard for you, Rach. I don't know how you cope, I really don't.' She gives me a long, appraising look. 'And I admire you for it, too. How you always seem to take everything in your stride, no matter what life throws at you . . .'

'I have my dark nights of the soul, too.' I shake my head. She seems to be echoing Stella's earlier sentiments, though. Maybe I just make it all look too easy? It isn't. Maybe that's my problem, in fact. Everyone around me – Annie-Jo, Bill, they all seem to have the impression that I can cope, perfectly well, with whatever life throws at me – so they don't offer to give me any help. But hell, Lily isn't usually this interested in my problems; what has brought this on?

'Still, it's good to see you again, sis,' I say. 'It's been . . . how long this time?'

'Three years,' she says automatically. 'You had just discovered that Stella was pregnant.'

Trust her to bring that up! I sit back carefully in the plush chair and fold out the creases in my skirt.

'Yep. Three years would be about right, then.' I give her what I hope passes for a nonchalant smile. 'And *you're* looking as fresh as ever.' I wonder if she's going to bring it up; the thing she wants to talk to me so urgently about. I wonder if she will or if I'm going to have to do it? What does she know?

'Oh, I might look good, but I feel like shite.' She rifles in her Louis Vuitton clutch bag for a tissue. 'I've not been at all well, to tell you the truth, Rachel. I'd have got in touch with you sooner if I had been. But things have been . . . rather unsettled, on the home front.'

'What? Have they? Everything's still okay with you and Guy, isn't it?' Guy McManus is Lily's husband of the last ten years. He's well-known as a stockbroker and a lover of the high life, much as Lily is. Neither of them have ever appeared to want children, and it's been a decision that has suited their lifestyle well. I look at her curiously. She isn't regretting that now, is she? Last time I saw her she was touting the idea of a possible adoption but I thought she'd gone cold on that. It sounded like a fad to me, the latest must-have accessory.

Maybe *this* is what she wants to speak about?

'Currently, we're separated,' she tells me starkly. 'I got tired of being humiliated by his . . . shall we say, indiscretions. Oh, I know he's always been the playboy but he's stopped being discreet about them any more. It's all in my face now. He even brought one of his floosies home a few weeks ago.'

'Surely *not*?' I look at her, horrified. I didn't realise

Guy had it in him to be so callous. I don't know him that well; we've not had much contact with each other of course. 'Heck, I'm sorry, sis.'

'And you know what that's like.' She dabs at the edges of her eyes with the tissue. 'It happened to you.'

I draw in a breath. Not exactly, I think. Bill never brought his mistress home. But I can't say anything, as I watch her blow her nose, this isn't the time to start scoring points. We may always have been rivals as kids, but when push comes to shove any residual feelings of jealousy I may harbour towards her blow away like gossamer in the wind. I don't *want* Lily to be hurt like this.

'Oh, Lily, I'm so sorry. When did all this happen?'

'It's been happening for a while,' she shrugs, and I catch something in her eyes. I'm not sure what it is. 'The thing is, something like this makes you stop and think, doesn't it, Rachel? I thought I had it all – the beautiful home, the handsome husband – but now . . . I feel like a playing piece on a Snakes and Ladders board. All those good years of my life spent climbing the ladder only to slide down some slippery snake right to the bottom again.' Her eyes harden. 'I want to know how *you* cope. You have a husband who's left you, a severely dependent child who is dying, and most of the time you're as poor as a church mouse. And yet look at you – you're positively radiant. I want to know what keeps you going. What do you still hope for? I mean, god, if I were you I think I would have topped myself years ago.'

These are rhetorical questions but she seems to be expecting some answers. I hold out my hands to her, shaking my head.

What do I want? It is simple. I want Shelley to be well again. I want her to live. But failing that, I want my daughter to be happy and to enjoy every single moment that she has left. That's why I've been prepared to lie and cheat to bring her out here. But there is something else I want, I think now. I want to make my peace with her father. I don't want to be angry with Bill any more. I want to be able to let him go gracefully so I can move on and find someone else to love. For a fleeting moment, my thoughts return to Frank.

'I mean, what is it still reasonable for women of our age to ask for?' My sister seems to be looking right through me. 'Are we still young enough to be desirable? What do *we* have to offer?' She sits back, spent. 'I want you to tell me how you managed to get through it,' she says at last.

'Your situation is very different.' There are no children involved, for starters. And I wonder if she really feels the emotional pain that I did, or whether she is merely furious at having been usurped. 'The heartache will take a while to subside, sure. But on a practical level, if he's prepared to keep letting you use his credit cards for your expenses . . .'

'No,' she says firmly. 'I want my independence from him. I have to . . . find something I can do. I need to earn my own money.'

I cast my mind back. I can't remember Lily having worked one single day in her life.

'Well, it's a tough old world out there.' I watch her take a sip of her diet soda with its thin lemon slice on the top. That single glass of carbonated water probably cost more than the whole bottle of wine I bought earlier for us to drink tonight.

'Daddy taught us both discipline, remember? I can work hard when I have to, Rachel, don't forget that.'

She is right there. Once upon a time our dad had made us work our backsides off to become the regional under-fifteens dancing champions. Lily worked hard once, to attain the impossibly perfect goals that had been set for her by somebody else. But finding a job that will maintain her in the lifestyle to which she has become accustomed might not prove so easy now. We aren't spring chickens any more, she and I. Those dizzy heights we achieved were all long ago now; so long ago.

'And you obviously aren't doing too badly for yourself.' She leans over and fingers the embroidered collar of my blouse admiringly. 'Are you working, currently?'

'I've got a couple of things on the go.' Well, that is half-true at least. I have Annie-Jo's work coming in this week. And I have Sol's work . . . well, it's been offered, even if I can't do it. Things are starting to open up for me at last. But it's taken a long time. My life has been anything but easy since Bill and I parted ways. I want to tell her that, but her eyes are elsewhere, thinking her own thoughts.

'But the truth is, I work when I can. Shelley's care takes up a lot of my time. I don't earn much.'

She nods appraisingly. 'I'm thinking of going into interior decorating. You know it's always been a passion of mine.'

I think of her house in Kensington and of the mansion of almost palatial proportions which she and Guy had restored in Edinburgh.

265

'I think you'd be very good at it.' I sip my tea. I imagine that people might have to be qualified in such things if they want to charge money for it. But what do I know? Maybe she'd blag it.

The tea tastes minty and fresh on my tongue. This meeting is turning out better than I'd hoped. Lily seems mellower, more vulnerable. Okay, she's managed to mention the failure of my marriage twice . . . but the good thing is that I don't feel stung by it, as I would have done in the past. Maybe I'm finally getting over it. Maybe this is just the effect on me of meeting Frank Dwight this morning.

My mind keeps rerunning the way he looked at me when he first came into the shop. I keep remembering the things we said to one another; the way my whole body jumped when we accidentally bumped shoulders as we walked along. This is crazy. It is some kind of teenage infatuation, I know that. But I don't even have his phone number so I can talk to him again. He never asked for mine.

'Everything all right?' My sister has been sitting observing me coolly with her hands neatly on her lap. She still has our mother's beautiful cheekbones and her high forehead; she also has Pandora's ability to home in on any lapse of attention, any area of weakness in her adversary.

'Sure.' I give her what I hope will pass for a reassuring smile.

'You look a bit distracted, that's all. I know it must have come as a shock to you, hearing about my marriage break-up. Don't worry, hon. I'll be okay.'

I look at her blankly. 'What?'

'Just don't say anything to anyone. I haven't told Mum about my separation yet. Okay?'

'Sure. Whatever you say.' I'm getting the beginnings of the headache that I always get whenever I spend time with either Lily or Pandora. They are both charmers extraordinaire. They each have the capacity to make whoever they are with feel special, even for just a few golden moments. But I know from long experience that neither of them has ever got the picture that the world doesn't revolve around them, and only them.

'If you mention it she'll only worry herself sick over me,' Lily continues. *Will she?* I wonder now. *Did she worry herself sick over me when my marriage failed?* 'And she was so excited when Bernie asked her to emigrate with him. He dotes on her, you know. He relies on her for everything. It must be so nice to feel – well, so *needed*, don't you think?'

You haven't got the foggiest. I clear my throat.

'Shelley didn't happen to mention, when you spoke to her, what time the kids were thinking of getting back?' She is in my head all the time. She's there automatically, even now. If we're out of contact for too long I feel uncomfortable.

'She didn't mention it,' Lily says. 'I caught them having lunch on the beach.' My sister sits back, crosses one elegant leg over the other. Someone has just walked into the hotel lobby now who's obviously grabbed her interest because suddenly her eyes are riveted elsewhere. I borrow Lily's phone (because Shelley has mine, the only working one we have between us) and Lily starts to reapply her lipstick.

Shelley doesn't pick up. I just get the 'your call has

been forwarded' message. I bat away the anxiety that threatens to rear its head. I'm not really worried. She is with Ellen and Jazzy, after all.

'She's fine,' I tell Lily at last. 'Well, no news is good news, right?'

'I don't know how you cope.' My sister's eyes move reluctantly back to me. 'It must be horrendous.'

'Not if you love someone . . .'

'No, even if you do. Look, honey, there's something you and I need to have a little talk about.' She leans in closer to me, even though there is no one near us. 'So even though I would have loved to have seen my niece, I'm rather glad you came alone today. Grown-up stuff, you know.'

'I'm all ears.' Okay, this is it now. Truth time. My past coming home to roost and all that.

'It's about that old tumbledown cottage Grandpa Seb used to live in. The one near the beach, remember?'

'Of course I remember.' I breathe out a quiet sigh of relief. 'We used to spend a few days of every summer down there.'

'As few as Pandora could get away with,' Lily laughs. 'It was so . . . unhygienic.'

'And now Mum has left it to you and me?' So, this is what our important meeting is all about, the property. For some reason it must mean a lot to her. I know Lily would never have called me otherwise.

'The thing is,' Lily is saying, 'I've been over to see it and it's . . . well, it's in pretty poor condition, I don't mind telling you. It will need major work doing to it before it can turn a profit, whether it be for rental or for sale. It's not going to come cheap.'

'I can barely afford to fix the leaks in my own roof, Lily. I haven't any spare cash to splash out on projects like renovation, particularly for a second house.' The chance would be a fine thing!

'That's just my point. We'll get a pittance for it if we sell it as it stands.' I watch her drum her immaculately manicured fingernails on the edge of her frosted drinking glass. How does she keep them looking so good all the time? An unkind voice whispers 'Because she never does anything with them.'

'I'm sorry, Lily. I'll have to take whatever I can. I wasn't expecting much.'

'How much?' she queries. 'Exactly how much are you expecting?'

I shrug. How should I know? I'm no expert on property prices in Cornwall.

'We'll have to get it looked over,' I say slowly. 'Get in some quotes.'

'I've taken the liberty of doing that.' She picks up her handbag. 'Where's my notepad?' She takes out a little electronic gadget that looks like an appointments diary. 'It's not worth much, though.' She frowns, punching in digits. 'Thing is, I could maybe buy you out on this, Rachel. It would give me something to get my teeth into. I need this to help me get over my divorce. What do you think?'

'I . . . don't know what to say, Lily. It sounds like a great idea. Can you afford it?'

Lily beams. 'I have some assets of my own, Rachel. A little nest egg I could use to get me through this. How does ten thousand sound to you?' She finishes punching her digits into the computer. How does it sound? It sounds like a lot of money. I remember our granddad's place as little more than a dive.

'Are you sure that's going to be fair on you, though?'

'Don't you worry about me. I'll make every penny back once I've renovated and sold it on, I'm sure of it. And,' she lays her hand gently on my arm, 'I know you've had a rough time since Bill left you. I'd like to do something to help your little family out, too, you know. Oh, I've missed you!' She changes tack in an instant. 'I've missed you all so much!' My sister leans over and hugs me again and I can feel the frailness of her bones beneath her elegant clothing. A rush of protective pity overwhelms me. My poor sister. She has always needed someone to watch out for her. How could Guy have done that to her? I watch her wipe a solitary tear away.

'Thank you so much for agreeing to this, Rachel. You don't know how much this means to me. I've never had . . .' she pulls a face here, 'I've never had children to dote on or to worry about, as you have. I've never had something that I could put all my heart and soul into – not since the dancing, anyway. I've missed out there. I know that was my choice. But maybe doing this will bring me the opportunity I need to bring some *meaning* back into my life. I've got you to thank for that.'

'Gosh, well, I wouldn't go over the top on that score, Lily. I'm sure it will give you a project to get you going, but . . .'

'No,' she shakes her head determinedly. 'It's important. I'm just glad you could see that.'

'I'm just glad you're willing to take over the paper-work,' I retort. But I can't deny that it makes me feel warm inside when my sister appreciates me like this. It gives me hope that everything can still be all right between us, even if we hardly ever see each other any more. I want it to be. Lily isn't so bad, she's just vain and foolish and a bit spoiled, really. We could still be good friends if we made it happen.

'I think this calls for more than an ordinary lunch.' Lily stands up. 'My treat. They don't do anything too great in here, despite the chef's rosettes. How d'you fancy Don Giovanni's? I'll order some champagne, too. To seal the deal.'

'What deal?'

'You agree to take the ten thousand, I take over the property, yes?'

'Well, sure, but . . .' I tuck my tatty handbag under my arm out of sight as we get up to go. 'Maybe we should celebrate . . . I don't know, us getting together again? You know, we could agree not to leave it so long next time, don't you think?'

She gives me a long look now, as if weighing me up somehow. Then she tucks her arm into mine.

'Of course that isn't going to happen, Rachel. We're both single women now, aren't we? And we single girls have got to stick together. We don't *need* any men, do we?' She says this with a brightness that is belied by the way her eyes swivel round to check out every likely-looking male who enters the hotel lobby. Maybe she doesn't need a man but she still wants one, clearly.

And maybe I do, too; more than I know?

By the time I get back to Maggie's late that afternoon there's a hand-delivered letter in a pale cream envelope waiting for me. It's from Frank.

Dear Rachel,
I don't know quite how to say this because I'm feeling a bit embarrassed, but I think I owe you an apology. I'm sorry for the way I left you this morning. I didn't mean to rush off and leave you like that. I'm not even sure why I did. I still enjoyed our walk together and hope we can be friends, after a fashion.
I'd be very happy if you would agree to meet me for lunch tomorrow (Wednesday)?
Yours,
Frank Dwight

Oh Frank, what are you doing to me?

Why are you doing this? Do you like me or don't you, are you 'available' or aren't you? I want to screw up the piece of paper and chuck it away right down into the bottom of the bin so I won't ever contact him again.

But I don't.

30

Rachel

Wednesday morning
Shelley is picking little bits of sugary plastic off her stick
of pink and white rock. She's been concentrating on this
task ever since we entered the Lost Gardens of Heligan
about half an hour ago. Why don't you just look up and
enjoy the beautiful scenery all around you? I want to say.
Or just *tell* me what you're aching to say to me so the
two of us can get on with the rest of our day?

'Okay.' I pull Bessie over and push gently on the brake.
'What is it that we both need to talk about?' The wooden
bench by the alcove where we've paused is vacant so I
take a pew beside her.

'Nuthin'.' Shelley shoots me a sullen glance. 'I've
nothing to talk about so why've we stopped?'

'We can always go back to Maggie's,' I say. 'If you'd
prefer?'

'Go home?' She glances at her watch. 'Whatever for?
You've just paid all that money to come in here, haven't
you?'

'It's just that you don't seem to be having a very good
time.'

273

'They're *plants*, Mum.' She motions all around us. Huge rhododendrons loom out at us beckoning us on into shadier pathways, dappled by sunlight, pink and lilac and deepest of mauve. Looking at plants isn't the way teenagers have a good time, she implies. 'Look, it's cool, okay? It's nice here. Even if everybody else around me is about one hundred years old. And I've got nothing to do till the twins come to pick me up later so we might as well . . .'

'You just don't seem to be very happy,' I put in. 'You wanted to come out here, didn't you? To Cornwall. You wanted us to spend some time together?'

'Yep.' She takes a bite out of her stick of rock candy and then covers up the rest in its cellophane wrapping and puts it away in her bag.

'You just seem . . . very *angry*, Shelley. Is it something I've done?'

She shakes her head.

'Something I haven't done?'

The thought that she's rumbled me crosses my mind ominously. Could she be aware that Bill isn't in on our little trip, and that he never agreed to it? After all, I never did get to find out what the hell Stella was referring to the night before we left when she said she knew 'all about my plan'.

Shelley lifts up her shoulders and then drops them heavily. She won't look at me. She won't even look vaguely in my direction.

'Okay, look, I'm just . . .' She scrapes her curly blonde hair away from her eyes and stares out over the vista of flowerbeds before us. 'I've just got some stuff on my mind, okay?'

'Care to share it?' I lean forward and look down at my hands. They are looking older than I remember. Even after five years the thin band of pale skin where my wedding ring used to be hasn't blended in yet. I put my hands up to catch the sunlight, perplexed.

I don't understand it. I am still somehow tied to him, and I don't want to be.

'I suppose I'd better,' she says ungraciously. 'But I warn you, you are not going to like it.'

'Just tell me first, is it medical?' I say this a little sharper than I intend, because that is my one all-consuming fear, of course. That she will start to get worse, just as everyone tells me she inevitably must.

There's a long pause and then she shakes her head, almost imperceptibly.

'Look, I need to . . . I need to be honest with you, Mum. I've got something to tell you, which I think you will understand but I'm not quite sure how you're going to take it. There's something I'm going to need your help with.'

Whatever is she on about?

'That's what mums are here for,' I tell her.

'Maybe,' she says cautiously. 'But this one might not be so easy.' She pauses. 'Did you know that Miriam asked her mum, not once, but twice, before she died, to switch her machines off?'

'Did she?' I take in a breath. I didn't know that.

'But her mum would never do it for her.'

'No, I can imagine that.'

'Would you?' she asks me starkly.

'No.' I say it too easily. It isn't what she wants to hear and I see her eyes widen in horror.

'What, even if I asked you?'

'It isn't going to come to that. You might be different. You're always telling me that it isn't going to come to that, not for you. You've got to keep thinking positive.'

'Thinking positive? Is that what you think I'm doing?' Her voice sounds strangled in her throat.

'Well, aren't you?' I look at her helplessly. 'If you don't tell me what you're feeling I can only go by what I see. You seemed so keen to come down here, Shell, so I . . . I moved heaven and earth to make it happen for you. But now we're here I don't feel you really want to be with me.'

'Come *on*,' she flares, 'don't tell me *you're* not dying to go off to your lunch date with that bloke Frank Dwight later on?'

'Is that what this is about then?' I fold my arms and lean back against the bench. The ferocity of her response has taken me aback a bit, I'll admit. 'Are you angry because I'm meeting up with Frank?'

'No.' A fat droning bee passes by, a little too close to her head for comfort and she dodges it.

'What then?'

'Oh, I don't know.'

'You shouldn't be, you know; you shouldn't begrudge me that. You never minded Dad marrying Stella, did you?'

'Oh, for heaven's sake!' she says. 'I don't give a toss about bloody Frank Dwight. I don't give a toss about Dad and bloody Stella either. If you two ballsed up your chances of having a good marriage together then that's just too bad, isn't it?'

'So you're angry about me and Dad splitting up?' I frown. That was over five years ago. Is she really still hanging on to that? One look at her face and I know that all this vitriolic spitting is about something else altogether. She's *scared*, that's what.

'I'm more worried about myself at the moment, to tell you the truth. I'm worried about how much support I'm going to have from the people around me at the end.'

'Shelley, you know I've always supported you. That isn't going to change.'

'You've supported me to *live*,' she corrects, and when her eyes lock on mine now they are remarkably cool and collected. 'I need to know you'll still be there when it's clear there isn't any mileage left in living. I want to know if you'll be prepared to let me go the best way possible for *me*; if you'll be there to help support me die.'

'Shelley, that is a *terrible* thing to say.' Even as the words leave my mouth I know that she's right, though. I've run and I've run but it's taken Shelley to bring it up – the one thing I didn't ever want to have to look at. But we have to. She's brought it up and the time is now. 'If things ever get to that stage . . .' I begin slowly, but she doesn't let me finish.

'We can't let things get to that stage, though, don't you see? It will be too late by then. If I get really bad I may not be able to tell you what I want you to do. We have to sort it out beforehand.'

'Okay,' I say through gritted teeth, 'we'll talk about it. I promise you. As soon as we get back home.'

'Don't look at me like that, please, Mum.' Her face is

distraught. 'We have to talk about this. We have to at least *start* talking about this. I need to, even if it's painful for you.'

'I'm sorry,' I say, 'I'm . . . god, I'm just . . . so sorry.'

'It's something you don't want to face, right? But you have to, just like you did when Dad left you.'

'I just think that focusing on the negative outcome might bring it on a little quicker,' I argue with her. 'You might have years of good life in you yet.'

'That's why Doctor Lavelle is ringing me every other day, is it?' She looks at me sharply.

'He's rung you too?' The guilt tightens in my throat.

'Loads of times. He's *desperate* for me to go in, isn't he?'

'We can't make assumptions about what he wants to see you for, though, honey.'

'Look, you haven't forgotten what happened to . . .' She looks up as a young couple walk by, glancing at us curiously, sensing the urgency in our voices. My own voice dips down a pitch or two.

'To Miriam, no, I haven't forgotten, and neither have you, clearly. But we can't just assume . . .'

'Oh I think we jolly well can.' She takes my mobile out of her bag to check for texts. Nothing from the twins yet, obviously, because she puts it away.

'You're depressed, Shelley,' my voice cracks. I'm stating the obvious. It doesn't help. If only she had a reason to want to live. If only she could see a *purpose* to her life, other than just waiting for the end of it to come.

She sighs quietly. So quietly that she fills me with more despair than if she had only had the energy left to still

278

be angry – with me, with life, anything at all. I can hear the lazy humming of the fat bee right overhead. The bush behind us is scented heavily, laden with a creamy burst of May flowers. I get a flash of my daughter as a toddler many years ago, her sticky fists full of these sweet-scented petals as she brought them to me to 'make her a birthday cake'. What wouldn't I give to be back in the days when it took so little to make her face light up with a smile like that? She watches me crumble one of the flowers in my hand and the sweet heavy scent of it releases our memories.

'Make me a cake?' she says. 'A *today* cake.' Don't wait for birthdays that may never come, she means. Just let's take today.

So I stand up and I find the strength somehow in my arms to push her back onto the main path again. The light catches the honey colour of her hair as we walk and I marvel at how beautiful my daughter is. She is, too. She is beautiful and she is grumpy. She is too young and she is too old. She is forever mine and yet I know that she will be mine for, oh, such a very, very short time.

I've got to concentrate on this moment, build up new memories, and it is bittersweet because my heart is bleeding still. Who was I fooling when I thought that the prospect of meeting Frank Dwight for lunch would cheer me up? He is nothing to me, nor I to him; only a momentary distraction to take away the pain she's just reminded me of, the discord that beats always inside my heart.

'Are you sure that you . . . you want to go out with the twins this afternoon?' The sun has dipped behind a cloud again. It's in and out, bright and then dark, making me run hot and cold with it. 'We could always do something together, I mean, just you and me.'

'We're doing something together now, Mum,' she points out. She wants to go out with the twins, obviously. That's good. It means that there is *something* she wants, even if it isn't me.

I shrug. 'If you're sure?'

'I didn't mean what I said earlier on.' She twists round in Bessie to look at me now. 'About you going for lunch with Frank. I *want* you to go, you know.'

'Thanks.' It doesn't matter any more, my heart's just not in it the way it was before. I won't tell her, though. There's just too much for me to think about now. I need some space to think.

There is *no way* I will be able to support her in the way she wants, if it comes to it in the end; I've fought too long and hard to keep her alive all these years. But, just for now, I can feel the sun on my face and my skin is warm. The air is full of birdsong and the gushing of sweet water over pebbles somewhere just beyond my view.

'Cheer up, Mum.' Shelley pulls a face at me from her chair. She doesn't add, 'It may never happen.'

That's because we both know it will.

31

Rachel

Wednesday afternoon
Maggie's garden is damp and dark this afternoon. Once you walk past the dahlia beds – she supplies local businesses and restaurants, she grows so many – you come to a choice of paths. One way leads to her herb garden, the other to the rose knot, and the third path I have yet to explore.

I won't today, though. It might have been warm earlier but now it's gotten too dull, a stiff breeze is threatening rain and I'll get wet. I remember the sheltered arbour tucked away inside the old stone wall that boundaries her herb garden so I make for that path instead. It's narrow, too narrow for a wheelchair so it's not a place I can come when Shelley's with me. The twins came for her about half an hour ago and they all went off laughing, wearing nothing but shorts and T-shirts because they're young and they don't feel the cold.

I don't regret cancelling Frank this lunchtime. I had to leave a message on his machine, though, and I hate it when I have to do that. You never know if the person's going to get it or not, do you? He could be sitting in that restaurant right now. Maybe he's looking towards the door every time it opens, waiting for me to come in?

Not that I imagine it will exactly break his heart when I don't.

Maggie raised an eyebrow when I went through the kitchen, but she didn't utter a word. She just carried on labelling her jam. I don't even want to imagine what she's thinking. I'd have been bad company for him today, anyway. I just need to hide away in a hole and lick my wounds. The shelter set into the stone wall and tucked away at the back of Maggie's garden is perfect. From here I can watch the lavender flower heads bending over unwillingly as the first drops of rain come spinning out of the sky. I can smell the sweet herby scent of water hitting earth; the lemon thyme and the oregano and the bright bushy-leaved clumps of basil. The downpour is relentless. In one instant everything is soaked, except me, safe in my shelter. *We've got to talk about this*, my daughter says to me; *we've got to at least start talking*.

But how can I start talking about *that*? How can I even begin to? I am like a warrior prepared for battle. My aim is to fight and survive. I can't even countenance the thought that this is one battle I can't win; that *she* can't win.

If Bill were here maybe he'd be able to talk her out of such nonsense thoughts. Girls always listen to their dads, don't they? They never listen in the same way to their mums. I know I never did. Pandora never made any sense to me; I always listened to my dad, though.

The rain is dripping right off the edge of my little arbour now. It's coming down so hard it's forming a curtain of water, trapping me in here. The water is so loud. I can hear it even when I pull my arms around my knees and put my head down so I can't see it any more.

I don't want to see it. I don't want to hear it. I wish everything would just go away and leave me alone, but my own thoughts betray me. They won't leave me alone. What happened this morning, it just keeps going round and round in my head. Shelley's trying to find a way to say goodbye to me. That's what this is all about, I know it deep in the heart of me. She's trying to find a way to make it okay, to find some safe way to let go of me, and *I can't do it*. Oh god, I can't. Not yet. It's too soon. It's too hard. How can I let go of her when I have built the whole of my world up around her?

If I let my daughter go then what do I have left?

It comes to everyone, I think; this time when children leave. It comes to everyone, not just to me. In my case it will be more final and more absolute, that is all. When Shelley leaves me she won't be coming back. I remember very well the day I first stepped out beyond the shadow of my own mother. I remember how scary that was. I remember all that it unleashed.

My head is starting to throb now; a deep, slow pain that runs along my temples feeling like a toothache in my whole face. The pain distracts me, at least. It slows down my thoughts. I'll find a way through this. There's got to be a way through. Think, Rachel, *think*. There's a solution for everything if only you look long enough and hard enough. There's got to be. Even when the solution is something you don't really want to look at. The answers are there. The answers are always there.

I tell myself this, like I always do; but when I think back now, *were* they?

No answer through the letterbox today. No letter from Gordon's parents accepting me as his new partner, and it's been two weeks already. How can it be taking so long? He told me that they liked me the best. He whispered it into my ear last time he saw me. He swore that they were writing to my parents to offer me the position as his dance partner.

Oh, what could be happening? My mother says nothing. Her face remains closed. I haven't heard anything, she snaps at me when I ask her. She looks like a cat who's just had its tail trodden on. Dad just shrugs his shoulders when I ask him. If they want you they'll write us, Rachel, that's the deal and I'll not be haranguing them so don't ask me.

Legrange's has been closed for two weeks due to the refitting of the new stages and the midterm break. I haven't seen Gordon in all that time. It's unbearable. Every day I wait for a letter and nothing comes. Why does nothing come? Why do I have to wait for such a long time and still nothing happens? What if . . . what if they have sent the letter and somebody's sitting on it? What if Pandora has secreted it away in that box of hers so that none of us know anything about it? Oh, it would suit her purpose very well to do that, if I think about it. If I'm offered the placement with Gordon then Lily has no one to dance with, and that is the very last thing my mother would want. I am the perfect foil for my sister; I help her to win the medals, that's what I've been told.

Well, I've had enough of it.

I'm checking out Pandora's secret box while she and Lily

are out having their hair done. If that letter is what I think it is then I'll present it to Dad when he gets in, and by the time Mum realises what I've done it will be too late for her to change anything.

My parents' room is dark when I go upstairs. The floor-boards in the top hallway let out a loud creak and give me a guilty fright, even though I'm the only one in the house. Nobody can hear me. Nobody knows I'm doing this. I don't have to worry.

But I leave the light off in my parents' bedroom just the same. I leave the curtains closed to, just as she left them, just in case anyone comes back home unexpectedly and wonders why I'm here. So I have to fumble around in the dark. The room is heavy with the scent of L'Air du Temps; the lingering note of her sticky hairspray clings to the clothes in Pandora's wardrobe. But she isn't there, I remind myself. She's out. And I have to look at that secret letter while she's out and be done before anybody comes back in and discovers me.

I shouldn't be prying in here, I know. The wardrobe is full of shoes and Pandora's tummy-tucking-in things and hair-curling machines. Her clothes hang majestically in the dry-cleaner's cellophane wrapping, untouched by dust, unruffled by anyone's hands, aloof, pristine; like her. These are her things. The secret inside that letter is her secret.

What if it's nothing to do with me? I feel a momentary flash of panic in the pit of my stomach, but I find the letter almost immediately. It is sitting right on the top, unguarded, unprotected, because of course she doesn't expect me to come in here poking and prying among her private things. I know it's the one because it has a strangely shaped envelope and the stamp has been stuck up in the very right-hand corner. I pick it up. The light is so dim I need to bring it close against my face to see who it's been addressed to.

My heart jumps with a little shock when I see the name. I was right.

It's addressed to Dad. To my dad. Not to her. And she hasn't shown it to him, has she? She's secreted it away in here so that he will never see it and never know anything about it till it's too late.

My fingers are trembling as I pull the thin sheet out. It's only one sheet and the message is brief. I can barely see it to read it, I'm feeling so strange. But when I do, I find I have to read it all over again and then again once more, disbelieving my own eyes. Can this really be what I think it is? I sink to my knees then, almost falling inside her wardrobe with the weight of what I've just learned. There's always an answer. But this letter only answers a question that I hadn't even begun to ask. It tells me more, oh, far more, than I ever wanted to know.

Oh god, to be able to turn back the clock and go back beyond that bedroom door and never, ever come in here and see what I've just seen! An answer; there must be an answer to this mess, I think. But where to look? And who to turn to, especially now that I know I cannot even turn to my dad. I have to do something. But what?

I have to do something. Yes, that's what I'm feeling now, too. I have to face up to something that's just too ugly to bear. The rain has subsided a little bit, though. I can hear it quietening down, just the pitter-patter-pitter as it drops off the large leaves of the fig tree. And the splash of someone's footsteps hastening down the path. Towards me.

'Hey.'

I look up abruptly. Who the hell is it now?

'*Frank?*'

By the look on his face he's as astonished to see me here as I am him.

'You okay?' His overcoat is completely drenched. So are the bottoms of his jeans. He's clutching a wet brown paper bag. He sees my eyes go to it and he waves it at me. 'Lunch,' he says. 'Want some?'

'What are *you* doing here?' I can't take my eyes off him. He looks different today somehow, but I can't place why. 'Did Maggie tell you I was out here?'

'She's out.' He shakes his head. 'The place was empty when I got in. Look, I'm sorry; I didn't mean to disturb you. It's an incredible coincidence but it seems that we've both chosen the same spot to come out to for a bit of peace and quiet.'

'Look, I'm sorry about our appointment,' I start guiltily. 'I did leave a message. On your phone.'

'Yeah. I got your message.' Actually, it was a very brief message I'd left. I never said why I'd changed my mind. I hadn't offered him any sort of explanation. I was a bit rude, really.

He offers me one of his sandwiches, which is tuna mayonnaise.

'I *hate* tuna,' I tell him. Hell, I'm beginning to sound like Shelley on a bad day. 'I'm sorry, I . . . what I meant to say was, no thanks.'

'You sounded a bit upset in your message.' He dismisses

287

my rudeness. 'Look, I, um . . .' Frank lets out a breath, 'I came here for a bit of quiet space. I'm guessing you did, too. I didn't realise anyone else knew about it,' he grins sheepishly, 'tucked away like it is. Most of Maggie's guests never venture down this far.'

But *you* know it, I think. And it seems you let yourself into Maggie's house when she wasn't here, too?

'I've been here before,' I say.

'So I see. What I'm saying is, if you'd like me to leave . . .'

'No, please don't. The rain's starting again. You'll get very wet if you go now.'

'I don't mind getting wet, Rachel.' I love his voice, I realise suddenly. I want him to stay around me because his voice makes me feel good. Something about the way he talks to me is intimate and bright and just interested. It reminds me that there are still people out there who might be interested in me and what I have to say and how I feel about things. He reminds me that I still matter as a person in my own right; that I'm still here.'You're welcome to stay, though. I'd *like* you to stay. If you want to, that is?' I snatch the proffered sandwich from his hand in a bid to keep him there. 'Frank, I owe you an apology. About today . . .'

'It's no big deal.'

No it isn't, I know it isn't. Not to him, anyway. I wish . . . I wish it *were*, though. I glance at him through my fringe, taking a bite of his sandwich because I don't know what else to do.

'Well, but I should have given you some sort of . . .' I wave the sandwich at him. 'Actually, this isn't so bad, this sandwich, what is it again?'

'Tuna mayonnaise,' he says without blinking.

'Tuna,' I say slowly. 'Well, anyway, I'm glad you're here, Frank.' Even though Maggie has already briefed me that you're not 'available', I remember suddenly. And what does it matter, since I'm not available either? I can never be available, not as long as Shelley still needs me.

'I'm glad you're here too.' He smiles suddenly and I catch a glimpse of the shy but oh-so-sweet stranger I saw yesterday. He sits down gingerly beside me, on the bench. 'So, are you having a good time in Cornwall, you and Shelley?'

'I'm not exactly sure,' I confess. 'I mean, I think I would be if we didn't have so much on our minds. It's kind of . . . difficult, for her, at the moment.'

'She's at that age,' he says sympathetically, though we both know that isn't what I'm talking about. 'Mags told me you were thinking about visiting Tintagel sometime this week?'

'Did she?'

So you and Mags have been talking about us, then? I think.

I shrug. 'We *were* going, but did Mags also tell you that her son-in-law is looking at my rickety old car at the moment?'

He shakes his head. 'You've got a problem with it? Look, I could always take you and Shelley down there myself if you like?'

'You *would*?' I feel my spirits lifting immeasurably as he says that. 'You really would?'

'If you'd like me to? Not tomorrow, I'm accounted for. But I'm free Friday if you've no other plans.'

'Friday is good.' I'm trying unbelievably hard to sound nonchalant, but inside my heart is singing. Why does he do this to me? How? My head doesn't understand it but my heart races on regardless.

'Look, if it's any help . . .' He leans in closer to me all of a sudden, across the green bench, 'I know exactly what you're going through, sweetheart.'

'You do?'

He uses 'sweetheart' as a form of general endearment, I know that. He'd use it to address a shop assistant or a child at a zebra crossing, I know – I know that, so why can't I stop my pulse from racing every time he uses it to address me?

'You know what I'm going through?'

'Not exactly,' he admits, 'but I do know a little. Maggie told me some more about your daughter's illness.'

'She did?'

'I asked her,' he confesses. 'After you and I spoke the other day. Rachel, I know it's not easy what you're going through right now. But you have to believe', he puts his hand on my shoulder, 'that you're doing whatever you can. Sometimes we just come to the end of what we can do. That's all. Maybe you can't do any more. Maybe that's the real battle you're facing right now?'

'How could you know that?' I blurt out. It's true, though, god, it's true. Can he see right through my heart and into my very soul? And, despite myself, I'm more aware of his hand on my shoulder than I am of anything else, every fibre of my being is focused just on the one spot, the place where he's touching my shoulder.

'Frank, how could you know what it's like for me?' I

290

can see in his eyes that he does know, though. His comments aren't merely the kind platitudes of a well-meaning stranger. *He knows.* I suddenly catch on. The sadness in his eyes when he looked at that family on the beach . . . 'Unless you've been in a similar situation yourself?'

'Something like it.'

'You have a daughter?' I breathe.

'No.' He shakes his head firmly. And we both look towards the bright water as it splashes on the red-brown tiles outside our shelter. Outside, the clouds are fragmenting. It's raining and the sun is coming through. I know my daughter will be looking for rainbows; it's what she always does. I remember how she used to cry and cry because I 'wouldn't take her to the place where the rainbows end, to the place where colours melt into the land' so she could see it for herself. I remember her promising me that when she was big enough that mean old mum couldn't stop her, she would go and find that place for herself!

'Shelley always wanted to be somewhere else,' I tell him softly now. 'She was the kind of kid who always had to know what was just behind and beyond wherever she happened to be at the time.' Frank gives a little laugh and his shoulders brush against mine as he draws nearer, seeking a drier spot on the bench. I want to question Frank more but there's a sudden wildness in his eyes and it warns me away, even as he looks up from studying the ground to lock his eyes on mine.

'We aren't in the same boat then, are we, Frank?'

'No, we aren't.' Frank puts his hand to his side now.

291

'But I know what's coming up for you, Rachel. I can see it as clearly as you see the sun coming right through those clouds out there. You haven't lost her yet but you have lost something, haven't you?'

'Lost something?' I give a little laugh, covering my face with my hands. Oh, yes. My marriage; the hopes I once had for a career; my self-esteem. But not *her*. I haven't lost her. Not yet.

I take in a long breath. 'I'm not defeated, Frank. I don't believe in giving up so easily. I'll fight to the bitter end to keep her alive.'

'I admire that in you, Rachel. You've got guts, I'll give you that. I'm just saying that sometimes . . .' his voice trails off, then picks up again, 'there comes a point when there is nothing left to fight. You keep on fighting but you find you're sparring with nothing but shadows. Sometimes you've just got to accept that whatever it is that was once there, it's now gone. That's all I'm saying.'

'*She's* not gone, though, is she? My daughter is still here. The way you talk, it's almost as if she were already gone and that's horrible. If you want to know what's really upset me this morning it's been my daughter's request that I . . . that I . . . oh, I don't even know how to say it, it's too horrible.'

Frank doesn't say a word. He's still leaning in towards me, listening.

'Yes?' He cocks his head to one side at last.

'She wanted to know if – assuming the worst comes to the worst – if I'd be prepared to have her life support machines switched off.'

292

'Rather than have her live on indefinitely in a vege-tative state?' I crinkle up the bag that held our sandwiches and look for a pocket to put it into. This is silly. Just silly talk. I don't have to listen to . . .

'I wouldn't put it quite like that.'

'How would you put it?'

'What do you mean?'

'I'm assuming that by the "worst has come to the worst" that's what you really mean, isn't it? That's what Shelley was referring to, in her worst scenario, yes?'

'I don't know, Frank. I haven't really thought about it. What parent would?'

'A parent that is forced to?' he offers. Something in his voice changes, then, and I stare at him stupidly.

'It happened to *you*, didn't it?'

Frank stares at the ground, his lips tight shut now. He's no longer thinking about me, but staring out over the flattened lavender beds. The water droplets, bright as gold on the narrow leaves, shine back at us.

'It's funny how people like you and I get pulled together in the world like two magnets, isn't it, Rachel?' When he looks at me now his eyes are shining softly but something inside them is twisted by private pain. 'When I first caught sight of you coming down that hill the other day, something inside of me, I swear, it *jumped*. I knew it when I saw you walking with your daughter inside the mall. I knew it when we first spoke, inside Maggie's shop.'

'What did you know?' I pull up a little closer to him on the bench. He's speaking so quietly I can barely hear him otherwise.

293

'I knew that we were two of a kind.' His hand closes briefly on mine. 'And who knows, maybe another time, in another place, we could have been more than just friends . . . ?' He drifts off.

I swallow, dumbfounded.

He smiles sadly. 'But it's . . . it's complicated, isn't it?'

In a daze, I watch him get up. 'Why *complicated*?' I voice helplessly.

Because he's already in a relationship, the answer comes back instantly. I see it in his eyes.

'I'm free,' I add boldly. 'Shelley's father and I are divorced.'

'I know.' I feel his hand squeeze mine now, almost imperceptibly. 'But there are many ways of not being free, aren't there, Rachel? And you're not, are you? If you're honest. And if I'm honest,' he leans in for an instant and I feel his goodbye, the gentle brush of his lips on my forehead, 'neither am I.'

32

Shelley

Wednesday afternoon

I wish I'd listened to Mum and brought a cardi out with me. Even though it doesn't make you look at all cool. But I'm bloody freezing. It won't stop raining. And this bus stop doesn't even have a shelter.

'We could have run all the way from the bowling centre,' Ellen looks at me regretfully, 'if only you could run.'

But if I could run at all, then I wouldn't be stuck on Bessie. And then I wouldn't have had to leave the bowling centre early, due to it being so crowded, would I? Ellen is sweet, though. She doesn't complain at all, even though she doesn't have to stay and go through all this with me. Her house isn't so very far from here, after all.

'Thing is, Mum's got her WI ladies in this afternoon,' she tells me now. 'We don't really want to go back there and get stuck with *them*, do we?'

We don't, but it's so wet and so cold. And the bus doesn't come, even though we wait for what feels like forever.

And then, just when we're about to give up and go to

Ellen's to join her mum and all the ladies having coffee, a miracle happens in the shape of Aunt Lily sailing by in a taxi. I feel so totally grateful when I see her. She makes the taxi stop and reverse all the way back to us, her eyes nearly popping out of her head when she discovers how drenched we are.

'What on earth is your mum *thinking* of, Shelley?' she says as soon as we squelch in, as if the weather was Mum's fault. 'You shouldn't be left out in the rain like that.'

'It's all right, Aunt Lily. I won't shrink.'

Ellen giggles hysterically and I kind of wish she wouldn't.

'Why didn't your mum pick you up?' Lily turns to look at us from the safety of her dry seat at the front. She's all in white today, in a ruffled skirt and cowboy boots. Her hair is tied up with a marcasite butterfly and she looks, I have to admit, really stunning. She's got the prettiest of eyes, Aunt Lily has. Mum says they are the same as mine. I wonder if I could ever have looked as good as she does? I suppose I'll never know.

Maybe Kieran would say so, though. I know he sees something in me that nobody else ever has.

God, this is hard.

Stop thinking about Kieran, stop thinking about him!

'Where is Rachel this afternoon? I'm hoping to catch her at home, actually. I've got some papers I need her to sign.'

What's she on about? Adults always think you're going to know what they're talking about; they always assume that somehow you should *care*. 'Mum'll be out with Frank just now, Aunt Lily.'

'With who, darling? Who's *Frank*?' My aunt turns her immaculately made-up aqua-green eyes on me. 'I didn't know your mum had any male friends down here.'

Sheesh. Why does she assume Mum's out with a 'male friend'? Frank could be the guy who's looking at our car for us, for all Lily knows.

'Just someone Maggie introduced her to,' I shrug.

'Good-looking?' She smiles a wide smile and flutters her eyelashes at us and Ellen giggles helplessly again. She's mesmerised; trapped like a butterfly under glass, I can see that. Lily kind of has that effect on people. Mum has always said her sister could charm the birds out of the trees.

'Not really.'

'Oh, Shelley, how can you say that?' Ellen pipes up now, hugging her knees with her arms shyly. 'Frank is, you know. *Very* handsome. And I've seen pictures of him when he was our age. Oh, Shelley, you would have just *died*.'

'I don't think so.' I haven't said anything to Ellen about Kieran yet. I'm trying my hardest not to think about him myself. It's better this way. I know it's for the best and I have to keep believing that or I won't do what I have to do.

'So, you two drowned rats were on your way back to the bed and breakfast where you're staying, I take it?' I nod, and Lily glances at the taxi driver. 'And is your mum planning on coming back there after her lunch with *Frank*, then?'

'I don't know, do I?'

'She probably will. Of course, I remember now why

297

your mum didn't pick you up. Her car's being seen to today, isn't it? Frank's bound to give her a lift back, if it's raining. I think I'll come in and wait it out with you girls. It's three o'clock already. I can't imagine they'll be that long, can you?'

'You'll lose your taxi,' I point out. She's *bored*, I think. She needs entertaining and she wants us to be the ones to provide it for her. I don't want her waiting with us for Mum, I think suddenly. I want to spend time listening to music with Ellen. I like Aunt Lily, I do, but she has a way of kind of taking over things. 'Why don't you just leave your papers so Mum can sign them and get back to you tomorrow?'

'No,' she shakes her head. 'My solicitor Myrtle needs them ASAP. She's going away for a few weeks.' Lily looks at me brightly. 'So best not to drag it out, eh? I love your *beads*, by the way,' she turns to Ellen now. 'Did you get them in town?'

I wish Aunt Lily would leave us alone and just talk to the driver about the weather like other grown-ups do. I fold my arms and stare out at the tree-lined country lanes as they chat on about jewellery and shoes and hair. She's hijacked Ellen. And when we get back to the house she'll hijack that guy Frank, too, if she possibly can. I hope Mum is still out with him and not at home after all. I hope they stay out till very late and Lily gets fed up and goes away. Lily is too frivolous for me, that's the trouble. She's too frivolous and I'm too serious. But how can we change what we are? Twenty minutes go by and then at last we're turning into the gravelled drive at Crouch's End and I spy a blue car there that I've never seen before.

Maggie's not at home when we get back. Mum's here, it turns out. And so is Frank. The kitchen is full of jam-jars, labelled and ready to go. There's a strange, almost awkward atmosphere in the air when we walk in, like we're disturbing something, but I can't imagine what.

'Frank, this is my sister, Liliana.' Mum glances at me, confused, like she's thinking, *What on earth did you bring my sister back here for?* I didn't, I didn't, I want to say. I shrug at her.

'Oh, it's *Lily*, poppet,' my aunt laughs softly, reaching out an immaculate soft hand to take Frank's. 'I had no idea I'd be intruding on anything, Rachel.' She turns wide eyes on her sister. 'Shelley said you'd be out. I shan't stay. I really don't want to break up your party.'

'Frank's just leaving,' Mum says stiffly. When you see the way he looks at Mum and she looks at him you can't help wondering why he isn't staying.

'Not on my account?' Lily looks from one to the other, and Frank – he's a nice guy really, I can see that – laughs softly.

'No, really. I was just going. See you two on Friday, then?' His look lingers for just long enough to convince me: he *likes* my mum! And Lily sees it too.

'So, I hear you're a friend of Maggie's?' she darts in, as if she knows Maggie at all; which is so annoying, because she doesn't.

'A long-time acquaintance,' he smiles.

Mum looks at the ground and swallows. She seems upset. Then I remember. What we talked about this morning, before I left to go off with the twins; of course, that's what's upset her, it's got to be. Maybe she was

talking it over with Frank and we just came in and interrupted them?

'Well, we'd better let Frank go,' I interject.

'You live locally, then?' Lily continues as if I hadn't
spoken.

I clear my throat.

'Mum said Frank was just leaving, Lily.'

'Because if you do perhaps you could show me round
the town sometime? The little local spots, the best places
to eat and so forth . . . ?'

Mum glances at me and I know she's thinking about
the number of times people automatically ignore me and
talk to her when I'm out with her in my chair. As if I
must be some imbecile, just because I cannot walk. Lily,
of course, knows better. Lily is ignoring me because she
doesn't want me ruining her pitch.

'On and off. I have a place down here.'

'And a place elsewhere too, from the sounds of it?'
She lowers her long eyelashes at him and I have to admit
to a reluctant admiration when I see how she does it,
even though I can sense she's hitting on him. She does
it so gracefully, with such a light touch; I've got to hand
it to her, really.

'Several places, actually. Toronto's my home base
though.' He picks up a folder from the kitchen worktop
which I recognise to be my mum's. 'It's been a real
pleasure to meet you ladies. Ellen, tell your parents I'll
be down to see them before I leave, I promise.'

Ellen trips over and gives him a shy hug.

'You *promise*, Frank?'

He crosses his heart. 'Would I let you down?'

Lily is still smiling at him. Mum isn't smiling at all. She still looks so sad. I wonder why he says he will see us both on Friday?

'Rachel, would you think me awful if I dashed off, too, darling? I just need you to sign these papers for me.' My aunt slaps an official-looking wad of papers down on the kitchen table. 'Where there's a cross marked. It's to do with the property,' she adds in response to Mum's blank look. 'Whenever you're ready.'

'I'll read them and sign them and get them to you soon.'

Lily looks agitated at that. 'You could just *sign* them, darling. It's all just what we agreed, after all. You know, what we spoke about yesterday.' She changes tack suddenly. 'Frank, I've just realised I'm so stupid, I let that taxi go. You wouldn't be a hero and drop me back into town, would you? I'm staying at the Royal Star Hotel. It's divine. Do you know it?'

'I know where it is,' he says neutrally.

'You won't stay?' Mum looks at Lily regretfully. 'I could do with the company, Lily. I'll order you a taxi a bit later if you like?'

'Can't stop, Rach.' Lily picks up her bag and looks brightly at Frank. 'I really have to get back. Give me a ring, though. We'll do dinner tomorrow evening, yes?'

'Shall I take you back too, Ellen?' Frank offers, but Ellen clings on to my arm. '*We're* spending the afternoon together,' she affirms. Normally I'd be pleased but I can sense a chaperone for Lily might be wise in the circumstances. *You can go if you like,* I plead with my eyes, but she doesn't take the hint.

301

'Are you sure you won't stay?' Mum looks at her sister hesitantly. I notice she doesn't look at Frank.

'Sadly, I've got to go.' Lily seems to have lasered in on her driver. 'I'd love to have stayed longer.'

'I thought you said you were,' I begin, frowning at her, but Mum gives me a tiny shake of her head. Let her go.

What's going on here? I want to yell at them all. Lily came down to see Mum but now she's buggering off with Frank. Mum was supposed to be having lunch with him and the air between them is crackling like it's bonfire night but now she seems quite prepared to let him go off with Lily without putting up a fight.

Who the hell is this Frank, anyway? I glance at Ellen, who is shivering in her soaked T-shirt and skirt by the radiator (which isn't on); we both need to get changed. But as soon as we're dry and comfy I will ask her about that man. If my mum's getting herself a boyfriend I suppose I'd better find out some stuff about him first.

33

Rachel

Wednesday night

Tonight the moon is restless, swathing herself about with clouds and then throwing them off as if she's too hot, too flustered, shedding her light and not shedding it, troubled by a halo of rain. I cannot sleep. It's 2 a.m. I've left my window open to catch the gusts of wind, hoping for something fresh that will blow these sticky cobwebs right out of my brain, but I can find no peace.

No peace in Maggie's garden from the sweet and pungent smell of the rain-washed herbs; no peace in the memory of Frank's quiet kiss on my forehead; no peace in the quiet smile that played about my sleeping daughter's lips. I checked on her at 1 a.m. but all was quiet. She's not lying awake like me, carrying on this fierce battle with anxiety deep inside her chest. She's already told me what she wants, and the telling of it has brought her a deeper peace than I've known in her for months. I can't begrudge her that gift – that quiet smile in her sleep – even if it's been bought at the price of my own disquiet.

So, she's told me what she wants.

She's told me and it binds me, I think, to *nothing*. I

don't have to accede to her wishes, do I? I can hear her out, but at the end of the day it's going to be me who makes those final choices, it isn't going to be Shelley.

And I have to be calm and logical about this. It's no use getting all worked up and hysterical.

It's raining again. It spits down onto the dark windowsill, catching my fingers with little frozen drops, and I ask God, where is the sunshine that I so desperately asked you for, before me and Shelley came out here? A little bit of warmth. A little bit of joy, that's all I asked for. We're into June in a few days, for heaven's sake, whatever's happened to global *warming*?

If only the weather would let up I'm sure I would find myself in a better place to *think*. When it's miserable like this, I feel miserable. The dullard moon clogs up my brain. I feel sulky; I feel angry.

If only I could sleep.

And what did Frank mean this morning, when he said all those things that he said? Something about there being nothing left to fight; you find yourself sparring with shadows?

I don't know what he *meant*.

Oh, it's all just words, isn't it? I don't know who he's lost, or why he felt he could empathise with me, but it didn't help. He didn't help me at all because he kissed me and said goodbye. Maybe it would have been okay if he hadn't kissed me. Frank serves to remind me, that's all. He reminds me of what I've lost – not only those things that I *had*, but all those things that I've lost that I might have had and now I never will. I can't afford to go down that route to the hell of self-pity, so I'm better off really. He just stirred up all the muddy waters of my emotions, just when everything was quietened down, settled like the untouched sediment of ages. I thought I'd got my mind clear. I thought I could keep everything simple but I can't. I can't, and I *have* to. If I don't keep things simple and logical and straightforward then I might not do the right thing by Shelley. I might make a mistake.

And in my life, I know, I have already made too many mistakes. Like, if I hadn't taken my eye off the ball, six, seven years ago, when Shelley was first sick, then maybe I never would have lost my husband? My children never would have lost their father and their home. I think that, and then again, I think – what else could I have done? Could I have clung on to him when he no longer had any mind to stay with us?

Come to that, will I be able to cling on to Shelley?

I've got to be fair to her in all of this. I've got to be fair to *us*.

And so, it rains. Even in the darkness, in the middle of the night when no one sees. And I remember the one thing that I don't want to remember: that sometimes the price of someone else's happiness and wellbeing – their *freedom* – is only bought at the price of us losing them. I'm thinking about Bill and I'm thinking about Shelley and I'm thinking about someone else, too.

I haven't forgotten my dad. How we sat on the low brick wall out the front of the house that night. He was smoking, I remember that. Pandora never allowed him to smoke inside the house. I knew it was the one place that I could be certain to catch him alone.

* * *

305

I held on to that letter for two weeks before I made up my mind what I would do with it. I wanted to shove it back, deep into the bottom of Pandora's box, back where it had come from, but I knew that I couldn't. I wanted to pretend that I had never seen it and I didn't know its contents and that the consequences of doing nothing wouldn't matter. But I knew that it would. And I knew that the injustice of keeping it quiet would grow like a boil inside me, just waiting to erupt.

I had to tell him. Even though I knew what it might bring down on us; the fallout that this would have for my whole family. I had to, because it was the only fair thing to do. And I had to be fair, even if it tore apart the whole fabric of my life. Even if it tore my heart up into shreds along with it.

I had to be fair.

And I felt guilty when I went out to him, sitting on that cold stone wall all by himself. As guilty as if it had been me who'd tried to hide the truth away from him, because I had held on to it for two long weeks without doing anything about it. I hadn't wanted him to know about it. Like Pandora, I had too much to lose.

And when I took it out of my pocket, crumpled and hot like an overused ten-pound note, and gave it to him, he didn't even know who it was from at first. He didn't recognise the handwriting.

'What's this, honeybunch? Your school report?' He'd taken one look at my face, pinched and white as no doubt it was, and I had heard him laugh softly. 'It'll never be that bad, will it, Rachaela? You've never been worried about it before.' And he'd stopped, not even opening it, his hand on my arm. 'Your mum's seen this, then?' – I'd nodded

dumbly, the truth as solid as a stone in my throat – 'and you're in trouble, pickle?'

I shook my head and next door's cat jumped onto the wall beside us, his spine arched up against his tail like the perfect letter N for 'No'. But in a sense I was in trouble once he read that letter; in truth, we all were.

'I found it in Mum's box.' I got the words out as he unfolded it at last and I saw his eyes, after reading the short paragraph that was there, flick upwards to the date.

'It's been in the house for a few weeks.'

'A few weeks?'

I watched as his eyes filled with tears. The accumulated ash at the end of his cigarette fell unheeded onto his leg. I wanted to brush it away but I found I couldn't move. Was it too late now? Had I brought it to him too late for it to make any difference?

'It's been in Mum's box, you say?'

'The one she keeps . . . at the back of her wardrobe.'

Dad had nodded, frowning. He didn't know about Mum's box. He never noticed such things. But he clearly got the picture.

'I'm so sorry, darling.' He folded the letter up. He put it carefully back into the creased envelope. 'I never wanted . . . you were never meant to know anything about this, any of you. I never thought it would go so far, that's all.' He cleared his throat as if he were about to launch into some sort of explanation and then he looked at me, looked into my face and saw I was just a thirteen-year-old and maybe that's what changed his mind. Maybe he thought the details of it weren't any of my business after all. 'Thank you for this.'

He put the envelope away in his pocket. Then he gave

me a quick hug. And in that hug I could feel that all his depression had lifted. There was a new energy in there; I don't know what it was — maybe hope? 'You did the right thing, kid,' he told me as we stood up. I watched him extinguish his fag-end underfoot and the cat jumped down off the wall, its tail erect, its head held up high and alert as if it had decided it had places to go after all, better places to be. 'Thank you, honey. I know that must have been hard for you. You do know what this is going to mean, don't you?'

I thought I knew. It was his passport to the freedom that he'd wanted. I knew what was going to happen after that. Maybe it was then that I concluded that because it was me who'd handed him that passport, I should be the one responsible for everything that happened afterwards?

It's 4 a.m. now. I can hear Maggie's grandfather clock in the hallway. All through the night it chimes, ever so low. I hear it even as I turn in my sleep. And soon the dawn will be breaking through the night-shift clouds. In another two hours or so Shelley will be awake, and then I'll go and make us some tea and we'll start the rounds of another day as if everything's the same as it was yesterday, but I know it isn't.

Something has changed. Deep in the core and the rhythm of our life something is no longer what it was, just like the day I handed Dad that letter. A decision has been made. A path has been set. I don't know now what it is, just like I didn't know then, but it's coming, I can feel it like the beating of a clock in my heart, drawing closer, ever closer to the moment when it will chime.

34

Shelley

Thursday afternoon

Okay, I've got the blasted laptop out just like Mum wants. She keeps insisting that I check to see if Annie-Jo has sent that work she said she would. She's been bugging me every day and I've been telling her that I've looked and it hasn't come in yet. I haven't actually been anywhere near the laptop, I don't dare. If there is an email from Kieran I will have to read it, I'll just HAVE to.

Mum has changed. Something is different about her, I don't know what. It's like I keep getting glimpses of this other side of her, just glimpses, and if I say anything she just snaps back into her normal self again so I can't quite get hold of it.

Maybe it's being here that's doing it. They always say people behave differently when they're on holiday, don't they? They say that being in a new place, doing new things, can bring out a whole other side of you.

I hadn't expected that. We're supposed to be here together so I can get to say goodbye to her. That's what I wanted to do. Like when I cleared out all my papers and Miriam's emails and stuff; I got things sorted. I wanted to do the same thing, but with my mum. Thing is, she may be physically present but she isn't really here at the moment. She's thinking about a lot of things but she doesn't say what. Yesterday I watched her looking out of the window for ten minutes altogether, not even aware I was there.

Finally, it's connecting up. Why is the Internet going so slowly today? If there's a message from Kieran I don't know what the hell I'm going to do. What the heck can I say to him; maybe I should just not reply at all? I really don't know what's best. If only I could come clean and speak to Mum. She might be able to give me some advice. I so wish I could.

Like today, at the Pony Centre. I almost told her, you know, about my plan. We were watching this cute little Shetland pony who was munching on some grass doing his own thing and then the rest of the herd just sort of galloped by and he got caught up and galloped off with them, and Mum said, 'Isn't that just typical of life in general: you're standing there minding your own business and then you get caught up in a tide that comes rushing past and before you know it you're with someone different, doing something else in some other different place that you never planned to be in.'

'You mean, like here with me?' I'd said, and she'd shaken her head.

'No, no, I planned to be here with you. I meant life in general; I wanted to be here with you.'

That's just my point, though, she isn't really here. Every time I try to talk to her it seems she has to drag her attention back to me from a very long way away.

310

Now she wants to go to Tintagel tomorrow. She's going with Frank, and I'm supposed to be going too. I wasn't even asked. I *like* Frank, but I can't help feeling that I'll be a bit of a spare lemon if I go along with them. Ellen has told me all about him and it's a real sad story. But I'm not bothered about Tintagel. I hear it's got lots of steps so I'll never make it up to the top unless someone volunteers to carry me all the way up!

Oh god, there's not one but FOUR emails from Kieran! And two from Surinda. And one from Annie-Jo; that's for Mum. I'll open that one first. Oops. It looks like quite a lot of work. Mum is not going to be best pleased, especially if she notices the date on the email and sees that this got sent on Monday. Hell, am I in trouble.

But I can't think about that now. It's hardly important. My stomach has turned to jelly just seeing all those messages from Krok@btonline. Hah! There's an email I didn't notice before; it's from Poppet24@hotmail.com, titled *Antiphospholipid Syndrome – Alert – contact Dr Lavelle. Urgent!* Yeah, sure, poppet honey, whoever you are. Straight away. So he can take me for some more bloody tests and get me in the bloody hospital, right? That's one to delete before my mum gets a look at it.

Now, Surinda: what does she want? I can look at hers.

From: **Surinda Chellaram**
To: **Shelley Wetherby**
Subject: **Stuff**
Hiya, girl. Hope you're not still mad at me? Are you having a good holiday in Cornwall? Just as well I didn't go with you because you wait till I tell you what's been happening here! You won't believe

it but it turns out Jallal's cousin (the one in the government) has actually MET Jay Surinham, the movie star, and they are on very good terms. Jay came to the cousin's birthday party last year, can you believe that? Looks like if I get in with this family I could get to meet some very fashionable people. I'm not saying that your Kieran isn't fashionable, but we're talking a different league, you know, girl. Jallal isn't too bad really, now he's cut his hair. When I'm his wife I'll have control over what he eats so we can get the blubber down a bit. I suppose they're all the same in the dark, aren't they? That's what Mum says, anyway. Who cares? I'm going to be married, and they're booking up the Jewel of India Hotel for the reception afterwards. If you can put off your Jump then you're invited to the wedding too of course (Jay Surinham might even be there – who knows?) Lots of love, Surinda.

Crikey, all change there then!

'If I can put off my jump,' she says! What does she think I'm planning on, a bungee-dive?

I'm glad things are working out for Surinda, though. She's a survivor, that one. I would have liked to have gone to her wedding, either with or without Jay Surinham being there. What's this 'ps' about?

PS: Hiya again.
Forgot to mention that I've been in touch with your bf about the BTB tickets – seeing as you won't be needing them – as I thought maybe me and Jallal could go. Do you mind? I suppose you've seen the date for the final show, which is this Sat coming

up, and as that's the day you're Jumping, you won't be seeing it, will you? No point wasting them, is there? Jallal said he was keen to meet my mate Kieran, too. What do you think? Let me know ASAP. All love, Surinda.

I could be excused for thinking that Surinda doesn't give a shit about the fact that I'm going to jump off a cliff this Saturday. How *dare* she contact Kieran about my tickets?

Now I'm really mad at her again. I really am. Hell, she didn't tell Kieran *why* I wouldn't be needing them, did she? I'm going to have to open his emails now just to see what she's said to him, aren't I?

She's *forced* me to have to open them, and I *so* didn't want to.

From: **Kieran O'Keefe**
To: **Shelley Wetherby**
Subject: **Your email**
My dearest Shelley, as you can imagine, receiving your email today was quite a shock, even though I knew you were trying to tell me on Saturday and I wouldn't listen. My darling, I am so sorry that I didn't listen to you properly. You've got to see why. I love you. I feel more strongly about you than I've ever felt about any girl in my life. I wish you could see that. Please don't end it like this. Please. Your own Kieran xxxx

Now I can't see a thing. My eyes have filled up with tears and I'm dripping them onto the keyboard and if I'm not careful it's going to break, just like my heart. Oh, Kieran, can't you see that I can't, I *can't* carry on with you because things are never going to get any better, they are only going to get worse?

From: **Kieran O'Keefe**
To: **Shelley Wetherby**
Subject: **Please reply!**
My darling Pixie,
Please reply to me. Please x 1000, don't just not ever talk to me again. I know you think you're doing this for the best. But how can you be sure this IS for the best? You can't be sure. I love you so much, my darling. I'm hoping that you didn't get my first email and that's why you haven't got back to me. I'm waiting for you. All my love, Kieran xxxx

From: **Kieran O'Keefe**
To: **Shelley Wetherby**
Subject: **Worried**
Darling Pixie,
I know I'll have to wait till you get back from your holiday as you can't be getting any emails where you are, but I'm still writing in case you can go to a cyber café and get them. Thing is, I'm worried. Your funny friend Surinda emailed me last night, asking if she could use your tickets for Saturday night's show. Of course she can if that's what you want, darling. I'd much rather it was you who was there but if you're still in Cornwall then I suppose there's no chance of it. (If you do get a chance to watch, they're showing it at 9 p.m. prime-time now, not seven o'clock, like before.) It's become a media phenomenon, hasn't it? I can't help notice the irony that you must be the only girl within 200 miles of

314

here who doesn't want to go out with me. But I
don't want any of them, you know that. Please
believe it because it's true. Well I'm rattling on
and you probably aren't getting any of these. I
wanted to say again that I Love You. I Love You.
I Love You.
Please get back to me as soon as you can. Always
and forever yours, Kieran xxxx

Email four (this one was sent just this morning):

From: **Kieran O'Keefe**
To: **Shelley Wetherby**
Subject: **Contact me, please**
Love you, Pixie. Counting the minutes till you get
this and reply to me, saying that you've changed
your mind. Granddad not too well so I won't be
around much tomorrow (what with the show and
all) so won't have a chance to write to you. Doesn't
mean I won't be thinking about you, sweetheart.
Could you please just put your phone on so I can
ring you at least? Yours always, Kieran xxxx

Oh god, oh god, why does it have to be like this?

'Shelley, darling, did you get round to checking the
Internet for me? Annie-Jo has probably forgotten, or
given the work to someone else by now, seeing as we're
away.'

'What?' God, why'd she have to come in right *now*?
She's got the worst bloody timing in the history of the
universe, my mum.

'Annie-Jo. The calligraphy.' Mum's standing there with
her hands on her hips, looking curiously in the direction

315

of the screen. I switch to screen-saver with a flick of a button.

'Who's that? Who's Kieran?'

'Mu-um!' I give her a hard look. 'That's my business, isn't it?'

'Sorry.'

'Annie-Jo's sent that thingy for you, okay? I'll print it off in Maggie's office.'

'She has?' Mum sounds disappointed. 'We're going to Tintagel tomorrow, don't forget.'

'I haven't forgotten.'

'Does it look like a lot of work?' she ventures. She's pulling her hair brush through her wet hair as we speak and I swear it's a different colour, more shiny than it is normally. She hasn't coloured her hair has she? I've never seen Mum do that before.

'Well, yes, actually.'

'Hell! When did she send it?' Mum stops her hair-brushing and leans over the screen even though there's currently nothing to see.

'Um . . . Monday,' I mumble, hoping that she won't hear that as I'm heading for the door, but she does.

'*Monday?* Shelley, you said you'd been checking every day! How could that have happened? How could she have sent it on Monday? And does she still want the work ready for Sunday?' She ties her hair up in an agitated movement with an elastic from her wrist.

'I think she said that she does, yes.' I keep my eyes mainly on the blank screen. If she's going to make a scene . . .

'I can't do it, though.' Mum's face has gone all red

316

and upset-looking now. 'I just . . . can't . . . do it for Sunday.'

'Don't, then. Say you've changed your mind. It is your holiday, after all.'

'Huh!' She rattles my bottle of tablets at me, as if to say, I'm still here on duty, you know. Earlier on she was busy cutting the ten-milligram tablets into halves because I'm supposed to have five-milligram ones but they didn't have any because the manufacturers have temporarily stopped making those. 'Did you check your blood pressure this morning?' she snaps.

'I do it every day,' I remind her. I don't know why. It never changes, really. I guess what she's saying is that this isn't a holiday for her, because how can it be if she's stuck here having to look after me?

'Do you realise what this *means*? I'll have to stay in all day tomorrow, Friday,' she continues, 'because it's your birthday on Saturday and we're travelling back on Sunday.'

'You might have other priorities on your mind by the end of the weekend.' I give her a dark look.

'What do you mean?' Mum's really irritated, and she's taking everything I say the wrong way. She's scooping all the bits of tablets into a bottle, the halved ones and the non-halved ones, as if she's not really thinking about what she's doing. 'Because if you're referring to *Frank*, I think that's pretty out of order.'

'I wasn't referring to Frank.' Why the hell would she think that I was? I was talking about me, of course, but she won't realise that.

'I think you were. Just because I want to go to Tintagel

317

with him tomorrow . . . it's all been ruined, now, do you realise that? My plans to go out with him have been completely *ruined*!'

'What's so special about Tintagel, anyway?'

She looks at me with an expression that suggests utter disbelief. Well, what *is* so special about it?

'Nothing,' she says through gritted teeth. 'Nothing is special about Tintagel at all. I just wanted to go out with Frank, that's all. He's a nice man. I just wanted to go out with a nice man, just for once in my life . . .'

'Keep your hair on . . .'

'And if I'd known about Annie-Jo's work I could have done it before.'

'Well you've been busy most days,' I point out. 'You went out with Frank that first morning, then you saw Lily for lunch, then you had lunch with Frank, then you . . .'

'I could have done it today, then, instead of which I've just *wasted* the day and got nothing done at all,' she scowls.

'Wasted?' I give her a look that matches her own. 'I thought that *today* we were spending some time together. I thought that you enjoyed being out with me today. I thought that was what this holiday was all about?'

Her eyebrows go down then and she frowns, and I'm not sure if she's angry at me or sad, but do you know what? To hell with her, I don't give a shit.

Kieran cares about me, he really does. He loves me properly, like people should be loved. Whereas Mum . . . like I said, she's changed, she's got more selfish. Maybe she's doing that 'remembering who she is' thing that Miriam's mum mentioned. I don't know.

I close the laptop down and take it out of the room, feeling the ache in my shoulders, which have hunched, and the ache in my throat where I feel I just want to cry and cry and cry.

'It seems as if', I hear Mum's arch tone coming from the room behind me, she always has to have the last word, 'you and I are having a real problem communicating, aren't we, miss?'

'And you think that's because I'm an impossible teenager and you just can't get through to me?'

'I'm not sure why it is.' Mum has come out onto the landing behind me and when I turn I see that she looks more sad than she does angry. She's not in any different place from me, really.

'Let's talk then, Mum.' My voice cracks. 'I mean, really talk. If you're ready for it?'

I hear her sigh. Her shoulders are hunched too. I get the impression she's been waiting for this.

'Okay, you remember I told you some time back that I wasn't prepared to end my life like Miriam?'

She nods, her eyes hooded, uncomprehending, and I continue.

'What would you say if I told you that I've decided to make *sure* that doesn't happen, by taking things into my own hands?'

'Well, that's what you were talking about yesterday, wasn't it? Euthanasia, they call it. But I'm not . . . I'm not going there with you. I said we'd talk about it but you haven't given me much time to think.'

'No, I don't mean that.'

'What do you mean?' The skin under her eyes looks

grey and strained in the landing's poor light. I guess we've come to it then; the point of no more pretending. I'm not sure, even here, even now, that I'm up for it.

'I mean,' I turn myself right round in my chair so she can see my face clearly and make no mistake about it, 'I mean that I made you bring me here under false pretences. I never intended to go home.'

'You want to stay on in Cornwall?' She's got that puzzled frown on her face again.

'In a manner of speaking. I'm going to . . . jump off a cliff, Mum. I'm going to end it here; that's all.'

'You're going to *what*?' She turns Bessie round towards her, gently, slowly. 'Say that again.'

'You heard it right first time, Mum. I've made my decision.'

'And you think I'm going to just stand by and let you do that?' She's got this look on her face – the sort of look I remember her getting one time when I was about five and I announced I needed to use the sharp kitchen scissors because I was planning to give myself a hair cut.

I sigh. 'No, of course not. I expect you'll do your very best to try to dissuade me. That's why I haven't said anything up till now. I didn't want to hear you going on at me.'

'What should I do?' she says quietly. 'What do you want me to do?'

Well, that's unexpected, at least. I have to pause to consider for a moment. I thought she was going to launch into a whole list of good reasons why I mustn't do it, why I must think about how *selfish* it would be . . .

'I want you to . . . let the final choice be mine,' I say

to her. 'That's all. I'm not going to last very much longer anyway, am I, Mum? Doctor Lavelle has been on the phone dozens of times recently, wanting me to go in again. I'm sorry, I should have told you, I know. But I didn't want to go in. They took Miriam in, remember? And look what happened to her.'

'That doesn't mean . . .'

'It *does*, Mum! Stop pretending. You know it does.'

We both just stop there for a moment, me drumming my fingers on the laptop, wanting to escape and her just – just silent, while she considers what I've just said.

'So you're just going to jump off a cliff instead?' she finishes. She looks all deflated. She looks like my battered old bear that I've had in my bed with me forever; all sunken in and bald somehow with the stuffing knocked right out of her. I can't actually bring myself to answer her right now. She stares at the computer screen blankly for a moment.

She won't do Annie-Jo's job now, I bet. And that's a shame, because her life is still going to need to go on even after mine has ended.

'When?' Her eyes lift darkly to mine, and that surprises me again because she's not fighting me at all. Is she really just accepting it?

'On my birthday. At six in the morning, the hour of my birth.'

A faint smile crosses her lips for an instant before it vanishes.

'You were born at six in the evening,' she tells me. 'Will that make a difference?'

I swallow hard. It does. For some reason that I cannot fathom at all, it *does*.

'I'll do it at six in the evening, then.' Even though that means it won't be quite as I envisioned it. It won't be the beginning of a new day, for one thing, it'll be the end of one. Oh well.

'Will you help me, Mum?'

She says nothing.

'Oh, and will you make sure Dad and Stella don't come down either? That might be a bit awkward.'

'They never were going to come down, Shelley.'

I shoot her a glance. Does she mean what I think she does?

'I made that up so you wouldn't let on to your dad we were coming here. He doesn't know. He would never have let you come. Turns out he was right.'

'Stella knew we were coming down, actually,' I tell her now. 'I let slip that evening on the phone before they came round. I told her not to say, though. I had a feeling Dad might not be in on this . . .'

'You *did*?' She draws in a breath. Clearly she's thinking Stella will have spilled the beans by now. But it's too late for anyone to stop me, far too late . . .

'It's better this way, Mum.'

For a very long time she says nothing at all but then I pull my master stroke. 'You know, letting me make that decision by myself, it's the only fair thing to do, Mum. It's the only bit of choice in the matter I've got left.' And then she looks at me and still her eyes are so dark, swimming with some emotion that I cannot fathom because it all seems so simple to me now.

35

Rachel

Thursday evening

Maggie's kitchen is quiet, and dark. I haven't put the lights on yet. It's 7 p.m. but it's the end of May, so why does it feel as if evening is drawing in so quickly? Maggie's out at choir practice so I have her ample kitchen to myself. I've been wrapping salmon fillets into neat tinfoil parcels for the Aga and it's strangely relaxing. I like working in the semi-dark. I like the deep stillness of the high ceilings, the dappled light that flutters in now and again from the garden. It calms my spirits and helps me to imagine that maybe things aren't as bad as they seem; perhaps Shelley didn't really mean those things that she said to me earlier on? About jumping to her end, and all that. She couldn't really have meant it.

Teenage bloody girls, eh?

Drama queens, the lot of them.

I pour out a solitary glass of red – cook's privilege – and console myself with the knowledge that many a mother has been here before me. Why can't we just hibernate them all like the tortoises? Put the teenagers away at age thirteen and bring them back at around twenty-one

323

or so when they've become sensible. *I* was never this bad, was I?

I brush past Pandora's smelly old box, which I've placed on the table where Lily can't possibly miss it. She gets to take all the memorabilia home tonight. Yay-bloody-hay.

The doorbell shatters my peace. I told Lily to come at six . She insisted on coming to dinner tonight. Yesterday I wanted her here. After Frank left, I could have done with someone to talk to. Tonight, I really don't care. But anyway, *six*, I said, so you can help me out with dinner.

When I get the door, she's holding a huge bouquet of scented flowers and a bottle of champagne. And she's positively beaming. At least someone's happy.

'Dinner's almost done,' I tell her dryly. 'Shelley's disappeared into her laptop.'

Hmmm, after shunning the machine for almost the entire week now Shelley's suddenly got lots to say to people. This has led to Annie-Jo's work being neglected, which is ruining the prospect of me going out tomorrow.

'Low carb, I hope?' Lily eyes the new potatoes boiling on the hob, suspiciously.

'Well, I don't know. Just eat the bits you want. Thanks for the flowers,' I tell her ungraciously. They look gorgeous, really gorgeous, but I'm going home in two and a half days, I think sourly.

'I thought you'd appreciate them.' My sister is already busy with the champagne cork. 'I don't suppose you get all that many these days?'

Only pictures of flowers, I think. I get a sudden flash

of Daniel's sunflower picture; the one he drew me for Mother's Day, and I bite my lip. God, I haven't even thought about Daniel! Unbelievable as it may seem, I haven't. How could my mind have been so crowded that I haven't had time to think about him even once?

'What's up, Rach?' Lily looks up at me abruptly.

'What's up?' I take the proffered champagne glass and sip it. Moët & Chandon. Not cheap supermarket fizz. Nice.

'What-is-up?' Lily sits down at the kitchen table. 'You don't look very happy. Have you heard from Frank at all?'

'No,' I shake my head. 'Should I have?'

She shrugs nonchalantly. She's wearing turquoise today; deep blue earrings that drop like sea-coloured pearls right down onto her shoulders. Her top is just off the shoulder, her skirt full at the hips so it serves to emphasise her tiny waist.

'I mentioned – I hope you don't mind – that we're eating in tonight. I hinted that he'd be more than welcome to join us.'

'You *did*?' I swallow the delicious champagne in a gulp as a shiver of anticipation tinged with annoyance passes through me. 'You invited him and you didn't think to tell me?' And there's you done up to the nines, as usual, and me looking frumpy and frustrated and hot and bothered from the cooking. 'I thought it was just us tonight,' I said irritably, 'and I haven't even had a shower yet.'

'You look fine.' She waves a dismissive hand. 'Besides, I thought you'd be pleased. I thought you liked him?'

'Did he . . . say anything to you?'

'Like what?' She's got her compact out of her purse and she's powdering her nose now, for heaven's sake!

'Look, you can wash the salad or something, Lily. If we've got guests coming I suppose we'd better be organised.' The thought of Frank turning up tonight flusters me beyond belief, and more so – I get a sudden flash of insight – because I don't want to share him with *her*.

'Oh, I don't suppose he's coming, if he hasn't rung.' The realisation of that deflates my sister a little. 'What's this?' Her eye alights on Pandora's box. 'Good grief, you brought it with you? All that way?'

'As it turns out, it was the *only* thing we brought,' I remind her.

'Well, fancy that.' My sister has no intention of making a start on that salad. She's leafing through yellowing photographs now, holding them up for me to see and laughing.

'D'you remember this one, darling? This was us in our hey-day. God, look at my waist, it was tiny! You were actually taller than me back then, do you realise?' She pauses to pour us both a second glass of champagne and I'm a bit shocked to see that we've both knocked our first glass back already. Slow down, Rachel. I get up and turn the hob off and the potatoes settle quietly to the bottom of the pan.

'Are you *sure* Frank said he would ring if he was coming?' I take the photo from her. Of course I realise, I was always taller than you, I think irritably. That was the whole reason why I had to be the 'boy' partner, or doesn't she remember that?

'He said he'd ring,' she says vaguely. 'I was rather hoping that he had, actually. Rachel, Frank's a *dream*, isn't he? And he's not poor either, from what I can gather. Quite a find, I'd say.'

'*My* find,' I remind her before I can stop myself.

'I see,' she says slowly. 'I wasn't quite clear if you two were actually . . . I mean, *are* you?'

'Are we what?'

'An item, so to speak?'

'Oh for heaven's sake, I've only just met him, Lily. Give me a chance, won't you?'

Back off, I want to tell her. Just back off for once in my life and give me a chance with someone I really, really like.

'I didn't hit on him, Rachel. He gave me a lift back. We chatted for a little bit. That was all.' Her wide blue eyes are open and innocent. I just wish they weren't sparkling at the memory of *what,* though?

Oh, Rachel, get a grip!

'I'm sorry.' The champagne is loosening me up, I can feel it. I need to just chill out a little and stop being so uptight. The kitchen is warm and mellower now that Lily has got up and lit some of Maggie's tall green candles and placed them on the wooden table. 'Sorry, Lily. I . . . just get a bit jumpy around you sometimes. You were always the sex siren, weren't you? Men can't help being attracted to you even if you're not trying. You're like a mermaid on a rock.'

'Calling them to their doom?' She smiles secretly, blowing out the match. 'Well, I think our Mr Dwight has got enough on his plate just now without the likes of me adding to his troubles, don't you think?'

'Does he?' I nibble at some cashew nuts, which she's tipped into a bowl, and I wonder what he's told her.

'Mmm.' She nods and pulls out another photo from the box. I must get my pink diary out before she takes the whole lot away tonight. 'He's cute. Do you remember *him*?'

She's frowning at the guy in the picture with intense concentration. I don't bloody believe it!

'Don't *you*?' I accuse.

'Not really. But I appear with him in a number of photos so I must have known who –'

'That's Gordon Ilkeley,' I remind her through clenched teeth. 'The guy we both auditioned for when his partner Amelie left.'

'I do remember Amelie,' she says infuriatingly. 'She had a hand-span of a waist and ivory-white skin. She went to live abroad, didn't she?' My sister sighs. 'I so envied her. I so wanted to go and live abroad, too.'

You've got to be *kidding* me.

My chair makes a loud scraping noise against the terracotta tiles as I push it out of the way, standing up. She doesn't remember Gordon? She doesn't even *remember* Gordon, after all that I had to risk to make him mine, after all that I threw away just for the chance to dance with him?

'Don't you remember how the letter came through, offering one of us the opportunity to partner him? It came through after Dad left.' It came for me, I remember now fiercely. The offer was *mine*. But by then Dad was on the verge of leaving. Mum was in charge and Mum insisted that Lily needed the chance more than I did.

Lily needed something to boost her confidence, Mum said, with things being so strained at home and all. At first I hadn't worried at all. I *knew* they wouldn't go for it. Gordon wanted *me*, he'd told me that. So did his parents. And there were other girls who'd auditioned who would have been next in place after me, not Lily. She had no chance of getting it.

But Gordon's parents had been so sure of my acceptance, they delayed too long before seeking confirmation of it. Dad had gone, and Mum wanted Gordon for Lily. By the time they got back to us all the other girls were already partnered off. It was unbelievable, but true. And when Mum made up some rubbish story about why I couldn't partner Gordon, they'd bought that too. They'd *had* to. Pandora was adamant they couldn't have me, and Lily was the only girl left still going free.

'I can't believe you don't remember that,' I mutter into the saucepan. I lift up the potatoes with a slotted spoon, one by one. I put them on a dish. I wonder with a sick feeling in my stomach if there is any chance Frank still might be coming. I fervently hope not.

'I can barely remember anything that happened around that time, actually.' My sister's voice has gone surprisingly quiet. 'It's only now that it's happened to me that I can see what she really must have gone through. And she had us to consider, don't forget.'

She sees it from Mum's point of view, she always has. I, on the other hand, have always taken Dad's part. Even, ironically enough now, when I find myself in the same position that Mum once was in.

'That's why I'm glad that Mum's found true love at

last,' Lily is saying softly. 'Even if it's taking her halfway round the world and away from us. It took her *years* to get over Dad leaving us, you know. They will have been separated for exactly thirty years in the autumn. She always said he was the love of her life.'

I turn to look at Lily, but she is staring into her drink, swirling the glass around so the bubbles rise up to the surface. Her face looks blank, but young, very young, as if the intervening years have all just dropped away for a second. I remember what she looked like then. I remember feeling sorry for her, even as I was determined that Gordon would be mine, but still sorry for her because she took Dad's leaving so badly.

'It was a real black time,' she continues. 'I think I've blanked most of it out, if I'm truthful. I don't remember the boy.'

She doesn't remember him. She doesn't. And she has no inkling of what I did to her, no idea of the awful, terrible thing I did to her in my rage and my grief, in my pathetic attempts to claw Gordon back for myself. I draw in a deep, shuddering breath and she looks at me strangely.

'You okay, sis?'

I nod silently. Then I bring the bowl of potatoes back to the table and sit down with a thump. 'No. I'm not.'

'I thought not. That's why I asked you when I came in.'

When I glance at my sister's face, stripped away as it is just now of all the years, I remember that once, a very long time ago, I had thought that we might be friends. Could I trust her now? I wondered. Now that she's laid bare again, remembering how bereft she was when Dad went, her own recent separation echoing the twist of the same knife?

I stare at the dish of potatoes on the table for a moment, wondering what on earth I was supposed to be doing with them. The smell of baking salmon, mixed with the high notes of the lemon juice it's been basted in and the sweet herby smell of the rosemary I sprinkled over it, reminds me.

'I've got to switch the oven off,' I tell her, but she stays me with a hand on my arm.

'What's wrong, Rachel? Is it *Shelley*?'

I look at her wordlessly.

'Those symptoms you've been looking out for, those things that you were telling me about – they've come on?'

'Not exactly.' I clear my throat. She's talking about Shelley. I wasn't even *thinking* about Shelley just now. I was caught up in some ancient childish drama that was over long ago, *years* ago, before Shelley was even born. What's wrong with me? That's the last time I guzzle that much alcohol in such a short space of time. I need to focus on the here and now, I think, I've got big decisions coming up and I need to be all correct and present. 'Well, no, the symptoms – they haven't. I don't see any change. It's just *her*. She's changed. She's so moody she wants . . . she wants to throw herself off the top of a cliff, Lily!'

'So do a lot of teenagers, honey. And the occasional adult.' She laughs blithely. Lily's voice is reassuring. 'But the vast majority of them are too self-obsessed to do anything about it.'

Her tone makes me laugh, despite myself. 'You sound disappointed!'

'Too many beautiful young things out there these days, darling. They all make *me* look old.'

'Lily!'

'It's the truth. It is. But anyway, about Shelley. It's her age, don't you see? I was just the same. Moody as hell, don't you remember me? Always sulking, wanting to find a quick way out rather than face up to anything?'

I did remember.

'Your case was different, though,' I remind my sister. 'You weren't faced with the death sentence that she is. In your case it was just words. Besides, you never threatened to top yourself.'

Lily smiles enigmatically and goes to switch off the oven. 'Are you sure about that?'

'Well, if you did threaten, then you never did anything about it, at least,' I retort.

'And neither has she, yet! It's all hot air and words, believe me. She's angry, and she's got a right to be, I'll grant you. More of a right than most of us. But Shelley's a fighter. She's a survivor, Rachel. Like you are. She'll never do it.'

'You think?' I watch Lily bringing the salmon to the table now, then digging out Maggie's fluted white crockery from the cupboards.

'No way, Jose. She's smarting. She's a teenager. It's what they do.'

'So you don't think I should put a twenty-four-hour watch on her?'

'What's she going to do?' My sister shrugs. 'She's not

332

exactly mobile, is she? She can't go up a cliff all by herself now, can she?'

'I guess.' Actually now that she mentions that I feel a huge sense of relief that she's right. Shelley *can't* do anything rash by herself. So I don't have to worry.

The green candles flicker softly on the long onyx candlesticks. They smell faintly of Christmas greenery and spices and the smell is out of place, I'm aware. They belong to another season, out of tune with the reality that is in front of us.

'The thing is, Lily, the thing that worries me the most is . . . what if she's *right*?'

My sister sits down opposite me and leans her elegant chin on her hands; watches me now from under hooded lids. 'How so? How could it be *right* for her to jump off a cliff?'

'Oh, it's not the cliff,' I tell her. 'Of course that isn't going to happen. It's the principle of it. It's difficult to explain . . .' I let out a long breath. I've got the strangest feeling I can sense all my innards twisted and jumbled inside. 'Every bone in my body screams *no*. Every atom of me screams *no*! She's got to be wrong. But then there's another part of me that understands perfectly well what she's saying.'

Lily waits, silent, for me to continue. Maybe it is the shadows from the flickering candles that are darkening her face, I don't know, but my words seem to have hit a nerve.

'I just think . . . maybe she's right. Why should I force her to suffer any more than she has to? Am I just being stubborn, standing in her way? Her scenario isn't the

333

same as that of any ordinary moody teenager, Lily, let's not pretend it is. The prospect for her end is that it will be horrible and probably lingering. Is it fair that I impose my will on hers, that I insist she go through it, just because of . . . because of some stupid, misplaced hope that something miraculous will come along at the last minute and save her, like some melodramatic Hollywood weepie? If I'm honest, I know that it won't.'

'So you're proposing to do *what*?' My sister sounds scandalised. 'Take her up the cliff-top and help tip her over? *You?*'

'No. No, of course not that. It's unthinkable. But I'm trying to see it from her side, Lily. We have to see it from her side.'

'Why do we have to?' Lily pours out the dregs of the champagne into her own glass. 'What she wants to do is wrong.'

It's wrong. And so much of this is wrong, I think. What's right about it? How easy for you to judge, Lily. I watch my sister as she teeters off to call Shelley to dinner. You won't have to be there at the end, Lily, but my daughter will. *I* will.

How can you really be so sure about what is the right or wrong thing to do?

36

Rachel

'There. She wasn't so bad, was she?' Lily remarks once dinner is over and Shelley has gone back to her laptop. Shelley was quiet tonight. I wouldn't say she was her usual self, but she didn't strike me as someone about to commit a desperate act, either.

'You don't think she'll do it, then?'

'Not a chance!'

We've finished off the bottle of red that I'd started earlier and my sister and I are both feeling distinctly drowsy. I can see her head drooping to one side every now and then. I make a half-hearted attempt to put the dishes into soapy water, mindful that this is not my house, but Lily dismisses the idea. 'That's what mornings are for.'

Then Lily continues, 'Not only is she not desperate enough – she seemed quite cheerful, in fact.'

'She's been looking more cheerful ever since she asked me to help her.'

Lily laughs loudly. 'You see? It's nonsense. Absolute nonsense.'

'She's so confused, Lily. I don't know what to do with her. Now she doesn't want to go to Tintagel either. I thought she'd really like that. But she's been asked out by one of the twins again and she wants to go, you heard her.'

'Let her go then. Leave Tintagel for the adults.' Lily raises an eyebrow meaningfully.

'Do you think I should?' We're both scraping the dreg-ends of the bowl of peanuts, licking our fingers for the saltiness – even Lily, who always scrutinises everything for calorific content before she eats it!

'No question about it.'

But there's something brewing away at the back of my mind. Some other reason why I won't be able to go now.

'Damn!' I remember Annie-Jo's email. 'I can't! I've got that work to do for Annie-Jo. I promised. She stuck her neck out to recommend me and I can't let her down now.'

'You must,' my sister corrects me immediately. 'You promised Frank too. He's expecting you to go with him tomorrow. He's lonely too, you know.'

He's lonely, yes, just like Maggie told me when I first met him. But he's still not available. And I need to be available for my daughter. Even if she doesn't want me around, I think, because she'd rather go out with the twins.

Oh hell, what do I do?

'I think I do remember this fella now.' Lily's wiped her fingers clean and now she's got out the photos of her and Gordon again – the ones I've managed to avoid looking at all this time. She concentrates hard with little screwed-up eyes over one of them, then gives up and digs in her handbag for her spectacles.

'You had a bit of a crush on him, I seem to recall?'

336

'A bit. Did you?' I ask her suddenly now. 'Did you ever fancy Gordon?'

'Was that his name?' Lily laughs wonderingly, despite the fact I'd already told her earlier. 'I'd really forgotten.' She puts her specs down on the table now, locks her beautiful green eyes on to mine, and leans in confidingly. 'Do you ever wonder how things would all have turned out if . . . if we hadn't given up the dancing when we did?'

'Not really.'

'What, not ever?' She smiles and her eyes seem dim and unfocused and I realise that she's had too much wine and so have I. I take a sip of water from a tumbler. 'Oh, I know I was no good at it. Not really. I mean, you were the one with all the talent, weren't you, darling?'

'If you say so.' I watch her over my water glass.

'You know so. Stop being so humble. It's infuriating. You were the real champion because you were the one with all the talent, but you did it all through gritted teeth. I had to get by on . . . oh, just prettiness and charm.' Her eyes narrow in on mine now.

'I hated being your partner.' The words are out before I can stop them but she doesn't appear to have heard me.

'You've always taken all your good fortune, everything you did naturally well, for granted. And, oh, how I envied you, Rachel, in so many ways! You've always known your own mind, for one thing.'

She's envied *me*?

'I have?'

'Of course you have. You've never compromised, have you? Being poor, for example.' She waves a lofty hand. 'It's never mattered to you. You made all your decisions

337

without being fettered to . . . to what people think of you, because you know what you're worth, you *know* it . . .'

Do I?

I pour my sister a glass of water and take in the mess of our dirty dishes on the side. I can hear the front door going. Maggie's back. Inwardly, I groan, because I'm going to have to be the one to clear up. Lily has clearly gone way past it. She's probably going to need to sleep on a couch for the night too, unless I can call for a cab and persuade the driver to see her into the hotel?

'I don't know what you mean about me making all my own decisions and knowing my mind and stuff.' If that were true I wouldn't be battling so much with what I'm facing right now, would I?

I gather up the plates and scrape the remains out into the bin. 'Nothing fazes you, Rachel,' my sister continues. 'Nothing ever has. Nothing ever will. Whatever happens, you cope. That's because you're naturally talented. When you're like me, unfortunately,' my sister plucks at her elegant turquoise blouse, rearranging it about her shoulders, 'you have to rely on other strategies.'

'Such as?'

'Such as persuading the naturally talented and better-off that they want to help you. That's something I learned from good old Dad. You find out what people's weaknesses are and you exploit them.'

I stop scraping the dishes, and stare at her, hard.

'That's not fair, Lily, and you know it. Our dad never exploited anyone.'

'Oh!' My sister rolls her eyes, suddenly irritable. 'He exploited *us*, you dumb-bell.'

338

'How can you say that? He tried to get us to achieve; to be the best we could be. That's what any good parent would do.'

'He wanted *you* to achieve, Rachel. There was never any question of greatness in it for me. He knew that. Mum knew it, even if you didn't.'

'That's just not true, Lily. He wanted us both to be good.'

'And when we couldn't be good any more?' Lily raises an eyebrow. 'He left.'

Oh, but he didn't leave us for that reason. I want to stop her and say, *Don't you know the real reason he left us?* Could she really not know? She still thinks it was because of the end of the dancing.

'Look, he left us because he was having an affair. He thought the woman wasn't interested in him any more but then she sent him a letter. A letter that made it perfectly clear that she was. Mum hid the letter away in her box, but I . . . I got it out and showed it to him and *that's* why he left.' I gabble out the words quickly, too quickly, and I see the blank, shocked look on her face being covered up almost instantly by something else. She finds it too painful, I see. She knows the truth; deep in her heart she has always known the truth. She prefers to believe the lie because it hurts her less.

'He left because we couldn't dance any more,' she repeats robotically, 'and that was my fault, Rachel. Do you remember what happened? How I . . . ended up in hospital? And after that I couldn't dance.'

'That wasn't your fault, though!' I grab her hands. She's got to know the truth, about this at least, even if

339

she won't accept the real reason why Dad left. She's got to know the truth about what I did.

'Oh, Rachel, Rachel. You can't save me from my sins, you know. They're mine. I want them. I need my sins!' She's cracking up, giggling in a stupid, hysterical way.

'Shush!' I put my finger to her lips. 'It wasn't your fault about the end of the dancing, you're going to have to believe me. It was *my* fault. No one's but mine.'

'So you say, Rachel. You think I don't see the whole truth, but neither, my dear sister, do you. Look, everyone has a blind spot.' She's struggling to speak coherently, making an effort to sit up straight in her chair. 'Everyone has their weakness that they don't see. It's their fatal flaw, if you like.'

'What are you talking about?'

'You, my darling. I'm talking about the bit you don't see. You feel too responsible for everyone. You're like Atlas, holding the whole world upon your shoulders,' she laughs.

'Well, do you want to know what yours is?'

'What?'

'You talk too much when you're drunk.'

I turn away in frustration. If she wants her imaginary sins so much perhaps I should bloody well let her keep them?

'Darling, that may be just about the *only* time when I've got anything to say that's really worth listening to.'

Atlas holding up the world, she says; but of course I am Atlas. I know too much about who did what and why they did it. I know that it was my own nosiness and desperation, poking around inside Pandora's box and revealing that letter to Dad, that split our family apart. I did my mum a disservice, too, I think now. Dad never even stayed with his mistress after all that. He went on and had another string of them, so Lily told me. He went away to the West Country, the last she heard of him, and slowly, with increasingly larger gaps between Christmas cards and birthdays remembered and then forgotten, he'd fizzled out of our lives.

I'd forgotten how it really was, and Lily doesn't want to know the truth, but Pandora's box has reminded me:

12 December 1978
I think, maybe, I have just seen my dad for the last time.

After we saw Lily, Dad and I went downstairs so he could have a smoke. We stood out there for ages and ages. I gave up holding the door open, thinking he might go back inside. I let it close to, and we left the bright hospital smell of antiseptic behind.

'Don't ask me,' Dad said. 'It's over. I was never cut out for this happy families lark. Your mother knew it when she married me.'

'I don't understand,' I told him.

He said, 'I know.'

There was this huge silence in the air between us. I could hear a child crying in a corridor far away. I could hear the engine of a motorbike revving up around the corner, the angry noise of speed.

I had to try real hard not to cry after that because it wasn't what he expected of me. I'm the strong, dependable one, he's always said so. He's expecting me to look after the others now – Ma and Lily – while he goes off and 'makes his escape', as he put it. I don't want him to escape, though. And I don't want to look after the others, either.

'I have to know why you're going,' I said to him. Was it because of her, because of the 'other woman'? Or was it something else? 'Are you leaving because of the accident? Is it because it's all over and we can't dance any more?' I grabbed hold of Dad's arm while he peered out from under the shelter of the doorway. He kept shaking out his umbrella, preparing to go.

'One day you'll look back on this and know it was the most courageous thing your old dad ever did,' he said to me. 'I'm not walking out on you, honey bunch. I'm freeing you. Sometimes you have to be cruel to be kind.'

I don't feel as if he's freed me, though. I feel as if I've suddenly got this huge weight on my shoulders.

I tugged as hard as I could on his arm but I knew that it was useless; I wasn't going to get any nearer to him than any of those raindrops that would soon be running harmlessly down the sides of that huge black umbrella.

I watched my dad stride out across the car park. He went past the drab rows of chrysanthemums huddled in their flowerpots. I watched him as he turned purposefully left towards the taxi ranks and disappeared out of my life for good, leaving Lily and Ma for me to 'look after for him'.

342

37

Rachel

Friday morning, 7 a.m.
When I wake up this Friday morning the mist is hanging over the beach like something out of an old black and white movie. There is a chill on the edge of the wind. Walking down to the beachfront at Summer Bay, nobody is about, and at 7 a.m., sitting on the damp sea wall with the muted sound of breaking waves behind me, I call up Annie-Jo's number.

She'll be in her fleecy white morning robe by now, I know, hustling some breakfast into her family, boiling up healthy eggs for them, organising pick-up rotas.

'Hello?' Her voice sounds early-morning cranky.

'Annie-Jo, it's *me*.' I'm so relieved to hear her voice it's pathetic. I want, oh I so desperately need, to be able to talk to her right now.

But she doesn't seem to know who *me* is. Of course she doesn't. Not any more.

'It's me, Rachel.' Pause. 'Shelley and Daniel's mum.'

'Oh, *Rachel*.' It's early, her reticence seems to imply; too early for a social call. And she's busy.

'Look, I'm sorry to call at this time, it's just, those invitations you wanted . . .'

'Oh, of course!' She sounds relieved. 'Oh, you've done them? That's great. When can I pick them up?'

'Not just yet, Annie-Jo. Um – is there any chance of extending the deadline?'

'None at all,' she says affirmatively. 'It was a rush job, I agree. But we both knew that at the outset.'

'Look, Annie-Jo, I've had to come away for a few days, though, that's the thing. I just wondered how long before you need them?' I'm thinking fast now. I'm thinking that I still need someone to pick up Daniel from scout camp because I won't be there to do it. And what if Bill – my first port of call – can't, or he decides to be difficult about it when he learns where I am? I needed to come clean with a lot of people sooner than this, I know. I meant to phone Bill yesterday, but all those things that Shelley said, they knocked me for six; I forgot what I was meant to be doing.

'Rachel,' there's a distinct chill coming down the phone right now, 'are you telling me that you won't have them ready in time? I went out on a limb to recommend you to the committee.'

'Oh no, I'm doing it today. It's just . . . I've rung you about something else altogether, actually.' I move along the wall, a bit further away from the bin. There's a tramp rummaging in among the refuse now and I don't want him talking to me.

'Thank goodness for that. I'm going to be taking my shower in a few minutes, Rachel, Michelle's got a recital on at the end of term so it's extra lessons on the clarinet over the hols – so could we be quick?'

344

'It's about Danny. When you pick up Josh from scout camp tomorrow, could you pick up Danny too? In fact, it would help me enormously if he could sleep over at yours tomorrow night.'

'What's going on?' she asks suspiciously now. 'Why can't you do it? Is there a problem with Shelley?'

'I'm sitting on the beachfront at Summer Bay in Trefolgew, Cornwall. I'm giving Shelley the birthday present that she asked me for – which was to come down here – but which Bill and I couldn't agree on, Annie-Jo, so I can't ask Bill.'

'Let's get this straight. *Michelle, darling, you still haven't put that clarinet back in its case and you're going to need it today* – sorry – where were we? I've been up all night puking,' she confides now. 'Rachel, you're telling me you're in Cornwall and Bill doesn't know you're there so he can't pick up Daniel?'

'No, he doesn't. You were up all night puking?' I say. 'Does that mean congratulations are in order?'

'Thanks,' she says shortly. 'But look,' there's a moment's hesitation, 'this doesn't sound at all like you, Rachel.'

It doesn't sound like the Rachel you used to know, I think now. She's right. But then Annie-Jo's not the same any more either, is she?

'Can you pick Danny up for me?' A boy with dark rings under his eyes staggers off the beachfront now. He's heading for the café across the road. He can't be any older than Shelley, I realise, and yet he's been up all night, boozing.

'Is everything . . . *okay*?' I note the change in her tone to one of concern. '*I said put that clarinet away Michelle!*'

345

The receiver is covered for a moment; the sounds at her end go muffled. When she comes back I can no longer hear the radio playing in the background.

'I'm having a bit of a hard time of it,' I admit, 'but this probably isn't the right time.'

'Rachel, we've been friends for a long while, haven't we? I have to be honest. I'm not sure that I'm comfortable going behind Bill's back like this.'

I take in a deep breath. I need her to help me now. I need her to know how bad things are, even if this isn't a good time to launch into this.

'Annie-Jo, Bill doesn't know we're here. But Bill couldn't see how important this trip was for Shelley. I could.' On the other hand, maybe I couldn't, I think now. Shelley tricked me, didn't she? It was important, but not for the reasons she led me to believe. 'Shelley . . . Shelley's in a bad way at the moment, Annie-Jo.'

'Oh my god, Rachel!' Her voice rises in pitch. 'Do you mean . . . ?'

'No, no. It's not that. It's something else. It's a sort of . . . depression, I guess.'

'That's only natural.'

'Yes, but she's . . .' my voice drops to a whisper, 'she's threatening to take her own life.'

'Oh, *Rachel*.' That shock again. 'That's terrible. Get her some help. Straight away. And Bill *must* be told.'

'No! I don't want to escalate this. I want to de-escalate. Bill will only make things a thousand times worse.'

'But there was a girl in Michelle's class – Shelley might know her – Rowan, she's called – anyway, she had a tiff with her boyfriend, and they found her last week, about to slit her wrists, it was a terrible business, she's had to have time off school for counselling and whatnot . . .'

A girl called Rowan had a tiff with her boyfriend? She needed to have time off school for counselling? What the hell is Annie-Jo on about?

And then it hits me. She doesn't understand. Of course she doesn't understand. How could she? Would I, if the boot were on the other foot?

'It's okay,' I tell her wearily. 'Really. I'm dealing with it, Annie-Jo. I just need a bit of support at your end. Will you pick Danny up for me?'

'Well, if I pick up Danny, knowing full well that Bill hasn't been informed, then it means I'm colluding with you, doesn't it?'

'But he doesn't have to know that you know.'

'It's still collusion, Rachel, and I'm not comfortable with it.'

'So you won't pick Danny up? You've got to pick Josh up anyway. And Danny's always over at yours. Come *on*, Annie-Jo!'

'I'll have to give this some thought, okay? Give me your number again. I'll ring you back later.'

I swallow, hard.

'Look, just stuff it,' I tell her. When had Annie-Jo become so sanctimonious? Suddenly I don't feel so duty-bound to do her calligraphy work any more. What just happened there? I'm furious with her, but I'm still gutted and that's the truth. I feel cheated somehow, bereft of somebody who used to be my friend. She's pregnant and she didn't even tell me. What's more, I don't think I even really care. I press the 'end call' button.

I punch in Solly's number now, praying that he'll pick up. Solly never picks up. He is permanently unavailable.

'Hel-lo,' he purrs into his cell phone.

'Oh, Solly, thank god!' If I hadn't thought he might still be in France I'd have rung him first. He already knows I'm here, for one thing.

'How's my girl? Enjoying the beach, darling?' He recognises my voice, too; oh joy!

'I'm good.' I shuffle off the cold stone wall. The little jaggedy edges are beginning to dig into my bottom and my legs. The mist feels like a wet breeze on my face. I lick my lips. 'Though it's not exactly sunny here.'

'And how is the birthday girl doing?'

'Huh! Do you really want to know?'

'Darling, I'm stuck in bed with the flu. I'm bored. Tell all, do. Oh, *thanks*, darling.'

Thanks? He doesn't mean me, I realise.

'You're back together, then?' His trip to Paris must have been a success, I think.

'Oh yes, we're back together,' he sighs.

'At least Justin can look after you while you're ill.'

'*Justin!*' he snorts. 'Justin wouldn't come near me with a barge pole right now. The boy's such a terrible hypochondriac. He doesn't *do* germs. Oh yes, I found him in Paris all right. That other bastard left him on the Champs Élysées without a sou after they had a tiff, would you believe? Lucky for Justin that I was hot on his trail, wasn't it?'

'So you rescued him,' I say. *And now he won't even hand you a tissue for the flu you've got.*

'Well, I *sort of* rescued him. I was *going* to rescue him

348

but then I discovered my credit card was missing and we were just about to call the police when who should I spot crossing the road just ahead of us?'

'Who?' Sacha Distel, I think. Catherine Deneuve. Jacques Chirac. I run out of well-known French names. 'Who did you see?'

He sighs, and I get a flash of what it must be like to live life as Solly. Here, sitting on this drab stone wall on this wet, grey morning by the deserted beach, I get a whiff of the scent of café au lait drunk at the elegant table of some pavement café along the boulevards of Paris; an accordion plays some melancholy song from the war years as Solly meets up at last with his wayward lover and then . . . some swanky French rock singer/actress/politician walks by. What a hard time he has of it.

'Adam,' he says. 'He'd come to Paris after me.'

'You've split up,' I remind Solly. 'Isn't that a little bit like stalking?'

'Not at all, darling! He'd brought me my credit card, hadn't he? I left it on the desk back at the shop. He works alternate days with me now, as you know. Anyway, he saw it and realised I'd get into a bit of a pickle without it.' He chuckles. I hear Adam chuckling in the background along with him.

'Oh, so it's *you and Adam* who are back together, not . . .'

'Precisely. I've been doing some rearranging of my priorities recently, Rachel. I've decided that Adam is . . .' his voice wobbles a bit here, 'Adam is the man I want to *grow old with*.' Solly clears his throat. I imagine him wiping away a sentimental tear. 'But apart from Adam – and Mrs Simmonds yesterday morning, of course – I haven't spoken to a soul. So tell me all your news, pray do.'

'Mrs Simmonds? What did *she* want with you?'

'Um, she couldn't find the reptile, apparently. She seems to think it's . . . no longer in her garden. I told her it was probably just hidden, you know. Like they do.'

'She's lost *Hattie*?' I can't afford to have minor domestic crises now. I grimace at the grey skies above me. I really want God to hear this: *Don't send any more crap my way until I've sorted out the major mess I'm currently in, okay?*

'No, no. I'm sure she's not lost. She just can't find it, that's all. It'll be there. She brought me up some rather dreadful chicken soup when she heard I was ill, too. Bless her.'

Chicken soup. Hattie's missing.

Focus, Rachel.

Solly is stuck in bed with the flu so he won't be able to pick Danny up for me. It's going to have to be Bill after all, isn't it? The *one* person I didn't want to have to ring and ask, damn it!

'But never mind all that. Are *you* two having a good time?'

'I'm not sure,' I tell him carefully. 'Actually I'm . . . I'm a little perplexed, to be honest. It turns out Shelley had a totally different agenda than what you and I thought she had.'

'She's meeting a lad down there, is she?' Solly sounds excited. I can hear him plumping up cushions, making

350

himself comfy in anticipation of my sordid revelations.

'No!'

'Oh.' He sounds disappointed. Why on earth would he think that Shelley had a boyfriend down here? Here, of all places? 'Fire away then,' he orders.

'She tells me she came down here with the intention of ending it all, Solly. She wants me to help her go off a cliff! Can you believe it?' I lower my voice as a dog-walking couple pass by and look back at me, wide-eyed. Christ, I never saw them coming.

'Oh, for heaven's sake, darling!'

'You don't think she means it, do you?'

'It's hardly likely. But I'd still be inclined to treat this as a call for help.'

'That's just it. The only help she wants is for getting up the cliff. It's crazy!'

'She's one determined young lady, isn't she?'

'You think I should be worried, Sol?'

There is a pause at the other end.

'If she's threatening stuff like that you can't ignore her. But on the other hand . . . can she do it by herself?'

'Solly, she's asked me to help her!'

'Oh that's rich.' He seems to find this pathetically amusing in that dark way that he has. 'I don't suppose there's too much to worry about then. Why don't you just bring her home, Rach?'

Because we came here for her birthday. Because we planned to leave on Sunday, and she's got stuff she wants to do here, and so do I. Because I don't believe she really means it. Oh, I don't know why!

You feel so far away, Solly, I think now. I need to see

the reassurance in your twinkling brown eyes. I need to feel your arms around me giving me a hug, because it's all too much, it really is. And everyone is just so far away. When I look along the length of the cold sea wall, everyone has gone: the dog-walking couple and the tramp who was digging around in the bin and the young lad who went by before with the dark, sleep-deprived eyes, they've all gone. Today I feel so very alone. Maybe we should just go home?

'I don't know what to do for the best, Sol. Everything seems so . . . so very unreal, since we got here. I don't feel quite right.'

'Come home,' he says comfortingly. 'Come back. Everything'll look different when you get back here, you know. Everything will go back to normal.'

He's right. If I go home everything will slot back into its usual place. Just like it always does. But what *is* normal, I wonder now? And do I want it any more?

I don't know if I do.

38

Rachel

Friday morning, 8 a.m.
Back at Crouch's End I can smell coffee on the boil; some folk are already starting to stir. Lily is still snoring gently. I can see her through the parlour window, draped like some elegant old-fashioned doll over the settee. The early walk has helped clear my head but there's no telling what hers will be like when she gets up.

'Frank phoned.' Maggie greets me on the doorstep, fetching the milk. 'He said he'd come round early, if you were okay with that – I told him you were already out walking.'

Maggie looks different this morning. She hasn't got her make-up on and she seems somehow more vulner-able without it.

'I couldn't sleep,' I admit. 'Look, Maggie, could you give me Frank's number? I need to ring him. This morning looks like it might be off after all.'

'Oh.' I catch a flicker of surprise. 'Are you sure? He'll be disappointed. He said he was bringing a picnic,' she adds, stacking the empties into the milk-tray. 'Oh, look, here he is now. You can tell him yourself.' We both turn round to watch as Frank's car pulls up onto her gravelled drive. 'I'll go and start reviving people with some coffee, shall I?'

I watch her disappear back inside, leaving me standing at the door to face Frank on my own, and my stomach constricts at the thought. I don't want to face him. What did he have to come so darned early for?

'Hi, Rachel.' There it is again. That smile.

'Frank.' I rub my hands together, the early-morning mist has made all my fingers so cold. 'Didn't expect to see you here quite so soon . . . the others aren't even up yet.' The others: Shelley and my sister, I think. And why does my sister have to be here? I wish she'd gone home last night.

'Tintagel is much better visited in the early morning,' he informs me. 'And as Mags said you were already up I thought I'd take advantage and maybe we could make an early start. But I don't want to rush you . . .'

'I had to make a few phone calls, so I went out.' I try to make my mouth smile back at him but I know that it doesn't reach my eyes. 'I needed to catch some folk before they left home.'

That sounds silly, even to me. I could make a phone call from anywhere, couldn't I? 'And I couldn't sleep,' I confess.

'Neither could I, Rachel.' He steps a bit closer, taking me by the arm. 'Do you want to stroll round the garden for a bit? Seeing as Shelley isn't up yet? Ever since yesterday I've been wanting to talk to you some more, to explain my situation. I know I've been a bit private. I don't just open up to anyone and everyone, not just like that. But I think you deserve to know.'

354

The pebbles underneath our feet are wet and slippery. They make a loud crunching sound as we walk past pink geraniums and roses, hollyhocks reaching skywards like banners of blue. Frank seems relaxed and at ease this morning. When I glance at him I know he's found some peace since yesterday, but me, if anything I'm only feeling more jittery.

'What I said yesterday, about being instantly attracted to you – I meant it, Rachel . . .'

But . . . ? The unspoken other half to his sentence hangs palpably in the air between us. You're going to tell me about the woman in your life now, I think. You're going to tell me that you've had a period of separation but now you're going to go back to her . . .

'Look.' He brightens up suddenly as a robin lands on the head of a little stone cherub. Maggie's garden is full of such garden ornaments. This one's piddling into a water fountain. 'Have you met Thomas yet?' Frank pats the cherub's arm affectionately. I shake my head.

'I thought Maggie might have introduced you.'

'Oh yes, she did. Of course.' Now I remember, she had stopped by this fountain a couple of days ago and showed him off to me. She's extraordinarily proud of her garden furniture. I think a cherub should have a more cherubic name, like Seraphiel or something more angelic, but I don't comment on that.

'Frank, you told me yesterday that you weren't really free,' I interrupt him now. 'I take it that means you're already with someone. And if that's the case, I think we'd better not take this any further. I mean, us going out together this morning, that sort of thing. You know I want to go . . .' and I do, oh, I so very much do, 'but I won't pretend that I'm not attracted to you. And if you're already with someone . . .'

'As I said, sweetheart, it's complicated.' He sits down on the wet wooden bench beside Thomas and I take a seat next to him. Somewhere above us in the yew tree behind the house a blackbird is calling; its song is high and sweet and haunting.

'I'm married, Rachel.'

I look up at him and there's a feeling of shock coursing through my body, even though I'd anticipated this. I won't be part of a triangle that helps to break up anybody else's marriage. I won't. I fight back the tears fiercely. I shake my head helplessly.

'Then it's not complicated at all,' I say at last. 'I won't see you any more, Frank. We can't go out together this morning. We're both developing, well, feelings for each other. It wouldn't be right.'

'You don't understand. She's said if she never sees me again it will be too soon. She's desperate for a divorce.'

'Give her one, then. Then you'll be free, won't you?' I say, more fiercely than I'd intended.

'I can't.'

No, of course not. Now he's going to tell me there's a child involved! Of course, and she won't let him see it, that's it. It all makes sense now, doesn't it? The look in his eyes the other morning when we came across those little kiddies running down towards the beach.

'You can't, *because*?'

'Because I can't divorce her like this. It can't end with this degree of acrimony hanging between us.'

356

'Because you still love her?' I accuse.

'I've never stopped caring for her, Rachel. Esme stopped loving me a long time ago. Because of what I did. I have to let her go, I know that. But how do I do that when she won't . . .'

Esme?

Did he say Esme?

Oh bloody hell. I'm suddenly hideously aware of the beautiful emerald-green cardigan that Maggie insisted I take yesterday afternoon when I felt cold. The one I'm wearing about my shoulders right now.

'Is this Esme's?' I ask faintly, plucking at my woollen sleeve. I know full well it is. It's still got her label inside, hasn't it?

'I bought that for her two Christmases ago.' Frank strokes my sleeve softly. 'And it looks just as beautiful on you, Rachel.'

'I don't look like her, do I?' A sudden horrific thought strikes me.

'Not in the slightest. She has blonde hair and a tiny frame. Even tinier now than she was before. She's lost a lot of weight.'

Since you two parted? I wonder now.

'So why does Maggie have all her clothes?'

'Because Maggie's her mother! Esme told Mags to just take them away. They don't fit her any more. And I think they remind her of . . . they remind her of an unhappy time.'

So Maggie's her mother. Which makes you Maggie's son-in-law, I think. God I always knew Maggie was private but this is taking it a bit too far . . .

'She hasn't . . . your wife hasn't got some terrible illness, has she? Like Shelley? When we first met, you said Shelley reminded you of someone . . .'

'Yes, it was my wife Shelley reminded me of, I'll admit. But Esme isn't sick the way Shelley is. She had to be admitted to a sanatorium for a while, after . . . after there was an accident involving her and my son.' When he speaks of Esme, when he says her name, I know that what he says is true: he still cares for her, truly, deeply. He loves her the way I would love him if he were free.

'You have a *son*, Frank?'

'I had a son.' His eyes go to the cherub standing over the fountain. 'Thomas.'

'He died?' I can't help probing even though I can see the pain in his eyes. 'In the accident?' I take in a breath. This is it, then, the thing that we have in common, he and I. Not quite yet, but soon.

'Not *in* it,' he corrects me quietly, 'but because of it. Look, please come with me to Tintagel this morning, Rachel.' He changes the subject abruptly, but I cannot claim that he hasn't been completely honest. He's told me about his son. My god, his son. And he hasn't pretended that there aren't any feelings left between him and Esme. He hasn't even pretended that he doesn't have deeper feelings beginning to form towards me.

'I want to,' I say slowly, 'you know I want to go out with you this morning, Frank. But if I do, I may be interfering in your . . . in your unfinished business with your wife.'

'I need to finish it, though, Rachel, don't you see? I

358

need to find someone who can help me do it. Esme finished with me two years ago. She made that clear then and she hasn't changed her mind. I need to find a way to get over her.'

Ah, but you need to do it yourself, I think.

'You can't use me to get over your wife, Frank. You have to get over her first.' The words come out without me wanting them to; they tumble out of my mouth like they're words I learned by rote for a play and they don't belong to me.

I'm lonely, I want to scream. I'm lonely, just like you are, and I know we could be good together, us two. I don't want to be sitting here telling you all this noble stuff about 'get over her first and then you'll be free' – and it might be the best thing to do by Esme, whom I've never met, it might be the noble thing to do, but I'll be damned if it's what I really want and that's the truth.

But my dad left Pandora when another woman couldn't find it in her heart to say 'no' to him. My own husband left me in just the same way. Who knows how things might have turned out if there hadn't been someone else there, so willing and so ready to step into the breach of those marriages?

The disappointment I see in his eyes is nothing but a shadow of my own.

'So you won't come out with me today then?' When he moves in it is without warning, my hands caught up against the buttons of his jacket as he pulls me in close. '*Please*, Rachel?' And then his mouth on my own, sweet and urgent, filling a void I had not even guessed was there. You can't do this, Frank.

'I can't!' I break free unwillingly. I want to, but it wouldn't be right. It wouldn't be fair.

'*Who* won't come out with you today?' There she is, right on cue. My sister in her borrowed wrap-around towelling robe, her hair tousled and sleepy-eyed. She looks as if she might have genuinely stumbled on us by accident, she looks so confused.

'I'm sorry,' she mutters, 'I have such a head on me this morning. Ugh!' She runs her hand through her hair. 'I needed some air. I'll just go round this corner and leave you in peace.'

But she doesn't go. She just stands there, the early-morning sun that's now filtering through the mist looking lovely on her face, her eyes closed, her whole body languid. And I know, even then, without either of them saying a word, that she will be taking my place on that trip to Tintagel this morning, because he is lonely and she is too, and because I am the only one with too many bloody stupid principles to allow myself any happiness in this world.

39

Shelley

Friday morning, 11 a.m.
'You shouldn't have let Lily go with Frank,' I accuse Mum. 'You always step aside for her, don't you?'

'What do you mean?' Mum is straightening out my bed. She's already smoothed out every little crease and crinkle on the duvet but she's still going at it. 'How could I have stopped her?'

'You could have gone with Frank yourself, for one thing.' I wheel Bessie over to the bottom of the bed and she stops smoothing the covers. Her eyes look bloodshot and strange this morning. I don't know if that's the two bottles she and Lily killed last night or if it's because she's been crying. Maggie told me Mum was up with the larks, walking the beachfront all alone. I know that I've given her too much to think about. I know that she's worried about me. I should never have told her anything, when I think about it now. I should have found some other way. I wasn't being very fair.

She's shaking her head at me now, half-laughing to herself, but not in a humorous way. 'Yes, Shelley, I should have gone out with him. And run the risk of having you sneak off to do some damage to yourself.'

'Oh come on!' She's the one being unfair now. 'I told you I wouldn't do it without you. I told you that. How could I, anyway? And it's tomorrow, not today.'

'I still won't leave you. The truth is, I should be taking you to see a doctor. I should be getting you some anti-depressants . . .'

'Do you believe that?'

Mum sits down on the edge of the bed, chewing her thumbnail, not seeing me.

'Do I believe what?'

'That this is all about me just being depressed. Because you'd be wrong, you know. It wouldn't make any difference how many tablets I swallowed down. It wouldn't change the way that I feel. And I still think you should have been the one to go with Frank this morning. He wanted you, not her. He was pretty upset with you when they went off.'

'How I choose to live my life is none of your business, Shelley.'

'*Oh yes it is! Every bit as much as how I choose to end my life is any of yours.*'

Mum looks at me, round-eyed. 'You're not going to end it, Shelley. Do you hear me? It isn't going to happen.'

'Oh, what's the use, Mum? What's the use of living for so many years? Look how many years *you've* lived. Every chance for happiness you ever get, you throw it away. Should I live to be one hundred, what good would it do me if I end up being like you?'

I watch her hand go over her mouth now, her eyes wide with shock. But it's the truth. She's got to hear it from me. No one else is ever going to tell her what I will.

'You're falling in love with Frank, Mum. He's falling for you. *Why* do you have to palm him off onto your sister?'

'Shelley, he's married,' she says in a shaky voice. 'He's not a free man.'

'I know he is. I heard his story from Ellen. But it's complicated, isn't it? Did he explain the whole situation to you?'

She laughs a little here, when I use the word *complicated*.

'He's explained everything, Shell. And I told him – as long as he's got a wife – I won't see him any more.'

'Then you're a bloody fool.' The words come out before I can stop them. She's giving this lovely man away to Lily, like a gilt-edged invitation on a plate. 'Lily doesn't deserve him, Mum. You do.'

She *knows*. She knows what he did, that's the thing. She hasn't said as much but that's the real reason. It's got to be. It's the thing that's driving a wedge between the two of them. When Ellen told me, I felt . . . I felt shocked and sad and I also felt happy as well. I knew then that Frank would be the right man for my mum, though; that there couldn't be anyone else.

'First of all, Lily deserves happiness every bit as much as I do, young lady. Her life's not all been a bed of roses, I promise you. If it hadn't been for some of the choices I made when we were younger then things might have turned out very differently for her as well. She has suffered, I can't deny that. And part of that was down to me, so I owe her more than you know.'

'I don't know what you're on about, Mum.' But I

363

know part of it. I've been reading her pink diary, haven't I? I haven't forgotten what I was reading earlier this morning . . .

15 December 1978
Last night we visited Lily on Hyacinth ward. Her arms were all bandaged up. Mum says she has broken bones in both wrists where she slipped. There was a vase filled with the hugest bunch of lilies and pink carnations and roses at the foot of her bed and she had metallic balloons in the shape of teddy-bears floating above her bedstead, with the words 'Get well soon' in tiny silver writing on them. Dad sent her all that.

Mum had got some special perfume for me to give her. I just stood at the foot of the bed with the bottle in my hand, feeling like a Judas, pretending to be nice. Mum and Dad and everyone else kept fussing around, more concerned than I'd ever seen them, 'because your sister is in such pain and she is being so brave'.

Maybe it is easier for her to be brave than it is for me, because I know exactly what is coming and she doesn't.

Our lives have been shattered; splintered like all those tiny little bits of bone I imagine must have been shattered in her wrists. Lily won't be dancing again, not for a very long time. And that means I won't be dancing either. Not with her, not with Gordon. Not with anyone, not now.

Feeling like a Judas, she says, as if it were somehow all her fault. As if it could be!

There must be more of a story in that diary than I've ever seen if Mum still feels so guilty about her sister. But that was all so long ago. Now is what counts. It's where we can make a difference. 'I don't know what you think you owe Lily,' I tell Mum, 'but if you know Frank's full story and you're still refusing to see him . . .'

'Let's talk about *you*, shall we, darling?' Mum turns on me and it's clear that Frank and Lily are the last things on her mind. 'I need to know – I just need to know that you didn't really mean what you said to me yesterday. That you haven't got so desperate as what you were saying.'

I sink my head into my hands now. It's pointless. She doesn't get it. She doesn't get where I'm coming from at all. It's the old generation gap thing, I guess. I should have known it would be like this.

From behind the black screen in front of my closed eyes I feel her get up and walk to the window and open the curtains. The light floods in and my picture turns orange.

'It's going to be a beautiful day after all,' she whispers, almost to herself. 'A perfect, crisp, clear summer's day.'

It is, too. When she pulls up the window I can hear the birds calling to one another in Maggie's leafy garden. I can hear the breeze rustling the curtains. I think it's going to be warm. Just how I wanted it. If only it can stay this way till tomorrow evening.

'Mum – you're right. If you don't want to get involved with Frank, that's your choice. I shouldn't interfere.' I lift my head from my hands and I see her turn to look at me now, her dark eyes shadowed by too much suffering.

I wish she could just break down and cry or something. That look in her eyes, I can't bear to see it. I want to make this all right for her, but I can't. 'Mum, I just want to be able to make *my own choices* too. Can you understand that? I don't want to suffer like Miriam did. It would be the worst thing you could do to me to force me to face death that way.'

'But what you're suggesting is unthinkable.'

'You're wrong. If we do nothing . . . if I come to Miriam's end, *that* is unthinkable for me.'

She takes in a long breath. She comes and sits back on the bed beside Bessie.

'I want to support you, you know that, Shelley. I want you to battle through whatever you have to battle through and to live as well as you can for as long as you can. But what you're asking me . . . it's impossible. What kind of parent would I be if I let you do that?'

'One that trusts me to make my own decisions.'

'Trust,' she says in a broken voice, 'I do trust you, Shelley. I do. But I can't let you do this. No way!'

'It's what I want, though, Mum.'

She shrugs. You don't always get what you want, she seems to say.

'And what about your brother? And your dad? Will you abandon them without so much as a goodbye?' Her voice rises bitterly.

'I've written to them, Mum. It's all sorted. This has got to be my decision. It has got to be. If I've got to face what Miriam faced then I want it to be on my own terms.'

'What do you mean?'

'I mean, I've got to know I had the chance to face it another way and that I decided not to take it.'

'You mean you might not jump? If I took you up there . . . you might not?'

'I guess we'll never know unless we try it, will we? I need to know I had that little bit of control, don't you see? That way, it's my decision how I face my end. I can't complain then, can I? I'll have done it my way. *Please*, Mum.' She flinches when I grasp hold of her hand. I know what it is I am asking of her. 'It's only fair. I want you to let me make the final decision.'

The look she gives me now, hard and dark, racked through with some kind of inner torment, is one that I will never forget. She inclines her head, ever so slightly.

'And I can trust you,' she demands now, her voice cracking, 'until tomorrow?'

'Of course you can. Who else would take me up there if not you?'

The relief I feel at this moment is washed out with a funny kind of deflated feeling. She's agreed to take me there. I can't believe it. Maybe she's lying? Surely my mum wouldn't really agree to what I've just asked her, no matter how much I begged her?

Her mobile goes off then, making us both jump out of our skins.

I can smell the aroma of frying bacon wafting in through the open window, and I feel hungry all of a sudden.

It's Dad, she mouths at me, her face looking blank and stricken at the same time. 'I'll take this privately, Shelley.'

367

I can hear him yelling something at her down the other end of the phone. I can't hear what he's saying, but when she leaves my bedroom and walks to the end of the corridor outside I can still hear her replies.

'Danny is *where*? What's he doing at home? He's supposed to be at scout camp. Oh, god. He took the bus back, you say? Oh, hell.' There's a pause and then she starts pacing up and down the corridor, her feet making the floorboards creak so I have to really listen up to get what she's saying. 'No, we're not at home at the moment, Bill. Oh, she *did*, did she?' She sounds angry. There is another pause. 'Well, if you rang Annie-Jo and she told you why we're here then there's nothing else to say about it is there? No, Shelley isn't being stupid, threatening anything. Don't be silly. Annie-Jo must have misunderstood me, that's all. We're coming home . . . tomorrow.' Her voice goes down a notch or two here but I can still just about make out her words. 'She's depressed, that's all. I'm planning on leaving here with her tomorrow, early. Yes, we'll be back by tomorrow evening, definitely. I'll pick up Danny from yours then. No, there's no need for you to come down here, Bill. I've got it all under control.' I hear her move further away and she's silent for a while as he must be saying his piece. When she answers, low, I can't hear what she's saying any more. Then I hear a click and wheel Bessie back towards the window so I'm away from the door.

'How is he?' I look innocently up as Mum comes back in.

'Danny got upset by something at camp and he's taken himself back home. *Damn* it!' She bangs her fist on the

368

windowsill. 'Why did that have to happen? Arkaela found him, but she couldn't contact us so she phoned Bill, naturally, and he phoned Annie-Jo, obviously . . .'

'Does she know?'

'I told her this morning.'

'Oh, shit. And what's up with poor Danny . . .'

'He's in a right old state, apparently, not aided by the fact that old Mrs S has lost his tortoise,' she continues in a daze.

'That's a bummer, but I should think that's the least of our worries,' I remind her. I want to ask her if she meant what she said to Dad right now about us leaving at first light, but then she'd know I was eavesdropping so I can't.

'It's probably just hiding,' I tell her when she doesn't answer.

'Danny's upset. Dad's upset. I'm upset!' She looks shaken. I bet Dad was really mean to her over the phone. I know what he's like. I bet she only let him speak to her like that because she feels so guilty at letting me come down here in the first place.

It's all my fault.

I know that.

I've got to put an end to all of this, and the sooner I can do it, the better.

40

Rachel

Friday afternoon

I *hate* it when Bill speaks to me the way he spoke to me this morning, so sarcastic – vitriolic would be a better word. As if he still holds me responsible for all that's wrong in the world. It doesn't bother him that Danny is going to have to stay with Mrs Simmonds till Shelley and I get back – *'It's a natural consequence, Rachel, of both his actions and yours. You can't expect me to pick up the tab.'* I thought all that would change once we were divorced. I thought maybe being on the receiving end of that particular strand of his character would be an acquisition passed on to his new wife, but to the contrary: *'I've got my plate full enough as it is, Rachel. Stella's rather fragile at the moment. We were still hoping to get away ourselves this weekend, as a matter of fact. I mentioned that last Sunday. I was still hoping that you might offer to take Nikolai for us, in fact . . .'* He'd spluttered on and on and my hands had gone white, clenching the phone so hard. At last he'd hung up, but his words have been ringing in my ears for the last two hours.

'Ouch!'

'You all right, my dear?' Maggie turns a concerned

face towards me from the kitchen door. She's got her secateurs in one hand, her cuttings basket in the other.

'I've-just-stubbed-my-toe,' I tell her between clenched teeth. Maggie hovers at the door, seeing me grimace.

'Why didn't you want to go with them, Rachel?'

'Shelley and Ellen wouldn't have wanted me along.' I force out a laugh. 'They were going to ogle some hunky surfers down at Smugglers' Cove, didn't they say?'

'You know very well I'm referring to Frank and your sister.' Maggie leans back against the door frame, a slight reprimand in her pursed lips.

'Three's a crowd,' I throw at her.

'You should have told your sister that,' she bats back.

Oh, her too? I've just had all that from Shelley, haven't I? I look at her curiously.

'He's married to Esme anyway, isn't he, Maggie?' I hesitate.

It feels strange, using Esme's name to Maggie since she's never mentioned her to me before. There is a strained silence between us for a moment, as if I have crossed some invisible line.

'How come you never mentioned that he was your son in law? I never . . . I never even knew about Esme.' I watch Maggie, usually so composed, as she bites back the tears.

'I never mention her, it's true,' she says at last. 'Because I find it too painful. I think about her all the time.' Maggie opens the kitchen door and steps out onto the patio. 'It looks like rain soon, Rachel. They said the sunshine wouldn't last. I must get my cuttings in.' Private to the last, obviously. She doesn't want to talk about it, then.

'I'll help you.' I take her basket and shadow her out into the rose arbour. 'Look, I'm sorry if I brought up something painful just then, Mags, but I just wish I could understand what was going on. I'm so confused. I didn't go with Frank this morning because I . . .' I feel my face flush slightly as I realise who I'm about to confess to. 'I'm starting to develop feelings towards him.'

Maggie looks at me sharply. Then her face relaxes into a smile. 'He's a sweet man,' she admits. 'I'm sorry. I didn't realise. You seemed so . . . so uptight when you came, I thought you two might help each other unwind, go for walks, you know.'

'Maggie,' I lay my hand on top of her own pale one, 'you have been the kindest person to me, and I do so appreciate it. And you're right, I have been a bit wound up since I got here.' *Since I got here! Since forever* . . . but the sympathy I see in her eyes is lethal. 'I feel I'm letting everyone down. No matter what I do, someone gets let down. Like, I'm supposed to be doing some calligraphy work for a friend today, but this morning I've just told her to get stuffed.'

'Do you *want* to do it?' She inclines her head to one side.

'I wanted the work,' I admit, 'because I need the gainful employment. Caring for Shelley twenty-four-seven is so exhausting and it feels so . . .' my voice goes small here, 'unrewarding.'

'It's endless,' she acknowledges.

'Until it ends,' I remind her. And which is worse?

'And Shelley's dad, Bill? Does he help you at all?' We're surrounded by roses, deepest of pink ones and huge scented orange ones and tiny, delicate, fit-on-the-top-of-a-cake ones. Maggie is carefully cutting the bottom of a long-stemmed rose and placing it lovingly into her basket as we speak.

'Bill is *furious* at the moment because, well, because first of all he never agreed that I could bring Shelley out here for her birthday – he wanted her at his for Saturday. He's only just learned that I brought her here anyway. Secondly, Danny – you remember, our little boy – he's just done a runner from scout camp and turned up at home with nobody there to look after him.'

'So it feels that no matter which way you turn there's something horrible waiting there for you?'

'There is, Maggie, there *is*. I feel so trapped. I just wish I could be free of it all. Even Shelley . . .'

'At least Shelley's having a good time.'

'Shelley has decided to end it all.' I give a grim laugh. 'Tomorrow. On her fifteenth birthday. Dramatic enough for you? Oh, and she wants me to help her do it by taking her up to the highest cliff-top.'

'Oh my dear.' Maggie pats my hand, her brows furrowed with concern now. 'But she seems to be having such a good time. She can't possibly mean it. She doesn't seem the slightest bit depressed, does she?'

'She isn't depressed, Mags. Hell, I don't think so. She's using logic, not her heart, to come to this. She reckons it'd be better to end it while she's still at this stage than to go through what may come on later.'

'But what about medical advances? What about having some hope for the future?'

I look at Maggie bleakly. 'Sometimes it isn't like that,

is it?' I take the secateurs from her and cut some more dusky-pink blooms from the tall bush. It's starting to spit and in a minute we'll be heading back in. 'Maggie, I'm just totally confused. I don't know what to think any more. Lily tells me one thing. Sol tells me another. Annie-Jo thinks I should tell Bill. Bill would say . . .'

'What would he say?'

'That I should book her into immediate psychiatric care.'

'It's a valid option.'

'Is it? To put her through another round of questioning; another set of medical loops and hoops? I don't know. What if she's just spouting off? I don't know what to do. I don't want to make this decision. Ouch!' She watches me, concerned, as I suck my thumb where I've just punctured it with one of those long rose stems.

'What does *she* want you to do?'

'She wants me to let her make the decision. She wants it to be her choice. That's what she said.' Bloody hell my thumb hurts.

'Can you do that? Maybe that is all she wants, you know. Maybe it's her way of facing the demons she knows she has to face.'

'How can I let her make that decision? How can I stand by and watch her do that and take no action to stop her? I can't, Maggie. You know that. You have a daughter yourself. Do you have any plasters?'

'I have,' Maggie agrees. 'Both some plasters – in my bathroom cabinet – and a daughter. And *I've* had to stand by and watch her throw her life away, and been pretty much helpless to stop her, you know.'

Only metaphorically, though, I think.

'Okay, let me get this straight.' She picks up my hand to examine what I've done and a bright drop of blood is showing from a thorn-prick. 'What are you actually scared of? Do you think she would really do it?'

'I don't know.'

'You *do* know. And she won't.' She lets my hand go.

'How can you be so sure?'

'Well, take Shelley out of the equation for a minute. Say you allowed yourself to do exactly what she asks you to do. You take her right up there. You give her the option. What are you really scared of?'

'That she'll do it, of course!' I hand her back the secateurs and she carries on cutting.

'But if you take out your worries about *her*, what are your worries about?'

'Oh for heaven's sake, Mags!'

'Go on.' She indicates for me to hold her basket so she can drop her flowers in.

'I'd be worried about me, I guess. I'll be bereft without her.'

Maggie sighs. 'You'd also be free, wouldn't you, Rachel? And that's what you want, isn't it?'

'Not that way. Never that way.'

'It's coming anyway, though, isn't it?'

I feel a prickle right through my skin when she says that, but she shakes her head at me, frowning.

'I'm playing devil's advocate for you, my dear. Think about it. Think about the unthinkable before it hits you like a bolt out of the blue one day when you're least expecting it. Okay, I think I'm done here . . .'

She peers at the roses that have now filled up her basket.

'Why didn't you tell me about Esme?' I fire at her now. We're moving away from her roses, taking the long way back via the kitchen garden. She still hasn't told me the first thing about Esme, I realise now. I don't even know why her daughter has come into my mind, except for this feeling I have that, in some strange way, we've been talking about Esme all along too. 'What happened to her, Mags? Why did she and Frank split up? Why does he still love her so much when she doesn't love him any more?'

It's to do with the child, Thomas; I've guessed that much. And Esme went into a sanatorium for a while – he told me that, too.

'You ask me about love,' Maggie laughs softly now, 'as if I might have answers regarding the greatest mystery of them all. Why does he still love her? I don't know. He does. When did she stop loving him?' Her faded grey eyes scan mine for a fleeting second. 'You'll have to ask him about that. I've no doubt he could tell you the precise second when that happened. Frank made a decision that my daughter could never abide by. He made it out of love but she could never see that. She couldn't forgive him.'

'He made a decision?' It has started to rain again, softly, dampening our hair with a fine mist of spray, and I slow my steps down because I sense once we get back into the house this conversation is over and Maggie may never talk about these subjects again.

'He . . . look, Rachel, he made a decision to let his child go; just as you're going to have to. After the car accident, Thomas was on life support for three months. He was never going to get any better. We all knew it. So Frank let them switch the machines off. It was for the best. We could all see that. But Esme couldn't see it. She's always been fragile, my little petal. She went out of her mind with grief, for a while. She couldn't let Thomas go; she couldn't mend.'

'Which is why Frank can't let her go, either? She's ill?' Oh Frank, poor Frank . . .

'Not any more, Rachel. She's met someone else. I don't like her new beau, to be honest, but that's none of my affair.' Maggie takes in a deep breath. She looks older all of a sudden, I see; so very much older.

'Is that what you meant just now when you said I should "think the unthinkable"?' I stop and watch her as she stoops to pluck up neat bunches of rosemary and oregano, pinching the leaves deftly between forefinger and thumb so as not to damage the plants.

'I mean, think about taking your freedom now; before another month passes. Once you stop giving up all the things that were meant to be for you, maybe then you'll find the freedom you want and when you do you won't feel so guilty about it.'

'Now you've lost me completely.' She sounds just like one of the Angel cards in her shop; it's just riddles to me, all riddles. 'Could I take a bunch of these home for my herb garden?' Her lavender smells heavenly. I want my garden to smell like that. I twist a sprig of it in my fingers, releasing the scent.

'You gave up on your dream of becoming an artist, didn't you?' she says softly.

377

'Well, I hardly had any option . . .'

'You gave up on your friend's calligraphy job this morning, too. And you gave up on your trip to Tintagel with Frank . . . ?'

'What's any of that got to do with anything?'

'Every time you "give up" on something that was meant to be for you, you give up a piece of yourself. I know it happens. I've seen it happen before. And if you just let it happen, if you just stand there and watch all the bits and pieces of your life drift by without you, then you end up feeling – well, as you do, trapped. You say you're longing for your freedom. I say if you don't watch out you won't have the first idea what to do with it when you get it.' Her face is wet, dampened by the rain, I wonder if that's what mine looks like, too? Would anyone wandering in here now think we'd both been crying?

'That's because I can only get my "freedom" when I lose something I'm not prepared to lose.'

'Of course not. But that's what we purchase with every loss, like it or not.'

'We purchase . . . what?'

'A space. A wilderness. A landscape where new things can grow.' She dips down and her hand brushes over the lilac head of a solitary tall thistle, a weed growing up through a crack in the paving.

'I don't like losing things, though.'

I don't want to purchase any new things with my loss. I want my old things. I want what I've already got. I want my daughter. I want my old friends, like Annie-Jo. I want to be friends with my sister.

I shrug. 'So you're saying I should . . . ?'

'Be free anyway. That way, whatever happens to Shelley, you won't be tied into it. You can't hold her a prisoner, you know. She's too old now. You can't keep her like you would an infant in a cot. Trust her to do whatever she needs to do and then accept whatever she does as coming from her.' She shivers, her thin top is soaked right through. I realise that I'm feeling cold, too.

'If I took her up the cliff-top, Maggie – which I won't, by the way – then I would be at least partially responsible because I'd have empowered her to do it.'

'She hasn't got the power, you're right,' Maggie looks at me sharply, 'but any other girl her age would certainly have the power, and so would also have the responsibility for their own actions. This isn't about her age, Rachel. It's about who takes responsibility, isn't it? And why should you imagine that it always has to be you?'

The light in her kitchen, once we go in, seems unbearably dim. I can smell the sweet lingering scent of the jam Maggie was cooking yesterday. The air feels sticky and close, and I know I'm going to have to go out again. I need to get changed into something dry and then . . . I need to go out. Somewhere. Anywhere. Where shall I go?

I cast my eyes around the kitchen, frowning, thinking furiously, and they alight on Pandora's box in the corner. And, placed on top of it, there are Lily's documents that I've still got to sign, for the handing over of the tumble-down property at number 11, Sycamore Drive.

That's when I decide exactly where it is I'm going on this grey afternoon that has suddenly opened up in front of me; I'm going on a trip down memory lane.

41

Rachel

Friday afternoon
What I didn't bargain on was that Memory Lane might have changed so much I'd need a navigational tool to help me get down there!

I stop and fill up with petrol. This is it, I think. This will be the tank that gets me back home tomorrow, providing the work that man did on the car holds up. And there's a kind of sadness in that, too, knowing that I won't be standing in this place again, waiting in this line to be served, picking up some sweets and a local map because I can't for the life of me remember how to get to Sycamore Drive. It isn't even where I expect it to be, on the map.

'Sycamore Drive?' The woman at the till – who claims to have lived here for the last ten years – calls 'out back' to her husband for confirmation.

'It's near the pig farm,' I tell her helpfully. 'There's a wooded area – it's a bit of a dump, really.' We used to scoot off down there as kids, looking for bits and pieces of other people's discarded rubbish, I remember now. We used to do that in the days before you had to worry about tetanus and dangers from infected needles and sad strangers that might be lurking behind every bush. 'But a great place for the kids to play,' I add. She looks at her husband doubtfully as he comes through, and he shakes his head.

'If it's where the old pig farm used to be,' he points a fat finger at the place on the map, now marked as 'recreational ground', 'then you're looking at the Queensbury development, aren't you?'

'Am I? Is that what it's called now?'

'That's what all this area down here is called.' He circles the place where the land meets the sea with his finger. 'The Queensbury Maritime Development Centre.'

'So . . . it's not *houses* any more? My granddad used to live there, years ago. He had a place that backed onto the scrubland just before the sea.' A place that creaked and groaned at night-time when the sea wind came up from the shore. A place with a little leaky attic room that smelt of damp and the feathers of seabirds and the shells that we'd collected down on the beach.

'Only *penthouses*.' The lady at the till throws me an arch grin. 'I don't reckon your granddad will be living in one of them, though. Unless he's very rich?'

'He's dead, actually. He hasn't lived there for a very long time. My mum had the house . . .'

'Oh, his place will have been torn down for the development then, years back. Some of them as inherited those old places hung on to them, and they got a penthouse in exchange, as I understand it. Those will be worth a pretty penny now, I'd warrant. Has your mum passed on and left it to you as her legacy, then, lass?'

381

'Pandora's legacy?' I laugh dryly. That would be all that's in her box, surely? 'No, she isn't dead. I was just in the area and I thought I'd look the old place up, that's all. But never mind the map, I shan't be needing that after all. Perhaps you could tell me, though, where I would find the nearest estate agent that handles property in the Queensbury development?'

17 April 1979
Mum didn't contest the divorce in the end. I wish she had. I wish she'd fought for Dad tooth and nail, hung on to him for all she was worth, but she didn't. It's as if all the life's gone out of her. She keeps saying she has to look after Lily, Lily's her top priority now. My sister hasn't been properly well for ages. Her wrists have healed up fine but the spark's gone out of her too.

I want to help them but I can't. Nothing I say helps. Nothing I do makes a difference. I offered Lily my blue necklace for keeps – the one with the sea-glass in it. I gave her my David Essex poster that she'd coveted forever, but they're both still in her bedroom where I left them. She doesn't even argue with me any more, and I never thought I'd miss that but I do. Gordon Ilkeley left for a place at a school in Surrey last term. I wrote to him twice. I even asked him to write a postcard to my sister (just to make her feel better), which he did, but even that didn't cheer her up.

Lily's been off school for ages. Mum says she is too depressed to go in. Maybe if we were still dancing we'd have something to do, something to aim for. It would get us out, anyway. But Mum says she can't afford it with Dad gone, and she hasn't the energy to be doing with all that any more.

And me? I'm trying to get my school grades back up to what they should be after so many years of neglecting them. I want to go to uni. I want to study art and, mostly, I want to get away from here as soon as I possibly can because I can't make Mum or Lily feel any better no matter what I do.

All I can think about all the time is — what do I have to do to put this right? I think it last thing at night, hoping to dream the answer so everything will be fresh and clear in the morning. I think it first thing when I wake up and no answer has been forthcoming. All I know is, the buck stops at my door and I can't live with it any more. I can't live with them.

So, just as soon as I possibly can, you can bet your bottom dollar, I'm going.

42

Rachel

Saturday morning, 10 a.m.

'Thank you so much for the diamond pendant you gave Shelley.' I watch my sister as she nibbles daintily on the edge of a croissant. 'That really was incredibly generous of you.'

'That's perfectly all right. My gorgeous niece will only be "fabulous fifteen" once, won't she?' Lily beams magnanimously at me. She's got a soft and satisfied glow about her today, and I should be happy for my sister but I'm not. I've got a horrible rankling feeling inside. I want her to tell me all about how it went with Frank yesterday, and at the same time I'm scared of what she might say.

On entirely another note, I still don't know what's going on with Shelley. She keeps looking at me in a funny way, but I don't know what she's thinking. Frank phoned at the crack of dawn to wish her Happy Birthday but I told him she was in the loo and we were at a motorway service stop. So he thinks we're on our way back to Maidstone. Ellen came round a little while ago to deliver her birthday gift. It was just a little thing – a hairgrip in the shape of a silver butterfly (just like the one Danny

384

got her for Christmas, in fact) – but it obviously meant a hell of a lot to Shelley. She kept turning it over in her palm, staring at it. 'It's a sign,' she said to me. She seemed quite overcome. She hasn't known Ellen that long, after all. 'It means I'm going to be all right,' she kept saying.

Oh, I suppose the birthday girl seems happy enough – if a little tense. She doesn't give the impression of someone about to commit a desperate act. She hasn't mentioned it at all, in fact, so I'm wondering if she might have changed her mind?

'Actually, I found that diamond pendant in Guy's jacket pocket six months ago,' Lily is saying to me now, 'he'd bought it for *her*, clearly, but I pretended to be delighted, thanking him profusely for getting me such a lovely gift. He had to hand it over, naturally.'

'You mean your husband bought it for his mistress?' I turn from the counter where I've been buttering some toast. My eyes open wide at the confession. Lily could have at least pretended she'd bought it herself! Still, it must have cost an arm and a leg, and I could see why she wouldn't want to keep it.

'Yep.'

'So, how was yesterday?' I bring over a couple of coffees and sit down opposite her.

'Lovely.' Lily dabs at her lips with a napkin. 'Very relaxing, actually.'

Relaxing? I thought there were millions of steps to climb to get up to Tintagel? How could she have found that relaxing?

'You two got along all right, then?'

My sister smiles languidly. How could there have ever been any question about that?

'Frank is . . . he's a really sweet man, Rachel. Going out with him yesterday was just the tonic I needed. I've been a bit low after, well, you know. Thank you for suggesting it. He's flying back to Toronto tomorrow, did you know?' She sips at the rim of her cup. 'Anyhow, did you manage to get much of that calligraphy work done?'

'No.' I shake my head ruefully. He's flying *home*? Damn! I didn't know that . . .

'I should have been a businesswoman, Rach. There were dozens of them at the hotel last night. Holding some sort of conference, I should think. But, my, you should have seen the clothes they were wearing – Balenciaga, Prada . . . and all with personal assistants to see to their every whim. It's the sort of lifestyle that would suit me to a tee.'

'If you ever decide to go to one of their conferences, maybe I'll come with you.' The comment is out of my mouth before I have the time to think about it.

'You will?' She looks at me curiously. 'What would *you* do?'

'I was thinking along the lines of . . . a little jewellery design business. It's something I've always wanted to do. But you know, one of these days . . .'

That laugh is so familiar. How could I have forgotten it? Is it more patronising or derogatory, I can't make up my mind. She stops up her mouth with the white napkin, at last.

'I don't think that's quite the level they're at, Rachel. These ladies aren't in it for *pin* money . . .'

386

'If it comes to that, there's got to be a bit more to it than what they wear,' I remind her stiffly. 'I'd imagine they'd have to put a bit of work in now and again, too.'

I'm smarting from her comment but I want to hear about her outing with Frank and she's pointedly not telling me. I can see that. I want to know what he said to her and what she said to him, and if they spoke about me at all.

Of course they didn't, though. Why would they? She certainly wouldn't have brought me up, and he must be pissed off as hell with me. And he's going home now and I've missed my chance and I feel so sad about that I could weep.

'That wouldn't be a problem . . . the work,' she smiles knowingly at me. 'You're thinking that I haven't got any brains, aren't you? But you know, in some ways it really is easier to be born talentless.'

'I wasn't thinking that,' I protest.

'When you're not talented, there's none of that pressure on you to succeed all the time,' she continues. 'There's no guilt if you don't succeed because nobody expected you to anyway. And there's less competition because nobody sees you as a threat in the first place.'

I laugh at this. There is a certain charm to her logic.

'Looks like you've got your route map to the top sorted out already,' I tell her, and then, without meaning to, I give my sister a hug. 'And anyway, you're not "talentless".'

I've got this feeling that, once we go our separate ways this time, it might be a very long while before I see my sister again.

'I wish you well, Lily, I really do. I hope . . . I hope you find all the happiness you deserve in the world.'

'You too,' she tells me. I can't help noticing her eyes look very bright.

'And, you know, what you said a moment ago about having all those expectations put on you if you have a talent for something, you're right. I never thought about it that way, but it's true.' I watch her breaking the rest of her croissant into minute little portions. 'Lily, I just want you to know . . . I just want to say that I'm so sorry that, well, you never got the chance to do the one thing you really loved. The dancing, I mean.'

'I have no regrets and no guilt about not making it in the dancing world, Rachel. The fact that I never achieved that, it wasn't all that important to me. It was you who had all the talent. But then,' she smiles disarmingly, 'we already *had* this conversation the other night, didn't we? Now,' she pushes out of her chair suddenly, and slides the house documents towards me. 'I must be tootling off, my dear. Will you sign these for me, please? I have to take them to Myrtle today.'

I take her pen. I can hear Ellen and Shelley in the hallway and my ears prick up. They aren't planning to go out again, are they? Not today. Especially not today. I feel uncomfortable about letting Shelley out of my sight at the moment.

'You have no idea what you saying that means to me.' I pull a smile at Lily now. 'I've always held on to this stupid idea that I kind of, well, *ruined* your life. If it hadn't been for me dropping you off that stage and you ending up in hospital with broken wrists . . .'

'Give it up.' Lily stands up now and hovers by my chair, waiting for me to be done. She checks her watch. 'You didn't drop me on purpose, did you? There was that faulty floorboard, remember?'

'Yes, I know that, but I can't help thinking that . . . Lily, this is going to sound so terrible, I know, but what if I *subconsciously* wanted you to fall?' Because you stole my boyfriend, I think now. That boy whose name you barely remember now, but who meant more to me than you'll ever know . . .

'Heaven's sake, Rachel, it's over, isn't it? Look!' She waggles her wrists in front of me. 'All better now.'

'I always felt guilty about it, that's all.'

She smiles at me. 'Maybe you *like* feeling guilty? Look, if it makes you feel any better, I thought you knew, that time I went to hospital with my wrists, that wasn't you . . . I did it myself. A cry for help, you know. I didn't want Dad to leave us for good. I wanted to make him come back and stay. Didn't work, though, did it? Quite the reverse. He couldn't wait to get away.'

'But . . . I dropped you!'

'An accident. And it didn't cause too much damage, Rachel. A really bad sprain, that's all. I did the other thing later, when I got to the hospital. Mum and Dad were arguing all the way to casualty, and that's when I found out, you know, what was really going on. When they left me there, that's when I did it. I cut my wrists. Not deep enough to cause any real damage, though.'

'*Mu*-um, me and Ellen are going out now!'

'No, you're not!' I yell at the girls in the hallway.

'Just for a walk . . .'

389

'No. Just you wait there till I can see you.'

I close the door so I can speak to my sister in private. What she's just told me feels like a blow right to the pit of my stomach.

'You did *what*?'

'A cry for attention, Rachel. That's all it was. Then I called the alarm button and all the nurses came running, so I was saved. I never *wanted* to die. Shelley doesn't either; that's why she's told you all her plans in advance. You're her alarm button, you see. Give her some attention and it'll all fade away. She's probably jealous about Frank, that's all.'

I want to go over and grab my sister by the shoulders and just shake her, but my legs are too wobbly so I just stay where I am.

They let me take the rap for it!

All these years, with me thinking that her injuries were all my fault, when they weren't! I don't want to believe her, but I can see in her eyes that she's telling me the truth.

'Why on earth didn't someone explain this to me earlier, Lily? I went through *hell*, thinking about what I'd put you through. The way everyone looked at me after that . . . they kept saying, *oh, you didn't mean it*, but that didn't change the way I felt.'

'It was the story Mum and Dad put out.' Lily shrugs, surprised at my reaction. 'You know how it is. Seeing as everyone had seen me go off to casualty anyway, they thought we didn't have to let everyone know our business, did we? Surely you can't have been holding on to guilt all these years over *that*? Who'd have thought it!

Well, it isn't like that. It never was. You have to update your childish view of things, Rachel.'

'Like . . . like the view I had of our grandfather's property, d'you mean? Remember the rainy summers we spent running in and out of that leaky tip?'

'Mum used to say it was just as wet inside as it was out.' Lily shudders at the memory. 'She went and stayed in a hotel in the end – and left us there – d'you remember?'

'I do. I have a hundred and one memories of that place. In fact, I went down there yesterday when you were out with Frank, to try to find it again, but do you know, I couldn't find it, Lily. Things have changed so much down there in recent years, haven't they? The area is unrecognisable.'

'Did you find it?' Her eyes go to the documents still on the kitchen table in front of me, to the pen I'm holding, still poised above the dotted line.

'I didn't,' I confess, and I see the relief flood through her shoulders.

I look up as Shelley opens up the door and peeks curiously round it.

'Ellen's godmother has a couple of tortoises she wants to get rid of to a good home. We want to go round and see them. I said maybe we could have them for Danny?'

I close my eyes. Tortoises for Danny. What next? Whatever next?

'Okay, go,' I breathe at last. 'Just go. Ellen, can you make sure she's back within the hour?'

'Of course, Mrs Wetherby,' Ellen smiles at me.

'Rachel,' Lily cuts in. 'Myrtle is getting on a plane this afternoon, I really need you to . . .'

'I found something else when I went out looking for Sycamore Drive, Lily.' I cut through her protestations. 'I found something beyond my wildest dreams, and I realised . . . do you know what I realised, Lily?'

'What?'

'I realised I've never really used my *imagination*. I've never stopped to think what things could be like, how things might change and grow and what they might become, if only I'd let them.'

'That's just a midlife crisis,' Lily tells me nervously. 'We all regret some things that we didn't do, those things we didn't become. Sometimes I feel that way about not having children, you know.'

'Do you?' I look at her curiously. 'It's strange, but after what you've just told me I've realised that I don't regret anything. The only thing there is to regret is the time I've wasted, worrying that maybe I should have been achieving more, *doing* more with my life. And why should I worry about that?' *Be at peace with your time*, I remember the Angel card from Maggie's shop, *and know that nothing is wasted*. It makes sense now; it really does.

'No indeed, you shouldn't.'

'The two most beautiful flowers in my garden are in full bloom. My son and my daughter.'

'You're proud of them,' Lily says softly, 'and you have every reason to be. Enjoy them while you can. I will never have that pleasure.' She leans forward and hugs me briefly, then taps the table with her fingernails. 'Now I really must go and get my skates on. The taxi will be

392

out there already. Can you put your paw print on that for me, darling?'

'I can't do that, Lily. We both know what that property is really worth. The penthouses lining Sycamore Drive must be worth a cool half a million each, with those stunning "sea views" and all. You wouldn't want me to go without my half of the inheritance, would you?'

Lily breathes out heavily. Outside, the taxi that's arrived for her gives an impatient honk. 'Girls,' she calls out to the two chattering in the hallway, 'tell him I'll be a few minutes, I'm just coming.'

'Look,' she sits down opposite me, her eyes steely now, but still hoping for a quick settlement, 'you've already got it all, Rachel. Everything you need. You have the two flowers in your garden, like you said. You have enough for your modest needs. I can't live like you do. I need more. I always have done. I'm like our mum.'

'And like her, you will always find a way to survive. There are plenty of talented people out there waiting for someone like you to come along and sponge off the back of them.'

'You've changed!' Lily gasps. 'You never used to be so grasping. You know I need the money. Do you really want me to have to go crawling back to Guy? How could you do this?'

'What you do with your life is your choice, Liliana. You're not my responsibility any more. I've realised today that you never really were.'

My sister snatches up the papers.

'You haven't heard the last of this, Rachel. We had an agreement. I'll have to see what Myrtle has to say about this. My taxi is waiting.' At the door, she turns on her heel. 'Oh, and if you see Frank again, tell him I loved his little tattoo. The honeypot one.'

'I've seen it,' I breathe. 'The one on his arm.'

'Not that one, darling, *this* one.' Lily points suggestively to a spot just below her navel.

'Do you mean that you two . . . ?'

'Oh, it was *raining*!' Lily smirks. 'My dress was getting wet and I didn't really have the shoes to go climbing all those blasted steps so we went back to his apartment instead. The man's a blessed miracle. He hasn't been with a woman for three *years*, Rachel.'

'Are you seriously telling me . . . look, I don't believe you. He told me he was still in love with his wife. He told me he . . .'

'You don't always want to pay too much attention to what men tell you, darling. Remember Bill?'

The taxi hoots again and this time my sister goes, pausing only to wave a cheery goodbye to the girls on her way out.

43

Rachel

Saturday afternoon, 5 p.m.
I want to turn back again to Frank's house. The winding road away from Crouch's End is calling me. I keep thinking, if I don't go there now I will never see Frank again; I will never get the chance to say goodbye.

I already know that goodbye will be all that there is left to say between us, and it seems so little a word, but, my god, does my heart ache to be able to say it. Even if – even if he *did* sleep with Lily.

Instead, I turn left, resisting the temptation to run to him even as he is preparing to leave, and I set my thoughts towards this evening, for it is my daughter's fifteenth birthday. Frank will be all packed up – maybe even on his way to the airport by now – but my daughter is still waiting for me, and I have a promise yet to fulfil to her. Probably the worst promise I've ever made to anyone in my life. I am going to have to trust her. I keep telling myself that.

I am going to have to trust her to choose life, because I can't be the one to make that choice for her.

I've got to focus.

Clearly I'm *not* paying proper attention to what I'm doing, because by the time I've jammed myself into the only available parking space left in front of the post office I realise that the dark green four-by-four beside me has taken up half of my space and the only way I can get out is through the passenger door.

The car looks vaguely familiar. On another day I might have left the driver a note on the windscreen. *Try and leave somebody else a bit of space, will you?* But it hardly matters. Nothing matters. I'm not even sure what I'm doing here at the post office, pausing to buy lettuce for these two tortoises, when nothing really matters.

Everything is going too fast, that's another thing. Can it really have been more than a moment ago that we'd sat out on the terrace at Maggie's, eating a decadent birthday breakfast of croissants smothered with fresh jam and cream? The sun had been shining then, and Shelley had thanked me profusely for the pink coral and red sea-glass bracelet I'd made for her. When I watched her face light up this morning I felt hope stirring for the first time in ages. She looked like someone who had just been released from a long and terrible prison sentence. She looked happier and more open and more joyous.

Foolishly, I've let myself believe that maybe she has changed her mind, that she is going to somehow let me off the hook. But she hasn't. Her text message from Ellen's phone came through a while back: *Pick me up from Ellen's, Mum, don't forget. I am waiting for you. It's time.* And then, a little later on: *Not at Ellen's any more, Mum, so just go home to Maggie's.*

Outside, the first fat raindrops are starting to splash

onto my car windscreen. I just sit here for a few moments, not wanting to get out. Why am I here? I keep forgetting. I have to buy something. Ah, yes: lettuce. I have to buy some lettuce for the two tortoises I've just picked up. But why the *hell*, when I think about it now, have I just gone and acquired the two reptiles in the first place? Just because Hattie has gone and I want to soften the blow for Daniel. Maybe these two will escape as well, and then my son will have to suffer the pain of more loss because, sooner or later, we all do.

Inside the post office shop, everything looks darker and dingier than usual. I realise, once my eyes get accustomed, that it's because there is no light. The woman has got a thin white candle lit in one corner, by the cigarettes.

'Electrics out,' she informs me when I take her my solitary lettuce. I don't know how to respond to her, but I can barely think. My mind is as clouded and leaden as the sky outside.

'Anything else?' She looks at me curiously as if she knows that I am dredging up every last ounce of energy just to be there. I wonder if she will be the one to quote to the papers, afterwards: '*The mother looked kind of odd, you know, as if she had a terrible secret on her mind. You wouldn't have thought it would be a priority for her to buy a lettuce. She clearly wasn't thinking right. Terrible business, that.*'

Out the door again and the green Volvo is still blocking my driver's entrance. I'm going to have to squeeze past that dripping forsythia bush to get in through the passenger seat. It doesn't matter, though.

Nothing matters. Today is a day of loss, and every-thing that matters to me is going to slip away as surely as the sea erases all traces of our footprints on the sand. We come and we go, and when each day starts anew it is just as if we have never been. I'm pondering on that when it comes back to me who the green four-by-four belongs to. Someone I have already lost, and who I don't know how I am going to cope with right now.

'*Rachel*, for god's sake, Rachel!' I turn in time to see my ex-husband racing out of the side exit of the post office, a newspaper over his head. He looks unshaven, dark rings under his eyes, the collar of his jacket rolled inwards as if he hasn't looked at himself before stepping out through the door. 'I've just been in there asking for directions to Maggie Hillman's place. I've forgotten the way, damn it.'

'Why?' It's a stupid question to ask. I clutch the lettuce in its damp paper bag closer to my chest. 'Bill,' I say, trying to keep my voice calm but it won't be steady; it betrays me, 'what are you doing here?'

'I think we both already know the answer to that. Where is she, Rachel?' His face is hard and white. His dark eyebrows are drawn together in a tight line of defence against me. 'Where is our daughter?' He empha-sises the word '*our*', evoking a reminder that it took the two of us to make her, that I could never have had her without him.

'She's back at Maggie's place, Bill,' I tell him. 'Where else would she be?'

'If you were to be believed, she would have already been most of the way back home by now. You lied to me about coming out here. You lied to me about coming home. What else are you lying to me about now?' He opens his back passenger door for me with a scowl. 'She'd better be where you say she is, Rachel. You're going to take me to her now and she'd just better be there.'

Bill slams his car into reverse before I've even shut the door, his wheels spinning in the soft mud hollow outside the shop. Too late, I think, I didn't need to have come in his car. We could have both made our own way to Maggie's. Now I was going to be given the third degree over misleading him. I could hardly blame him either.

'I hope you've got a damn good explanation for this, Rachel.'

'She didn't want to come home.' I'm still struggling with my seatbelt, which is stuck, and he is driving down the narrow lanes like a maniac. I can feel his wheels skidding on the oil-rainy road. 'She just didn't want to get back before her birthday was over.'

'Not good enough, Rachel. That doesn't explain why you felt the need to lie to me about it.' His voice is high and hard and no doubt that conversation with Annie-Jo has got to him. She shouldn't have said anything but she probably thought that she was doing the right thing. I'd have done the same, in her shoes. 'I don't know what you're so upset about . . .' I begin.

'Oh, I think you do,' he snarls at me. 'Where the hell *is* this place, anyway? It seems further away than I remember . . .'

'Second on the left from here. It's a very small turning, remember? It's marked towards Scudhill's Grange.'

'As you know, I already spoke to Annie-Jo, Rachel, and

she told me everything: what Shelley planned to do on her birthday. The *cliff*. She told me you were planning to go as far as take her up there. I didn't believe her, Rachel. I told her she was wrong. You would never do that.

'And you yourself, reassured me. But when I rang back a second time this morning and found out from Shelley that you hadn't left at all, that you *weren't* leaving, nor had any intention of doing so, only minutes after you'd already told me you were on the road . . .' His voice breaks. 'What were you *thinking*, Rachel? I knew then that something had to be very, very wrong. You'd already covered up the fact that you'd planned to bring her away. You've been lying to me from the very beginning.'

Shelley *told* him? I sit there, stunned, for a moment. Had that been deliberate, I wonder now, or just a mistake? I never knew she spoke to him this morning. She must have picked up the phone and not said anything.

'I'm sorry about that,' I interject. 'I should have been honest with you from the start. I just didn't have the courage a week ago.'

'You didn't have the courage to be honest with me this morning either,' he reminds me. '*Shit!*' He swerves then as we narrowly miss a car going in the opposite direction every bit as fast as he is. 'I've clocked ninety miles an hour most of the way down here,' he confesses. 'I've had to cancel this morning's meeting. *And* my plans to take Stella away this weekend. You've had me scared half to death wondering what was going on. What *is* going on, Rachel?'

Bill pulls into a muddy lay-by, slamming the brakes

on hard, making my head jerk back. 'You're going to stop playing games with me now. Tell me where our daughter is. Tell me she's all right.'

'She's at Maggie's, of course. I had to pop out to buy something.' I still have the lettuce in my hands. I've been squeezing it so tight there can't be much more left of it than shreds any more. The tortoises, I suddenly remember irrelevantly, are still in the back of my car.

'I want to know if it's true, what Annie-Jo told me, what you and Shelley were planning?'

'Annie-Jo doesn't know the full truth. She must have surmised some of it. You can't imagine that I would want to hurt my own daughter in any way?'

How am I ever going to tell him?

'No.' Bill's body is rigid and stiff. He reminds me of a barrier; like some piece of metal that has been moulded into a fence. Of course he won't believe it. But he is furious with me, his anger a dark cloud that evaporates into the air between us, and it scares me.

'No, I can't imagine that, but I can . . . I can *believe* it, though.' His voice has suddenly gone very low. 'I don't know how or why, but something in me tells me that you've changed. You're not the same any more. If you only knew what I've had to go through to get down here . . .' He pauses suddenly and pulls out his phone, checking it for text messages. As his eyes scan the tiny green writing I watch the bead of sweat that has formed over his brow roll down in a tiny droplet to disappear into his eyebrow. 'Nikolai's gone to his grandmother's now. Screaming blue murder, I shouldn't wonder. I can hardly blame him. I wouldn't want to spend any time with the insane old

401

bat either.' He seems to be talking more to himself than to me.

'Where is Stella?' I begin, but that serves to remind him that I am there, and the look he gives me warns me into silence again. It feels so familiar, all this: sitting here in the car with him, feeling him steaming and me not daring to say anything. My throat always seems to close up whenever I am faced with Bill. That's why I didn't tell him the truth at the very beginning. That's why I sneaked us away in silence, so as not to have to listen to him ranting at me, even though I'd known I'd have to pay for it sooner or later. Even though I'd known it was wrong.

'My *wife*,' he deliberately doesn't use her name to me, separating the two of us out, I notice, 'has needed to go away for some rest. She is exhausted. Mentally and emotionally exhausted with having to deal with . . . with what life has thrown at her.' I wonder now what life could possibly have thrown at her that is *worse* than what it has thrown at me. Bill, perhaps? There is nothing really wrong with Nikolai that I can see. Nothing that couldn't be sourced directly back to the root of his mother's 'nerves'.

'I'm sorry to hear life has been so hard on her.' My voice is suddenly cooler than I usually use with Bill. Something – what is it? – that invisible link that binds two people together who have once had a relationship, it just goes *snap*, right at that moment, sitting there in the car. Bill carries on, he doesn't notice it, but I do.

'She's on the verge of a breakdown, Rachel, if you must know. Abandoning them both at this moment to come racing down here to deal with your lies and your incompetence were *not* top of my agenda.'

'You didn't need to come,' I tell him quietly. 'Our daughter is in no danger from me.'

That much is true. I would throw myself off the top of that damn cliff if I knew it would stop her from doing it to herself. The wind buffets the side of his car gently. For a moment the clouds pull back overhead like some great curtains parting, but behind them there is no sun, only more grey sky, only higher levels of squally clouds, and in his eyes I can see the impatience behind his desperation, the willingness to turn too quickly and throw up his hands in the air in frustration, pointing at me, always at me, to be the one who must be totally to blame.

'I needed to come,' he tells me, 'because she is my daughter too. Do you think I don't *care*?' He jabs at the button of the glove box till the door falls open and a half-empty bottle of mineral water rolls out. He drinks down some water without offering me any. 'I have had to leave my distraught wife and son because you couldn't handle what you needed to, without me. You couldn't stick to our agreements, and you couldn't clear up your own mess.' He thinks he is some knight in shining armour, I realise now, charging to save his daughter from his evil witch of a mother. He thinks, he really thinks, that he can save the day; that there really *is* any way to save the day. He swallows some more water noisily and I bite my tongue, letting him have his rant. Part of me hopes that he is right.

Soon he starts up the car again, and before long we turn left towards Scudhill's Grange. Someone else's car has been there this night. I can make out the deep wheel tracks in the gravel just out front of Maggie's house where someone's car has been reversed. Could it have been Frank, coming to say goodbye, while I'd been stuck in the post office buying lettuce and then trapped in Bill's car? Shelley will know. Oh god, let it have been Frank. My eyes fill with tears, which I wipe away quickly. I don't want anyone to see.

Bill gets out and slams his car door shut without waiting for me. I feel fragile and taut and the noise of it slamming goes right through me. Perhaps Bill *is* a knight in shining armour, after all? Maybe Shelley will see her dad and she will change her mind about everything; she will come round like a little puss-cat the way girls do for their dads when they won't do it for their mothers. He'll say, 'Come along now and stop all this nonsense', and, hey presto, she just will.

Maybe that's part of what being Pandora's daughter does for me. No matter what life throws at me, there is always this other bit going, 'Ah, yes, but hope springs eternal'. My legs are trembling as I get out of the car at last, a nauseous feeling stirring deep in the pit of my stomach. Inside the porch I can hear raised voices, Bill panicking, shouting at someone I cannot see.

44

Shelley

Saturday afternoon, 5.10 p.m.

From: **Surinda Chellaram**
To: **Shelley Wetherby**
Subject: **RE: Jump**

Hiya, Shell. If you go for the Jump, this may be the last email you ever get from me, so I'm letting you know I'm thinking about you and wishing you all the very best. That Kitchener's Point you described sounds fearsome. I hope it all happens quick and clean, just like you're wanting, and you don't have to suffer in any way. You deserve that much, at least. I've been thinking about you a lot, girl. I've been realising your bravery in what you're going to do. That takes guts.

Things here are not so good. I don't want to go into details, but man, they're like, pretty bad. Some men think just because the wedding date is set that means they got rights over the bride, if you see what I mean. Jallal came in and tried it on Tuesday night, and I've had a real bad time of it ever since. When I saw him in there – you know, in the flesh – I don't know what came over me, but it's made me go all funny. I won't go into details (sorry to bother you with this, you got enough on your mind, I know). But I just wanted you to know, you're doing the right thing. I wish now I had run away while I had the chance. I wish I had done it. Things have gone too far now, and I can't. But if I had my freedom over again, I'd make a different choice, I'd go for the other option, even if it wasn't comfortable. Just wanted to let you know that. I'll be watching your boy Kieran on the telly tonight (he never did send them tickets through), so I'll cheer him on for you as you won't be able to. All best wishes, your friend, Surinda Xxx

I can't do this any more. I can't. This waiting here for Mum to come and get me; it's worse than any death sentence. What the hell was she thinking of, anyway, going to get those tortoises? I know I was the one who told her she should. I know that, but well, she shouldn't have paid any attention to me, should she? I need her here now. I need to be able to say stuff, all those last-minute things that condemned people are supposed to come up and say at the last minute – I don't know what.

Not that I feel much like talking. I've had a tight throat all day, and this horrid sickly feeling in the pit of my stomach like you get before you take an exam. I don't have all that courage that Surinda thinks I have. I'm a coward at heart. Maybe if I weren't a coward I'd be preparing to face the end that will come naturally instead of just running away from it.

On the other hand, Surinda is right. She's really regretting that she took the easy option, isn't she? I said all along I wouldn't do that, I wasn't going to take the Miriam path, I can't. Look, everything is set for it now. I'm going through with it.

What if Mum . . . what if Mum really meant what I overheard her saying to Dad on the phone last night, though? She said she'd bring me home today. Maybe she still thinks she is? So she's not coming to get me? She's not going to keep her promise. She MUST, though. No, I can't think like that. She'll come.

I'm only sorry that the *Beat the Bank* show wasn't on last night instead of tonight. I'd have loved to have seen Kieran win his million. He IS going to win it, too. I know he is. I can feel it in the middle of my bones. He's going to win that million pounds and then he'll find some other girl, someone lovely, someone 'healthy and whole' who will make him happier than I ever could. He'll find someone even if he isn't stinking rich, of course, because he's lovely and he deserves it.

I don't have any tears left now.

'Hey, Shell, can I see your laptop?' Jazzy's back. I thought he and Ellen had gone out for the night. They had this other party to go to; for her best friend. Ellen didn't want to go, but I made her. Mum said she would pick me up from here.

Jazzy's looking a bit glazy-eyed. He's probably been smoking. He leans over me a little too unsteadily, a little too close. I wish Mum would hurry up and come back.

'What's that?'

'An email from a friend.' No more emails from Kieran and I've got to stop looking. He said he wouldn't email me any more, didn't he? I don't know why I keep hoping to hear from him again. It doesn't matter any more, anyway.

'No, I meant *that*.' He points at Mum's little pink diary that I've been looking through ever since Ellen went out. I thought I might as well, especially since there ain't going to be no tomorrow. It's cleared up a lot of questions for me that were never going to be cleared up otherwise. Like what is really going on between Mum and Lily. Sitting there having dinner with them last night, all I could sense was this tense politeness between them, covering up a huge, gaping raw wound of guilt. I recognised what it was straight off because I feel pretty guilty myself about what I'm planning to do tonight.

I snap the laptop shut. Jazzy veers backwards a little as the screen disappears. He stares at the smooth silver surface of the laptop for a moment, his eyes tiny black pearls, and he ruffles up his already-scruffy hair.

'Why do you smoke that stuff?' I turn from him, catching a whiff of his slightly sweet smell.

'I can handle it, man.' Jazzy's voice is slightly slurred. Maybe he's been drinking, too? 'Hey, what was that?' His attention is turned by a huge flash of lightning that bursts across Maggie's huge bay windows like a screamer at a firework display. 'Whoa, man, that is seriously cool.' Jazzy leaves me and goes to lean against the windowsill. The afternoon has got very dark now. It isn't much past five o'clock, but the storm clouds have made the sky very black.

'How'd you like to go out in that?' Jazzy yelps. He's started prancing round like a demented puppy.

'I would, actually.'

'She would, actually.' A leery kind of grin spreads across Jazzy's face. 'Then I'm at your service, *madame*.' He makes an exaggeratedly low bow. 'And where would *madame* like to go?'

'Up to Kitchener's Point, Jazzy. Would you take me there?'

Jazzy ruffles his hair some more and I see that it's glistening wet with the rain. He's already been out there, prancing around in the weather like a demon.

'Sure I will, if it's what *madame* wants.'

I glance at my watch. Mum's taking too long. She should have been here already. Maybe she's changed her mind, that's the thing. She knows full well there is no way I can carry out my plan without her help. That's probably it, now that I think about it!

Mum isn't coming. She's going to let me sit here, stewing, till I come to my senses.

'It's brilliant out here.' Jazzy has opened the front door and he's standing in the lamplight by the porch, his eyes tight shut as the wind whips the rain into his face. 'Kitchener's Point will be pretty hairy tonight.' He opens his eyes and gives me a look that goes right through me. 'It'll be a blast.'

'Let's go, then.' I say it before I've had a moment to think. I don't want any more time to think.

And Jazzy grabs hold of Bessie's handlebars and shoves Bessie and me out into the night, handling us like he would a wheelbarrow full of logs, jolting me on the steps on the way down, but I don't care any more.

It is Time.

*   *   *

409

'You never told me this thing would be so heavy,' Jazzy is complaining. He's been bumping me over every single pothole and stone standing in our path for twenty minutes now and I can hear his breath coming short and quick.

'Slow down, then,' I snap at him. 'I didn't tell you to run, did I?'

Jazzy just grunts in reply. I don't look back at him. I'm too concerned with hanging on here because I get the impression he might tip me out before I even get a chance to jump, at this rate.

This is so far from what I imagined it would be like at the end that it's almost laughable. It's like some kind of grisly comedy sketch. It's all so dark and so hurried and so . . . so seamy. But I've got this urge inside and I can't deny it. It's like something's pushing me down this route towards the end, some sort of self-preservation device (strange as that sounds!), and I know, in my heart, that my mum will never help me do it. Never. Perhaps it's better this way.

I'll come back through Suko and tell them, once I get there, what it's really like on the other side. I'll let them know that I'm perfectly okay. Bump, bump, bump.

'You're rattling my teeth out of my head,' I complain, but Jazzy isn't listening. When I glance back at him his eyes are like two darkly glowing lamps in his head. He's forgotten all about me, I think. He's away with the fairies, somewhere else. I think he's disappointed because there hasn't been any more lightning. The wind is really whipping the rain into our faces now, it's got really gusty. I can smell the sea, salty and fierce and strong, an aroma of rolled-up sand and shells and seaweed and dark fish that have come from some other land very far away. I'll be gone in an instant. No hanging around with the waves as high as they are tonight. All over, no fuss. I mustn't panic. I must stay calm. Remember Miriam.

I wonder if Jazzy will stick around to help me with my plan? I clear my throat to ask him, but he begins to sing before I can do so, an old sailor song I think it must be, something about mermaids and lost men at sea and then something very, VERY rude at the end. He laughs.

'*Madame*, you have arrived at your destination. Please mind the . . . the cliff.' He bursts into hysterical giggles. 'Man, I need to take a leak. I'm . . . I'm . .' He looks around, even in the state he's in, for somewhere to do it. It must be instinct, but he doesn't want to just whip it out in front of me, I can tell. I'm surprised he even cares.

We're at the top of Kitchener's Point. It's a cruel-looking, sharp-edged drop of god knows how many hundred feet. There's a whole bunch of jaggedy rocks waiting for you at the bottom, assuming that the sea doesn't get you first. Jazzy is looking up at the moon, which has temporarily unveiled itself from behind one of the storm clouds. 'The moon's in Scorpio,' he informs me. His expression is completely blank. He unzips his trousers.

'Not here!' I yell at him. 'I'm in front, remember?' He shrugs and turns away from me, stumbling a little way down the path where we've just come up. 'Go home, Jazzy,' I call after him. I feel strangely protective towards him now. I wouldn't want him to fall down this damn cliff before I do. I'm going to have enough on my conscience as it is.

'What?'

411

'I said, go home! Go back to your nan's place, it's nearer. Jazzy, can you hear me?'

'All right, man, I'm going. I'm going.' I hope he makes it. I watch his progress for a few anxious moments till the path turns downwards, away from the cliff edge, away from the point where his careless stumbling feet might lead to disaster. He's gone, and that Scorpio moon is clouded over again. I listen to the sea roaring and tonight it sounds angry to me. This wasn't how I planned it, but oh well. It's Time.

If I use Bessie's handlebars I can just about hoist myself up to standing. I did it that day in front of my mirror, didn't I? I can do it again. It doesn't have to be for all that long. I'm not going to get more than one stab at it, I know that. Once I collapse, my legs won't be strong enough to get me up again.

Bloody stupid, useless, worthless legs!

Still, this is my choice. Crap set of choices, admittedly, but this is the best one.

Okay, he's gone, so what am I waiting for?

I hoist myself up, feeling my elbows trembling violently, my heart going like a hammer, but it won't take long. I grit my teeth. No, it won't take long.

'Hey!' a voice yells out from the pathway behind me – damn, damn and double-damn it! It's Jazzy back again. 'Hey, Shelley; ShelleyPixie?'

I collapse back into the chair, my blood freezing up at that name. There is only one person who EVER calls me that name and he's due to go on live TV in front of one and a half million people tonight, so what the – ?

'Shelley, my god, what are you doing? Why didn't you

answer any of my emails? Why the hell are you out here all alone on a night like . . . ?'

'Kieran, you've got no business being here.' I turn to face him, the love of my short life, and his face looks sad and angry and shocked all at once, and I feel so ashamed.

'Have I not?' he demands. 'What the hell did you think you were doing?'

I feel like a child caught out stealing sweets in a newsagent's shop but I brazen it out.

'What the hell do YOU care?' I retort. My arms are still trembling like crazy from my effort, adrenaline pumping through my body making me stronger and harder than usual, on edge.

'Go on, do it then.' Kieran folds his arms and looks at me cynically. 'Just do it.'

'Well I will.' My voice rises up, over the wind. 'In a minute. As soon as I find out what you're doing here?'

'What d'you think?' He places his hands firmly over my wrists, as if with handcuffs, snapping me into my chair. 'I'm saving you.'

'But I don't want saving! I'm here on purpose. How the hell did you find out, anyway?' This seems like a really stupid conversation to be having. I can't believe we're actually having it.

'Your friend Surinda emailed me. She seemed to be under the impression that I already *knew* what you were planning tonight at Kitchener's Point. But she wanted to check. It's been on her conscience, she said. Then she asked me *again* if she could have some show tickets as she said that you wouldn't be needing yours.' His voice is wobbly. He's gutted, but he's also angry.

413

'And neither will anyone else if you don't do the show tonight,' I point out. 'Wasn't it going out *live*?' I can't believe he's done this! He's ruined his chance to win a million just to come out here, for me. And what for? I ask myself. His gesture isn't going to make any difference, in the long run. He can't save me from this disease, can he?

He shrugs. 'What does it matter? Do you really think I could go on telly to try and win some money when my girl is planning to top herself?'

'I'm sorry, Kieran. You never should have found out about it. You weren't meant to know.'

'Until I got wind of it some other way – through Solly, for example?'

'Oh god.' I rub my face with my hands. 'Look, forget about me, Kieran. You've still got everything going for you. I haven't, you know. I haven't anything to offer you.'

Behind me the ominous rumblings of another burst of thunder herald that the storm isn't over yet. 'I thought you'd just give up if I didn't answer your emails. I thought you'd just forget about me.'

'How little you know me, Shelley.'

'I'm sorry,' I repeat, pathetically. 'How the hell did you find me?'

'I used a map to find Kitchener's Point. Your helpful friend, the stoned lad, passed me on the way down. He told me he'd left you at the top.'

'And it was Surinda who told you that I – ?'

'She told me. As a friend, she said. And all about the terrible life she's got with her husband-to-be . . . Look, sweetheart, I can't pretend that I'm not angry with you.

414

I'm mad as hell. I want to kill you myself, in fact. But . . .
I have to know why? Surely you know what doing this
would *do* to all those people who love you?' He's crouched
down now so that his face is at my level, his hands
unclenched now, stroking my arms, and I feel all my
resolve just drain out of me. How could I possibly hurt
him like this?

I close my eyes to block him out. 'I know what NOT
doing it will do to all the people who love me.' My voice
comes out a mere whisper, a croak. 'And, anyway, you
don't love me. You love some image that you have of me,
that's all. I think you're still grieving for your mum and
dad, and that's the truth.' God, that is mean of me. I
can't believe I said that, but it's what I think.

'What's that, sweetheart?' When I open my eyes, he's
crying soundlessly, tears just running down his face.

'Let me go,' I say to him at last. 'Just let me go. This
way it will be quick. I won't have to suffer. And nobody
will have to watch me. I want it to be dignified. I want
it to be my *choice*.'

Then Kieran pulls me out of my chair. He lifts me up
so fast that he takes all my breath away, one hand on the
small of my back, supporting me, the other hand under
my arm, so that my weight falls against him.

'Have a look.' He tips me nearer to the edge of
Kitchener's Point so that I can see the black swirling
waves underneath. 'You make sure to have a real good
look at it before you make that decision.'

It doesn't look nice. It doesn't look the way that I'd
dreamed it would look. It isn't peaceful and welcoming;
it isn't gentle.

415

Kieran, on the other hand, is so close that I feel his heart thudding against my chest, the taut muscles of the length of his body strong and firm against me. I feel his strength. Oh, to be so healthy; to be able to stand so strong and firm, to know that your body is a good one, fit to support your life. I love him for all that he is. I wish that I could be like it.

For a few long minutes he just holds me here against his own warmth, then, turning my face towards his with gentle fingers, he kisses me for one last, tender time. In that kiss I know all the love of a man that I will ever need to know in a lifetime. He fills up my heart with this kiss so that it's brimming right up to the top, so that even here, even at the end of my hours, I feel full up with joy.

I could do it now; really I could, feeling as happy as this.

'Make your choice, my love,' he says at last. I couldn't have hoped for a better, more loving way to go, no better person to be here with me at the end.

I look backwards away from him, over to the edge. Kieran picks me up and takes me there, right to the brink. The sea looks dark and angry. I feel a huge shiver go right through me now. The sea looks *cold*. I nod at him, and I see his eyes close briefly, acknowledging my decision.

'You won't be needing this any more, then.' He turns and, with his free hand, holding on to Bessie's handle-bars with surprising strength, he hurls her right over the edge.

I gasp at that. I can't help myself. It feels like a physical shock has gone right through my body. He's thrown Bessie over, Oh my god!

I watch her fall. In one instant, she's gone, crashed against the rocks and submerged, a heap of glinting metal and broken wheels in the darkness. She's gone. My chair. My support all this time. I feel so angry with him that he's done that; I can feel tears welling up in my eyes. I want to *hit* him for doing that. I *need* her; how could he do that to me?

And then I remember. I don't need her any more. I won't be needing her. She's suffered the same fate as me, that's all.

I swallow hard. When I look at him, I see that he's waiting. He's still waiting for me to make my choice. All I have to do is let him go. My legs are little candy-floss sticks, thin and brittle, and my body is as wispy and insubstantial as threads of pink sugar, ready to blow away on the breeze. His body, his warm, strong body that clings so close to my own, makes me feel strong, though; it makes me feel that I could conquer the world, if only . . .

'Well?' he says at last. 'It's got to be your choice, my beloved. Have you made it?'

I turn back towards him with a shudder and a sigh. His lips are still waiting. His rain-soaked face watches my own as I nuzzle his neck gently.

'I've made it,' I tell him in his ear.

Now there is only one thing left to do, and I know I will need more courage than I have ever needed before in order to do it.

45

Rachel

Saturday evening

'She's gone, damn it. There's a boy in there about her age.' Bill's eyes are wild. 'He looks stoned out of his head. He said he left her outside somewhere, about an hour ago. He can't say where, the bloody idiot. What did you leave her with *him* for? Are you completely mad?'

'I didn't leave her with him. She doesn't know any druggy boys, what are you . . .' My heart stops then as I see Jazzy appear, glazy-eyed at the doorway. 'She wouldn't have gone out anywhere with *him*, Bill. She was waiting for me. He must be mistaken. Maybe she never came home from Ellen's. Or could she have gone to the Royal Star Hotel, where Lily is? I don't know!'

'The Royal Star? Didn't we pass that a few minutes back? Shit.' His voice rises in panic as he jumps back into the car.

'Why don't I ring Lily first?' I start to make the call but Bill points to the seat beside him, indicating that I'd better get in. *Now*.

'He said he left her on a cliff-top.' He looks at me darkly. 'Does the Star overlook the sea?'

'Yes, it does. But he must be mistaken. It's at the bottom of a cliff, not the top. The frontage leads out onto its own private beach. Let's go there.'

'Who is he, Rachel?' Bill pulls the steering wheel round hard and I can tell that this journey isn't going to be any more comfortable than the one out here.

'He's Maggie's grandson. Shelley's been spending a lot of time with him and his sister Ellen. Are you sure Ellen wasn't in there? She might have a better idea where . . .'

'He said there wasn't anyone else at home. Just ring your sister, all right?'

'I *am*. She isn't picking up.'

'And what about this Ellen girl? I take it you've got her number, seeing as Shelley's been spending so much time with her? And doesn't Shelley have a phone? I bought her one last Christmas,' he remembers irritably.

No I don't have Ellen's number! And Shelley's phone is still packed away in the luggage I shoved into the cupboard under the stairs the night before we left. She's been texting me from Ellen's phone hasn't she?

'Let me get this straight, Rachel. I'm confused.' He flicks the windscreen wipers onto fast mode, their harsh clunk-clunk as they hit the windscreen matching the pace of his driving.

'So. You brought Shelley down here because . . . why?'

'She wanted to come.' I don't want to talk to him any more. I don't even want to be with him. I need to find my daughter and he isn't helping. He isn't *helping*.

'And you knew why she wanted to come?'

'I didn't have the first idea of her real reason. Not then.'

419

'Not then, but afterwards, though? When did she tell you?' He pulls aggressively into a lay-by to let another car go by down the narrow two-way road. I can hear the screeching sound of wet tree branches as they scratch all the way down the side of the car.

'Yesterday,' I breathe.

'So why didn't you get her some help yesterday, you stupid woman? What if . . . what if we're too late now?'

'Take that for me, will you?' he barks suddenly as his mobile starts up with some ridiculous ring tone, Beethoven's Fifth or something. 'I'm driving. If it's Stella tell her . . . well, tell her I'll ring her as soon as I can.'

'Hello. Is Bill there? It's Maria.' The breathy voice sounds strangely familiar but I can't place it.

'It's Maria,' I echo to him.

'It's for *you*,' he cusses. 'It's that crazy Maria woman who keeps ringing me just because she can't get hold of you. She's one of your people. What the hell she's doing with my number god only knows . . .'

'Uh. Hello? He can't take it right now I'm afraid. This is Rachel.'

'Rachel, oh my dear. I haven't been able to get hold of you. There have been such developments! It's Maria here. Look, you must make an appointment to see Doctor Lavelle as soon as you can.'

My heart sinks. It's got to be one of the practice nurses again. My head is clogged up. I can't think properly. I'm as battered as the windscreen in front of me, pelted by rain.

'We're away at the moment.'

420

'Come back, then,' the bloody woman insists. Really, this is hardly the *time* . . .

'Look, who is this? I've already had several phone calls from Doctor Lavelle. Can't this wait?'

'It's Maria!' she shrieks, and, 'No, it can't wait. This could be a matter of life or death, Rachel.'

I'm kind of in that situation already.

She pauses, then, 'Oh, you've spoken to Doctor Lavelle already, then?'

'Oh for goodness' sake! Who are you? And why are you hassling me like this? And why are you calling on my ex-husband's phone?'

'Shelley gave us this number ages ago so Miriam could contact her when she was staying with her dad,' Maria tells me now.

Maria – Miriam's mum. Of course!

'I didn't realise you'd already spoken to Doctor Lavelle. I'm sorry. They've all been going spare trying to get hold of you. They contacted me, in case I knew a way. I even tried emailing Shelley . . .'

'I've . . . I've had a few messages through, Maria. But I haven't actually spoken to Doctor Lavelle,' I confess now.

'You haven't? Then you've got to stop all medication straight away. Shelley might not be on the right one.'

'You went through all this with Miriam, didn't you?' I remind her now. 'And, as I recall, you were of the opinion then that it was the change in medication prescribed by Doctor Lavelle that really caused her downturn?'

'Maybe I was wrong, though? One of the members of my little support group has just put in to sue Doctor Ganz for misdiagnosis . . .'

'Doctor Ganz?' I swallow hard. 'To *sue* Doctor Ganz, did you say? But I thought you were his greatest supporter?'

'I understand now that we may have been misled,' she replies stonily. 'If he has misdiagnosed the condition then the medication he's put them on could be what's caused their symptoms in the first place.'

'Misdiagnosis? Oh, holy heavens above . . .' This can't be true. Surely it can't be true?

'From what I hear, Doctor Lavelle has recalled the two other people Ganz was treating – the Aussie girl and the old bloke. The girl is a *possible* misdiagnosis, they say. The old fella isn't. As for my daughter . . . we'll never know now, will we?'

'No.' There is a pause. 'I'm sorry, Maria. Could you start explaining this to me all over again? I want to make sure I understand you right.'

'Rachel, there is a condition called "Hughes Syndrome". I don't know if you've ever heard of it?'

'Hughes? No, I haven't.'

'Well, they call it sticky blood syndrome. It's to do with antiphospholipids in the blood; it makes the blood become thick. Sometimes the symptoms are very similar to those used to diagnose MS. Like I said, they've already found one of Doctor Ganz's patients who had that. It's just possible the girls were misdiagnosed, too. I'm sorry if Shelley's father feels I've been pestering him. I'd heard that no one had been able to contact you yet, that's all,' she says primly.

'Thank you, Maria. Thanks so much. Look, I . . . I can't talk just now. I'll call you back, okay?'

'Misdiagnosis? What misdiagnosis?' Bill's voice is dark and flat. While I've been talking to Maria he has stopped the car in a lay-by. We're a few minutes past the Royal Star Hotel, but from where we are we can look out onto the sea.

'It's possible. From what Maria is telling me now. Someone is suing Doctor Ganz over it, apparently, so they must have evidence . . . '

He doesn't answer me. He just stares out of the windscreen, battling with some inner demons I can only guess at.

'It's rough out there tonight,' he says. From the corner of my eye I can just pick out a crowd gathering down on the dark shore – some campers, maybe, having a party?

'This suing Doctor Ganz business, though . . . it's probably just some parent deranged by grief.' His voice is trembling. 'There'll be no substance to it.'

'But it's possible, Bill.'

'You really think, after all this time, it's possible?' He gives me a long, dark look. 'That Shelley could have been misdiagnosed by Doctor Ganz? I thought you said he was the expert in this field? What about all her symptoms?'

'The medication could have caused some of them,' I tell him. 'It *is* possible,' I say cautiously. 'We've got to make an appointment to see Doctor Lavelle ASAP. And keep her off all medication till then.'

'But why on earth hasn't Doctor Lavelle contacted you *himself*?' Bill's face looks contorted in the half-light. This doesn't seem like a good time to tell him that Dr Lavelle has been trying . . .

'We might, oh, Bill, we might . . . do you think there's still a chance we might be able to save her yet?' I don't even dare to think that this could be true. It's too much to take all this on right now, it really is. 'Bill? Bill . . . there could just be some hope.'

For a moment, as I turn to look at him, I remember us as we used to be. His face looks so young, unmasked in the half-light. We had shared dreams, once, shared hopes for what our future might hold. And now, with this one brief phone call, Maria has rekindled a hope that I imagined to be long past rekindling. Does he feel it, too?

But Bill isn't looking at me any more. His fingers are drumming on the steering wheel in a robotic trance. His head is turned, looking out of the window way over to the right where there seems to be some sort of commotion going on, down on the beach. The crowd that has gathered, even on this squally night, is considerable. I think there were some boy scouts camping down there, but they don't sound as if they are having a party.

The flashing yellow lights that herald the arrival of, first, an ambulance and then a police car pass by our own parked car at speed.

When he turns to look at me, Bill's face is still twisted and dark. We both know what he is thinking. Neither of us can move.

'We may be too late,' is all Bill replies. I watch him climb out of the car at last on shaky legs.

'What's the problem down there?' I hear him calling to one of the scouts, and his voice is almost lost to the wind.

'They think someone may have taken a dive,' the lad

yells back at him. He points up at the white cliff-face in front of him. 'From up there. A handicapped person, they say. They've found the wheelchair but there's no body been recovered yet.'

The police are beginning to cordon off an area at the base of the cliff, but when I clamber out of the passenger seat and put my face over the sea wall I can make out the wheelchair he's referring to, collapsed on one side.

'It looks like Bessie. Oh my god.' I clutch at Bill's arm. 'It looks like Bessie.'

Bill looks at me in horror. His lips curl into a thin line of loathing.

'Are you telling me that it's *hers*?'

I nod. It is. I know it is.

'Perhaps you should go a bit nearer and see. You'll have to tell the police . . .'

'No!' I step back. Not yet. I don't want to get sucked into a round of form-filling and detail-giving police procedures. Not till I know for sure that she's gone.

'What the *hell*, Rachel! Come back!' I hear Bill's heavy footstep behind me. He's breathing hard, his eyes bulging out of their sockets. When he catches up with me he nearly pulls my arm off.

'You're going back there and you're going to tell the police what you know. Don't you try and run away from this now and leave it all to me.'

When I turn to face him now, my fear, which has felt like bile, a sickness rising up from my stomach, suddenly melts away into thin air. I am only struck by the realisation of how this man, who used to be my husband, could be so incredibly *stupid*.

'I want to make sure she's not still up there,' I tell him now, breathless. But he's not listening to me.

'You knew she was planning this,' he throws at me. 'Anyone else would have put her in some secure place till she came to her senses. If you'd done that she'd be fine right now. She'd have a chance of getting a new diagnosis from the doctor. But no, you wouldn't do that, would you? Maybe you *wanted* her to fall so you could be free of her . . .'

'I should have hospitalised her, you mean? Put a lock on her twenty-four-seven till she aligned her reality with mine? No, Bill,' I get into the driver's seat, 'I never wanted her to do this. How could you imagine that would set me free? Walking away didn't set *you* free, did it? If she's really gone and done this thing then I . . . I don't know how I will ever recover from it either, but I don't regret that I didn't lock her up and stop her. I trusted her to wait for me. I don't regret that either. Now if all you've got to throw at me are words of blame then you can piss off and I'll go by myself and find out whether she's still up there or not.' I turn the key in the ignition.

'You've changed, Rachel.' His face is aghast as he gets into the passenger seat beside me. His hands are in his pockets, his shoulders all hunched, I notice. 'What's happened to you? You never used to be such a . . . such a . . .' Words fail him.

'No, I didn't.' I glance at him as I set the car into reverse and pull us out and onto the road that will take us up to the top. 'But I am now. I *have* changed.'

I don't know how I recognise the road that will take me right up to the cliff-top, but I do. Something takes over that is stronger than me, more assured and more powerful than me. The fuzziness in my brain clears as if by magic. The rain stops lashing the windscreen long enough for me to take the car up the narrow and little-used path to the top. I'm probably not even supposed to be here, I realise. This rough road has been hewed out for emergency vehicles only. Well, tonight this is an emergency vehicle and my trip is an emergency, because I can save her yet. Something deep inside me tells me that she hasn't gone yet, that she's still alive.

When we get as far as we can go, I pull the car to a stop and we get out. There are no lights up here. There is nothing but a remarkably bright, small moon. The muddied pathway, with the tracks of small wheels engraved into it, shows me that Bessie has indeed been pushed up this way tonight. We have a little way to walk before we get to the edge at the top, the place where the chair would have been launched from, and we walk along in silence. Bill walks four paces behind me. He does not utter a word but I can feel him every step of the way. Not a word, but I feel him stalking like a panther, dark and silent, intent on his purpose, and I am not altogether sure, if we get to the top and she is not there, if he will not see fit to push me over too.

There is another car coming up the path behind us. I can hear it now, the engine labouring to make the last muddied part of the track. A police car? A warden of some sort? Someone to tell us that we shouldn't be up here with the car, that we aren't allowed to come this way? It doesn't matter. We're here now.

We're here, at the top.

427

And she isn't.

And it's then that the power surge I felt all the way up here just drains out of me. Behind me I hear a muffled sob from Bill, a long moan; the sound of a darkness that has long been held in check being slowly released. I turn to look at him, pity and sorrow softening my heart, but I only see a face contorted by rage and loathing.

'I blame *you* for this.' His growl warns me to stay where I am. 'This is all your doing. You killed her, as good as if you'd pushed her over the edge yourself.'

'No, I didn't, Bill. Keep a grip on yourself, man.'

I don't even see his fist coming. When it hits the side of my face it is like a rock. It sends me spinning backwards in shock and pain. I fall on my side and the muddied path softens the blow but the ground is cold and soft and wet. At first I don't feel any pain. I have only one thought in my head.

Where is my daughter?

She is not gone; not yet. I know this, because I am her mother.

'Hey, you there.' A man's voice checks Bill as he towers over me. He turns to look and I crawl painfully out of his reach as he faces the other man. 'What's going on here?'

I can feel the slippery hot wetness of blood as it runs down my face from a gash.

'Help me, over here, please.'

'Oh dear god! *You* did this to her?' I cannot see him, but I can hear the outrage in the newcomer's voice, and I thank the lord for guardian angels as he addresses Bill with contempt.

428

I don't hear very much of what Bill replies to him then. There is some sort of altercation going on between them, but as I lie there, on one side, facing the adjacent cliff-top, a dark figure catches my eye.

It is then that I see my daughter. She is not alone. She is with a man, I think. They are standing very close together. He is holding her close to him. It is as if he has known her for a very long time. I blink. My eyes are so wet. It is still raining. What am I seeing? Am I really seeing it?

'My nose. My god, man, you've broken my nose.' I can hear Bill yelping like a spoiled schoolboy, losing a fight, but I don't bother to look at him, my eyes are locked elsewhere.

She doesn't look at me either, when I wave to her, for she, too, is otherwise engrossed. I notice the two of them keep looking over their shoulders at the sheer cliff-drop beneath them. I call out, but my voice is like a feeble bird's cry, lost to the wind.

They are so very near to the cliff's edge. Too close for comfort. Anyone seeing them would know at a glance what they are thinking, what's on their minds. But the policemen and the ambulance men below me don't look up to the right spot where the young people are. They're looking in the wrong place. I shout and yell at them in vain but none of them heed my warnings, none of them look over to see me and neither does Shelley.

I can save you now, I want to yell at her. It's going to be okay. Don't do it, Shelley, just don't do it.

And then a helicopter flies over our heads and I can hear someone hailing us over a loudspeaker to 'come down immediately'. They've seen her, I think! Someone has spotted her and they're taking some action at last!

The helicopter flies so near I have to cover up my face and ears to protect myself from the wind.

'Oh god, oh god,' Bill is crying. He's on the ground now, covered in mud just like I am. Then my saviour comes to offer me his arm and I take my eyes off my daughter.

'Oh, sweetheart! Jazzy told me where he left her.'

'*Frank?* You came back to the house?' I take in Frank in amazement. 'How did you know where to find me?'

'I didn't!'

'You're supposed to be en route to the airport, aren't you? I thought you were flying back home tonight? I thought I'd never get to say goodbye . . .'

'I couldn't do it, Rachel. I just couldn't do it. I had to see you . . . but when I got to the house all I found was Jazzy, in a bad way. He told me where he'd left her.'

'Oh Frank, she's . . . I thought she was gone but she isn't, she's . . . she's over there . . .'

I turn to show him, pointing to the cliff-top where she was, perched so precariously on the edge with that man, but I can't find the place any more. I look and I look but I just can't find it.

Frank pulls me to my feet.

'The helicopter has spotted them, sweetheart. It's landing. They're going to be all right.'

Are they? That rather depends on what they them-selves have decided, doesn't it? I wonder who the young man is, who was holding her so gently, so lovingly, just a moment before.

430

'We've just heard . . . she might have been misdiagnosed, Frank. There's a chance. It's a slim one, I know, but it's still a chance . . .'

He wipes at his eyes fiercely then. I know that he is thinking about his son.

'Leave him.' He jerks his head towards Bill who is still lying on the ground, groaning, holding his nose. Frank's arms about my shoulders are warm and steadying. 'You don't need him any more. He's not so hurt he can't get himself to a casualty department. And you're not responsible for him, either,' he adds as I start to protest.

He's right.

Things might work out all right yet. *If* that chopper can get to the two young people in time. *If* it turns out that there really has been a mix-up in the diagnosis.

So many 'ifs'; so many slim chances for happiness. But I think I understand now that whatever happens, however life turns out in the end, I owe it to myself to reach out for mine.

I feel Frank's warm mouth close briefly on my own.

I don't mind about my sister any more. She was probably lying, anyway, just like she always did.

I don't mind about Bill.

Frank throws his heavy overcoat over my shivering shoulders and I look behind me one last time, as we stumble back down the cliff pathway. It is then that I catch sight of her: my love, my beloved daughter who is the queen of my heart, and my heart stops once more.

46

Shelley

When at last I saw her fall, it was exactly as I had imagined it would be. Her face was a white flash of shock, eyes wide open and full of surprise. I watched her hair riding up in tumultuous curls behind her, the light filtering through every strand, all in slow motion like some scene from a film where they slow everything down to savour every last agonising detail.

All the while that she fell I had the worst feeling in the pit of my stomach. It was the knowing that, oh god, I did that. It's my fault. I should never have let her go. I could have saved her but I didn't. I can't believe that I didn't. And the shocked, horrified part of me that had let her go turned on the bit of me that had wanted her to fall all along.

You needed to be free of all this. How many times have you thought that? You needed her to fall so that you could be free, didn't you, Rachel? So you just let it happen. By the sins of our commission and omission . . .

You were responsible for her safety and her wellbeing and you knew this was going to happen and you just let it.

And I could not deny it.

How many nights had I lain awake fantasising about just such a scenario, my escape route from the prison that my life had so long ago become? Would it have made any difference if I had not succumbed to temptation and looked into Pandora's box? I really cannot say. I'm feeling too numb now. My world has crumbled, everything has gone. I don't know anything at all any more.

And so she fell and I did nothing. And why? Because although I loved her, as long as we were yoked together I could never be free.

I always wanted to fly. I thought: what must it be like to go hurtling through the sky at any time – through daylight or through dusk – to feel the buffeting of the wind against your sides, the exhilaration of the drop.

For a brief moment I catch the scent of sea-spray, the tang of salt against my lips; Kieran's face looking white. The Scorpio moon shines so pale on his skin, washing him out. I don't know if I've made the right decision. I wonder if my mother will think so?

A thousand fractured, disjointed thoughts tumble through my head, a dozen per second. I wonder if she will ever decide to go through Pandora's box. I wonder if she will ever get to read the pink diary I took out of it. I feel my fingers curl around the roughened edges of the old journal and I hang on to it for all I'm worth. When she catches up with me I'll still be holding on to this. This is the whole reason why I made the decision I had to. In the end, I made it not for me and not for

Kieran and not for anybody else, but only for her. And I made it because of what I read in this pink diary.

'I love you,' Kieran mouths at me before he turns his face away. The noise of the chopper engine is too loud for us to say any more. The pilot says that by helicopter we should make it to Springdale Studios before an hour is up. I couldn't believe it when the producers of Kieran's show rang him up and, discovering where he was, ('*Cornwall, bloody Cornwall, mate?*') made the decision to send a 'special form of transport' down for him, just to make sure he made it back in time for tonight's show.

'Come with me?' he had begged me. 'You can ring your mum on the way.'

It's not something I would ordinarily have done; flying off in a chopper with a bloke my mum has never met, and today of all days when she's supposed to be meeting me for me to go and take the Jump.

Oh, it's crazy, all this is crazy, I know, but Kieran's got to leave and in my heart I know I'm doing the right thing, going with him. Because in the end I know that what Mum wrote in her diary about someone else altogether is still true about her, for me.

'*As long as we are yoked together I shall never be free.*'

And I've got to the point where I have to be free. I have to.

She wrote it about her sister Lily, I know; after Lily slipped off the stage when they were dancing. She blamed herself for that. She blamed herself for showing her dad that letter from his mistress so he had the excuse to leave them all, I know that too. She blamed herself for Lily's injuries because she'd sensed, a moment before it happened, that Lily was off-balance and she'd known she was going to fall. But Mum had hesitated. She'd thought about that boy Gordon Ilkeley; about how Pandora was trying to palm Lily off onto him as a partner, instead of it being Mum. The hesitation had run through her mind just for that one second, but it had been enough.

So in the end, I couldn't do it after all.

She'd only blame herself, and I couldn't put Mum through that cycle of guilt all over again.

And then there was that sea; that rough and angry sea. It looked so fierce and so unkind. It wasn't how I wanted it to be, it wasn't what I'd imagined, after all.

So, it's life for me, then. I choose life. Whatever that means, however long it will be for, and whatever it will bring me.

Right at this moment, it's brought me Kieran. We're sitting squashed up together in the back of this cool helicopter and he's holding my hand so tightly I think he might be about to faint. I don't know if it's the shock of finding me like he did or if it's apprehension over the million pounds he's about to play for.

Maybe it's just the chopper ride.

He won't look out of the window, but I do. My eyes are glued to the panorama of inlets and coves, the choppy, rain-lashed sea, the coastal lights like a bright pearl necklace lighting up the shoreline of the land below us.

It's six o'clock, the hour I was born, and so I'm there. I officially did it. I've reached fifteen and guess what? I'm doing exactly what I always wanted to do.

I'm flying!

Points for Discussion on *Pandora's Box*

- Consider the mother-daughter relationships within *Pandora's Box*. Are they satisfactory and/or troubling?

- At 15 years old Shelley decides to take her life; do you think she is too young to make such a big decision? Which do you consider to be of the most importance: Shelley's maintaining her dignity or her prolonging her life?

- 'You needed to be free of all this. How many times have you thought this? You needed her to fall so that you could be free, didn't you, Rachel? So you just let it happen. By the sins of our commission and omissions.' Do you agree with Rachel's subconscious thoughts?

- Look at the ideas of hope and medical fact. Bearing this in mind, do you think that miracles are possible? What would you consider some real-life miracles to be?

- Rachel carries the guilt of her sister Lily's accident for most of the novel. Does this affect her judgements and her actions with those around her?

- What is Rachel's attraction to Frank built on? Is there a future for their relationship?

- What role does the theme of loss play within this novel?

- Rachel and Shelley fight to conserve some sort of 'normal' existence. Is this the best way to tackle this situation? How does Shelley's illness and this whole situation affect Daniel?

- Bill and Rachel have very different approaches to raising children. What are their values, concerns and priorities?

- Is Shelley and Kieran's relationship genuine? Or are they using each other as an outlet to deal with their own personal issues? Is it a good idea for either of them to be in a committed relationship?

- Look at the role of friendship in the novel. Examine the roles that Solly, Annie-Jo, Surinda and Maggie play.

- Do you think that opening 'Pandora's box' brings some sort of hope to Rachel and Shelley?

- Unspoken thoughts are revealed and documented in Rachel and Shelley's diary's and emails. How is the written word both liberating and restrictive? What purposes do the diary entries and the emails serve to the author and to the readers?